Battle of Ash and Flame

By Ellie Fowler

For everyone who thought
they were on their path,
but the universe had other plans.

Content Notes:

This book is written for an 18+ audience and has several potentially difficult themes. Please note the possible triggers in the back of the book before reading - your mental health matters!

A note from the author on time:

Creating a planet in a system with multiple suns presented some challenges. Its orbit needed to occur further away from the suns in order to be habitable.

Through a lot of awkward, theoretical, and probably completely wrong attempts at astronomical calculations, I found the time it takes for this world to complete a full orbit is nearly four times as long as Earth.

Because of this world's base-12 system, decades and centuries are calculated a bit differently as well.

If, like me, math is not your favorite, do not panic. None of this changes the plot.

But for clarity's sake, I wanted to offer some definitions to help you orient to the odd flow of time in this new world:

Annum (plural annae): a full orbit around the suns, with all four seasons. This is approximately four earth years

Season: approximately one earth year, twelve mooncycles

Mooncycle: this world's equivalent of a month, based on the moon's phases, four weeks

Duosnight: two weeks, twelve days

Week: this world has six days in a week

Day: thirty Earth hours. The extra few hours create space for the midday rest (noonrest) and the nighttime wake (moonwake)

Duocentury: 144 annae, 576 seasons

Duodecade: 12 annae, 48 seasons

Battle of Ash and Flame

Chapter 1

The assassin leaned against a pillar, his arms crossed. The alleyway's putrid stench was a tangy mix of metallic fumes and stagnant rot. The hedge buffered the sights and sounds from the busy thoroughfare, but it stifled airflow and scents hung thick around the temple ruins.

Muffled sounds of horses and carts were bustling on the other side of the brush. The reminders of death and disease were unwelcome and few bothered to glance past the natural barrier. Behind the ruins was nothing but the remains of a holy forest, making for a perfect location for an ambush.

A hood covered the man's features, but he was turned with his gaze fixed on the back entrance of an infirmary. The only movement in the past two hours was from a couple of assistant life-tenders, grumbling as they emptied chamber pots and surgery basins into the waste pits. None noticed the harbinger of death, as his midnight indigo cloak blended into the foliage around him.

The bright yellow sun had just dipped below the horizon. Its smaller sister lingered, casting an ominous red tone down the street. It was almost time. The assassin remained a statue as the second sun slipped away, abandoning the world to shadow. Nighttime creatures began to emerge, scratching through the piles of filth.

The door opened and multiple life-tenders and their assistants emerged, dressed in traditional healer's garb. The sudden chatter caused a few rodents to scurry back into the woods. The assassin uncrossed his arms and crouched, peering through the leaves to get a view of the healers' faces in the torchlight. He remained hidden as the last of the afternoon shift trickled out, arguing with each other about which pub would have the better ale this evening. Their laughter faded and the assassin was left alone in the dank alleyway.

After a few moments, he rocked back on his heels and stood up. A breeze caught his cloak as he stepped away from the dark brush. The wind was singing. The assassin tensed and pivoted back to face the door as it opened one final time.

A lanky man stepped out and stretched his arms, rolling his neck from side to side. He wandered into the middle of the alley, watching the stars beginning to wink into the sky. After a few moments, he pivoted to leave and unknowingly turned his back on his attacker.

The assassin sprang forward, wrapping one hand around the man's mouth and the other arm around his chest. The man struggled as he was dragged down the alleyway and into the woods.

Once they were far enough away to not be heard, the assassin shoved the man into a clearing. "Judgment has come, aether-weaver." The assassin pulled back his hood and the healer gasped. A silver mask, shaped like a *trillin* beast, covered the top half of the assassin's face. His golden eyes were framed by feline features, carved in a predatory gaze. The long, threatening tusks hung down each side, emphasizing his bloodthirsty grin.

The man began to shake and dropped to his knees. "S- so the rumors are true." The breeze brushed against the trees, a fevered dance.

The assassin smirked and licked his lips. "Whatever you have heard is nonsense. You have been chosen as a worthy sacrifice to build our power. Your death is a vital step in healing the lands and reuniting humans."

The aether-weaver scrambled backwards toward the treeline. The assassin flicked his wrist and the healer's feet sank into the ground, cementing the man to the spot. He grimaced at being trapped and lifted his arms, chanting ancient words. "*Raeshio aeki raewi.*" Emerald smoke billowed out from his aura.

The air howled and lashed around them. The assassin's grin grew wider and he tilted his head, a predator sizing up prey. "Good, show me your power! This is one fight you cannot win." He threw his head back and cackled at the spiraling gusts building around them. The aether-weaver gritted his teeth and hissed the enchantment over and over.

The assassin stepped closer, raising his hands, and muttered. "*Gokaw budzug.*" Instantly, brown smoke hissed from around him and the winds went silent. Stagnant stillness pressed down, making breathing difficult. The lack of air movement created an oppressive barrier and sounds seemed muffled in the vacuum.

The assassin gripped the man's hair and stepped behind him. He pulled a knife from his belt and held it to the healer's throat, pressing until a bead of red formed.

"N- no, please, I am doing so much for our people as a life-tender. I beg you..." The aether-weaver rasped as his eyes filled with tears.

The harbinger of death patted his cheek and chuckled. "Do not worry, my son. Your death will serve your people more than your healing skills."

The healer whimpered, an echo of his timid plea. The assassin pulled the man's head back and made a single, swift stroke across his throat. A slight gurgle escaped the healer's mouth before he slumped forward.

The assassin turned and walked into the treeline. He spent a moment searching, then reached into a tree trunk and pulled out a bag. He rummaged through his supplies, humming an ominous tune, before pulling out a shell bigger than his hand and a bright blue gemstone.

He walked back over to the aether-weaver's lifeless body, placing the shell underneath the drip of blood from the man's neck. As he placed the stone in the center of the shell, light surrounded the aether-weaver and the air began to stir. It whirled, whispering to the harbinger of death.

The assassin turned. He narrowed his eyes and bared his teeth as he looked directly at her...

Princess Linneya shot up, gasping. Her entire body ached and her eyes darted around her room. Both suns were up, their combined golden glow streaming through her windows and highlighting the cheerful patterns on the wall. Mint and rosemary wafted through the space, attempting to brush away the tangy scent of her nightmares. The soft furs and wool blankets provided a pocket of warmth protecting her from the morning chill, but after the fevered heat of the murder in her dream, Linneya found their insulation stifling. She kicked off the layers and threw her legs over the side of the bed, willing the cool air to bring her to a calmer state.

She brushed her messy, dirty blonde hair back from her sweaty face and padded over to get herself some water. Her hand shook as she poured the drink. This season, she had dreamt of the assassin at least once a week. The dreams always came during second sleep and nothing she did during moonwake seemed to change the outcome.

Stories of elemental hunters were part of their campfire ghost tales ever since she was a child. As an elemental flame-talker, Linneya was more terrified of them than the *tioksh* creatures - massive predators with dark brown fur and paws the size of a man's head. One of her father's guards had an unfortunate encounter with one and considered himself lucky that he only lost a leg. Legends claimed the *tioksh* could turn white in the winter season and disappear into the blizzards. While those beasts had given her nightmares for annae, no elemental hunters had haunted her dreams until now.

Linneya shook her head, as if the motion would shed the terror still aching in her bones. She squinted, looking out her window to the bustling courtyard below, and groaned. She had slept longer than she realized and would need to rush downstairs to help.

Her mother, Queen Altheia, was already supervising the final decorations for today's caravan from the neighboring kingdom, Enthor. The queen glided around, adjusting details and delegating tasks. Princess Eleanor, Linneya's younger sister, was following behind their mother, flitting amongst the courtiers. Linneya watched as Eleanor flicked her hair over her shoulder, her curls waving in the wind like golden wheat. She chattered and laughed with everyone. Eleanor had never met a stranger. Her charms would serve her well. Linneya managed to avoid the marriage exchange this time, but Eleanor had begged for the chance to pick a husband from amongst the Enthorian nobles.

As detailed in the duocenturies-old peace treaty between Enthor and Aelor, every five seasons there would be an exchange of women in one of the kingdoms. The women volunteered, but were expected leave their homeland to marry. Linneya shivered at the thought of being separated from her family all for a man one chose over the course of two days.

Because of previous attempts to subvert the treaty, all participants were required to be betrothed at the end of the exchange or be stripped of their titles and humiliated. So far, with a bit of finagling, the treaty worked and peace reigned. Having wives from the neighboring kingdom created a sense of family and strengthened the bond between the two nations. Enthor and Aelor thrived as allies in the human realms. Other countries respected their combined resources and conflicts were almost nonexistent.

But lately, unrest was growing. Threats from the southern kingdom of Serathor added to worries around the worsening droughts. The Aelorian council wanted both of the princesses married off to high ranking nobles in Enthor to solidify the alliance, but Linneya could not bring herself to leave. Not when war might be coming and her healing powers could save so many lives.

Tapping at the door signaled the maids were ready to prepare her for the day's events. They bustled in, bringing the scent of cedar with the freshly steamed dress. Their soft, deferential murmurs brought tranquility and familiarity to the space. It was easy to slip into a pleasant daydream as they braided her hair, the scent of her clothing transporting her to her favorite clearing in the woods.

As the maids fixed her blue and white dress, her eyes fell on the book she had borrowed from the palace library. She was finished reading it and it would be better to go ahead and return the book now, while it was on her mind. The maids completed her outfit with jewelry and an icy blue tiara that matched her eyes, then Linneya snatched the book and headed downstairs.

She made her way to the library. The heavy wooden door creaked as she entered the room. The dark wood paneling and rich green walls made this room her favorite haunt. Fond memories of hours tucked away in the books, exploring the magics of other worlds, brought a smile to the princess' face. The sweet smell of ancient parchment wafted to her, like comforting greetings from old friends. She stepped toward the shelves and shivered, as the fireplaces were left empty until after noonrest. She placed the book in its proper place and turned to leave.

Raised voices caused her to hesitate, hand on the door. Her father, King Varilon, was grumbling, a rough tone to his voice. She slowly peeked through the crack at the door. He was in deep conversation with Lord Caelin, his chief advisor.

The king was tall with auburn hair that was turning white along the sides. His blue eyes were lined with wrinkles from annae of strong emotion - both happiness and worry. The king's frame was still bulky, reminiscent of his days as head of his brother's kingsguard. Linneya always suspected he had been an assassin before his elder brother abdicated, but her father never would reveal anything about his previous role.

His advisor was mumbling in a dark tone and the king was a statue, intent on absorbing every detail. "When he had not returned home after first sleep, his wife called for a search party. They found his body in the clearing behind Rasha's temple ruins." Lord Caelin was hunched over, as if the weight of the annae bent his spine. He wrung his wiry hands as he spoke, more from habit than anxiousness. "No one saw anything, but he always worked late. They say his throat was slit and his body was drained of blood."

Bile rose in Linneya's throat. The man in her dream last night had been killed in a similar way. She worried her bottom lip between her teeth. Surely it was a coincidence.

"For now, let us keep this between ourselves. I do not want to worry anyone over what could turn out to be an unrelated murder."

Lord Caelin nodded and sighed. "The message indicated more news would arrive with my investigator this evening. I will meet with him and find out any details that might give us more insight."

The men were quiet for a few moments. King Varilon hacked into his kerchief before continuing. "Between this and the soldiers traversing fjords undetected... King Shumor is planning something."

"I agree, sire. The droughts are making everyone more anxious. Food is becoming scarce in some of the Southern kingdoms. It is possible Serathor's king is becoming desperate."

The king grunted. "It is likely an excuse. He has never forgiven us for refusing to back his conquest of Altheia's homeland. When we made it clear his son would never marry our daughter, he vowed our destruction. Now that he has awakened more dragons than is safe, he can follow through on his threat."

The blood drained from Linneya's face. Before she was born, her parents had agreed to wed their firstborn daughter to King Shumor's son, the heir to the Serathor throne. When King Shumor razed Queen Altheia's homeland, he decimated the capital. No one survived the four days of fiery torture the conqueror inflicted on its residents.

Her parents then rescinded the royal marriage agreement. Linneya did not know that Serathor's king threatened them for doing so. No children were born at the time, no formal documents had been signed. It should have been the end of the matter.

King Varilon and Lord Caelin wandered back down the hallway, talking in hushed voices. Linneya was rooted to the spot, stunned.

Could last night's nightmare have been a coincidence? Was it related to the murder? Was King Shumor sending a message?

She took a deep breath and pressed her palms to her eyes. The aromatics of the library settled her thoughts and she let out a sigh. There would be time to worry about the dreams later. Today she had to focus on staying invisible and not being discovered as the legendary flame-talker.

As a flame-talker who nurtured the light side of her elemental connection, she could heal burns. Not just tiny oil splatters, either. Early on, her parents realized she was able to channel an unusual amount of the flame element when Lord Caelin's house burned down and Linneya was able to heal the man of burns that the most talented life-tenders had deemed fatal.

They managed to keep it a secret, but she was quickly introduced to healers that could train her in the light side of her element. Her powers might be the only thing to save them when Serathor came with their dragons. Her life-tending skills mixed with her affinity gave her purpose, value, even if no one could know their princess was the source of almost miraculous healing ability.

She had begged the council to not force her to marry and go to Enthor. None of them knew why, and many were worried about the political fallout of the firstborn princess refusing to wed an Enthorian noble - again. Linneya had been courting a duke the last time she was eligible for the exchange, so no one had fussed then.

Now, she was older and had no advantageous suitor to buffer the council's request. Many argued that only offering Eleanor would seem like a snub. With a little pressure from Lord Caelin they made an exception to the list. For now, she was free to stay and protect her people. At least, as long as no one found out about her abilities.

King Varilon had warned her that Enthor would have the power to claim her if they discovered her value as a flame-talker. Enthor was closer to Serathor's borders and would see her abilities as a necessary addition to their forces. Her father could not risk the Enthorian court's fury, as their armies outnumbered Aelor's three to one. The only reason she was not being dragged off already? Her parents had the foresight to keep her powers a secret.

Only a couple of King Varilon's closest advisors were privy to the knowledge. Her brother, Prince Aiden, had caught her leaving the infirmary once and followed her until she took off her disguise, but Eleanor still did not know. For this exchange, the king had admonished Linneya to keep her head down and stay quiet. As a middle child of the sovereign, she was accustomed to staying out of the way and was happy to be relegated to the sidelines.

Linneya took one more steadying breath full of aged parchment and made her way to meet her family outside.

The courtyard had been decorated with grand displays of rare flowers and gold ornaments. The flowers perfumed the air and plush carpeted runners had been placed along the entrance. A full orchestra was setting up at the far end, tuning their instruments and laughing at the antics of one of their fellow musicians. Courtiers were milling about, placing final touches on the decor.

As the family gathered on the steps that led to the front palace entrance, King Varilon stood apart from the others, observing the chaos. His stillness was in stark contrast to his wife. Queen Altheia was a flurry of movement fussing over everyone. She was petite, but her mannerisms were commanding. Her salt and pepper hair flowed freely, dancing as if it had a mind of its own. When Altheia saw her daughter arrive, she brightened.

The queen hugged Linneya, then stepped back and began assessing. "Dear, you are dressed too plain to be the eldest princess. I am forever having to remove excess jewelry from Eleanor, but you are another challenge altogether! At least put this brooch on for me."

Eleanor rolled her eyes and pursed her lips at her mother's comment. Linneya just smiled and nodded, taking the ornament. She had taken to dressing in plainer styles whenever possible. The droughts were becoming worrisome and she struggled to reconcile their finery with some of the poverty she saw working at the infirmary in the capital. On a normal day she would have refused, but she knew better than to argue with her mother over her attire at official functions. She turned away, affixing the brooch to her dress.

Her older brother was approaching. Aiden was taller than their father. He had inherited King Varilon's auburn hair which he wore long. His green eyes were piercing. The way he held his athletic frame hinted at his status as king in the making. For all of his handsomeness and grand presence, he was still unmarried. There was almost always a gaggle of women nearby, vying for his attention, and he was always oblivious.

Aiden smirked as he swaggered to her side. "Are you going to spend the festival looking mopey while I have to make up for the lack of personality?"

She grinned up at him. "Absolutely. It's your time to shine."

Eleanor leaned over. "Nuh unh. Both of you need to step back and let me have my spotlight. I plan on picking out the handsomest of the crew and charming him before anyone else even has a chance."

Aiden chuckled and swatted at Eleanor's braids. She hissed and ducked before trying to smack him back. Linneya was quite literally caught in the middle, trying to settle them before a tiara went flying or a shoe got scuffed. Eleanor was the youngest of them at twenty two seasons, yet some patterns from childhood never changed.

Her shoulders relaxed as they settled into their normal rhythm: her peacekeeping between two boisterous personalities. Eleanor sniped and Aiden bantered. Between her two siblings, the chances of anyone noticing Linneya were slim. As long as she made it through the banquet, masquerade, and choosing ceremony without incident, she would be free. Two days and she would be back in her woods, foraging for healing medicines. Linneya took a deep breath and straightened up while Aiden moved to the place of honor beside her father and mother.

As the first signs of the caravan came into view, the orchestra began a tune. The Enthorian caravan took Linneya's breath away. The carriages holding the women were made of polished mahogany with gold detail. Each of the carriages were pulled by two black horses whose manes were braided and not a speck of dirt hinted at the full mooncycle of travel they had endured. The men were on horseback, each horse clothed in a navy blue mantle with ornate stitching.

As they entered the courtyard, the laughter and chattering amongst the welcoming committee died down. The buzz of energy was palpable.

Everyone remained rooted to their assigned place and craned their necks to catch the first glimpses of the newcomers.

As the caravan came to a halt, their leader dismounted. The man was dressed in a crimson outfit that complemented his rich umber skin. His tunic stretched over muscular, broad shoulders and his lithe movements nodded to his warrior training. He turned toward Linneya's father, striding up to greet the royal family. His dark eyes and even darker hair made her forget to breathe. Her heart raced at the intense expression on his face. The man had a vicious countenance, but seemed right at home with her parents.

He bowed to King Varilon and exchanged pleasantries. As he turned to Queen Altheia, he bowed and kissed her hand. She pulled him into a hug, whispered something into his ear, and he smiled. Her mother's response was surprising. She had not mentioned that they would know anyone in this season's spousal exchange.

The leader relaxed and turned toward Aiden. The two grinned and embraced, laughing about something she could not quite catch. *They must have been in the same company during last season's shadow raids*, Linneya thought. *Sharvach*, wolf-like shadow creatures with stag horns, had once enslaved the human realms. Now, the raids on the shadowlands helped to keep the creatures from orchestrating another attack. Aiden's participation last fall had ended early after a particularly brutal fight and he had come home bragging insufferably about his exploits.

As the rest of the men disembarked, they began to open the carriages and the women filed out. Beside her, Eleanor was jittery with excitement. Linneya did not blame her sister. After all, these men represented her marriage prospects. At least if Eleanor was happy, the next few days would fly by.

"Oh, is their leader not marvelous?!" she blurted.

Linneya shushed her and tried to maintain composure, but it was too late. The man stopped mid-sentence and was looking toward the two of them, his eyes narrowing.

His stare gripped her, the bright clarity of his gaze causing warmth to flush up the back of her neck. *Marvelous* hardly did him justice. Sure, she had courted warriors before. Some even knocked her off her feet at first sight, but this was deeper. She was entranced. Captivated.

He maintained eye contact so long it was disconcerting, but she set her jaw. Determined not to flinch from his inspection, she held his stare and one corner of his mouth curved upwards. She watched him for signs that he was experiencing the same urge to close the distance between them, but there was nothing concrete. An unnerving crawling sensation made its way up her spine, his silent refusal to bend unsettling and intriguing her.

Aiden made another comment, which forced the leader to return his attention to the prince. It took a few breaths for Linneya to steady herself. Her brother and the leader began walking toward the main entrance hall, laughing about a shared memory. She was embarrassed by the unspoken exchange, but curiosity won out and her eyes followed him. His relaxed demeanor and steady posture suggested he was unfazed. A natural leader, one who was born to command armies.

Her mother broke her daydreaming, motioning her and Eleanor forward to greet the others. They fell in line and made their way back to the sprawling palace. As the majority of the caravan departed to their rooms, King Varilon led the elite guests into a private audience in his stateroom. The walls were dark gray stone and the lack of windows created a heavy ambiance. The shadows were broken by bright white, larger-than-life marble statues of the previous leaders of Aelor. The spectral effigies lent a mystical feel to the setup. The wood smoke from the majestic fireplace scented the air.

They gathered around the inglenook, a charming group of noblewomen surrounding Linneya. She made her way around the room, attempting to give each new face a few moments of her time. The newcomers seemed eager to intermingle and Linneya was pleased to make introductions. After a bit, she was able to take up an inconspicuous spot by a statue of her great-grandfather and observe the room.

While most were chatting happily and getting to know one another, one woman sulking in the corner caught her eye. The woman was petite with dark hair and a pinched face, as if she had eaten something sour.

Linneya walked over and offered a warm smile. "I do not believe we have been introduced, I am Princess Linneya."

The woman pursed her lips and narrowed her eyes. "Lady Alayne."

"It's wonderful to meet you. Is there something I can do to help?"

Lady Alayne raised her eyebrows. "You? Help?" she scoffed.

Linneya stepped back, surprised by the abrasiveness, "I only meant -"

She was cut off by Lady Alayne's piercing condemnation, "As the eldest princess, you shirk your duty and yet you expect me to be eager to make your acquaintance?"

Linneya's head spun. Alayne's voice continued to rise as more conversations ceased and their participants turned toward the outburst. "The rumors around your decision to not take part in your duties leave much to the imagination. Your lack of a husband and refusal to participate in this exchange suggest your reputation is sullied. No one in their right mind would choose such a disruption of tradition at such a time as this. You might as well burn the treaty between Aelor and Enthor for your insolence."

"You refuse to strengthen the bond between kingdoms, even as the droughts in the Southward kingdoms continue to strain everyone's economy. Serathor is beginning to threaten us both and your refusal to take an Enthorian man as your husband is an affront."

Linneya's eyes darted around for a friendly face but found none. The leader studied the commotion, a smirk on his face. She flushed as their gazes met and he narrowed his eyes. She was failing at staying in the background and this dark enigma of a man was flustering her and making things worse.

Turning back to Lady Alayne, she stuttered. "I - I apologize."

The woman scoffed, "mere words, child."

Linneya raised her eyebrows. Alayne could not be more than a few seasons older. Linneya wished for a witty retort, but when she opened her mouth her voice cracked and Alayne snickered.

So much for not drawing attention to herself.

"Lady Alayne, I believe there has been a misunderstanding." Linneya's shoulders relaxed and she released the breath she was holding as the sound of her mother's voice cut through the tension. Lady Alayne quickly curtsied and murmured an apology. While she still held her lips in a tight line, arguing with the queen was unconscionable.

Queen Altheia offered a soft smile. "The decision to allow Linneya to stay is complex and extends beyond ceremony and tradition. Surely a century of peace cannot be ruined because of one person's need to remain with their family." Prince Aiden walked up and stood beside his mother, glaring at Lady Alayne as if he were daring her to keep pushing.

At that moment, the butler announced noonrest, putting an end to the topic. King Varilon clapped his hands and the tension dissipated at everyone's desire to get settled.

Although many appeared satisfied with the queen's answer, the woman still appeared to be annoyed. Linneya was unnerved by her eagerness to point out the offense. Was she making the right choice? Would Eleanor be enough to smooth over the diplomatic blunder of her remaining behind?

Chapter 2

Noonrest and the afternoon's activities were a blur. Before Linneya realized it, the gong sounded to signal the beginning of the banquet. The dining entrance glowed with the light of a few dozen candles arranged into crystal chandeliers. The scents of savory and sweet glazes wafted through the hallway.

Several of the newcomers milled about, mixing with the usual populations of nobles. Eleanor was already basking in her flock of suitors. Aiden was also gathering a bit of a following, even though he was not part of the exchange and had not made any declaration to suggest he was ready to find a wife. Linneya fought a smile at the grimace of discomfort on his face.

Her brother's eyes darted around the room, looking for an escape. When he locked on her, he cracked a tight smile. "Ladies, excuse me. I must attend to my sister."

He dodged the clingy hands of a couple of the bolder women and sidled up to Linneya. "Thank the Creators. I suspect Eleanor put them on my scent to keep them away from her pool of suitors until she can pick her favorite." He shuddered and shook his head. "Whenever she puts her mind to something, she is a force to be reckoned with."

Linneya snickered and took his proffered arm. "Our little sister is a spitfire, for sure. But she is not cruel. She knew you could hold your own." The gong sounded and their butler announced the dinner. Aiden grinned and led her into the low light of the dining hall.

As Linneya found her seat at the table, she began taking in the splendor. Her mother had commissioned the finest embroidery, a creative mix of swirls and motifs across the smooth silk tablecloths. The design offered Enthorian and Aelorian elements intertwined in a symbolic union.

King Varilon clapped and the stragglers hurried to sit. Servants lit eloquent centerpieces up and down the table and the room burst into color. The tapestries on the wall seemed to come alive in the candlelight. Stories of elemental magic, alliances with creatures and beings, battles won, and treaties signed had been woven into vivid legends.

As servants presented the first course of smoked salmon, she shook off her gloomy thoughts and turned to her father's advisor. Lord Caelin was terrible to drone on about historical matters, but his devotion to banal facts was known to have saved the kingdom more than once. Besides, Linneya loved his rambling stories and was committed to showing him the respect he deserved.

He smiled and whispered to her. "Dear Linneya, you know we are proud of you for putting off your marriage prospects to serve your country. Your abilities and healing skills are so valuable, but I also worry you are missing an important chance to find a match. Are you feeling left out of the festivities?"

"Not at all, sir. This outdated mess holds no fascination for me. Besides, healing is my calling, not succumbing to these ridiculous customs."

"Oh no! You must not make light of this. The genius of your ancestors' treaty created a strong bond between our kingdoms. One that has not been broken in almost a duocentury. I know some of you youngsters believe this is an affront to women to make them be the ones to leave home, but the entire event is a choice and..."

As Lord Caelin launched into a monologue on the benefits of the marriage exchange, Linneya nodded and offered a polite smile. Many of his arguments were as antiquated as the treaties that bound the noble houses of Enthor and Aelor, but the man deserved respect, and debating him over dinner would only bring attention she did not need.

After a while, he seemed satisfied that his point was made and settled into enjoying the food. Linneya scanned the room to see how her loved ones were faring. The booming voice of her brother pulled her eyes toward the far end of the table. He was regaling his entire section with an embellished tale of his first *tioksh* kill. She had heard it many times, each retelling becoming wilder and more dramatic.

Miming the final strikes, he created a scene worthy of legend. As everyone applauded, Aiden caught her eye and winked. His boisterousness was encouraging and Linneya could not help but laugh at his antics.

As she was grinning, her eyes looked to the left of her brother and met the amused gaze of the Enthorian leader. For a moment, a warmth she did not expect surrounded her. Seated between her father and Aiden, the leader fit right in. He was perfectly at ease - even regal.

As their eyes locked, his expression iced over faster than the lake in a blizzard. Heat flushed her cheeks and she snapped her attention back to her meal.

She took another bite and forced her focus elsewhere. Two seats to her left, Eleanor was giggling madly at a handsome young man. Already infatuated, she would no doubt spend the rest of the evening hanging on to his every word. Her eyes glittered as the man leaned in, feigning an intimate moment for the sake of flirting.

For a moment, a pang of jealousy flitted through her. It was less about the attention her sister was receiving and more about how easily Eleanor enjoyed this man's advances. Her face held no sign of worry or hesitation. She held no shame and had no stinging experience with rejection. She knew her value, her worth. Linneya had weathered her own share of heartbreak, but Eleanor was always the one shattering her suitors' hopes.

Further down the table, her best friend Mariel was talking animatedly with one of the officers. Mariel walked with a limp from a childhood injury and had been overlooked when she reached marriageable age. Her entire family celebrated when she was accepted to go to Enthor and now Mariel was wasting no time in making conversation with possible matches.

It pleased Linneya to see her friend so comfortable in the face of such uncertainty. Mariel was a kind soul. This opportunity was not a guarantee for her happiness, but the stability it would most likely bring was welcome.

Servants cleared their plates and presented the main course, cutting her ruminations short. Her stomach twisted at the stuffed quail in mushroom sauce and a variety of exotic vegetables. Such extravagance could not be sustainable in the face of the looming droughts.

"These mushrooms appear to be imported, but I cannot place the spice."

Linneya turned to her left, studying her new conversation partner. It was no wonder Eleanor was infatuated. He had sandy hair and a lopsided grin. The glimmering gemstone in his gold brooch complemented the color of his eyes: brown with gold flecks. His lips quirked up as if he was enjoying her inspection.

She dipped her chin in greeting. "It is the carramon in the sauce. The seeds are roasted and ground into a powder. We harvest limited quantities from our forest each annum. It lasts us a couple of seasons and rarely is available outside our nation."

"Well, it is a fantastic delicacy. I am Orrain. You must be Eleanor's sister?"

"Yes, I am Linneya." His demeanor made her hesitant, something lurked underneath his act. However it was her responsibility to make him feel welcome, so she smiled back politely.

As they picked over the meal and made small talk, Linneya relaxed. Orrain enjoyed talking and she was happy to let him carry the conversation. "My brother was also expected to come, but he ended up in trouble for cowardice."

Linneya's eyebrows raised and she took a sip of wine to try to cover her surprise at Orrain's candidness. "Oh, yes, another man challenged him to a duel and Johann made a spectacle of his acceptance. Then the actual day came and he never showed. His second attempted to step in to preserve honor - and was wounded."

As she coughed into her goblet, he smirked as if he was pleased by her shock. He showed no signs of embarrassment as he plowed on. "Everyone lived, but our king forbade Johann from representing Enthor after such a mess." Orrain smirked and tore off a piece of bread, dipping it in the honeybutter.

Linneya grimaced. "How can such a brutal custom be upheld as honorable?"

He flapped his hand. "Oh, no one takes it seriously. Most of the time our duels and trials by combat are ceremonial. Johann's second was injured out of bad luck more than anything. His ear being sliced looked more gruesome than it was - only the top half couldn't be saved."

Queasy and desperate to change the subject, Linneya enquired about the Enthorian newcomers. Orrain was more than happy to share the gossip and his seething review of many of the party. She was able to mostly tune him out and returned to her meal.

"... but Darryn frustrated our king by refusing to join the official caravan," he gestured toward the leader.

Darryn - finally, a name for the dark-haired leader with that intense gaze. Linneya leaned in, ready for some answers about the enigmatic man who flustered her with a single glance. "Why is he here, then?"

"Our king ordered him to come, even though he refuses to be a part of the exchange. It's probably because he knows Prince Aiden so well, but I have also heard that King Birron hoped he would match anyway." Orrain snorted, "It's almost as if everyone forgets he has sworn his fealty to the Knights of Falorian. There's no room for a wife."

Linneya narrowed her eyes. The legendary knights were feared for their brutality and barbaric customs. She opened her mouth to ask more, but Orrain continued down the table, pointing out his fellow travelers and naming off other interesting tidbits. Linneya remained lost in thought, studying Darryn's mannerisms. *He does not fit the horrifying stories of a Falorian knight...*

Whispers of the knights' brutality fueled many late-night tales between Linneya and her siblings. No one knew why they chose to attack the towns they did, but when they showed up you could count on them razing entire buildings in minutes. Sometimes they even aligned with the fae and other beings to complete their destruction. The knights were highly trained, focused on bringing about complete desolation to whomever they targeted. Linneya witnessed enough terror from survivors to know that they were ruthless. They were so skilled that not once had she heard of unintentional casualties.

She analyzed what she knew of Darryn. He was dark and moved like a warrior, but did not seem to fit the savagery described by the survivors of Falorian attacks. Even now, he leaned forward and inclined his head to show interest in something one of the dimmest, dullest nobles was saying. Darryn offered a polite nod to the man, even when everyone else had pretended to be otherwise engaged.

The servants presenting a fruit dish interrupted her thoughts again. Linneya smiled, realizing her mother had made sure her favorite dish was on the menu for the evening. The multi-colored berries were slightly chilled and served with a creamy cheese sauce. These were probably berries Linneya had picked herself and the thought made warmth bloom through her chest.

As she settled in for the new course, a man stepped through into the dining hall. He was still wearing a hood and dressed in *tioksh* furs, as if he had come from the fae lands. He signaled in her direction and it startled her.

"Ah, princess, you will excuse me. My investigator has returned." Lord Caelin stood, nodding toward the man.

Linneya knitted her brows and Lord Caelin patted her shoulder with his gnarled hand. "Nothing to worry about, my dear. Whatever he has found will not be a concern for tonight. Enjoy your friends." She smiled, but a knot was forming in her stomach. Even the berries and cream could no longer tempt her.

Linneya spent the rest of the banquet talking to Orrain and Eleanor. The more she watched him dote on her sister, the more she grew to like his boisterous behavior. On more than one occasion, he had them laughing so hard that Darryn glared down the table toward them.

He could try to intimidate her, but he would not succeed. She lifted her chin and continued enjoying her sister's success. After all, life should not stop because one handsome stranger seemed irked.

As the servants cleared away the remnants of the banquet, everyone meandered into the ballroom. The walls were alabaster with gold accents and white marble columns lined each side, separating the dance floor from areas where guests could gather and visit. The scent of baking spices and wood smoke filled the air. The bright banners and colorful arrangements accented the luminous energy that resonated throughout the space. Even at night, the torches reflected off the gold accents and made the room feel almost sunlit. The musicians had been set up on a platform at the far end and small refreshment tables stood at convenient intervals, scattered in the alcoves.

A full ensemble was already playing a lighthearted waltz, and Linneya's parents took to the floor to open the dance. King Varilon swept Queen Altheia into his arms and grinned. His black suit with gold embroidery complemented her pale pink, lacy gown. The queen's cheeks flushed as he whispered something in her ear. He laughed and the two flew across the floor as if they had been born dancing.

As Orrain led Eleanor onto the dance floor, he caught Linneya's eye and winked. She laughed, pleased with her sister's choice of beau. Queen Altheia beamed at the two of them dancing every time they came into her view. The seating arrangements at dinner must have been carefully planned; her mother was proud of the results.

Everyone seemed to be relaxing into the rhythm of the exchange. Three interested suitors surrounded Mariel. Aiden hid in a corner chattering with one of his friends.

Surrounded by the joy of family and the familiar radiance of the ballroom, Linneya should have felt at peace. However, her stomach was twisting into more knots, crocheting a blanket out of her insides. Lady Alayne was whispering to another courtier by the fireplace, both pursing their lips and shooting glances toward Linneya. Lord Caelin was with the inspector and several ambassadors, wringing his hands and shaking his head. She could not dispel the sensation that something was wrong. The uneasiness from last night's assassin dream enveloped her like a winter cloak.

A song ended and Orrain made his way to her. He grinned and held out his hand. "Shall we dance?"

Linneya's shoulders relaxed. At least for a few minutes, she could enjoy the company of jollier folk. She smiled and nodded, allowing him to lead her to the dance floor.

The tune picked up to a complicated rhythm and she became breathless as they twirled and dipped. A warmth swelled in her chest as the music led them into a giddy trance. By the end of the dance, they were both laughing so hard they struggled to stay upright.

"Well, Linneya, I expected to be able to chat with you but the musicians had other ideas." He grinned without letting go of her waist. "Might I interest you in one more?"

She chuckled and fell back into step. "Surely one more will not hurt." The music slowed and they began to sway, catching their breath. Orrain began looking toward the other end of the ballroom and tensed his jaw. She followed his gaze, finding Eleanor giggling in the arms of another potential suitor.

"My sister is rarely serious. Most of this evening will be her enjoying herself, not pursuing her dance partner. Based on her actions at dinner, she will be back in your arms before you know it."

Orrain blinked a few times, fidgeting with the brooch at his collar, then looked back down at Linneya with a sheepish grin on his face. "You caught me. I am a bit enamored with your sister and hope I am afforded an opportunity to get to know her better."

Linneya patted his arm. "I am certain that she will give you a fair chance. I do not want to ruin the suspense, but I do believe she is more than a bit enamored with you. My advice? Do not keep secrets from her and make it known you love her for her - not for her title."

His face flushed and he nodded, looking back at Eleanor. Turning to Linneya, Orrain studied her face. "If I tell you a secret, will you promise to keep it between us? Just for now?"

She pursed her lips, considering, then nodded and he leaned in. "I am an elemental - a ground-tamer." He pulled back, studying her response with his eyes bright and head tilted. "Would you still wish that on your sister?"

Linneya threw her head back and laughed. "I thought you were going to tell me about something sordid! Of course, you want to keep your status as an elemental a secret. Please also know the family would not hold it against you. We do not see elementals as a liability."

He grinned and that warmth grew larger in her chest. Having a brother who could understand the frustration of having an elemental affinity would be a delight.

The rest of the dance flew by and Orrain parted from her with a swift kiss on her cheek. Linneya patted his shoulder and glided off the dance floor, allowing the music and rhythm to carry her to one of the refreshment tables. The lavender sweetcakes and bowls of fruit were scattered amongst goblets of tart lemonade. She snagged a drink and watched the others dancing as she cooled off.

As she sipped on the lemonade, her mother drifted over and placed a hand on her arm. "Linneya, dear, come with me, I want to introduce you to your brother's friend, Darryn."

Linneya choked on the drink and sputtered, the sour liquid burning her nose. "Oh, no thank you. I think I already know enough about the man."

Queen Altheia's eyebrows raised. "Nonsense, his sister is a reputable healer and I believe the two of you will have much to discuss. Just because you are not looking for a husband does not mean you cannot make friends."

She gripped her daughter's wrist and began tugging Linneya to the next alcove, where Darryn and Lord Caelin were huddled together. Their jaws were set as if they were deep in a discussion. She protested again, but it was too late.

The queen dragged a reluctant Linneya into the space and both men straightened up before bowing. Queen Altheia smiled. "Gentlemen, I wanted to introduce my daughter to Darryn." She nodded to him. "The princess is a healer and loves the outdoors. I believe you have many things in common and should take some time to become better acquainted." The queen turned on her heel and left before anyone could respond.

Linneya fidgeted with her necklace as Darryn's attention locked on her. His stare heated her core. Lord Caelin beamed and clapped his hands. "Our queen has marvelous ideas! Do not let me stop you - Darryn, you must dance with our dear princess."

The knight clenched his jaw and a darkness passed over his eyes. "No, thank you. I am not here to find a wife."

Heat crept up Linneya's cheeks and she fixed her gaze on Orrain and Eleanor, becoming fascinated with their waltz. Lord Caelin pressed on. "It is not as if one dance will bind you together. Neither of you is here to find a mate and it only seems logical that you befriend each other to pass the time. Dear sir, is your sister not an herbalist as well? Perhaps you two can -"

"I said no," Darryn bit out. "I am not here to cater to women whose questionable reputations leave them without a partner."

Linneya gaped at him. What had she done to deserve such a sharp condemnation? Surely he did not take Lady Alayne's earlier declaration seriously.

Lord Caelin drew himself up to his full height, preparing to defend her. She interjected before her father's advisor could respond. "Sir, I do not believe you have all of the facts. My reputation is neither questionable nor am I without dance partners. This was solely my mother's attempt to give us a chance to learn more about each other."

Darryn cocked his head to the side and a small smirk crept across his lips. "Is that so, princess? Well then, it's a pity we do not have time to debate the facts. I might enjoy learning more about you."

His smile threatened to undo her. She worked to steady her breathing and petitioned the Creators for an excuse to escape. As Darryn stepped closer to her, Aiden burst into the alcove, panting as if he had been running. "Lia! I have been looking everywhere for you. You promised me a dance - why are you hiding now?"

Linneya's arms dropped to her side and she grinned as a wave of relief washed over her. "Of course. My apologies." She took his outstretched hand as her brother nodded to the knight and Lord Caelin.

Darryn turned and announced to no one in particular, "If you will excuse me, I believe it is time for me to retire to my quarters."

Linneya smirked and Aiden ground out a smile before he turned to guide her back into the grand ballroom. As the dance began, Darryn stalked toward the back exit. His grimace distorted his face and his eyes were dark. Even after everything, Linneya wanted him to turn around, come back, and sweep her out of her brother's arms. She bit her lip and tried to squash the longing.

"Sorry about Mother. I told her not to push him on you. She wants him to feel welcome with us, but that should not fall on your shoulders." Aiden said, guiding her into the dance.

Her eyes turned back to her brother. "Why have you never mentioned him before? How can Mother care about him so much when he has never even been here?"

He shrugged. "I think she knew his parents - a long time ago. She has a soft spot for him, especially since we became so close during the raids. He was an important part of my squad and saved my life more than once. In that last fight with the *sharvachs*, he risked his life to make sure we all got out in one piece."

She hummed a noncommittal sound and they glided across the floor, focusing on the music. The mysterious, brutal knight had saved her brother's life. Her face flushed as she recalled his brusque manner when addressing her earlier. The tug to know more was betraying her.

Linneya sighed and squashed the curiosity down. A momentary attraction was not worth the upheaval it could create if he started asking questions. At least she would never have to see him after the exchange concluded.

The rest of the evening was a blur. Battle lines formed as the suitors fought to lay claim to their betrothed. Hearts were breaking and hope was brewing. Lady Alayne danced with a courtier while his jilted lover glared at them from an alcove. Eleanor and Orrain were inseparable, yet several other suitors followed her around, searching for a moment to gain her attention. It was a comfort to think there was only one more day before things could go back to normal.

Chapter 3

The morning of the masquerade brought a light frost. Linneya struggled to peel back the soft wool blankets and dress for the day's activities. The schedule included brunch and a promenade centered around the couples who would use the time to solidify their matches. She planned to avoid it all, if possible. As long as her mother did not catch her, she could get out of the palace and focus on the foraging that needed to be done.

Linneya hurried to dress. With any luck, her mother would not be up yet and she would sneak out without having to face a debate on the benefits of showing up for the morning's formal activities. She pulled on a practical set of trousers and a rough shirt, packed her bag, and left the room.

Slowly walking down the hall, Linneya peered into the dining area before entering. Eleanor was already at the breakfast table, dressed to steal the show. The blue fabric of her dress matched her eyes. The delicate lace that lined the sleeves was her own handiwork - the perfect conversation starter. She was primed to capture the hearts of any men who showed interest, though Linneya suspected the ultimate target was Orrain. King

Varilon buried himself in paperwork, as always, while sipping on tea. No one else had yet arrived, so skipping breakfast would be relatively easy. Deciding to grab something to go, Linneya leaned over the serving platters on the buffet and snatched an apple and a piece of toast

King Varilon glanced up from the letters he was reading and surveyed Linneya's outfit. "Are you not joining us this morning?"

"It feels like a full frost is coming, Father. I need to pick the rest of these elyre berries for tincturing."

King Varilon nodded and returned to the missive in front of him. Eleanor continued chasing the strawberries around her plate while not so subtly watching the door. Linneya chose to make her exit before anyone else might question her absence at breakfast.

She snuck through the hunting entrance, pulled on boots, and strolled outside. The crisp air promised an enjoyable foraging trip, as long as she could dodge the few humans who might dissuade her from her mission. The further from the palace she walked, the more the tension released from her body. She munched on her apple and meandered into the woods. This is where she belonged: among the trees and plants, doing her part to care for her people and prepare for their needs. The purple and red leaves rustling in the breeze and the birds singing in the brush warmed her soul - she had purpose here.

Even though her flame-talker status caused her mother to worry, King Varilon continued to allow Linneya the freedom to roam. If anyone exposed her secret elemental abilities to heal burns and wield fire, these foraging trips would be over. A bounty would be placed on her power and elemental hunters would stop at nothing to harvest her abilities.

If her dreams of the assassin turned out to be real, there could be bigger threats. The psychic, Creators-blessed powers were even more coveted. She shuddered at the thought of being labeled a dream-walker, pulling her cloak tightly around her.

She veered off the well-trodden path, heading toward the cave that marked the beginning of the elyre bushes. The cave system was vast and a bit ominous, but she had fond memories of the time she and Aiden had spent exploring and mapping out different areas when they were little. As a child, she never imagined the knowledge would be tucked away as an option to keep her safe. The caves were her first choice if she had to hide to avoid being captured and killed by elemental hunters.

As she wandered further into the woods, a bird began singing a tune that she did not recognize. At first, it was one bird. Then two.

More joined in, repeating the new tones. Curious, she changed her path in search of the murmuration. The song became clearer as she approached. To keep from scaring the new birds, she crouched down and gradually crept forward. Her eyes widened as the clearing came into view. The whistling came from a man seated under a mother oak tree, his back turned to her.

This man was warbling to the birds. He was teaching them a new song. His sword lay in the moss beside him, while he fixated on one particular sparrow that was singing animatedly in response to his communication.

Hidden in the brush, her eyes lingered on his frame. His shirt stretched tight over his back, clinging to his muscles as if it struggled to contain his strength. A warm sensation grew in her abdomen as she watched him, but she was more curious about his whistling and chirping than his physique. It was too rhythmic to be random. After a few moments, she stood up to introduce herself. But the man turned and her breath caught.

Darryn. Linneya's cheeks flushed and she whirled to escape before he noticed her. Her foot caught on a root and she tumbled to the ground, scattering the toast and foraging supplies from her bag. A stinging cut on her right arm caused her to wince, but there was no time to worry about it. In vain, she scrambled to recover everything and run. As she crammed the last items in her bag, she heard leaves crunching behind her.

Cold metal pressed against her neck and Linneya froze. "Well, what is this?" She shivered at Darryn's rich, dark growl - or perhaps it was the threat of the sword at her throat. "Did your mistress send you to spy on me to try to discover how to win my favor? I did not think Aelorian women would stoop to such absurd attempts at capturing a mate."

Linneya turned a deeper shade of red, furious at the insult. He stepped around to face her, pressing the point of the sword under her chin and forcing her to look up. His eyebrows raised and he dropped his weapon to his side, "Princess?"

She rocked back on her heels and dropped her gaze to her arms, trying to control her breathing. Taking stock of her torn sleeve and the underlying cut, she mumbled, "Yes, it's me."

He reached out and helped her stand. She busied herself with dusting the dirt off her trousers to hide her shaking. Darryn crossed his arms, inspecting her and the chaotic aftermath of her escape attempt with a bemused smile.

After a few breaths, he broke the silence. "Why are you not at the formal brunch? Did you plan this, thinking that spying on me would win you a shot at courtship? Or did you just happen to be on a stroll and take advantage of the moment?"

Straightening up, Linneya snapped, "Not every woman is desperate for a husband. I heard the birds singing an unusual tune and followed their song. I did not realize it was you, *sir*. I had no intention of vying for your attention and I have not set out to win your affection. It never occurred to me that you would abandon the role of honored guest and be out here trying to become one with nature instead."

Darryn smirked and turned to walk back into the clearing, motioning for her to follow. "Back home, there is a brace of starlings that talk to me whenever I am in our woods. I have been practicing with the sword this morning, but when I took a break I wanted to see if the birds here were as friendly."

She stomped into the glade. The gash on her right arm throbbed and she wished she was anywhere but here - with him. "A Falorian knight, communing with the birds like a child. Will wonders never cease?"

His smile tightened as he crossed his arms. "It is a useful skill to have. These birds can warn us of incoming threats: beast or being."

Linneya plopped down on a tree root the size of a small chair and began rummaging through her bag for a bandage and her wound tincture. "They did not seem to warn you of my presence. It would appear that your bird friends are more interested in socializing than strategizing."

Darryn chuckled and stepped toward her, "As I said, they warn of incoming threats. I do not think you count, princess." He kneeled in front of her as she pulled out gauze and a nearly empty tincture bottle.

"Here, let me." He took her hand, easing back the sleeve and exposing her cut arm. A slight breeze drifted around them and Linneya caught the scent of citrus and cedar. Her stomach fluttered and she became light-headed. She resisted the urge to reach out and run her fingers up his arms.

As Darryn inspected the wound, his lips pressed together and his eyes narrowed. "This is rather deep and needs to be cleaned. Where is that medicine you had?"

His concern was touching, but he was the leader of the Enthorian caravan and sworn to a vicious knighthood. Avoiding his attention was necessary if she wanted her elemental affinity to remain secret. She flinched, withdrew from his touch, and stood up. "I do not have enough. There's a stream over this knoll where I can wash. I will be on my way."

The knight shook his head and stepped back. "I will go with you. It's the least I can do."

She shrugged and stalked off toward the stream. Darryn grabbed his sword and followed. She groaned inwardly, wishing he would let it go.

After his insulting words about her *questionable reputation* yesterday at the ball, it seemed ridiculous that he insisted on accompanying her. As they crested the hill, she sped up, hoping he would leave her once he saw she could fend for herself. Instead, she almost tripped over another exposed root, causing him to reach out and catch her.

"Whoa, princess. No need to add a bloody nose to your injuries."

She turned around and yanked away from him. "Do not talk to me like I am one of your horses. Just because you assume my reputation is poor does not mean you can talk to me as if I am an animal. I am still a princess of Aelor."

Darryn let his arms drop. "I hold no ill will toward you." He leaned back and smirked. "However, I cannot be held hostage in a public space where rumors can so easily start. My refusal to dance was strategic, not a commentary on you."

"Strategic?" Linneya scoffed. "So your commentary around my suitability was strategy? Not bad manners?"

He huffed a laugh. "Perhaps it is a bit of both. Nonetheless, I am not the right fit for you."

She pursed her lips and knitted her eyebrows together. She was not looking for anyone, but his words wounded her pride. "How could you even know? You snubbed me off over one dance."

His eyes darkened and her heart skipped a beat as he tucked a stray lock of hair behind her ear. "Are you making an offer? Do you think you want to take me on? My bloodlust leaves me rough around the edges. I imagine you think you can polish me up and show me off to your noble friends. I warn you, I am not a task to be taken on lightly."

Linneya rolled her eyes. "That is one thing on which we agree."

He shrugged. "I did not think my words would bother you. Your brother calls you formidable and I was certain you would not be phased by my lowly opinion."

News of Aiden's praise boosted her spirit. Still, she frowned and crossed her arms, ignoring the sting of the gash. "You could have left my reputation unscathed."

He studied her closely. "At the time, it seemed to be the only way to stop the conversation. I am sorry it hurt you. I may be well versed in military strategy, but sometimes my social tactics fall short."

Linneya pursed her lips. "I see." His gaze caused her stomach to flutter. She needed to stay away, to remain neutral, but she found herself being drawn in. "Is the music you were teaching the birds some sort of strategy as well?"

He blinked toward the sky. "It's the song my mother sang to me as a lullaby. Having my bird friends echo it to me brings her back, if only for a moment." His face glazed over as he began walking again and searched the trees for the birds. She was surprised to realize she was softening toward him. Perhaps they could be friends - just friends - and things could still work out in her favor.

They walked in silence the rest of the way down the hill. The stream was crystal clear and minnows scurried around the bottom. The cool, inviting water trickled over several larger rocks, creating a gentle splashing sound that added to the soothing environment.

She pulled out some supplies and began tending to her wound. Darryn knelt beside her as she washed the gash. His touch was warm and gentle as he helped her bandage her arm. This dangerous and violent man, part of a group that destroyed entire cities, was on his knees and tenderly caring for her. She fought a smile.

As they finished, he glanced up with a gleam in his eye. "You never did tell me - if not spying on me, what were you doing in these woods?"

Linneya dropped her arm, ignoring the growing tug in her chest. "I was trying to forage for elyre berries. They are vital for a tincture I make to help with the winter season illnesses."

Darryn's face brightened, "So, you are a healer. My sister would love to meet you. She is always gushing about the unusual variety of plants that can be found around your capital. Let me forage with you and you can give me some stories to take home."

The knight needed to go. There was no point in telling him foraging stories or bonding over her healing work. But she could not stop herself from wanting to hear more. She offered a small smile and nodded. "Tell me more about your sister."

He grinned and launched into a description as they began to walk away from the stream, talking animatedly about her interests and her love of all flora and fauna. This led to a discussion of different healing methods, and inevitably the elemental affinities came to the forefront of the conversation.

"There are rumors that Aelor has the most powerful flame-talker on either continent. They should be trained in their combat abilities." Darryn studied her face as if he hoped for a reaction.

"Yet they prefer to focus on their healing power and the value it brings." Linneya focused on the path and frowned, trying to seem bored. They were supposed to be talking about plants, not political nonsense.

"Ah, so there is a flame-talker - and you know who they are." He smirked.

"I did not say that. I said they prefer their healing to the damage from combat power, but I know nothing else about their abilities. Ah - here it is."

The purple bushes were still full of the sour red berries that she was after. Linneya showed him which berries were ready to harvest and they went to work. They stayed in comfortable silence for almost an hour. Every once in a while, Darryn would whistle his tune and the birds would sing back. Her foraging sack was full and the suns were almost overhead before he broke the tranquility.

"You avoided my question earlier. Do you know who the flame-talker is?" He pressed.

Still staring at the brush, Linneya bit her lip. This was her fault for letting him follow her. She arranged her features in a display of ignorance before turning to meet his gaze. "The elementals stay hidden from most of us to protect themselves and their healing power, but why does it matter who it is? The person will be able to heal both Aelorian and Enthorian troops when the time comes. What more do you need to know?"

"It's going to matter if the prophesied appears and sides with the wrong people. The flame-talker may be a key element to stopping Serathor from destroying our countries. If the flame-talker is trained for combat instead of hidden and used for healing abilities, we stand a chance at survival. You should know this better than anyone. It's the lesson learned from the mistakes made in your mother's home country."

Her jaw dropped at his audacity. How could he so flippantly criticize the destruction of her maternal grandparents' kingdom? Serathanian armies razed Queen Althea's tiny homeland when they plowed through the Southern realms in search of larger conquests. Linneya occasionally overheard whispers that the elemental mages could have saved the small nation, but no one dared explicitly blame the queen's parents and their strategy.

"How dare you make such a tasteless comment! The flame-talker remains anonymous to protect themselves from anyone who would try to claim their power as their own. There is no need for them to embrace darkness and learn how to kill people. On top of that, you know nothing of the *mistakes* that my grandparents may or may not have made. There is more that goes into leading people than fighting."

He clenched his jaw and stared into the distance. "You claim to understand the responsibilities of leadership and yet you so easily dismiss me as crass. You will learn, princess. Light cannot exist without darkness. Healing the land and reuniting realms will come from sacrifice. Hopefully, you wise up before it is too late."

Linneya shivered at his words and studied him. "I am more than you give me credit for. My decision to stay at home and not pursue a husband is because of my dedication to leading and helping my people. It's exhausting to meet all of the speculation from those who claim to be our allies."

Darryn shook his head. "There is something you are not telling me. How are you nearly thirty, a princess, and unwed? You cannot claim it is only due to an unselfish need to take care of your people. That is not everything. What are you too ashamed to admit?"

She crossed her arms and turned her face away, blinking back tears of frustration. The man teased out a sore spot like a needle in an open wound. It would be easier to confess her role as flame-talker, if for no other reason than to stop him from looking at her with such pity.

Still, she needed to stay hidden. A sigh escaped her lips and he stepped closer.

Darryn reached up, picking a leaf out of her hair. His eyes met hers with an intensity that caused her breath to catch. The breeze picked up, swirling around the two of them. He gently placed his hands on her upper arms and squeezed. She stared at his lips, wondering what he tasted like. *Citrus and cedar...*

The knight leaned in, closing the distance between them and dropping his gaze to her mouth. Her heart beat a rhythm of excitement, but she grimaced and clamped her mouth into a sharp smile. Backing away, Linneya dropped her gaze. "I must return to my rooms. The masquerade..."

A shadow flickered across his face before he released her. "Of course. I will see you later this evening princess. Please, save a dance for me."

Linneya spun around and marched off before she changed her mind. He fell in step behind her and they silently made their way back to the palace. At the gate, she nodded to him and turned to walk to the royal apartment entrance. She shivered, feeling his gaze burning into her back until she entered the side door.

Chapter 4

That afternoon, Linneya was jittery with anticipation. Instead of dreading another night of dodging gossips and meddling courtiers, she daydreamed of dancing. Her maid was working on her hair and her feet kept swaying and tapping. Even waltzing with...

No, she would not think of Darryn. She shook her head and her maid tsked, grabbing her scalp and holding her straight. "I am sorry," she muttered. Her light gold gown was accented with deeper gold lace and her mask was black with the same tatted pattern.

As the maids were putting the finishing pins into her hair, Queen Altheia peeked into the dressing room. "Might I come in?"

"Of course, mother," Linneya smiled. Queen Altheia walked into the room, easing the door shut. "I saw you returning from the forest with Darryn this morning."

Heat crept up her cheeks. "Yes, I ran across him training in the woods and he offered to accompany me to pick elyre berries."

Her mother nodded to her arm and pursed her lips. "Is that how you got cut?"

Linneya sighed and sidestepped that awkward conversation while a maid wove her mask's ribbons into her hair. "Sort of, but I am curious, how much do you think Darryn knows about the flame-talker? He was pressing me for details and believes they should be trained." She shooed the maids out, hoping the queen would give her a real answer once they were alone.

"I doubt he knows much more than anyone else. His mother told me that his father was fascinated by elemental magic, but I did not know him. Darryn's work as a Falorian knight has likely caused him to be interested in the darker, more confrontational aspects of your power."

Linneya turned to face her mother while tying her mask. "He suggested that Grandmama and Granddaddy could have survived and saved their country if they had trained their elementals as soldiers instead of healers."

It was Altheia's turn to sigh. "Many people believed your grandparents should have forced the elementals to fight in the final battle. There are a lot of rumors that it could have changed the tide. Your father and I witnessed it, Linneya. The devastation wrought by Serathor could not have been stopped. Sure, one more battle might have been won, but Serathor's forces would have eventually won out."

"Until the day that Rynor was destroyed, my family focused on serving others the best they could. My mother and father made the brave choice to let the elementals escape with the refugees in hopes that the healing knowledge would live on. Sometimes the best decisions are the ones that keep others alive." Altheia's gaze was distant and there were tears in her eyes.

However, there was also a slight smile on her lips as if the memories were bittersweet.

Linneya laid a hand on her mother's arm. "I am grateful that you and Father made it out."

Altheia placed a hand over Linneya's. "As am I." She turned to her daughter, smiling. "The three of you make all the struggle worth it. I am so pleased with how things are working out for Eleanor. Now if I could get you and Aiden settled, I would feel my work is done."

Linneya shook her head and grinned. "I am happy with my lot. I want to be here, not married off and unable to use my power to protect our people."

Before Queen Altheia replied, the bells rang signaling dinner. Her mother patted her cheek and stood. "Time to go, dear." Linneya adjusted her mask one final time, linked arms with her mother, and they made their way to the dining hall.

As the guests lingered in the hallway, Linneya searched for the man she knew she should not be missing. "Princess." A rich baritone voice made her shiver.

She turned around and gasped. The blood drained from her face. She was staring into a silver mask - the *trillin* tusks transported her back to her nightmare assassin.

Darryn's lips pursed at her reaction. "Are you well?"

"Where did you find such a mask?" She struggled to keep her voice steady.

Darryn grinned from underneath the beast's visage. "This thing? It's one of the popular masks offered by Enthor's greatest artist, Sharya. There are at least four other people wearing it. Unoriginal, I know, but I had not planned on being at the masquerade tonight."

Linneya glanced around. Within moments she saw two others with the identical design. Her shoulders relaxed and she drew in a breath, steadying herself. Darryn cocked his head, but did not press further. Before she thought of anything else to say, dinner was announced and he led her into the dining hall.

The second evening was a quick affair designed to give the possible couples one more chance at intermingling. Linneya was seated between her brother and Darryn - no doubt her mother's doing. She spent most of the time laughing at her brother's boisterous storytelling and avoiding Darryn's gaze.

Twice, she gave into temptation and he locked eyes with her. Both times she swore her face nearly caught fire. The *trillin* mask was eerie, but the man beneath it made her blood sing. Relief only came after her father announced the end of dinner and gestured for everyone to continue the merriment through dancing.

Linneya headed into the ballroom and settled into her favorite alcove. The familiar scent of warm spices wafted through the room. The seat she chose allowed her to see most of the dance floor and the music echoed perfectly into that particular corner. She was relaxing and enjoying the sounds of merriment until an unwelcome figure blocked her view.

She looked up to find Lady Alayne in a dainty lace mask that barely covered her features. She sat down beside Linneya, crossing her arms. "I am sorry we got off on the wrong foot the other day. I have been frustrated by certain events and spoke out of turn. I would like us to have a chance to be friends."

Linneya's stomach churned. Even now, this woman's body language did not suggest she was friendly. However, she nodded. "Thank you, I look forward to getting to know you as you get settled in here."

"Since we are now friends, please let me confide in you. Darryn is not who he seems. He will suggest he does not have the right to be among the elite, but he is more worthy of a crown than anyone else I know."

Linneya cocked her head to the side. "Lady Alayne, thank you for this information, but please know that I am not in search of a mate at this time. Besides, my crown is only an extension of my father's. Once Aiden ascends to the throne, my power significantly wanes."

Lady Alayne pursed her lips. "That is all the more reason I find it difficult to believe you are avoiding securing a husband and your place amongst the nobility."

"Thank you for your feedback, friend." Linneya bit back a stronger retort and stood up to leave. The woman crossed her arms, but at that moment the song ended and Orrain strode into the alcove.

"Ah, Linneya, let us dance!" He held out his hand and she took it. Orrain ignored Lady Alayne but Linneya gave one final nod to the woman before he swept her onto the dance floor.

The song was one of her favorites; it always evoked a sense of summer winds. Their dancing was simple but swift and Linneya relaxed into the repetitive movement.

"How are you finding our palace, dear sir?"

Orrain grinned. "It is lovely, although I struggle to pay attention to much else when your sister is nearby."

"Ah, she is quite a beauty."

"Yes, no one else will do for me."

Linneya's chest warmed at his confession. She was thrilled to see someone who could match Eleanor for wit and energy. They wheeled around on the floor, bantering about the couples that were forming, taking bets on who was beneath each mask. Linneya was weightless as they spun. The dance ended, they bowed to each other, and she twirled her way to the edge of the floor, laughing.

As she spun off the dance floor, she slipped and stumbled into the arms of a stranger. To keep from collapsing into a pile, she grabbed his forearms and gasped an apology.

"It's alright. I was coming over to ask you if I might have this next dance?" The rumbling voice was familiar. Startled, Linneya stepped back to see his face. That damned mask. Darryn. Beneath the silver, his eyes seemed to turn an even deeper shade of sable.

Her palms tingled where they touched his arms, wishing she could explore him further, but she was acutely aware of the reality of their situation. Even if he felt the same, she could not leave her people. Even if he admitted their mutual attraction, he could not leave his sworn duties as a Falorian knight.

She took a deep breath. "What happened to strategy? Are you not afraid of dancing with a ruined woman, sir?"

He just smirked and gestured toward the dance floor. Speechless, she took his hand and allowed him to lead her to their place. He drew her close as the slow waltz began and a shiver of anticipation ran down her spine. How was this the same man that only yesterday was glaring down the table toward her?

"How is your cut?" He brushed around the bandaged part of her arm, avoiding the area directly over the gash. His touch left goosebumps in its wake.

She cleared her throat. "I believe it will heal quickly. Thank you." He nodded and they settled into an awkward silence. The urge was there to press closer, to feel supported by his strength. The thought made her heart flutter.

After a few moments, Darryn leaned in. "I noticed you were speaking with Lady Alayne again," he smirked. "Were you trying to reason with her about your choice to stay home?" Her cheeks began burning and Darryn seemed proud of his handiwork.

"I had no idea there were so many people opposed to my staying here," she retorted.

"Oh, it's not everyone. Lady Alayne is upset because her family had her convinced that I would be her best opportunity and now she is angry. It was complete rubbish, lots of mental gymnastics, something to do with traditional ancestral lineage." He studied Linneya's confused expression. "I have no intention of marriage. I am happy with my decision to live for war and vengeance. I swore my final, permanent oaths to become Falorian and then Alayne's family scrambled to enroll her for this exchange. She is humiliated and lashing out at your good fortune."

Linneya replied, "Well, I can understand her frustration. Choosing such a barbaric brotherhood is a strange way to live." She pursed her lips. "She also thinks you deserve a crown."

The sound of his laugh made her breath catch. "You cannot believe everything you hear, princess."

"But you are a Falorian knight?"

He smirked. "I am. Some find the brutality to be hard to stomach, but I welcome it. As a castaway son of disgraced nobility, I have no responsibilities to ensure the line and can risk it all for a bit of dark adventure. I embrace my deadly talents and, in turn, I have saved many."

"After how fast you put a sword at my throat this morning, nothing would surprise me."

He chuckled and pressed close, until his words tickled her ear. "You were in no danger. I think you know that. I would even wager you liked it."

She worked to steady her breathing. "You are hiding something."

Darryn pulled back and frowned at her. "Princess, two can play at that game. You question me as if I should be forthcoming with my life and decisions, yet I can see you are not being completely truthful with yours. You are harboring a secret and do not find me worthy of your confidence."

Her stomach fluttered and her mouth gaped open as his stare gripped her. Linneya wanted to say more - to tell him everything and trust him with her safety. However, revealing her truth meant she would be forced to go to Enthor and marry someone. Someone, but it would not be him. He had no intention of finding a partner and she had no intention of being taken from her kingdom.

Likely, he had chosen to dance with her because she was a safe choice. The knight knew she would not throw herself at him. The song ended and she dropped her eyes, turning to flee. He swiftly grabbed her wrist and warmth spread up her arm from his touch.

"I know you cannot understand, Linneya, but I am meant for a life of darkness. My choices have served my family well - even if others do not approve." His imploring gaze left Linneya conflicted. He seemed earnest and yet he was proud of his place in such a vicious group.

For a moment, she wondered if he sensed what his touch did to her - if perhaps he felt the spark between them. In the next breath she chided herself for the fanciful thoughts. Darryn would be gone tomorrow and she would return to the infirmary, anonymously healing and giving back to her people in whatever ways she could until Serathor attacked.

She gathered herself and responded cooly, "How can I think harshly of you? I've made similar choices to serve my kingdom without concern for my future security."

He smiled hesitantly and dropped his arm. She was conflicted and almost wished he would sweep her into an embrace, admitting he could feel the heat between them as well. Linneya hurried away from the dance floor, relieved that she only had to wrestle through the rest of the evening's festivities. Then he would be gone and things would be less confusing.

After another hour or so, King Varilon gestured for the musicians to clear off the platform for the choosing ceremony. Tradition dictated that it was less elaborate than the other events. The practical approach highlighted the nature of the exchange and its underlying commitments. Dry and unromantic, this was Linneya's least favorite part of the whole affair.

As her father read out the names of each of the suitors, they came forward to claim their bride. Linneya held her position by her mother and kept her face as blank as possible. Twice, Linneya caught Darryn looking her way. His face was a mask: no emotion betrayed what his thoughts were on the whole ordeal.

One small hiccup occurred when a local nobleman tried to claim one of the local women as his own. The treaty did not allow for the pairing, especially since the man had joined the exchange willingly and she was not participating. After a brief argument with some council members, he finally relented and announced his second choice, Lady Alayne. Alayne sneered at the slight but accepted his hand. Linneya grimaced - her new 'friend' was likely to not take this twist of fate well.

As King Varilon called Orrain up, the man wasted no time in making his wishes known. Eleanor's cheeks turned bright red and she embraced him before taking his hand. Mariel was chosen by a Lord Straion and both were grinning like children at one of the midseason festivals.

Then, as fast as it began, the entire ordeal was over. The humming sound of a throng of courtiers enveloped Linneya. She could not stop smiling at the energy that buzzed through the room. Eleanor's laugh trilled above most of the noise, her fluttering and giddiness drawing many of the onlookers to celebrate with her. Linneya felt full of happiness for her sister but struggled to ignore the tug of her own heart.

That sensation caused her to scan the room, looking for the one man who was off-limits. He was moving toward her and their eyes locked. A shiver went down Linneya's spine. Not ready to face that final goodbye, she turned and moved toward Mariel and her new beau.

Her friend grabbed her arm. "Lia! You just missed Mother. Come, meet Straion."

Linneya inclined her head toward Lord Straion. He was tall with light brown hair that he kept braided back. His eyes were hazel and he sported a scar that bisected his left eyebrow. The man's lips curled up at the sides as if he was permanently in on a joke.

She took his outstretched hand. "It is good to formally meet you. I am excited for both of you. Mariel is a treasure."

The man kissed the back of her knuckles and grinned. "I could tell that from the moment I laid eyes on her." He squeezed Mariel close and pressed his lips to her forehead. "She is my crown jewel."

Mariel gazed at him with a lovestruck grin. Linneya was pleased to see such happiness from such a short courtship. They exchanged a few more pleasantries, discussing Straion's home and the journey back to Enthor. Straion demanded she come visit as soon as possible and became giddy at finding out that King Varilon was a musician.

"I play anything with strings! I have always loved the fae's music. Their sacred thamu harps are beautiful."

She grinned and promised to show him their music room at some point. Straion looked ready to faint and he stumbled over his gratitude. Mariel mouthed her thanks as Linneya moved to the side so others could offer their congratulations.

After a few more minutes of celebrating, everyone began meandering outside toward the bonfires in the courtyard. The remaining red light from the setting, smaller sun made everything glow. Cushioned benches and hewn logs had been scattered in between the fires and groups of people were already claiming the best spots. The younger children started playing a game of tag, stumbling and weaving around the seated adults. Their laughter rose with the glowing embers into the night sky. Linneya's shoulders softened and a smile formed on her face at the sounds of celebration. Relief washed over her as she realized that she was on the other side of this ordeal.

She hurried toward the ale. Tonight, she would drink to her heart's content. The banquets were over, the choosing ceremony complete, now their lives could return to normal. The only thread that was not neatly fixed was Darryn. His burning gaze was branding her back and she twisted around. She searched the crowd and locked eyes with him.

As if he read her thoughts, he began making his way over. Linneya turned to stare into the flames and took a deep breath to calm the butterflies in her stomach. Fire always calmed her, as if her affinity could feel the closeness of the element. She inhaled the bitter aroma of the ale, then took a swig.

A tug in her chest told her that he had arrived. She hoped that he would make a quick comment and move on to another form of amusement. Instead, Darryn stood by her side and turned to gaze into the flames himself. The silence between them was comfortable and she prayed he would leave the painful parts unsaid.

He spoke first. "Tomorrow we leave for Enthor. I must confess, my time here has been more enjoyable than I anticipated."

She bit her lip and he pressed on. "What would you say if I asked to write?"

Her breathing became shallow and the courtyard faded away with his question. She studied his face, but his features revealed nothing about his intent. She took another sip of the ale, pretending to mull it over. "I would be happy to write to you. While I doubt I am a source of much entertainment, I am sure your adventures as a Falorian knight will make for fascinating letters."

He chuckled, "I am certain I will be required to ask after your experience on plants for my sister. I also want to hear about your life. What you do, how your healing skills serve your country, all of it."

"Then it is a deal. I look forward to your letters." She smiled. "I also expected this exchange to be difficult, but I can say I am pleased. Eleanor found companionship and I found a friend."

Color crept into his cheeks at the word *friend*. "Your entire family seems pleased with the results of this exchange."

"We have been lucky. Instead of being forced into marriage alliances with others, we have been allowed to forge our own path." She turned to him, "Mother saw to that after I was almost pledged to the wrong man. Eleanor wanted to join this time and my family is happy for her success."

He ran his hand through his hair, hesitating before asking, "So what of your path? Where will you go from here?"

Linneya took in the sight of her people and their celebrations. Her parents were beaming as they made their way through the crowd. Some younger men were pulling out instruments and debating what songs their impromptu ensemble would play. More children were joining the chaotic game of tag. Sounds of joy rang out, the scent of wood smoke hung thick, and she was certain this was home. But her soul was singing for this man next to her. The ale was not helping matters, but she took another long gulp.

As long as she did not make eye contact with Darryn, she thought she could survive this goodbye.

She wondered what would happen if she confessed her elemental power. Her stomach dropped at the thought. Would he understand? Would it change anything?

Interrupting her musings, he pivoted and blocked her view of the bonfire. Linneya gasped as he leaned down and gave her an intense look of pleading. "You claim this is all for duty, but you deserve so much more. I hate you will not let me in on your secret. If there's truly something that makes you undesirable, the right man will forgive you, princess."

Linneya's jaw dropped and her heart raced under his gaze. How could he think she harbored that kind of secret? Then again, she had not told him the truth.

She took a deep breath, set her tankard of ale on a nearby log, and reached for his arm to steady herself. The world fell away as she stared into his eyes. It was time to tell him everything. "Darryn, I -"

A scream jolted her back to reality. Darryn spun around, positioning himself between Linneya and danger. Disoriented, she peered around his outstretched arm and blood drained from her face. A toddler who was trying to play tag with the bigger kids lost his balance and fell face-first into the hot embers. His mother continued to scream as she reached toward the bonfire and dragged the child away by the heel, smothering his flaming tunic with a cushion. Her black hair had a single white streak, a curtain that hid the boy from view as she took in the damage. Wide-eyed and trembling, she began cradling her child and desperately tried to soothe his cries.

In three steps, Darryn closed the distance and knelt beside the mother. He turned to Linneya. "Guide me to the infirmary. This child might live if we can get him to the flame-talker."

She set her jaw and shook her head. "It's too far to walk, let me take care of him. Bring him over here and set him on this cushion. Then you can call for a coach to take him."

Darryn hesitated, looking as if he might argue. Linneya pursed her lips and snapped, "Quickly! Time matters - the longer this takes, the less the healing will be effective."

He relented, bundling the screeching boy into his cloak and brought him to her. "Keep him as comfortable as possible" he growled, before rushing toward the palace entryway.

But she knew it could not wait. The faster she could start healing him with her flame-talker ability, the better off this poor child would be. She sprang into action, reciting the enchantment that would activate her healing abilities. *"Krehth aeki raewi."*

Her hands shook as she worked over the boy's tiny body. Even as some of the less burned areas healed, blisters began forming in the worst sections. The characteristic warmth and light that came with her flame-talking abilities was sputtering. Something was not right.

She began breathing harder - the magic was not working. Linneya's eyes darted, trying to figure out what was stopping her flame-talker powers from fully healing this poor toddler. Her stomach twisted into knots as her eyes landed on the tankard and she realized the buzz from the ale she had been drinking was slowing the healing process.

The child was kicking and whimpering, losing the battle with consciousness. The whispers of the nobles around her were distracting - her secret was out. Gritting her teeth, she forged ahead. Alcohol might make this harder, but she was certain she would eventually be able to fully channel her powers. After what felt like a lifetime, the blisters began to recede.

Finally, the toddler began to relax and his breathing slowed. The glowing energy around her helped to remove the damage and her healing slowly restored his skin and tissue to their soft, baby-like state.

As he fell asleep, Linneya stood up, wiping her clammy hands on her skirt. She began searching for more ale, as the toddler's mother was still visibly shaking from the shock and needed something to help her steady herself. Before she could pour a pint, a familiar burning gaze pressed into her back and she froze.

The crunching of boots told her that Darryn had returned. Her mouth went dry and she slowly turned to face him. "So this is what you were hiding, *flame-talker*." He nearly spit the last word.

Linneya's heart thrashed against her ribs as Darryn's sharp tone hit her. She was too exhausted from the elemental healing to respond. She made eye contact, her flat expression mirroring the numbness spreading inside. His eyebrows knit together and his mouth formed a tight line. The shock and fury on his face told her he would not be the man to forgive her this secret. She wanted to argue, to beg, to make him see her, but it was too late.

The murmurs coming from the nobles still around the fire told her there was no chance of containing knowledge of her power any longer. Linneya's heart sank as she began to imagine the diplomatic mess that her abilities would create. The mood was somber. Quiet.

Too quiet.

Darryn had been moments away from being her friend, possibly more, but fate forced her to choose. Even with the consequences, she had made the right choice. Raising her chin, she turned away from Darryn, who was still frozen in judgment of the revelation he just witnessed.

She faced the mother. "Let us get this little one checked out at the infirmary. They can make sure there is nothing else to worry about." As she walked away with the mother and baby, his gaze burned into her, hotter than the bonfire. Linneya struggled to contain her panic. The child was fine, for that she was grateful, but what would become of her?

Chapter 5

At the infirmary, Linneya guided the mother to a futon while the healers checked the toddler in the exam room. The walls of the waiting area were painted with the celestial storytellers. Even as a child, Linneya was enraptured, almost reverent, when looking at the murals.

Like the tapestries, they now seemed alive. The twins that always faced opposite directions loomed from their mountain peak. The fiery goddess of war stood on the bow of a ship and pointed ahead, casting judgment.

Her heart tugged her forward to one particular panel, the seer in the cave. A shriveled, hooded figure hunched over a single candle. Most wanted the seer to tell them what was in store for their lives. Linneya was more curious about why the seer chose that cave, one that was said to be found only by the treacherous path beyond the sacred mountain.

A small whimper brought Linneya back to the present. The toddler's mother was still shaking and occasionally her tears would spill over. Linneya walked over and placed a hand on the woman's shoulder. "Let me make you some tea."

The woman nodded and managed a small smile. Linneya walked down the hallway to the largest apothecary preparatory room and began rummaging. The musty scent of dried leaves centered her, creating a sense of peace. She located the herbs needed for a relaxation blend, placed the leaves in a teapot, and began grinding the bark and roots. Her shoulders relaxed as the familiar rhythm of the mortar and pestle sent vibrations resonating up her arm.

She began to heat the water, staring at the flames flickering around the kettle. Her mind whipped up worry while she waited. Memories of Darryn's glare sent shivers up her spine. Visions of Serathor burning her people while she sat in some fine lord's fancy manor in Enthor plagued her. She shook her head to clear the sensation and turned back to preparing the tea. Her father would know what to do once she was back at the palace. She poured the boiling water over her herbal blend, threw two cups on the tray, and made her way back to the waiting area.

The toddler's mother was still pale and her eyes were droopy. Linneya stopped in front of her, poured them both some tea, and handed the woman her cup. "Drink this. It will calm your nerves." The woman nodded in thanks, taking the cup in both hands and breathing in the tea's scent.

One of the healers stepped out of the room, smiling. He was of a slight build and had reddish brown hair the color of the dirt paths painted on the walls. His eyes twinkled and his sharp gaze reminded Linneya of a hawk. The mother straightened up as the life-tender walked toward them. Linneya's heart sped up and she wrung her hands.

The hawk-eyed healer stopped in front of them. "Madam, your boy will be fine. There are no signs of burns or damage to his tissues. It was a celestial blessing that our princess was right there." He inclined his head toward Linneya and gratitude flooded her chest for the child's healing. The mother smiled and cried out in relief as another healer brought the toddler back to her.

The mother grabbed Linneya's hands in hers and squeezed. "Thank you, princess. My child owes his life to you. We are forever grateful." Warmth spread through Linneya's body and she smiled and nodded to the mother. The woman turned back to her child, grinning and speaking to him in their own special babble. Linneya waved to the healer and made her exit.

As she walked out and shut the door, she spied her brother. Aiden was leaning in a doorway with his arms crossed and a frown on his face. Their eyes met and he nodded toward an open room. She sucked in air and braced herself. Neither of them spoke as they headed into what appeared to be extra storage space for the apothecary. She grabbed a torch from the hallway and secured it into the brackets inside the room to give them more light.

Aiden shut the door behind them and let out a deep sigh. "Oh, Linneya. I am so sorry." He ran his hands through his hair as he paced around the space.

Linneya crossed her arms and studied the jars full of herbs that lined the back wall. "Have you heard anything yet from Father? I am wondering how we can keep this from becoming a problem."

He shook his head, "Mother is the one that found me and sent me here. I do not know if there is a way to stop Darryn from demanding you return with them."

Her heart sank. The thought of having to pack up and leave for some unknown man twisted her stomach into knots. "Do you know who they are likely to force me to marry?" She dragged her fingers through the dust on the shelves, hoping her brother could not see the shame creeping onto her face.

Aiden stared into the distance and narrowed his eyes. "Technically you are required to be betrothed to a noble before leaving here. It is written into the treaty to keep anyone from trying to weasel out of the exchange once the numbers are set." He cocked his head and smirked. "We both know there is only one person still available."

"So, Darryn." Her heart began thumping hard. He nodded and Linneya groaned, sinking onto a stool. She tried to ignore the excited tingling in her core. The situation was a disappointing outcome, no matter how strong of a pull she felt toward the man.

Aiden placed his hands on her shoulders and held her gaze. "Listen, if you are compelled to marry Darryn, do not allow him to bully you. I have seen the two of you together, this could be a wonderful thing. He is part of a brutal Falorian unit, but his heart is good. I do not say that lightly. I fought with him in the raids and would trust him with your life. He may have dark secrets in his past, but he will keep you safe. Now that everyone knows of your powers, you need someone who can protect you in Enthor."

Linneya put her head in her hands. "I thought that escaping a betrothal to King Shumor's son was the only terrible fate I would have to dodge. This arranged marriage treaty is horrible. Promise me that you will put a stop to this tradition once you ascend the throne."

He smiled sadly, "My ascension is likely to shake the foundations of our monarchy. I cannot make a promise to abolish this on top of everything else that must change."

Linneya nodded. Aelor's small population and desolate landscape had made it less welcoming. The people were more suspicious and the culture was slower to change than the larger countries, such as Enthor.

Aiden was always defying convention here and there, making room for Aelorians who had previously been overlooked or shunned. He would change policy for many things, but even kings had to choose their battles. Although some were inescapable, like the looming threat from Shumor. A shiver spiraled up her spine at the thought of all those who might die in her absence.

Tears welled up in her eyes. "If King Shumor's dragons ride into battle, people are going to die. People I could have saved." She took a shaky breath as wetness spilled down her cheeks.

He brushed them away with the back of his hand. "Linneya, you cannot save everyone, everywhere." He sighed. "Yes, there will be devastating loss, but there is nothing to be done. All you can do is go where fate would have you and do the best you can for the people at your new home. Keep yourself safe and fight to protect others from Serathor's conquests."

She grasped his arm. "Perhaps you can talk to Darryn. Convince him to bring me back here when we expect an attack?"

Aiden shook his head. "That is not likely. He has a duty to his king. I suspect he has direct orders to bring any useful elementals back with him to defend Enthor. He cannot openly defy King Birron. The king may be jovial and lighthearted on the surface, but anyone who angers him ends up brutally murdered. Ever since he took over their temples and named himself godking, he has been vengeful."

Her heart sank even further. "Darryn seems to openly defy every other convention. If he really wanted to, he would find the loophole that could keep me here without King Birron's wrath." She grumbled.

He chuckled. "Always the optimist. Come on, the carriage is waiting for us. Father will have more answers."

Aiden was silent for the entire ride back. Linneya was grateful for the time to think. If she was going to marry Darryn, maybe things would not be so dire. She flushed at the memory of their dance earlier that evening. How could only a few hours change things so much?

They arrived back as the moon was peeking over the horizon. Aiden helped her down from the carriage and pulled her into a hug. "Whatever happens, know I am here for you." Linneya nodded, blinking back tears, and turned toward the palace entrance.

Linneya plodded down the long hallway toward her King Varilon's study. Her mind whirled, desperate to make sense of the unknown. Surely her father could protect her from whatever the fallout. Almost immediately, she snickered at her false hope. There would be no fixing this - Aiden had made that clear. Darryn would not be much help, either. Enthor's king was volatile and could not be easily defied. Orders or not, she was unsure that he would help her. Darryn's angry expression was frozen in her mind and she shivered.

As she approached her father's study, she heard raised voices. She hurried forward, ready to open the door, until a particular growl stopped her.

"This is an affront to Enthor. You have withheld valuable information that our king cannot ignore." Frozen, Linneya stood outside the study, listening to the tense discussion already occurring between her father and Darryn.

"Darryn, you must see how important it is for us to protect Linneya. Her affinity holds great potential, but that potential breeds fear in some. She only harnesses the light side of the power. Her work as a healer could save so many when King Shumor unleashes his dragons."

Darryn sighed, "If I had known about this sooner, I could have carried the child to a private place and let her heal him in secrecy. However, there were too many witnesses to her power tonight. It is impossible to ignore. I cannot refuse to honor both our kingdoms' treaty and direct orders from King Birron to return with any powerful elementals we find. She must take Eleanor's place and come with us back to Enthor. "

Linneya's worry churned her stomach like ruined meat. The thought of marrying Orrain and denying her sister the happiness she deserved was unbearable.

"Your coming here and refusing a wife is also in direct defiance of the treaty. If you demand to take her, you must marry her and let both girls go instead of leaving Eleanor here. I cannot allow my daughters to suffer so."

Darryn huffed. "You cannot expect me to go against my sworn oaths for something as mundane as your daughters' emotions. This is the curse of nobility: we must place duty above enjoyment. The lack of sacrifice in the ruling class is part of why this land is drying up."

Linneya's heart sank. Darryn's words cut deep and she struggled to believe he was so unfeeling. The crack made by the open door was large enough that she peeked through to see his expression.

King Varilon stood up and moved out from behind his desk. Standing in front of Darryn, he placed his hand on the man's shoulder. "Orrain is not likely to take losing Eleanor well and my daughter would be crushed. Not to mention, Linneya and Orrain would not be well suited. The answer is simple: ask for Linneya's hand."

Darryn shook his head. "If you do not feel Orrain will work, then we can find another man. Any of the nobles will gladly take on the princess. Enthor would be proud to host both princesses."

The king grimaced. "And what of the noblewoman left behind? What of her family? Her future? I will not allow my failure to protect Linneya to harm another one of my subjects. Sacrifice is necessary, but this suffering is not. I saw the two of you coming out of the forest this morning. Your actions suggest you have developed feelings for my daughter."

"Feelings or not, I cannot give your daughter a life befitting a princess. I am a brute, my bloodlust drowns out any chance of peace for myself. Linneya must come with us - you know the war that may come to our shores and we will need her healing power," Darryn insisted.

"Yes, war will eventually come to your shores. King Shumor cannot be stopped. You are the warrior, a Falorian knight, and better positioned than Orrain to protect Linneya."

Her heart pounded in her ears. Unable to take anymore, Linneya burst into the study. "Father, I am sorry." Darryn clenched his fists and stepped out of her way as she hurried to the king's side.

King Varilon gently took her hands in his. "You did what was right for that poor babe. Our duty as leaders is to do our best for our subjects. You did the right thing." He turned, "I ask you one more time, Darryn, please reconsider. Take Linneya for yourself and allow Eleanor to wed Orrain."

Darryn's expression was unreadable as he scanned her flushed face. "Again, I cannot agree to marry your daughter. It is due to my shortcomings, not hers. I am sorry, but she must take Eleanor's place."

Linneya gritted her teeth. "Fine," she ground out, "based on what I have heard, I have no choice in this matter. I will go and keep the peace, but I want you to know I blame you for any death or damage that arises from my absence here."

His face twisted at her condemnation and she thought regret flickered across his features. "Fine, princess. Come with me, we can discuss the details further."

She looked toward her father and her stomach knotted at the sight of his furrowed brow. He waved to them, dismissing them from his study, and sank into his chair. If Darryn heard the groan and rattling cough that emanated from the room as they left, he did not show it.

Instead, he stormed down the hallway, heading for the hunting entrance. He pushed open the doors and pivoted toward the gardens. His long legs covered almost inhuman distances with each stride, and Linneya stumbled on the loose stone lining the path as she tried to keep up.

"Darryn, slow down" she huffed.

She tripped into him as he wheeled around. Darryn grabbed her arms and snarled. "Why did you hide this from me? I might have been able to protect you."

Linneya sighed and studied the rocks at her feet. She struggled to find words that would not sound accusatory. "The more people that know, the more danger I am in. You know elementals are being hunted for sport. Besides, my family needs me here. My people need me for my healing abilities. There was no benefit to being so open about my power."

He let go and shook his head. "You can learn how to harness your element and fight. I will train you to protect yourself once we are in Enthor. There may come a time in which you are the one saving us all."

Her eyes blurred from the tears and she shook her head. "I am not *that* strong. I may have some healing abilities, but I am no one's hero."

Darryn placed his hand on her cheek and brought his forehead to hers. She shivered at his touch. "After what I saw tonight, I can confirm you are one of the most formidable elementals alive. No one heals extensive burns that fast without significant signs of fatigue. If you had just told me you were an elemental, I might have been able to keep this from happening. We could have pretended to go to the infirmary and given you a private place to work."

She closed her eyes, breathing in his citrus and cedar scent. After a moment, she pulled back. Her voice shook. "I decided to tell you at the bonfire, but I did not get the chance."

Darryn dropped his arm and straightened up. "How convenient. Well, it would seem fate had other plans." He sighed and shook his head. "There is nothing left to say. You must return with us. I will see you safe and protected. You *will* be Orrain's bride and you *will* train to wield the darkness in your flame element like the powerful warrior you are, *princess*." His sharp tone left no room for discussion. He turned on his heel and stormed away, leaving her stunned.

The burning tears in her eyes spilled over. Trembling, she collapsed onto the closest bench and sobbed. A crunching sound on the path caused her to look up. Her sister was standing over her, wide-eyed and shaking.

"You - Orrain's bride?" Eleanor's nostrils flared and she balled her petite hands into fists. "You couldn't let me have this one thing, could you?"

"No, that is not - " Linneya wiped her eyes and stood up, reaching for her sister.

Eleanor wrenched away and jabbed a finger at her. "I always knew you would ruin things for me. You have always been so jealous of me. I am prettier and you cannot stand it. Now you have manipulated Father and Sir Darryn into having you take my place. You couldn't manage to catch anyone's attention with me around, so now you are trying to take my husband."

The flush crept up her cheeks at the accusation. "How dare you! This has nothing to do with who is getting attention. They have found out I am a flame-talker and now Darryn is forcing me to marry Orrain. I do not want this. I want to stay here and help protect our people."

Eleanor scoffed. "Oh, sure. You - the fabled flame-talker. I heard about your stunt at the bonfire. Just because you had some potion that kept the child from hurting as much does not mean you fooled me. Orrain will not stand for this. He wants me, not you. This is not over, Linneya."

In a movement that mirrored Darryn's exit, Eleanor spun around in a huff. Linneya sat back down on the bench and fatigue washed over her. She wanted to make a plan to fix this, but she was numb and her thoughts were too hazy.

The afternoon servants filing out through the gardens to head home pulled her from her melancholy. She stood up and retraced her steps to the palace. Tonight she would pack and prepare to leave, but she would be including some of her foraging supplies and other survival tools. Linneya would do everything in her power to be prepared to escape her fate, given the opportunity.

Chapter 6

Linneya shivered, more from dread than from the morning chill. She was of little help as the carriages were being packed, especially since her mind was still reeling from the sudden change of plans. She tried to comfort herself with thoughts of escape, but her musings were ensnared in a thick haze of fatigue. She stood there, stiff and shaking, wishing she had been able to sleep for a few more hours.

Her place was here, with her people - not in a foreign country a full mooncycle's journey away.

She winced at the day's greetings. The first light peeking over the horizon was too bright. The sound of the birds beginning to sing was too shrill. She was stiff from the sleepless night and exhausted from trying to figure out how to escape this mess.

Friends and loved ones were hugging, crying, and promising to write. In stark contrast, her father and mother huddled together with their advisors, deliberating on how to reverse this last-minute decision. There was so much hope in the farewells being spoken around her, but she was tumbling into complete despair.

Aiden and Darryn stood nearby, huddled in intense debate. Aiden's face was pinched and his arms were crossed. Darryn was gesturing southward - toward Enthor - and shrugging. She suspected that the conversation was a final attempt by her brother to stop this. While she loved her brother for it, Linneya also recognized it was futile. Darryn's decision would stand and she would become a bride in Enthor.

Mariel and Straion were saying their goodbyes. He was grinning from ear to ear and Mariel was looking at him with starry eyes. Warmth bloomed in Linneya's chest at Mariel's beaming face. As Straion pulled his betrothed close, Linneya managed a small smile. She was glad to see her friend in what appeared to be a promising arrangement.

A slamming door caused her to jump. Orrain stalked toward the caravan with a grimace on his face. Eleanor was so enraged by the turn of events that she refused to come down, so he had gone up to bid her farewell. It was a bad omen that her sister could not forgive the unexpected - and unwelcome - reversal of fate. Shaking, Linneya turned to her mother and father and said her final goodbyes, then walked toward the carriage.

Darryn broke away from Aiden and strode to her side. He placed a hand on her shoulder. "I am sorry it has come to this."

Linneya shrugged him off and raised her eyebrows, not wanting to speak for fear of adding to her troubles. Arousing suspicion would make it more difficult for her to escape once she had the chance. He offered her his hand as she climbed into the carriage. She stiffened at his facade of concern. He knew this would mean people would die, and he still insisted.

She stepped into the carriage, taking a seat beside Mariel. Darryn closed the door, refusing to meet Linneya's gaze. Shucking off the sense of dread, Linneya grasped Mariel's hands. Whatever awaited her in Enthor, at least she was not alone.

"Lia, I know this is not the way you had hoped to find a husband, and I know you feel torn because of your duties, but I am grateful that we are going to be together in Enthor."

Linneya smiled at her friend. Mariel had a knack for soothing one's worry. Her foot was crushed as a child and she struggled to run or go on adventures in the forest with the others as they grew up. What she lacked in physical ability, she made up for in perceptiveness. She seemed to know when Linneya needed distraction and when she needed quiet.

A shout from outside the carriage signaled that the caravan was departing. The driver whistled to the horses and there was a lurch as they began moving. Linneya settled in for what promised to be an uneventful mooncycle-long journey to Enthor's capital. She looked forward to the time that she and Mariel would have on the road, at least until escape was possible.

As if on cue, Mariel started reliving her experiences from the past three days. A lightness began to bloom in Linneya's chest at the familiarity of listening to her friend. Mariel was going over every detail and gushing about the excitement of starting this new life.

As Mariel continued chattering about her adventure, Linneya stared out the window to memorize as much as she could about their surroundings, just in case she got a chance to escape and needed to trace her way home. There were so many people that she lamented ever having an opportunity to slip away. The men riding their horses blocked most of the view, making it hard to see much about the landscape.

Instead, she watched for Darryn. Even though he would be at the front of the caravan, she wished he was riding alongside their carriage. A pang went through her chest, a longing.

Linneya sighed and Mariel patted her hand. "This is all going to work out exactly the way it needs to, Linneya. You are a powerful force, no one can deny your strength."

Linneya smiled, unwilling to divulge the tumultuous storm that was brewing inside. Desperate to change the subject, she redirected the conversation to Mariel's good fortune. "So, tell me about Straion."

Her friend's dark brown eyes lit up and she launched into details about their brief courtship. "Is his smile not the most lovely thing? When he asked me to dance, I thought I would melt. He has the kindest mind..." Content to let her friend gush, Linneya defaulted to a serene expression and occasional exclamation.

After catching up, they settled into a comfortable silence. As the afternoon wore on, fog began to move in along with an icy wind. The chill that settled on Linneya caused her to pull her shawl close and shiver. She could no longer see any of the surrounding landscape. Mariel nodded off and Linneya closed her eyes, relaxing back into the seat. The swaying of the carriage lulled her to sleep. Dreams of bonfires, silver masks, and dancing haunted her until evening.

Linneya started as the carriage ground to a halt. Blinking into the darkness, she felt around for the latch to open the door. Before she got to it, the carriage door sprung open and light from a torch blinded her. A man poked his head into their space. "Mari?" Linneya rubbed her eyes. "Ah princess, excuse me. I am looking for my betrothed." As her vision adjusted, she saw Straion grinning in the doorway. He held out his hand and helped her out of the carriage and then stepped inside. Linneya heard Mariel giggling and she scurried away to give them some privacy.

The suns were nearly set, but there was just enough light illuminating the clearing. Insects were humming a rhythmic pulse and the wind whispered gently through the trees. A damp smell suggested a wetland nearby.

She made her way to the supply cart. Others were milling around, grabbing necessary gear to set up for the night. Linneya began rummaging for a tent pack to set up for her and Mariel. A familiar voice rumbled, "Princess, could I help you with that?"

Linneya turned around and pursed her lips. Darryn reached around her, picking up a pack from the cart and dangling it in front of her. She yanked the pack away from him. "I am perfectly capable of setting up a tent, thank you."

He chuckled. "These tents are a bit more complex. They require two people to erect. Let me help you."

Linneya turned and scoured the groups forming around them, desperate to find anyone else who could help. She spotted Mariel working with Straion to build the campfire. Orrain was nowhere in sight. Causing a scene would call more attention to her and make it harder for her to escape once she had the chance. She gritted her teeth and mumbled. "Fine, let us set this up."

Darryn smirked and started walking toward a clear spot to build the tent. She followed, trying to ignore the pleased sensation that was growing in her core. She set her jaw, resolved to stay indifferent toward the man who forced this on her.

He motioned to a spot next to a tent that had already been pitched. Her eyes bulged at the massive size of the shelter. The knight was right; it would take two to set it up. Darryn silently handed her part of the frame and they went to work spreading out the pieces.

The bulk of the structure came together rather easily. They worked together in companionable silence and a sense of warm contentedness spread throughout her body. Linneya went to pick up the tent cover and three separate pieces of canvas fell out. "What are these panels?"

Darryn glanced at the cloth, his lips pulling up at the sides. "They are to divide the three rooms in your tent."

Linneya's eyes widened at the realization. "Three rooms?" She stepped back, placing her hands on her hips. "Do you not think these tents are a bit... overdone for this journey?"

He laughed and the sound made her blood sing. "I do. They are ridiculous. However, our king demanded that we make sure the women traveled in style. He seems to have forgotten that they take quite a bit of work to put up and take down. We have to stop early and end up leaving late every day. It adds a couple of extra days on our journey, but King Birron would have nothing less."

She grinned and shook her head. The entire setup was ludicrous. Several people struggled with the poles. One tent collapsed with two people inside, everyone clamoring to get back out from under the heavy canvas. The sight made her giggle. "Well, far be it from me to defy the king's orders."

His smile grew even wider and she tossed him one of the panels. They worked to adjust the frame to accept each panel and then secured the domepiece to the top. When they finished stretching the outer layers of the canvas around the frame, Darryn hammered the corner posts in place to secure the cover. Linneya watched as he worked, noting how his rolled up sleeves accented his muscles. She bit her lip as she marked the sweat glistening on his chiseled arms. It was becoming impossible to want to keep her distance.

As he finished the last post, they both stepped back to admire their handiwork. She grinned and poked at the tent cover. "Well, it will not keep predators out, but it sure makes for a fancy setup."

His hands balled into fists. "If you run into predators, you scream. I will be by your side immediately."

Her grin fell and her eyebrows pulled together in confusion. Why was he so concerned with her welfare? It did not seem to matter yesterday when her father practically begged him to marry her. "I am certain we are safe, sir." Linneya bit out.

He placed one hand on the post behind her and leaned in. "If *anyone* bothers you, I am right next door." She shivered as his breath tickled her ear. She was torn between moaning and clawing his eyes out.

A twig snapped and they both jumped. Orrain was standing a few feet away with his arms crossed. "Darryn, I believe I need some alone time with my betrothed. Do you mind?"

The knight straightened up, smirking. Without looking at Linneya, he turned on his heel and stalked off to his tent. Orrain rolled his eyes and strolled over to where she stood.

Smiling, Orrain put a hand on her arm. "I know this is not what we would have wanted for each other, but I promise to do the best I can to help you be happy."

Linneya looked up at him and sighed. "I am sorry it happened this way, but at least we can find some sort of camaraderie in our elemental powers."

He nodded, staring off into the woods. She touched his sleeve and continued, "Do you think we could come back once we are wed to help defend Aelor?"

He laughed softly. "Oh, no dear. No wife of mine fights. You will be well attended and will stay busy with helping me grow my influence in the capital."

"But my people are in danger-" He held a hand up to stop her pleas, then wrapped his arms around her and hugged.

"Lia, I said no. Absolutely not." Her body tensed at his touch, but she forced herself to relax into his embrace. After what felt like an appropriate amount of time, she tried to pull back but he gripped her tighter. There was no room for debate, no room for what she needed. She stopped struggling and chewed on her bottom lip, waiting for him to release her.

Finally, he planted a kiss on the top of her head and dropped his arms, turning to leave. She could feel a familiar burning sensation boring into her back. As Orrain sauntered away, Linneya turned and caught a glimpse of Darryn's expression. His jaw was set and his eyes were narrowed. He was framed by the pitch black of the cold forest. She stepped toward him, but he rearranged his features into a mask of boredom and turned back to the campfire.

She crossed her arms and ground her teeth. He was the reason she was stuck here. Why did he get to act petulant when this was all his fault? Her stomach twisted in knots at the thought. Before she worked up the courage to confront him, Mariel appeared at her side. "Come, Lia. Straion and I saved you some stew."

Her friend's eagerness was infectious. A warmth grew in Linneya's chest and she grinned. "Alright, let us eat and toast to new beginnings." She turned her back on the icy darkness of the forest and allowed herself to be consumed by the celebratory warmth of friends.

For the first week, the caravan's progress was uneventful. The scenery slowly changed from dark, dense forests to more open fields and lakes scattered in between smaller forested areas. Linneya began to suspect that Darryn had ordered for her to be watched at all times. Or maybe it was because people were fascinated by her power. Someone was always nearby, pretending not to pay attention to her.

Days were spent in the carriage with Mariel and occasionally Straion riding with them. Much to everyone's amusement, one time an ornery healer popped in unannounced to bicker over a medicinal preparation with Linneya. Orrain never spent much time near her and was becoming increasingly snippy. Nights were full of storytelling, games, and the more adventurous couples sneaking off to get to know one another better.

Dinners around the campfires were informal, with everyone sharing gossip and exciting news. Sometimes the conversation turned dreary in the red glow of the evening light. Whispers of the Serathanian threats were traded amongst the caravan. Linneya's heart would race whenever someone mentioned King Shumor, the dragons, or rumors of Serathor's scouts. Most of the nobles were convinced there would be war soon, within the next annum. No one mentioned assassins or exsanguinated elementals and Linneya decided her nightmares were nothing more than manifestations of her fears.

The travel was dull, but it gave her time to consider her options. She was closely watched during the day, but it seemed possible to slip off during second sleep and make her way back to Aelor. The winter season would be settling in soon, with bitter cold winds that would make traveling alone next to impossible. It would be at least ten mooncycles before the spring season suns would begin to warm the land. If she left now, she would struggle less against the weather, but could she abandon Mariel? At least now they were together and the days were enjoyable.

She stared out of the carriage, noting the stream that was a stone's throw from their current road. Perhaps she should stay with the caravan a little longer and make sure her friend was alright. She chewed the inside of her cheek and tugged at the rough curtains as she marked the water feature as a possible one-week landmark for her trek back.

A sigh startled her from her reverie. Linneya swiveled toward her best friend. Mariel was looking at her with her brow furrowed and her lips turned down. Linneya blinked rapidly and leaned in. "Are you alright, Mari?"

Mariel sighed again and shook off the frown, smiling sadly. "Yes, but I am worried about you. Lia, you cannot blame yourself for what has happened. The fate of Aelor does not solely rest on your shoulders - even with your flame-talking abilities."

Linneya took her friend's hands and squeezed her thanks. In such a moment, she was grateful for her friend's intuitive comments.

The carriage shuddered as it stopped. Linneya was surprised it was already time for noonrest. Both she and Mariel hopped out and made their way to where Straion, Darryn, and some of the others were unpacking a picnic.

Orrain joined the group just long enough to snag a handful of dried fruits and hard cheeses. He stalked off toward the carriages without acknowledging any of them. Linneya let out a breath of relief at the sight of him retreating. He had become unbearable with his odd mood swings.

The day was unseasonably warm and a chance to rest in the shade was welcome. After they were done eating, Straion flopped out on the ground and shaded his eyes from the suns. "What would it take to hold the caravan up while we found a place to swim? It's so damned hot."

Darryn gestured toward a stand of trees. "There is a stream right over that hill, just beyond that grove." Linneya raised her eyebrows at him, silently questioning how he could know so much about this part of Aelor. He shrugged at her expression. "At least, I assume that is where the stream we crossed earlier flows. The trees are thicker in that direction."

Mariel jumped up, almost stumbling in her excitement. "The four of us should go! Lia, come on, it is probably the only chance we will have to stretch our legs today."

Linneya took her hand and they sauntered off in the direction the knight indicated. The wooded area had a fresh, resinous smell that emanated from aethereal everblue trees. Straion and Darryn lumbered behind them, chatting.

As they crested the hill, the sound of trickling water made Mariel squeal in delight. "Listen to that! Even its sound is so refreshing." Down below, the spring widened into a shallow pool. The water sparkled in the noontime sunslight.

Straion took off his shirt and flung it to the side. Mariel bit her lip, gazing at her betrothed. Linneya giggled at her expression and Mariel turned red. "Stop it! I cannot help if I struck gold. I just - oh!"

Mariel was cut off as Straion snuck up behind her and picked her up into his arms. Linneya threw her head back and laughed as her friend squealed. Straion marched straight into the water, tossing her shoes back to shore and carrying Mariel until the pool was almost waist high.

Linneya grabbed their shoes and Straion's shirt, tucking them safely to one side. The heat on her back was familiar, and she turned around to meet Darryn's gaze. "Are you joining us in the water? I can put your things over here."

He chuckled and stepped toward her. "Why? Are you hoping to catch a glance of my bare chest? Sorry, princess. I keep this under wraps."

She crossed her arms and huffed, halfway joking. "I was trying to be helpful. If you do not want to play nice, that is on you."

He closed the distance between them and ran a knuckle across her cheek and jawline. Heat flooded her veins, and she was unsure whether she wanted to devour him or slap him. One side of his mouth crooked up, as if he could tell what she was thinking. Before she could respond, he turned and walked into the water - fully clothed.

She followed and gasped as the water licked at her legs. It was cold, sharp enough to bite, but satisfying on such a warm day. The four of them swam for a few minutes, enjoying the chill of the water and the heat from the sunslight.

A green glint near a boulder caught Linneya's eye. Curiosity seized her and she wandered further into the stream. Mariel called out to her, "what are you looking at, Lia?"

The green rock was partially submerged in the gray mud, but Linneya was able to pry it free with a satisfying squelching noise. Mariel came up to her as she rinsed it. Linneya rubbed one side with her thumb, the rough surface showing vibrant flecks of green. "It is dirty, but I am certain that it could be cut and polished into something beautiful."

Straion sloshed over, excited. "Might I see? Rocks are a hobby of mine." She nodded and he took it and held it up to the light. "What an amazing find!" He licked it and Linneya raised her eyebrows while Mariel giggled. "How unusual. This is a massive gem, but I have never seen anything like it. What are you going to do with it?"

A flash of memory, Orrain confessing his ground-tamer abilities during their first dance, flitted through her mind. She was drawn to flame because of her affinities, perhaps Orrain had a similar connection with stone. "I think I will give it to Orrain. When we get back to Enthor, he can have it cut and polished. It may not be valuable, but it is bound to be gorgeous." Linneya thought Darryn's jaw pulsed, but she ignored it. The man could keep on being angsty, he had no one to blame but himself.

Others from the caravan were wandering over and exclaiming at the sight of the spring. The four of them made their way back to the bank and grabbed their things. Mariel and Straion headed back to their carriage, whispering in each other's ear. A small sting of jealousy crept into Linneya's chest. Their relationship was blossoming in an easy manner. Unlike hers.

Speaking of her betrothed, Orrain was nowhere to be seen. She snuck over to his horse and brushed her hand across its soft, burnt sugar coat. The warm, grassy scents of the animal caused a sense of calm to wash over her. He nickered in greeting and she shushed him, giggling. "Hush, honey, I just want to give your master something to smile about."

She unlaced his largest saddlebag and pushed open the top flap. Wrapped in dark wool, almost hidden, a small sliver of metallic glinted in the suns. Curious, Linneya pushed aside the cloth and groaned. *Another one of those ridiculous trillin masks.* Its feline glare roiled her stomach.

She covered the mask back up and placed the rock on top. She began lacing the bag shut, grinding her teeth at the unwelcome reminder of her nightmares. A hand grabbed her wrist and she started at Orrain's sharp tone. "What are you doing?"

"Oh, I put a gemstone in there. It's rough, but the green tone suggests it would polish up and be beautiful. I wanted to surprise you."

He narrowed his eyes and tightened his grip. "Snooping in my bags is not the way to surprise me, Linneya."

She huffed a laugh. "Okay, I will remember that." He would not let go and after a moment she realized he was not joking. Orrain's eyes were vacant and his hand was a steel manacle around her arm. She finally ripped her wrist from him. He snorted and turned back to his horse, dismissing her, and she turned to leave.

Heat crept up Linneya's cheeks. Surely there was nothing *that* private in his knapsack. Someone coughed and she turned, startled. Darryn was standing a few feet away, watching. He marked her rubbing her wrist and his jaw pulsed. She set her lips in a hard line and marched past him, refusing to entertain his anger.

Chapter 7

That evening, Orrain had returned to a more normal disposition. He sauntered over, helping Linneya out of the carriage. "Lia, I did not get a chance to properly thank you for your gift. It will be a beautiful addition to my collection. I will help you set up the tent and then we can eat together."

Linneya hesitated before smiling. "Of course. I am happy to hear you enjoy stones. When I thought about how flame draws me to it, I wondered if you might be the same with ground."

Orrain gave her a bemused look and gestured toward the wagon with the tents. They walked together, grabbing the supplies they needed before finding a spot to erect the monstrosity.

The forest sang its lullaby as the suns drew lower in the sky. The woodsmoke from the bonfire hung thick. Someone began whistling a traditional song of praise to the twins and others joined in.

As Linneya and Orrain began to put together the frame, a dark figure was looming. Darryn had his arms crossed, glaring at the two of them. His brooding was irritating. He had alluded to his bloodlust as if he was dangerous, but so far all she had seen was him moping about as if he had no control over the situation.

She wanted to go over to him, shake sense into him, and then get lost in his body. Warmth drenched her core as she envisioned his strong hands wrapping around her waist and pressing her against him. His lips on hers, tongue claiming her as a shiver ran up her spine...

"Heads up!" Orrain tossed her a canvas divider and she caught it, barely avoiding it slapping her face. Linneya shook her head. Daydreams of the man that effectively forced her into this captive state were pointless.

They completed the tent in record time. Orrain slung his arm across her shoulder and steered her to where the others were digging into dinner. They stepped into line, Linneya taking in their surroundings. The beautiful purple trees glowed with the red hues of the second setting sun. The aromatics of wood smoke and hearty spices from the stew permeated the clearing.

A sudden disruption of raised voices caused Linneya to jump. The ornery healer was squawking at one of the younger men. "What nonsense! You forget yourself. I was there when we rebuilt Rathen. There was nothing. No buildings remained fully intact from Tirathel. The only things that survived unscathed were the catacombs." The man dropped his gaze, appropriately chastised, but the healer kept haranguing him with details.

Linneya's eyes widened. Enthor's capital was over a duocentury old. The previous city, Tirathel, was only whispered about in legends. She turned to Orrain "How could they know that?"

Orrain grinned. "That healer, Falryn, is over six hundred seasons old. While most elementals live an extra twenty or thirty, their rare combination of elemental affinities causes them to age at a slower rate than a normal human. The most gifted of the elementals are rumored to be practically immortal."

Linneya chewed on her bottom lip. She had never met an elemental with more than one affinity. The healer moved with the grace of someone who had only seen two duodecades - not even a full one hundred seasons.

Once she had her bowl of stew, she settled on a log next to Orrain. Clouds gathered in the sky, as if it would rain at any moment. The icy wind had them all huddled around the campfire as Falryn told legendary stories of magic, creatures, and myth.

Falryn was in the midst of explaining the threat against elementals. "Some say the seer has given a prophecy that explains the fate of humankind. Rumor has it that King Shumor believes it means Serathor will be restored to its original splendor. He has been hunting for the elemental who can harness all five elements: mist, ground, flame, aether, and vine. He believes this person is prophesied to secure his rule and lead his armies to conquer all of the human realm."

One woman spoke up. "I heard he is experimenting on elementals." At her announcement, a murmur rustled through the group. Linneya shivered and Orrain pulled her suffocatingly close.

Falryn pursed their lips. "Yes, there is a strong likelihood he is capturing elementals to study. Many people have disappeared around the same time Shumor's scouts were nearby."

Mariel leaned forward. "But, why? What is the purpose of experimenting? Would it not be easier to use threats or mind control?"

Darryn growled before Falryn could respond. "Powers extend life. One belief is that if the king controls enough elementals, he will become immortal. The allure is from both power as well as infinite life."

One of the men scoffed. "Then why are hunters murdering the elementals? It seems like such a waste to eliminate that kind of power."

Linneya shivered as a vision of the silver *trillin* mask flashed before her eyes. She almost whispered the words. "Hunters do not kill people to eradicate power. They do it to absorb the power for themselves." Heads turned and stared at her.

Falryn raised their eyebrows. "Most people are not aware they have that ability. Yes, it is believed that these hunters can use gemstones to absorb the power of any elementals they murder. Then, whoever wields the stone can use the elemental power stored within."

Orrain interjected, "Not just any gemstones. They use stones from the Other that can hold the elemental energy."

Ice chilled her veins. She had heard the Other mentioned only a few times. It was a world apart from theirs. Rarely did someone venture to the Other. It was a difficult journey and not everyone completed it. There were a few portals in different human kingdoms, heavily guarded by knights handpicked by their respective kings. Legends also suggested the Creators sometimes gifted a person with the ability to walk between the worlds, although Linneya had never heard of someone possessing this power.

Falryn nodded. "That is one possible theory. Other sources suggest that it is not about the source of the stone, but about elaborate rituals performed after the stone has been drenched in the blood of the dying elemental."

Linneya was not sure, but it seemed as if Orrain tensed at the correction. A vein bulged in his neck, dancing with his pulse. He did not press the point further and Falryn continued. "It is hard to separate rumor from fact with these hunters. Most speak of them in hushed tones as if staying quiet would keep their families from harm. Evil like this is allowed to spread when we are silent."

Orrain declared, "It would be so much easier if King Birron would grant us license to kill them on sight." Linneya scoffed at his bravado. He turned to her, narrowing his eyes. "What? It is the quickest way to eliminate the problem."

She shook her head. "More killing is never the answer to widespread issues. It would be better for trained knights to capture and interrogate the hunters to learn more about their techniques and strategies. Eventually, better plans could be put into place depending on what was discovered. It would stop unnecessary bloodshed and help the kingdoms discover what is needed to eradicate the hunters."

He clenched his jaw and stared past her. Falryn lifted their chin and tilted their head, studying Linneya. Darryn's eyes burned into her, though she refused to meet his gaze.

Mariel broke the silence. "Are the hunters after Creators-blessed as well?"

Orrain sprung up and stalked off to the edge of the woods. Falryn tracked his movement before rolling their eyes and turning back to Mariel, "Elementals are easier to find. Their affinities can affect the natural world even when they are not expecting it. Creators-blessed magic is all psychic. Unless someone has disclosed their gifts, it is harder to discover who has those powers."

Linneya caught Darryn looking at her again. He raised his eyebrows and smirked, jerking his chin in the direction of Orrain. It was as if he was suggesting she needed to go soothe him. Heat crept up her cheeks. It felt odd to stay, but she dreaded having to pacify Orrain's ego. She reluctantly stood to follow her betrothed.

Orrain was a statue, staring off into the dark as if in a trance with his fists clenched. Linneya stopped beside him and touched his arm. He turned his back and started to walk away. She followed him into the woods, stumbling to keep up with his long strides. "Orrain, what is wrong?"

No answer. He kept crashing through the brush and she struggled behind him. For several minutes, he ignored her and pushed deeper into the trees. The dense foliage blocked most of the fading light. The overcast sky made navigation difficult and Linneya began to worry that they had gone too far.

Linneya glanced back toward the campfire. She could no longer see its flames and she chewed on her bottom lip. "Orrain, if we go much further we might end up lost. I cannot see camp. Oooh!" She tripped over an exposed root and fell into his back.

He whirled around and bared his teeth. "Do not ever contradict me in front of the others. Never again. Do you understand?"

She stumbled backward and her jaw dropped. "Contradict you? We were just debating -"

"No, you tried to make me look foolish." He snapped, jabbing a finger at her. His other hand twisted around his gold brooch. "In leaving Eleanor behind and agreeing to marry you, I have rescued you from looking like a traitorous cow in front of the king of Enthor. The least you could do is take my side." His chest heaved and the wildness in his eyes made her cringe.

Linneya's thoughts whirled as she struggled to understand. Embarrassment clashed with confusion and she tried to respond. "Oh, okay. I am sorry. I am grateful for what you are doing. I would like us to have a chance at a peaceful life together. I will try harder. Again, I am sorry."

Orrain stared at her, a snarl on his lips. She was afraid to move or speak further. After what seemed like an eternity, he turned on his heel and stalked deeper into the woods.

At first, she thought he would come right back. After several minutes, it became clear he had left her. Abandoned her. Everyone would think they were together and no one would be looking for them for hours. She began shaking and tears filled her eyes. *What just happened? Why would he speak to me like that?* The questions burned like bile in the back of her throat. Linneya started walking back toward the camp.

Breathing became a chore. Brambles cut at her hands and face. She struggled to put one foot in front of the other.

She pressed forward until she came to a clearing. She stopped for a moment and sat on a mossy rock. Her breath came fast and shallow. She tried to steady herself and settle the spinning thoughts. The conversation kept replaying, parts of it louder or softer. She had to live with this man. Had to make a home with him, for life. The nightmarish thought made her shudder and tears spilled over.

The cold began to settle into her bones. She would have to start moving or end up sick from the chill. She stood up, oriented herself to where camp must be, and carried on. Thorns scratched and twisted against her legs, mimicking the pain squeezing her heart. She shook her head, unable to face what this meant.

Crashing through the brush, the exhaustion cut into her muscles, screaming at her to stop. Her legs began shaking and her breath came in short gasps.

How far from camp had Orrain led them? Surely the tents were close, but she still could not see the fire. She stumbled and pushed aside a sapling. She came to a second clearing and found another moss-covered rock.

"No, this is the same rock. Same clearing. By the shadowed void, what am I going to do?" Linneya shivered and wrapped her arms around herself. Getting lost in the wilderness was not part of the plan. She craned her neck toward the skies, but the clouds still obscured the stars. She had no way to determine which direction she needed to go.

Disoriented, Linneya succumbed to her tears. Sobs ripped from her throat and she slid down the rock to the ground. The shock of the evening washed over her, waves of an incoming tide that threatened to drown her if she did not move. The panic shut off any survival skills Aiden had taught her. She curled herself into a ball, pressing her legs to her chest.

The discomfort of the forest floor barely registered. Insects crawled over her as if she was just another boulder. Her arms and legs became numb and she closed her eyes. Panic devoured her. Linneya could have laid there days.. or maybe it was a few minutes...

"Linneya! Orrain!" Shouts came from nearby. A crashing sound caused her to float back into consciousness.

"I am here," she croaked, unable to move. Desperation in the voices rallied her. A dark grumbling curse spilled from the mouth of her sweetest enemy.

"Here," she managed a little louder.

The clattering stopped and she heard a sharp intake of breath.

"I will kill him." A voice growled and strong hands sat her up. She was wrapped in the soft warmth of a blanket and the smell of citrus and cedar made her wrench open her eyes.

"Orrain is still out there, D- Darryn." She could not stop her teeth from chattering.

He frowned, looking out into the woods. "The man can take care of himself. I am getting you back to camp." Before she protested, the knight swung her up into his arms. She sighed, leaning into his strength, and shut her eyes again.

Within moments, the smell of wood smoke and sounds of relieved exclamations prodded her senses. Mariel sobbed with relief as Falryn barked commands. Arms squeezed around her, sturdy and secure, and all faded into the aether.

The warmth of a damp cloth on her forehead startled her awake. She was still being held, citrus and cedar enveloping her liminal consciousness. The sounds of another person moving about the tent made her open her eyes, looking for who was with her. She tried to twist around to see and Darryn's arms tensed. "Linneya?"

All she could do was mumble. Linneya buried her head back into his chest, listening to the comforting rhythm of his heartbeat. Falryn's voice cut through the fog. "She is waking up. You can put her down now. Let me do what I do best. Lay her down."

Darryn tightened his grip and his heartbeat became more insistent. Falryn chuckled. "Boy, you made the wrong decision with this one."

"Will she be okay?" He shifted, settling Linneya on the cot and moving himself to sit next to her.

"Physically, yes. That man is a snake though. She will not survive his evil." Falryn finished mixing a concoction and held the vial full of purple sludge out for Linneya. "Take this, girl. It will help you sleep and be ready to go in the morning. You may sleep through moonwake, but you will feel much better come dawn."

Linneya nodded, taking the vial, and sniffed at the substance. Her nose wrinkled and she cleared her throat. Darryn chuckled. "Falryn's remedies are potent, but they work well. Best to take it all at once if you can."

She knocked back the bitter tincture, coughing as the astringent aftertaste caught in her throat. Falryn nodded in approval, taking the vial and packing their supplies up. "Rest. You are well, only a little shocked and chilled. Tomorrow you will be able to travel just fine." A rare shadow of a smile graced the healer's face before they left the tent.

Darryn stared after Falryn, lost in thought. Linneya sighed, sinking back onto her cot. At the sound, he turned back to her. "Sleep, princess. I will not let anyone bother you. I will stay until Mariel returns."

She did not respond. Falryn's tincture began weaving sleep into her eyes. The last thing she felt was the warmth of his fingers stroking through her hair.

When her dreams came, the assassin had returned. He was crouched in a tree at the base of the mountain, waiting. His eyes were locked on a stronghold, one of the fabled halls of the Southern dwarven realms.

The grinding of stone and clanging of the forge vibrated the ground. A light drizzle pattered against the *trillin* mask, but the harbinger of death paid no attention. Petrichor mixed with limestone dust to create a loamy, metallic aroma. The warmth of spring was muggy, but the occasional breeze provided relief.

The rain suddenly turned violent, thunder crashing so hard the branches of the tree shook. A woman stormed out of a small door to the side of the front gates. She ran her fingers through her inky black hair and growled into the red glow of the evening second sunlight. She was short and stocky with a gleam in her eye that would make a lesser man cower.

She stomped in his direction. The assassin dropped from a tree branch, landing in front of her. "Vine-bender! You have been chosen."

The woman rolled her eyes and snapped, "Chaanren, if this is your idea of a fresh prank, you need to think again. Get more creative and pick better timing. By the shadowed void, tonight is not the night to try me."

She moved toward him, head held high. The assassin cackled and pulled out his blade. She stopped dead in her tracks and her eyes widened. "You are not Chaanren."

"No, woman. Your judgment has come and you have been chosen as a worthy sacrifice." He crept toward her, his teeth glinting in a menacing grin beneath the mask.

The woman hissed and the assassin stopped in his tracks, faltering. "You are not the vine-bender."

Her hands shook as she raised them, aqua colored smoke billowing from her arms. "What does that matter? *Kwaesh aeki raewi.*" A torrent of rain fell as she turned to run, making it impossible to see where she was headed.

The harbinger growled. "*Raeshio boshog.*" Immediately the deluge stopped. The air around him turned drier than the arid desert, sapping moisture into a void. The woman was gone.

He sniffed the air and stalked into the woods. "Mist-whisperer, do not play this game. You will lose." He stopped, looking around at the brush and tracks on the ground. The assassin adjusted his path, looking up into trees and kicking over dead stumps.

He raised his hands. "This is your last chance to surrender! I do not have all night. Come peacefully or be dragged like a coward." After a moment's pause, he shouted more of the ancient spells. "*Raeshio pfee.*"

The words conjured a whirlwind, twisting the tree tops and shaking the underbrush. The assassin's hood ripped back away from his head and he stumbled back against the force. Yet the woman was nowhere to be found. He prowled forward, growling. "*Raeshio pfee shatarki.*"

The whirlwind returned, twisting trees out of the ground by their roots. The cracking sound cut through the air like ice shattering as it melts in the spring. A scream came from the pile of timber as the air settled.

He trudged forward, wrenching limbs and splintered logs out of his path. The aromas of different chips of woods mixed together in a fragrant bouquet. He moved a final branch to reveal the woman, disentangling herself from the destruction. She spit on him as she scrambled to get away. "You foul beast! Nothing about Serathor's plans will come to fruition."

The assassin backhanded her, sending her to her knees. "Your power will be used to reclaim lands and restore balance! The sacrifices we are making will lead the world forward to prosperity. Accept your place with bravery and let us get on with the ritual."

He leaned down and grabbed her hair, dragging her back to a cleared area. The woman shrieked and twisted, scratching at his face. He held her at a distance and continued methodically searching until he found his knapsack. The harbinger pulled out a red gemstone and shell and laid them on the ground.

He kicked her knees from behind, forcing her to kneel. Then he swiftly sliced her neck. She fell into his arms and blood dripped onto the rock. The woman gargled, glaring at him as she slowly faded. He brushed the hair out of her eyes, almost as if he admired her spark. As her life force faded into the stone, the drizzle picked back up, slowly becoming a steady downpour.

The rain hissed to the assassin, a sound of betrayal and fear. His eyes darted around, searching wildly through the downpour. Then the harbinger of death looked directly at her and pointed a single, accusatory finger.

Chapter 8

Linneya woke up in a cold sweat, shaking. She had not dreamt of the assassin since leaving home. The covers were suffocating and she threw them off of her.

The events of the previous night hit her and her stomach turned. Nauseous and disoriented, she jumped up and ran outside. She made it to the edge of camp before she lost last night's stew in the brush. She pushed her hair out of her face, surprised to find most of it braided back.

She rubbed her eyes and wiped her mouth before looking around. It was still dark, but the barest amount of pink was beginning to peek over the horizon. The camp was quiet as she walked to a nearby log, downwind from her sick, and placed her head between her knees.

Memories from last night were still racing through her mind. Fighting with Orrain. Frigid, lost in the woods. Her head throbbed. Jumbled up pieces flooded her brain until she remembered being scooped up into the warmth of Darryn's arms.

She sat up and hugged herself. He had carried her to safety and stayed with her until Mariel returned. Flashbacks of his strength and concern sent tingling down her spine. He was worried about her and it was confusing.

A rustling sound caused her to jump. A large, shadowy figure was walking toward her from the woods. She stood up and began backing toward the tent, the lingering terror from her dreams tugging at her stomach again.

She squinted as the man came closer. "Orrain?" Her shoulders dropped from her ears when she realized it was him. His clothing was disheveled and his eyes were wide with dark circles underneath, but he otherwise seemed unphased from his night in the woods.

He walked up to her and grabbed her hands, pulling them to his chest. "Linneya, I am sorry. I loved Eleanor and am still struggling with losing her. There is so much pressure and I do not always respond well to feeling slighted."

Linneya clamped her teeth together, afraid to say the wrong thing. His face was arranged into a contrite expression, but his words seemed rehearsed. She felt bile rising again, disgusted by his facade.

He continued pleading. "Lia -" She pulled a hand back, holding it up to stop him. She took a deep breath, but no words came. He lowered her other hand, gripping it tight at his side. They stood in uncomfortable silence for several minutes, listening to the birds waking and calling to each other. The large sun broke the horizon, the icy light bathing everything in an aethereal glow.

A cough caused them both to swivel toward the tents. Mariel stepped out and stretched, yawning. Linneya slipped her hand out of Orrain's grasp and motioned toward her friend. "I should go help Mari pack up."

His face was unreadable. She turned and stalked back to the tent. As many times as they had taken the ostentatious thing down, it was now easy work. Straion sauntered up as the women finished. He grabbed Mariel from behind and she dissolved into a fit of giggles at his touch.

Linneya tried to smile, but the expression did not reach her eyes. The worry of being yoked to a man who thought so little of her hurt her heart. All she wanted was to have the freedom to return home and fight against Serathor. She would have to escape before they made it to Enthor's capital and Orrain locked her away.

She climbed into the carriage and yawned. Mariel followed, bringing several warm furs and blankets. "After last night, I felt like you might need a more comfortable setup." Linneya squealed her thanks and curled into a ball, tucking the furs around her.

The carriage door opened and Linneya sat back up, groaning. The thought of entertaining Orrain after the previous evening's events weighed heavy. Instead, a jolt of sensation rushed to her core when she was met with a rich baritone.

"Mariel, Linneya. I thought I would ride with you today, if that is alright." Darryn's face was a welcome relief. He nodded to the women and Linneya steadied her breathing.

Mariel grinned. "Yes, please join us! I meant to thank you again for finding dear Lia and caring for her last night." Linneya could only stare as the man climbed in and plopped down next to her.

"It was my honor. I could never have lived with myself if something had happened to our darling princess." He tugged at her braid and heat crept up her cheeks.

Mariel chuckled and craned her neck, peering out the window. "I might see if Straion wants company today. He is always begging me to ride with him on one of the extra horses." Linneya's mouth went slack when Mariel waved at them and hopped out. Her friend had no business leaving her alone with this man when her every instinct cried out for him.

Darryn seemed unphased by the privacy. Linneya silently cursed him for how calm he was being. He started pulling the furs and blankets up. "What is all this?"

Linneya chuckled at the awkward mess. "Mariel brought me stuff so I could make a nest and sleep. After last night's debacle, she guessed I would want a chance to nap. She was right." She stifled a yawn with the back of her hand.

He grinned and motioned to her. "Well, you can build me into your nest." He pulled some of the furs onto his lap and patted his leg. "Let me be your pillow."

She tilted her head, considering him. His offer was oddly intimate, but there was no sign of malice or wickedness on his features. The carriage lurched forward as their caravan started off for the day. Mariel was definitely not coming back and at least he could keep her braced on the seat while she slept.

Without saying anything, she started arranging the blankets. He grinned as she laid down and settled in. The soft, plush furs were soothing against her cheek. Darryn's fingers undid her braid and brushed through her hair. His touch caused her stomach to flutter and she sighed.

It felt so natural - so safe. The opposite of Orrain's demands. Even though this man had forced her to come with them, he tried to be gentle toward her. Perhaps he was beginning to feel more for her. Maybe he would reconsider being her way out of this mess.

"Thank you for rescuing me," Linneya sighed.

"What kind of knight would I be if I did not help one of our dear elementals stay safe?" He murmured, his voice so soft she was unsure he meant for her to hear it.

At his admission of duty, a sinking feeling of disappointment slipped through her fogginess. She was too tired to respond and she fell into the inky black of dreamless sleep for most of the day.

Darryn let her nap and only woke her once the tents were set up and dinner was ready. Orrain glared as the knight helped her down from the carriage, but she ignored it. They grabbed their dinner of dried fruit and cheese and headed toward the bonfire.

Falryn's campside stories continued to be the highlight of the journey. The healer took pride in introducing the Aelorian women to Enthor's legends. Most were similar to the tales Linneya grew up with, but Falryn's age meant enriched details and unusual twists. This evening, they had decided to tell the creation legends.

As Linneya and Darryn approached, Falryn was weaving together the story of elemental magic. "The Arduin spread throughout the world, offering different affinities to the divine ancestors of the sentient species. The dwarves inherited knowledge of Ground. Merpeople were gifted knowledge of Mist. Fawns were descendents of those who wielded Vine. Humans' ancestors were taught the magic of Flame. Fae descended from those who harnessed Aether."

"Over the duocenturies, the magic intermingled. Some of it came from interspecies relationships. Other parts came from the sharing of knowledge. Studying one's affinity and sister elements allowed for more skilled warriors to emerge. The light aspects of each element are more subtle, therefore the development of the healing arts took longer. We are still finding new ways to use the gifts from the Arduin."

"What about psychic magic? The Creators-blessed?" Mariel leaned in, enraptured.

Falryn grinned. "Yes, girl, the psychic powers descend from the Creators: Substantia, Motus, and Libra. Anything that bends the mind is said to come from their gifts. I believe the Creators-blessed are almost as prolific as elementals.

Linneya cocked her head. "I thought psychic magic was only given to those born under full eclipses?" Eleanor had been born under a red sun eclipse and Linneya had been fascinated with the lore ever since.

Falryn shook their head. "Not quite. Psychic magic is almost a guarantee to shadow-children. However, others can receive Creators-blessed magic. It is a more subtle magic and much is still unknown. Because they are able to hide their power more effectively, the Creators-blessed have not been as readily studied as elementals."

The evening passed with quiet chatter among friends. A tight sensation solidified in Linneya's shoulders, a sense of unease lingering from the night before. She occasionally felt Darryn's gaze burning into her back, a reminder of her dashed hopes. While she would miss Mariel and feared Orrain's retaliation, it was time for her to escape.

The next day, they stopped for noonrest at the top of a hill. The wind was blustery, wafting the sweet scents of grass around their eating area. The light meal of soup and bread tasted stale and desiccated, like wood shavings. Her mouth was dry and fuzzy from anxiousness. She was dressed in a practical tunic, trousers, and a warm coat. The carriages were out of sight, stationed behind a stand of trees. She could get back, get her things, and perhaps she could make a mad dash for it before anyone realized she was missing.

This would be her chance to get away.

She finished her lunch and wandered toward the trees, trying to seem as aimless as possible. On a glance back toward the group, Mariel and Straion were huddled together, whispering lovers' secrets. Orrain had his back turned to her, playing a card game with some of the other men. Darryn was nowhere to be seen.

She picked up her pace as she reached the trees, her pulse pounding in her ears. Dizzying excitement made her stumble, but she managed to keep going. All she needed was her small sack of items from the carriage, then she could disappear. Just as she thought about breaking into a run, fingers wrapped around one of her wrists and yanked her back.

"So glad to finally have you alone." A horrid chill went down her spine as she recognized Orrain's voice. He spun her around and leaned in, pressing a kiss just behind her ear. He leered at her and his hand wandered down to her chest. Linneya's stomach dropped and she twisted away from his groping. "What are you doing?"

Orrain smirked and grabbed her upper arm. "What is wrong? We are betrothed. I deserve to know what I am getting out of this deal." His eyes dragged down her body, lingering on her curves.

She grimaced at the scraping, intrusive sensation of his gaze. "Once we are married, you will have full access. However I must protest your current actions." Today's escape attempt might have been thwarted, but hope remained that she would somehow be free of this man before permanent damage could be done.

"Eleanor would have gladly done as I wanted." He hissed and tightened his grip on her upper arm.

"I am not my sister." She spat.

"Much to my disappointment, you are correct." He clamped down on her arm so hard she was certain it would bruise. "However, if we plan on being husband and wife, you need to act your part." He grabbed the back of her neck and crushed his lips to hers.

Linneya wrenched away, sputtering. Orrain bared his teeth and gripped her shoulders. She shoved at him. "You cannot treat me like this! Yes, we are to be wed and I expect to fulfill my duties, but you must show some decorum."

Orrain dropped his hands and pulled a dagger from his waistband. She froze, her entire focus on the weapon. He smirked and began tapping the blade against his palm. "I warned you about slighting me, Lia." A chill went down her spine. Her stomach dropped when he reached back up, tucking a stray lock of hair behind her ear and whispered, "I will devour you right here, right now. Do not -"

A growl cut him off. "Take your hands off the princess or I will remove them for you." Linneya turned around to find Darryn towering over them. His mouth was set in a grim line and his eyes burned with fury. His hand was on his sword, prepared to draw it at a moment's notice.

Orrain huffed a laugh and turned his nose up at Darryn. "What is it to you? She is to be my wife and I will do with her as I please."

"I guarantee her safety, knave." Darryn's eyes darkened and he leaned in, threatening in an almost-whisper, "Even after you are wed, if you lay one finger on her without her permission, you are a dead man."

Orrain shoved his chest and Linneya started shaking. This was too much. She retreated away from their arguing, finding a log to sit on. She could still see them bickering, but at least she could not hear them volley meaningless words. Orrain spat on the ground and jabbed a finger toward her rescuer. Darryn stepped closer, reaching for a hidden dagger.

Orrain threw his hands up and stormed off. He saw Linneya and made a vulgar gesture. If she had been less infuriated, it might have been comical.

Tears burned in her eyes and her chest squeezed. She had thought she was slipping off unnoticed, but instead she had put herself in what could have been an awful situation. She rubbed her face with her hands, trying to clear her head.

Darryn pressed a hand to her shoulder. She jumped, trembling at his touch. He dropped his hand, but knelt beside her and frowned. "Linneya, what do you need?"

She glared up at him through narrowed, wet eyes. "I need freedom. You forced this fate on me and gave me no say in the matter. Now I have to marry *him* and find a way to keep myself sane. All while knowing my people suffer. Stop trying to fix this. You had your chance to make things right, but instead you forced me into this role."

He momentarily cringed as if her words stung, the action so brief she might have imagined it. But then he rolled his eyes and stood up. "You are not the only one that is forced to play a part here, princess. Forgive me for thinking you had more grit than this."

She gasped through her sobs and grabbed his sleeve. "We could have been betrothed and none of this would be happening. Why did you refuse to protect me? I could have married you and returned home to save my people."

He hissed, his eyes darkening with what seemed like regret. "This is me protecting you. I cannot be wed. My vows do not allow it. Being near you is pain enough without us damned for being bound. My family would never approve and you would be ruined. I would do anything to see you safe, but that includes not selfishly claiming your life." He reached down and placed a hand on her cheek.

Linneya recoiled from his touch. "Stop giving me hope that you might still find me a way out of this. One moment you treat me as if you care, then turn around the next and act as if I am diseased."

He wrapped his hand in her hair, gripping its roots at the base of her neck. She gasped as he pulled her close and held firm. "We cannot be together but that does not mean I do not want you." He leaned down and ran his nose up her jawline. Her blood heated as he whispered in her ear. "Creators, I want you. I fear the day that my self control breaks. I am dangerous for you, Linneya."

She grabbed his tunic and leaned back. "Is it safe for me to be with Orrain? He is volatile, Darryn. Nothing I say calms him." Her chin trembled and tears burned in the back of her eyes.

Darryn frowned and brushed his hand through her hair, considering her. Then he sighed and reached into his cloak. He drew out a small blade with a leather sheath. "Keep this with you at all times. Tie this to your thigh, tuck it under your pillow, whatever it takes."

Her fingers trembled as she took the dagger. The dark handle was carved with an intricate design of vines and flowers. She wiped her eyes and took a deep breath. "Thank you, sir." He nodded and left her alone with her racing pulse and spinning mind.

Over the next few days, Orrain's increasing aggression made Linneya more determined than ever to get away. If she left soon, surely she could make it back to Loraen before the icy winter winds moved in. Once she was home, she was certain that she could signal Aiden to her presence in the caves. He would help her figure out a plan to stay hidden until Serathor attacked. She shivered at the thought of spending a full winter season in Aelor without the warmth of the palace, but the alternative was being helplessly trapped in Enthor with a furious, unwilling husband and the heavy guilt of knowing her people needed her.

Even worse than the winter chill, she dreaded the idea of having to return to Orrain once the fights were over. He would be infuriated, but at least her people would be safe.

As if her thoughts summoned the man, the carriage door burst open and Orrain climbed in. "Hello ladies. I will ride with you today."

Mariel smiled politely, but Linneya ground her teeth into more of a grimace and braced herself for a day of hiding her annoyance. Orrain sat down beside her and wrapped his arm around her shoulders, locking her in place. She rolled her eyes for Mariel's benefit and her friend's mouth tugged up at one side. The sparkle in Mariel's eyes told Linneya her friend would at least laugh with her to try to diffuse the tension.

After all, her father had always said it was better to embrace absurdity than to be consumed by misery.

"Are you ladies ready to see your new homes?" Orrain peered out the windows as if he did not care what their answers would be.

Mariel beamed. "Straion's residence is near the river. I am so excited to be able to wake up to the views. I never thought I would be running my own house, much less anything so grand.

Orrain puffed his chest out and lifted his chin. "Straion's house is an adorable little place. My home is closer to the palace. Our mansion is built into a hillside and everyone remarks on how formidable it seems." Mariel waggled her eyebrows to Linneya, but he ploughed on without noticing. "We dine with aristocratic families every evening. Linneya, we will be expected to entertain the highest nobility in the realms. Be ready to earn your place at my side."

His bizarre posturing was almost too much. Mariel nodded and maintained a straight face. Linneya had to cover her giggles with a coughing fit.

"I will do everything I can to maintain my status as a respectable *princess*." She emphasized the word, hoping he would remember that she did not need to earn a place. She was born to it.

He began fiddling with his gold brooch, pulling on it as if the weight of the brown stone was heavy on his throat. His eyes darted outside the carriage, watching the passing scenery. "You were a princess in Aelor, but you will be my wife in Enthor. I expect to give you the best, but you must do the same for me."

"Well, when you put it that way, dear." Linneya rolled her eyes. It was Mariel's turn to hide her amusement behind a cough. Linneya was afraid to make eye contact with her friend. Orrain continued to stare out of the carriage window. His lips were set in a thin line but he seemed oblivious to the women and their amusement.

A shout from the front of the caravan stopped their conversation. The carriage ground to a halt and the sounds of an argument drifted toward them. Orrain shook his head and clenched his jaw. "Something sounds off. Ladies, if you will excuse me..." Before either of them responded, he jumped out of the carriage and slammed the door.

Only then did Linneya dare look at Mariel. The two of them dissolved into a pile of giggles. "Thank the Creators, I was about to burst!" Mariel wiped tears of mirth from her eyes.

Linneya gasped in between laughs. "Earn my place!"

Mariel shook her finger in a mocking gesture. "It is a formidable mansion and you will respect my evening formalities!" They grabbed each other's arms for support as they howled.

Linneya was grateful for the levity. Everything had felt so heavy lately and having a cathartic laugh was refreshing. Once they caught their breath, Mariel sobered, pursing her lips. "As amusing as this morning has been, I worry about what Orrain is thinking. His mind is not kind or gentle. He acts like you are a bargaining chip for him."

Linneya waved a hand, not wanting to worry Mariel further even as her stomach dropped. "He is angry that he lost his choice of bride. Once we get settled in, he will get into a routine and things will be better."

Mariel shook her head, but did not say anything else. After a moment she grinned. When she looked back at Linneya, they once again burst into laughter.

Shouts and sounds of steel clanging grew louder, sobering them. The air in the carriage became stale and warm. Linneya began to wonder what was causing the men to fight so viciously amongst themselves. Mariel was biting at her thumbnail and bouncing her leg. "Lia, something does not seem right."

Linneya opened her mouth to respond, but jumped as Orrain threw the carriage door back open. His eyes were wide and he was panting. "Come on, both of you. Bandits are attacking. We need to go - now!"

Mariel gasped and froze. Linneya slid out of the carriage and shuddered. They were surrounded by a flurry of weapons and shouts. She turned back around, reached in the carriage, and grabbed her friend's wrist. "We have to get out of this carriage. If any of them realize we are still in here, it will be a death trap." Mariel's eyes snapped to hers and she nodded, finally able to move.

The three of them began running toward the treeline. Mariel struggled, but Linneya stayed by her side. As they reached the forest, Orrain turned to Mariel and pointed toward the front of the caravan. "Straion was just up ahead last time I saw him. If you hurry, you may be able to get to him."

"Should we not stick together?" Linneya panted, but it was too late. Mariel had already run into the fighting, scrambling in the direction Orrain had indicated.

Linneya's jaw dropped. Orrain gestured to her. "Come on, we need to find you a place to hide so I can fight."

"But Mariel - "

He narrowed his eyes. "Now."

She gritted her teeth, but acquiesced. The last thing she needed was Orrain turning on her in the midst of a bandit attack. He pointed into the woods. "This way. Maybe there will be some thick brush you can hide in until this is over."

A cackle startled Linneya. One of the bandits had broken off from the fight and was following them. "Orrain..."

"Come on, faster!" Orrain grabbed her wrist and yanked. She tried to run harder, but she could not keep pace with him. She grimaced as Darryn's dagger slipped off her leg. Not that she had much advantage before, but now she was completely unarmed.

"Keep up, Linneya." Orrain barked as he tugged on her arm and pulled her in front of him. The bandit was gaining on them and laughing maniacally at their escape attempt.

A shove from behind surprised Linneya and she stumbled. She tried to regain her footing, but her foot collapsed into a divot in the ground, causing her to fall. Her teeth clanged together as her jaw bashed into an exposed tree root and her vision went blurry.

She twisted around, reaching out and searching for help, expecting Orrain to be there. Instead, he was already ten feet in front of her. He had not stopped, had not looked back. The abandonment burned like bile rising in her throat. Linneya gaped as he continued to flee.

A dark cackling told her the fighter was standing at her feet. She turned over slowly, looking up. The man towered over her, his soured body reeking of blood and adrenaline. His hulking frame was covered in ratty clothing that was streaked with mud, as if it had never been washed.

Her eyes darted around, looking for an escape as she tried to slow her breathing. He bent over and grabbed her hair, pulling her into a halfway-seated position. She gasped at the pain and swatted at him.

"So much for your protection, woman. I do not think I have ever seen a man sacrifice a female so fast. What did you do to piss him off?" He leered at her and licked his lips. The rotten stench of his breath brought tears to Linneya's eyes.

Red tendrils of smoke crept from her fingers. Her hands splayed out to each side, rifling through the weeds in search of any sort of heavy rock. Almost as if the ground heard her thoughts, a small tremor shook the area and a stone rolled up, nudging her hand. *Thank the Creators.* Linneya gripped it as the fighter continued to hover over her, smirking.

"Not one to talk, eh? No matter. let us see if you scream." He shoved her down and crawled on top of her, ripping at her tunic. She gasped and flailed, gathering up as much force as she could, and slammed the rock toward his face.

The crunch of the stone connecting with the fighter's skull told Linneya she had hit her mark. The man's eyes bulged before he collapsed and began twitching. For a moment, she laid there, stunned and panting. The scent of iron scorched her nostrils and she sat up. The bandit was groaning and shaking as blood pooled underneath his head.

The reality of the past few minutes sank in. Her pulse pounded in her head, heat rising. Fear turned into rage as she crawled over to him. She hoisted the rock above her head and slammed it down again and again, the force of impact stinging her palm. The fighter went still as his life force finally drained from him and Linneya crumpled to the ground.

Chapter 9

Shaking, Linneya took stock of her injuries. Her jaw throbbed and her ankle was beginning to swell. Covered in blood, she checked her body for deep cuts but she found nothing. It appeared all the blood was the fighter's.

Then she lifted her eyes and surveyed her surroundings. She was completely alone. Things had grown quiet and she guessed the bandits had been defeated. Her heart began to race as her thoughts whirled.

This fight brought the impending threat of Serathor back to the forefront of her mind. They were likely to follow through on their threat to attack Aelor within the annum. Thorns twisted around her heart, part of her mourning the loss of her role as healer to her people.

Could she sneak back to the carriage for her travel bag? Would she be able to escape without notice? Probably, but she was too injured to make the week's journey back to her home. Linneya sighed, brushing her hair out of her face and flexing her ankle.

If nothing else, she needed to be armed. It was possible that more bandits were hiding in the woods, stragglers who had gotten away before the fight was finished. Linneya began searching the space, looking for her lost dagger. The dense blue and purple foliage surrounding her hid any sign of the blade. She began retracing her steps, pausing to glance under thick tangles of brush in case the earlier tremor had made the dagger move. After all, it had been a rough enough quake that the stone rolled to her hand.

A glint of silver steel under an unusually red bush caught her eye. Leaves covered the item and she dove to brush them back. A smile nearly split her face in two as she pulled the dagger out from beneath the plant. Linneya strapped the dagger to her thigh and some of the tension left her. Such a tiny thing, but somehow its pressure against her leg was a source of comfort.

Stumbling back to the caravan, Linneya's eyes widened as she took in the carnage. Dead bodies littered the road and several carriages were beyond repair. Tangy scents of blood and bile poisoned the air. Several women were huddled together, crying. There were so many injured that the caravan's two healers were struggling. Both were arms deep in a bloody mess, stitching wounds and setting broken bones.

Linneya desperately searched the wreckage for her friend. Her eyes scanned the area and she tensed at the thought of Mariel injured. Her breathing tightened as she desperately searched for her friend. She stumbled over a carriage shaft, almost falling face-first into the mud. Then, she heard a telltale laugh and let out a breath she did not realize she was holding.

Mariel was with Straion, eyes crinkled with mirth, and sipping from a canteen. As she saw Linneya approaching, her smile widened and she strode forward. "Lia, thank goodness! We were starting to wonder what happened. Orrain said you had gotten separated, he claimed he was going to find you. Oh, my - why are you limping? Is that your blood? Are you hurt badly?"

Loud jeers erupted from a crowd forming around the front of the caravan, drowning out Linneya's assurances that her ankle would be fine. Darryn's voice boomed above the chatter. Straion grinned at her surprised expression. "He has captured their leader. This was not a typical bandit attack and Darryn is determined to figure out who is behind it."

"They definitely seemed more... civilized in their fighting skills than I expected from a ragtag group." Linneya gnawed on the inside of her cheek, cringing at the memory of being pinned underneath the bandit she killed.

Mariel grabbed her hand and the three of them made their way to the crowd. Linneya wrestled her way to the front. The bandit was battered and bloodied. He was on his knees, hands tied in front of him. Darryn had a handful of the man's greasy hair knotted into his fist. Blood leaked down Darryn's shoulder, as if he had a wound from the fighting. The man screamed and Linneya's jaw dropped. Darryn was pressing the point of the knife into the bandit's ear and twisting.

"Who sent you?"

"Sent us? We are bandits! We had heard tell that a caravan of nobles was headed this way. It seemed like the perfect opportunity."

"Then why did you not run away once you realized how well-armed we are?" Darryn rotated the blade in his hand and pressed it into where the man's ear connected with his head, causing a thin stream of blood to run down the bandit's jaw. "I do not believe you. Tell me now. Who. Sent. You?"

The man bared his teeth and snarled. "There is nothing to tell. We *are* bandits and your caravan was too much of a prize to pass up. This was an opportunity to acquire riches beyond what our village makes in an annae... we had to try."

Darryn smirked and began sawing, bit by bit. The bandit thrashed and screamed underneath his grip. The veins in Darryn's arms strained as he subdued him. He slowly carved the man's ear off and Linneya hugged herself, watching the carnage unfold.

The ear dropped to the ground, splashing in a puddle of the bandit's blood. Mariel gasped and Linneya cringed, feeling bile rising in her throat. But then Darryn straightened up, turning to face them.

His face was contorted, a mix of pleasure and darkness. Her eyes widened and her soul was transfixed. His bloodlust shone through as he interrogated the man. "If that were true, you would not fight to the death. Bandits are after loot, not honor."

The bandit wheezed, cackling through the stream of blood. Darryn pulled the man's head back, baring his neck. He placed the knife against the man's throat and growled, "Last chance, bastard." Mariel's hands covered her face and Straion pulled her into his arms. Linneya was mesmerized, her breath coming faster as she watched Darryn's vicious methods. He was beautiful and roguish. Her fingers twitched and she wished she could stand beside him, protecting their people.

The bandit began to roar, his whole body shaking. "You know who sent us. We will not be the last. The flame-talker will be captured and both of your countries will fall to the true king!" Linneya groaned and Darryn's head snapped up, searching for the sound.

His eyes burned with a dark molten flame as he locked onto her. She set her jaw and steadied her breathing. A hint of a smile curved on his lips. The world fell away and silence enveloped them.

The intensity of his stare sent a shiver up her spine. Linneya no longer heard the crowd's taunting or the bandit's screaming. Darryn cocked his head to the side, almost as if he was asking her permission to execute the man. She narrowed her eyes. This bandit had instigated the attack that killed several and hurt many others. What right did he have to mercy?

She gave him the slightest nod. A wicked grin spread across the knight's face and he held her gaze as he sliced. Blood sprayed and the nobles cheered. A cascade of crimson flowed from the bandit's neck. She did not dare blink as Darryn released the man's hair. The bandit slumped over and hit the ground with a thud. Darryn turned away, breaking the spell, and she let out a breath.

Next to her, Mariel groaned. Straion chuckled, "Not one for blood, my love?" She shook her head and turned to Linneya. "My stomach hurts after all that. I think I need some spicymint tea. Are you alright if we head back?"

Linneya nodded and watched them walk off, Straion protectively holding Mariel as if he could stop the carnage from seeping into her bones. Orrain was standing with two men she did not recognize, cackling at some joke. Darryn was somberly cleaning his sword and directing men to clean up the rest of the bodies.

His expression was burned into her memory. The warmth that flowed through her body when he held her stare was reminiscent of her flame-talker abilities activating. His bloodlust called to her in a way that terrified her and gave her newfound purpose. Perhaps it was because now she had taken a life. She shook her head and brushed the hair out of her face. There would be time to figure this all out later. For now, she needed to check with Falryn to see how she could help.

She turned away from the dead bandit and gingerly picked her way back through the wreckage. The healers were still working on battle wounds, unphased by Darryn's show of power. Linneya limped up to Falryn and the healer barely acknowledged her. Their mouth was set in a tight line while they worked on suturing a gash. "Where are you injured, girl?"

She grabbed a cloth and wiped some of the blood from her face and arms. "I am alright, it all looks worse than it is. Most if this is not my blood. I have only turned my ankle. I was coming to see if you needed me to gather any plants."

Relief flooded Falryn's face as they finally made eye contact. "Thank you, yes. We are running low on arnycia. There is a creek to the west, just follow the suns and you should easily find a patch."

Linneya nodded, picking up a harvesting basket and hobbling toward the treeline. Arnycia was vital for wound healing; the white flowers could be crushed and pack a wound to keep out heat and seal the damage without scarring. It was bitter and terrible in tea, but topically it offered quick relief from pain.

As she reached the forest's edge, rowdy laughter caused her to turn back toward the camp. Orrain was still wrapped up in conversation with those men. Her body shook at the sight of him. He lounged against a broken carriage wheel, laughing at something one of the others was saying. Linneya hobbled off, hoping he would not see her.

Why had he pushed her down? Orrain had not struck her as a coward. Had it been purposeful or did the bandit's words taint her memory of the event?

A lump rose in her throat as a looming image of the bandit surfaced. His mocking tone rang in her ears. *"I do not think I have ever seen a man sacrifice a woman so fast."*

Thoughts swirled in her head, a dizzying whirlwind of emotion. Fear. Shame. The squelching of an ear being sliced. Excitement. The crunch of rock against skull. She tried to focus on the peaceful sounds of nature, but even the hissing insects seemed to be screaming her condemnation. *Murderessss.*

The creek was easy enough to find and Linneya began limping beside the stream, searching for the bright white flowers of arnycia. The pain in her ankle was getting worse, but it was a welcome distraction from the mounting storm of thoughts.

A mother oak with several hulking, partially exposed roots was nearby. The silver bark was knotted and grooved, as if the tree itself had drawn a map of a mythological world into its trunk. She sank onto one of the roots that was shaped like a loveseat to catch her breath and check her injury. She groaned at the pulsating ache coming from her ankle, flexing it.

The loud, rushing of water suggested a waterfall was not far. After a few minutes, she picked back up and headed that direction. She left her basket at the tree, hobbling toward the source of the sounds. The roaring grew louder as she made her way downstream. Her breath caught as she rounded a corner and spied a waterfall that plunged further down than anything she had seen before.

The cascading water sprayed into the air, creating rainbows. The strong red and orange hues of falllight stole the show, but small glimmers of blue and purple hinted at the changing season. The petrichor wafting from the fresh mist brought memories bubbling up of her childhood. She blinked back tears as she thought of her parents, of Aiden and Eleanor, and of the times they had spent exploring the streams and waterfalls around Loraen.

Out of the corner of her eye, Linneya spied the fluttering of white petals. Arnycia. She grinned and turned, limping back to the mother oak for her harvesting basket. She leaned over to pick it up and froze. The crunching sound behind her was not subtle. Linneya whirled around, half expecting to see a straggler from the fight. Instead, she met with Orrain's towering figure. Her heart leapt into her throat and her chest tightened.

He tilted his head slightly and crossed his arms. "I am glad to see you are alright. When you fell, I hated that I could not do anything to save you."

Her eyes narrowed and she gritted her teeth. "You pushed me. You left me."

Orrain rolled his eyes. "You must have hit your head when you fell. I tried to wake you up, but when you would not move I knew I had to save myself." He explained as if speaking to a child.

Linneya shook her head and raised her voice, furious at his refusal to acknowledge the damage he had done. "I was not knocked out. I watched you run away! You sacrificed me to save yourself from that brute!"

Something shifted in Orrain's expression. His features seemed to rearrange as his eyes narrowed. "When you talk like that, people will assume that you are attempting to ruin my reputation to escape this marriage. You are going to end up labeled a spoiled brat who babbles delusional nonsense. A pariah."

She scoffed. His constant belittling was becoming too much. "I guess we will find out."

Orrain stiffened and wiped his mouth. He stepped forward and unsheathed his sword, pointing it toward her. The tip of his weapon touched her chest and he pressed, leering as her false bravado melted. The stinging sensation gave way to sharp warmth and a thin stream of blood began to trickle down her chest.

Trembling and wide-eyed, she dropped everything and backed up, stopping only once her back scraped into the rough oak bark. He sneered. "This is why I preferred your sister. She would have known how she should behave. You tell those lies to anyone in Enthor and I will split you open from navel to throat."

"They are not lies! You pushed me down like a coward. If this ends with you killing me, go ahead and do it here. I am done." One glance at Orrain's infuriated expression told her the words found their mark.

Linneya closed her eyes, ready for death. A fine mist sprayed from the creek and she took solace in its freshness as she faced oblivion. Would it be complete darkness or is there something beyond? Perhaps her grandparents would be waiting for her. Would the Creators allow her peace or would she be expected to return to experience another life? She began to float out of her body, acceding to her meaningless fate.

An inhale and swish told her the killing blow was imminent. Time slowed. Her final breath was scented with citrus and cedar.

A loud clang jolted her back. Her breath caught as she opened her eyes. Darryn was a wall between her and Orrain. The knight was stalking toward the man like a wolf closing in on its prey. "You dare to raise a weapon against the princess? You dare to harm your betrothed? You dare to threaten the flame-talker, an asset to your country? Any one of these is a punishable offense."

Orrain snarled, "You know she is not the flame-talker. After her little stunt at the bonfire, Eleanor came to me and begged me to step in. She told me Linneya faked it to take her place in the exchange. I ignored her request because I knew the older sister would come with more prestige. I did not realize that I was linking myself with such a whore. Now stand aside and let me kill her. I will go back for the other one to pacify the Aelorians and we can say this one died at the hands of a straggler."

Darryn bared his teeth and spat, "You will pay for this." Without another word, he lunged forward and lifted his sword to strike. Orrain parried, but Darryn was too strong. He pressed his advantage, causing Orrain to stumble back toward the creek.

Linneya backed away from the two men, barely able to stand on her injured ankle. Her heart pounded in her ears and the pain made her dizzy. There was no safe place to watch her fate play out. The rocks nearby offered some amount of shelter, so she scrambled to hide in the outcrop.

Darryn tried to subdue Orrain without landing a killing blow. The man fought hard, but Darryn moved as if the sword were an extension of his body. Occasionally, Darryn would stumble from a rock or mound of dirt shifting unexpectedly. Dark smoke seeping from Orrain suggested he was invoking his ground-tamer power to trip up his opponent.

Darryn pushed forward with a steady gaze, feinting and lunging as Orrain strained to keep up. One punch landed square in Orrain's chest, causing his prized brooch to fall into the mud. The next move, Darryn struck his cheek with the flat of the blade and Orrain cursed, spinning around.

Then, Darryn crumpled to the ground as Orrain landed a cut on his hamstring. The knight rose almost immediately, but his demeanor shifted. Bright red began blooming on Darryn's tan tunic. His shoulder wound had reopened, blood beginning to soak his shirt.

With a roar, Darryn lunged and swung back into action in one fluid movement. Orrain was struggling to keep up. Darryn's nostrils flared as he struck Orrain with the hilt. Orrain staggered back and snapped, "I will never surrender to you, royal bastard. You will have to kill me."

The blood continued to pour from Darryn's wound and with it his stamina. Linneya's heart wrenched, thudding a desperate plea for her to somehow protect him. She gripped the rough rock so tight it stung her palms. He stumbled again, this time from fatigue, and his breathing became labored. His strikes became slower and held less power.

Linneya tried to stand again, but the pain was too much. She sank back down and began chewing on her bottom lip. Her mouth was dry and her breath shallow. The slower Darryn became, the more her stomach twisted in knots.

Orrain blocked and parried Darryn's next blow, sweeping both their swords to the right. As Darryn recovered his position, Orrain sprang forward. Smirking, he landed a punch on Darryn's injured shoulder and knocked the sword from his hand.

Linneya cried out. Darryn turned toward her, giving Orrain the chance to sweep his leg. Linneya grimaced as his frame hit the ground with a thump. Orrain smirked at her outburst, stepping on Darryn's injured shoulder and causing him to groan. He pointed his sword at her. "Do not worry love. You are next. It will all be over soon."

"Get up, get up, get up!" She whispered, gritting her teeth. As if he heard her, Darryn rallied and grabbed Orrain's ankle to throw him off balance. He was too weak and Orrain barely stumbled before stomping down hard on Darryn's wound.

Darryn tried again. Orrain dodged his hands this time and stepped back, repositioning his sword above Darryn's chest. He brandished his weapon, ready to pierce Darryn's heart and end any hope Linneya had of escaping. She vibrated, smoke seeping from her palms as if she could call on her flame affinity and stop this.

Leaning forward, he bared his teeth at the knight and growled, "You never could learn to stay out of my way."

At that moment, the sound of rushing water became louder. Surging water raged over the creek banks, knocking Orrain off his feet. He barely had time to grab onto an exposed root. Darryn roared and scrambled to his knees, thrashing about on the bank for a way to save his former friend. In the last moments before Orrain was swept downstream, his eyes bulged and he again bared his teeth at them, shouting some curse drowned out by the crashing water.

Then Orrain lost his grip and was gone.

Chapter 10

The water returned to its normal flow, but Linneya still heard rushing in her ears. She remained frozen, staring at the spot where Orrain had been only moments ago, as if she could will him back with her thoughts.

Darryn was kneeling on the river bank with his head hung low. He was breathing hard and shaking. She tried to stand to go to him, but the moment she put weight on her ankle the pain became unbearable. The world spun and she groaned, sitting back down.

The sound stirred Darryn from his dazed state. His eyes darted around, looking for Linneya. The moment they made eye contact, he rushed over and began checking her. "Are you hurt anywhere? When I heard you telling him to kill you, I saw red."

"You followed me?"

"I followed Orrain. This attack was suspicious but Orrain seemed less than surprised by it all. When I saw him sneaking away, I wanted to see where he was headed."

His fingers lightly touched her chin, turning her head so that he could examine the bruise on her cheek. He clenched his jaw and growled. "That cad deserved so much worse. Pushing you down so he could escape instead of fighting... he should have been held in the dungeons and tortured instead of given a swift death."

Linneya's eyes burned as tears welled up. His fingers brushed down her neck and across her shoulders, leaving trails of goosebumps in their wake. She pulled away from him, drawing her knees to her chest. "This is too much. I cannot keep going." She buried her face in her hands, shaking her head.

He frowned and pulled her to him. She clutched at his tunic, gasping for breath. Darryn stroked her hair and let her sob. She leaned into his warmth, resting against his strength until the grief washed out of her.

"Let us get you back to the caravan. Falryn can check your ankle and we can find you some clean clothes." He went to pick her up, but grimaced and clutched his shoulder.

Linneya pushed him back with a frown. "Stop, you are injured too. I can walk if we find a stick for me to lean on. However, I cannot go back yet. I need to pick some arnycia for Falryn before we return." She scanned the blood covering her outfit and mumbled, "I would not mind having a moment to rinse off, either."

Darryn nodded and stood, offering her a hand. "We should find you a spot to bathe and I will harvest the flowers." She took it and stood, wobbling a bit. He placed her hand in the crook of his arm and started slowly guiding her back down the rocks.

As they walked toward the stream, a gold shimmer caught her eye. "Oh, wait." She stopped and bent down. Orrain's brooch was halfway buried in the mud. She pried it out of the muck and studied it while chewing on her lip.

Darryn knitted his brow as she examined the brown stone. "Shall we continue?" Linneya nodded and they shuffled up the stream.

After a moment, they found a spot where the water pooled and the bank was sloped enough for Linneya to navigate. Darryn let her go at the water's edge but hesitated. "Are you okay to clean up by yourself?" She raised her eyebrows and his cheeks turned pink. "I meant since we have just been attacked and your ankle is injured..."

She smiled. "Thank you. I believe I will be alright."

He nodded. "I'll be over that ridge. Do not hesitate to yell for me if you start to feel uncomfortable."

Once she was alone, Linneya undressed and quickly dipped in the stream. The cool water soothed the throbbing of her temples. A fresh pine scent tinted the breeze, encouraging her to breathe deep and just be. She sighed and began floating in the crystal-clear water. The peaceful woods sang with the rhythmic sounds of woodland creatures chittering and birds whistling. The tension of the attacks she had endured today washed away with the dried blood of the man she murdered.

But still, the insects hissed. *Murderessss.*

Her chest tightened and the silence began to feel crushing. The more she tried to relax, the more dreadful thoughts crept in. The stones at the bottom of the creek seemed to mock her, mimicking her weapon of choice.

The reverberations of the bandit's skull crunching were imprinted into her hands.

Even more, Orrain was dead. He had turned out to be villainous, but Linneya did not feel better at the thought. She imagined his body crashing against the rocks at the bottom of the waterfall. It made her cringe.

She tried to shake the visual from her mind, but it would not budge. She began trembling and tears threatened to spill. When she tried to stand in the water, the throbbing in her ankle intensified. She shuddered and crouched back into the water, swimming her way toward a mossy boulder.

The fatigue washed over her, offering an icy numbness. Linneya welcomed the escape from the flood of emotion. She clambered onto the rock, curling into herself, and let her mind muddle.

Several minutes later, Darryn returned with a basket full of arnycia and a bundle of cloth. He waved the bundle like a flag of victory while looking anywhere but the pool of water. "Sir Jolom found me foraging and went back to find you a towel, blanket, and fresh clothing. I will set them down by your other clothes and be back in a moment."

His voice was muffled and Linneya could not respond. When she did not answer, he peered toward the pond. His eyes fell on her, in a fetal position on the rock. "Creators, Linneya! What are you doing?"

He rushed to her, half running, half swimming. He crashed through the water, reaching her and brushing the hair out of her face. A warmth washed over her skin as he covered her with the blanket. "You have to sit up. Shit, I shouldn't have left you after so much shock. Sit up, Linneya." He started vigorously rubbing her back, bringing a stinging sensation.

Sharp irritation flooded her veins. His panting was too loud. He had kicked up mud and now her crystal clear water was ugly with silt. Everything about him was intolerable. She sat up with a jolt and shoved his hands back. "Stop it! Leave me be."

He chuckled and reached for her. "Anger is good. Be furious. Kick and scream. Hate me, if you must. Just do not shut down. You are too important." He rubbed circles on the back of her hands with his thumbs.

She huffed. "Too important to Enthor."

He pressed his lips together as if he wanted to say more, but thought better of it. He brushed hair out of her eyes and started running his hands up and down her arms, a grounding sensation. Linneya glared at him and his calm presence, but after a few minutes, the annoyance drained away. She sighed and closed her eyes. "I am sorry. This is so much."

Darryn nodded, rubbing circles on the back of her hands with his thumbs. "Let us head back to the others. The healers will have some supplies to bind your ankle and we need to get these flowers back to Falryn."

She slipped back into the water and they made their way to the bank. Her feet hit the mud and pain radiated up her leg. "Darryn, my ankle -" she gasped, unable to complete a thought through the throbbing.

He wrapped his right arm around her waist. "Lean into me, princess."

Too tired to argue, she sank into his body. He gave her space on the bank so she could dress in clean clothes, then pulled her back to him. His powerful frame enveloped her, giving her the support she needed to make their way out of the forest.

Back at the caravan, Darryn deposited her with the healers and went to speak with his men. He motioned toward the stream and Straion and another man with graying hair took off in that direction. She shivered at the thought of what they might find at the bottom of the waterfall.

Falryn raised an eyebrow as Linneya handed them the basket of arnycia. "Where is Orrain?" Linneya shook her head, unable to speak. The healer's lips tightened into a thin line and they flared their nostrils. "Well, I am sure he deserved it. Let me see your ankle."

Darryn walked over to them as the healer finished binding Linneya's ankle. Falryn glared at his shoulder and forced him into a seat to rebandage his wound. Around their muttering and cursing, Darryn recounted the afternoon's events. Falryn barely reacted, even at the news of Orrain's death.

"I sent Straion and Jolom to see if they can locate his body." He tested his range of motion as Falryn finished tying the bandages.

"If you will leave it alone, it will heal, but if you keep tearing the wound open it is going to be impossible for it to set." Falryn poked him in his chest. "I always said you reminded me of Luthin, boy. His fate was intertwined and he ignored it. Do not go making the same mistakes."

Darryn groaned and winced. "Stop with your fantastical tales. Not all of us are meant to be reincarnated gods."

Linneya cocked her head to the side. "Luthin?"

Falryn grinned, their eyes shifting between the two of them. "Yes, in Enthorian legend Luthin and Payera are demigods that saved the human race from the shadow creatures, the *sharvach*. Luthin saw the harm the corrupt Arduin council was doing and tried to stop it."

"Luthin rejected the heartsong that connected him to Payera, which left him too weak to fight the council and doomed the human race. The council was betrayed by the creatures and the human realms were enslaved for over a duocentury. Only after Luthin and Payera were reincarnated and accepted their fate were they able to defeat the *sharvach* and save Enthor."

Linneya blushed at the insinuation in Falryn's gaze. Aelor had a similar tale. Luthath and Pajra were immortalized in the night's sky - two wandering stars forever circling each other in an intricate dance. Being compared to a demigod and the mighty role the two played in saving humans made her shiver. Was there more to Falryn's ramblings or was the healer only teasing?

Falryn crossed their arms and nodded toward Darryn. "What do you make of this attack? Do we need to be concerned for the rest of the journey?"

He shook his head. "This entire situation is so odd. The leader's declaration that someone was after our flame-talker was not surprising, but why here? Why now?"

Linneya quirked a brow. "Do you think they were hired? I wondered if they were fanatics or something. It seems like mercenaries would cave after the torture you inflicted."

He grinned and leaned forward. "I told you - my bloodlust is strong. Do you believe me now, princess?"

Her heart sped up at his nearness and her cheeks turned red. Falryn sniggered and Darryn shot them a scathing look.

The conversation stopped as Straion and Jolom returned. The somber expressions caused Linneya to shiver. Orrain's death felt like an omen; she was not meant to be here.

"His body was caught on a fallen tree. We tried to get to him, but when we got close, the log shifted and he was swept further downstream. We only recovered a boot and his belt." Straion held up Orrain's empty scabbard and muddy shoe. Falryn shook their head and moseyed back toward their supplies to pack up.

A muscle twitched in Darryn's jaw and he nodded, turning to Jolom. "Ride ahead. King Birron needs to be made aware of these odd circumstances. We do not want him caught unawares that the princess is without a betrothal. He will want to rectify it immediately."

The man inclined his head slightly and stalked off. Another eagerly jogged up, panting as he stopped in front of Darryn. "Sir, four carriages are damaged from the bandits ransacking our supplies. Some of the women have been placed in other carriages, but we will have to continue with the rest of them on horseback. Everyone has been placed with a horse or with their betrothed except..." He frowned and gave Linneya a sideways glance.

Darryn nodded. "Thank you. I will take care of it." The man's shoulders relaxed as if he was relieved and he stalked off, shouting orders to the other men. Darryn grabbed Linneya's wrist and pulled her toward his horse.

Darryn began removing his horse's saddle, handing it off to one of the men for safekeeping on the supplies wagon, and tossed blankets over the steed's back. Linneya turned to him and crossed her arms. "Okay, where is my horse?"

His eyes sparkled and he smirked. "You are riding with me, princess." He finished securing the straps across the blankets and led his horse to a fallen tree, gesturing for her to mount. The dark, majestic animal had been named Doshar, an ancient fae word for mountain, for a reason.

She grimaced, but followed him. "Can't you let me have a horse? I can ride well enough. One of the carriage horses should suffice."

He shook his head. "Those horses are bred and trained for the harness and tack used on these carriages. I cannot risk you getting injured when one of them does not take kindly to you being on his back."

Linneya sighed in defeat. "Alright." She secretly was pleased by the idea of being close to him, even though his hesitation toward marriage still stung.

Darryn grinned and held out his hand to help her onto his steed. She hobbled past his outstretched arm and climbed up on the log. With only a little struggle, she helped herself onto the horse. He chuckled and followed suit, adjusting her a bit more forward to make room for them both.

The rest of the caravan began to move and Darryn clicked his tongue, nudging Doshar forward. As they fell into place, he reached around her waist and pulled her back against his chest. The lack of saddle felt unusual, as if she could slip at any moment, but his arms held her securely in place. His citrus and cedar scent enveloped her and her shoulders relaxed. She sighed and he squeezed. "While I hate these circumstances, princess, I am glad to have you in my arms." The smile in his voice was evident.

Her breath caught but she did not respond. For the next several hours they traveled in comfortable silence. Mariel was close by on Straion's horse, giggling as he whispered in her ear. Falryn rode up to them three different times to comment on a plant, pointing out unusual species to Linneya. Darryn occasionally whistled to the birds, singing their tunes back to them.

Linneya tried to enjoy the scenery without thinking about what lay ahead. What did arriving at Enthor mean for her? With Orrain dead, she was technically in violation of the treaty. She doubted King Birron would mind. He would just as easily marry her off to another noble. One as bad, if not worse, than her former intended.

She needed someone who would listen to her and be willing to rally others to help Aelor in the fight against Serathor and their dragons. Now that her flame-talking abilities were known, she could not risk being placed with a power hungry noble. She needed a husband that would see her as more than an elemental. More than a broodmare that would give his children powers.

She shivered at the thought and Darryn leaned down. "Are you cold, princess?" His warm breath tickled her ear.

Linneya shook her head. Tears burned her eyes and she twisted to face him. "Please, let me go home. I cannot stand the thought of being auctioned off to some lecherous fool for my abilities."

He waved her concerns away. "Johann will honor this contract and see you safely cared for. You have nothing to fear in Enthor, flame-talker or not." Darryn's expression softened when he saw the way she grimaced at Orrain's brother's name. "Truly, princess, you will be safe. I swear it."

She chewed on her lip and faced forward. "Orrain was bad and you let me be promised to him."

His arm tightened around her waist. "That was a mistake I will not make again."

Heat spread across her body, a mixture of longing and frustration. "Orrain told me of Johann's refusal to fight in a duel. What little I know of the man suggests he lacks honor. How can you leave me to his whims?"

Darryn growled. "I will kill anyone who refuses to treat you well. They will die a slow and painful death. Your power is important and we cannot afford to lose you."

Desperation bubbled over. "If you cannot afford to lose me, protect me yourself. Why can we not make an alliance? We can be married, I can aid my family, and then once the battles have been fought I will settle down and focus on doing everything I can to be what you need in a wife. I will train to fight my own battles, sign a contract - anything."

"A contract could not save you from the consequences of being bound to me. I have already told you, Linneya, you would not like it if you tried to take me on. I cannot marry you, but I will train you for combat."

She rolled her eyes and opened her mouth to respond. At the same moment, a shout from the head of the caravan indicated it was time to set up camp for the night. She clamped her mouth shut and slid off the horse at the first available moment.

A chill settled over the roadside clearing as they set up the tents. A thick fog formed, leaving Linneya with goosebumps. The mist in the air glowed orange from the fire. Once dinner was prepared, she bade Mariel goodnight and took her stew into their tent. She half finished the bowl and nodded off on top of her blankets.

Linneya rolled over and squinted her eyes, disoriented. The full moon, radiating through the fog, created a soft light in the tent. Her body ached from the previous day's fighting and horse riding. She stretched, willing her muscles to stop burning. Her hand hit her bag as she twisted to one side and it knocked over, scattering its contents across her pallet.

Gold glinted from one of the items. She reached for Orrain's brooch as everything came rushing back. Conflicted feelings churned her stomach. The relief of not being bound to such a harsh man clashed with the worry of not knowing if his brother could be worse. Her eyes ached from tears and the cool night air beckoned.

Linneya grabbed her walking stick and headed outside. The smell of burned wood in the smouldering fire scorched her nostrils. She sighed and a soothing baritone voice reached her ears.

"Princess." Darryn was sitting on a log by the fire, staring upward, as if he could see past the fog. He dipped his chin and craned his neck, looking back toward the sky as she sat down next to him.

"What are you thinking, Darryn?"

"I am thinking about home. My sister, Shailyn. How relaxing it will be to sleep in my own bed."

She nudged him with her shoulder. "Tell me more about your sister."

He chuckled. "Shay is opinionated and feisty. She does not hold to convention and I love her for it. She has such energy. Her positive demeanor could be mistaken for innocence, but she is no stranger to suffering. She chooses to continue to be sunny, even in the face of everything we went through when she was a baby."

Linneya smiled at his obvious affection for his sister. He continued. "She cannot help but bring in strays. Her love for all living things is a blessing and a curse."

Darryn shivered - *shivered* - at a memory. "She has this devil of a *hiduh* who hides underneath furniture and attacks me for the fun of it. He is a terror but she loves him fiercely and I cannot bring myself to throw him out."

She threw her head back and laughed. A *hiduh* was a miniature feline with a face like a *trillin* and a long feathered tail. The cute little animals were common house pets, but his reaction suggested this one was vicious. The thought of this nearly invincible warrior being bested by a tiny, furry creature was hilarious.

Darryn shook his head and chuckled. "You laugh now, princess. However, once you are settled, I invite you to come meet my sister and her little beast for yourself. Then you can tell me how funny his attacks are."

Linneya gasped, trying to catch her breath. "I would love to meet her and her pet. I would almost pay to see you shirking from the tiny thing." He groaned for comic effect and she giggled, wiping the tears from her eyes. The promise of meeting his sister and having a friend in the capital warmed her heart.

Darryn reached over and brushed a lock of hair out of her face. His touch lit a fire in her core. She bit her lip as he leaned in, his gaze lowering to her mouth. His jaw pulsed as she ran her hand up his arm. She wanted him to choose her and end this torture.

But something shifted. A momentary hesitation glazed over his features. He closed his eyes, sighed, and looked away. "Princess, I should head back to my tent. We will be in Enthor soon. Get some sleep."

The fire in her core morphed into shame. Her throat tightened and her eyes blurred. She stood up, brushing past him without a word, and quickly escaped back to her tent for second sleep.

The rest of the trip was uneventful. Linneya settled into a comfortable routine, riding with Darryn and swapping stories of their siblings. She ignored how her heart raced when Darryn would press her close and whisper in her ear. There was no point in acknowledging it; whatever poor excuse he had told himself, his mind was made up.

The suns were barely up when they arrived at Rathen, Enthor's capital. The cool breeze hinted at the impending winter season, but there was enough warmth in the air to keep the wind from biting. They crossed the river bridge and the capital came into view, a colorful island surrounded by a sea of forest.

She vaguely remembered the time her father brought them all on a state visit. The city's grand entrance had not changed from when she was a child. The blue and purple trees around the city made the white walls glow.

Birron had been a teenager, a few seasons older than Linneya. She remembered a lanky prince with a sallow complexion. He had bossed them all around with dramatic gestures and silly demands. He treated his place of authority like he was playing a casual game of *Hajut*, haphazardly sacrificing pieces across the board.

His father had passed within one and a half annae of their visit - only six seasons. If the ostentatious tents they had stayed in on the journey here were any sign of his reign, he had not changed much since ascending the throne. Still, she prayed to the Creators that Birron had sobered into a wiser king.

As they passed through the primary city gate, a loud roar erupted from a gigantic arena. Linneya started and Darryn chuckled. "King Birron said he would host a week of games in the amphitheatre in honor of the upcoming weddings. Sounds like we have arrived just in time."

"We have only visited once before, but I do not remember the arena being so loud." She marveled at the hustle and bustle of the markets. The pathways leading to the palace were lined with merchants from several countries, bells ringing and stall-owners shouting. Linneya recognized some of the same fae fur traders that would visit Aelor. Enthor's North Islanders offered wooden trinkets and woven baskets. The merfolk of the western seas brought a variety of spices and spirits. The rich, heady aromas from the spices mixed with the smoky buttered scents of the food stalls. Linneya's mouth watered as they made their way down the path.

Noticeably missing were the booths dedicated to traders of the South. Serathor's conquests had destroyed many realms, and the rising empire did not participate in free trade with other human countries. Linneya remembered vivid woven tapestries depicting Southern life and carved leather goods with dedications to foreign deities. Their absence now caused an ache in her throat.

Darryn snaked one arm around her waist, pulling her closer as they turned a corner. The palace loomed ahead and Linneya sucked in a deep breath. Its polished, white sandstone was carved into intricate patterns. As a child, she had been enamored with the murals on the walls that surrounded the estate. Tales of dragons and their riders spoke of a time when Enthor had a firemountain.

Her heart sank when the rest of the walls came into view. Carvings of the Arduin deities and the Storytellers had been destroyed, leaving only depictions of Matu. "What happened?" Linneya half-whispered, dejected by the sight of the ruined bas-reliefs.

Darryn sighed. "King Birron claims himself the reincarnation of Matu, but at first there was resistance. An early rebellion arose, claiming they should be able to follow whichever deities they preferred. He became irate when his sister was murdered by their zealots. After she died, he was inconsolable. In a drunken rage one night, he demanded all other deities be removed from the palace. King Birron oversaw the destruction, forcing stone masons out of their bed to see it done. The next day he regretted it, but it was too late."

They dismounted in the courtyard. Darryn gripped her waist as she slid off Doshar. Mariel and Straion were close by and the four of them drew together in a huddle.

"King Birron is, um, a bit unusual, but the welcoming ceremony is always quick and the food afterward is fantastic." Straion grinned at Mariel and Linneya. Mariel gripped his arm and gaped at the towering palace. While the buildings in Aelor were smaller and easy to keep warm, Enthor's temperate climate allowed for sprawling structures and grand architecture.

Linneya was shaking from fear. What if the king decided to give her to an old, decrepit privy council member? She shuddered and turned to pull out the cane she had been using. Her ankle was better, but not well.

Darryn offered her his arm. "Leave the walking stick and lean on me, princess."

She flashed him a grateful smile and could have sworn a darker shade crept up his neck. The guards were announcing their presence and Linneya had no time to decipher Darryn's newfound awkwardness. It was time to meet with King Birron and find out her fate.

Chapter 11

The throne room was covered in polished, pale sandstone. The muted gold hues glistened in the light of the sunsbeams streaming through the windows. Incense burned from hanging copper censers, coating the room with a tangy, resinous smoke.

A gigantic sculpture of King Birron was placed behind the throne. It depicted him in place of Matu. The Arduin fertility deity was associated with the light of the suns and a bountiful harvest. Priests were positioned on both sides of the statue, holding sheaves of grain, a silent reminder of their approval of the divine monarch.

King Birron was short with dark features. He had braided his black beard into a long, cylindrical weave in the style depicted of the Arduin. He sat on a throne made of green dragonglass. The stone was considered precious, as the only way to acquire it was if a dragon breathed fire on the island beaches east of the continent. A solid piece this size spoke of the dragon power wielded by the king's ancestors, in a time when Enthor's firemountain was active in the North Islands and dragons nested near its crater.

Rumors of the king's attempts to position himself as a godking had reached her family in Loraen, but Linneya was stunned to see how bold the man was becoming. Kings had suggested they were descendents of deities before, but to claim to be the reincarnation of a powerful Arduin such as Matu threatened the way religion had been practiced for duocenturies.

King Birron's consort took the place of honor beside his throne. He was blonde and stocky. Clothed in the king's colors of red and purple, his presentation emphasized his designation as the king's favorite. The queen stood beside the consort, willow-y and pale. Her icy hair hung like a sheet, hiding much of her expression. Her gray, long-sleeved dress was out of place in the still-warmer temperatures. She seemed to accept her role as lesser, even though her half-fae royal blood made her more formidable than nearly anyone else in the human realms. The swell of her stomach hinted that King Birron would have his first heir soon - if the baby was a male. She was stoic; no hint of emotion betrayed her thoughts. The queen might have been bored, but a slight spark in her eye indicated it was a calculated move to hide underlying turmoil.

The king was in a heated debate with an advisor as everyone from the caravan settled into their places in the throne room. His eyes were narrowed and his mouth was contorted into a snarl. The advisor flinched as he delivered whatever words were unwelcome to the king.

The king's countenance shifted to one of delight as he spied the princess. He stood, shoved the advisor aside, and clapped. "Dear Linneya, lovely to have you with us again. I see you have finally chosen our finest warrior as a mate!"

Linneya's face went red. Darryn rubbed the back of his neck and grimaced. She shook her head and responded, "No, your majesty. Darryn has been my escort since things became... more complicated."

King Birron nodded to them both, lips pursed as if he was bursting with questions. "We will talk after the welcoming ceremony." The queen shifted her gaze to examine Linneya, staring daggers from the dais.

She smiled halfheartedly toward them both and gripped Darryn's arm even harder. Mixed emotions coursed through her veins, burning her from the inside out. His decisions trapped her here, making her little more than royal bait for a greedy noble. In the same breath, she wanted to follow the tug of her heart and find out how extraordinary they could be together. If he had just agreed to be her ally and marry her, this would all be better. *Much* better.

She shivered at the thought of being pressed against him as they had been while riding, her back to his front. A whiff of his citrus and cedar scent sent her further into the daydream, but the reality of her situation sobered her almost as fast.

She trusted Darryn to keep her from physical harm, but he seemed to be unconcerned with her pleas to find a better solution. Thoughts continued to whirl like uncontrolled aether as the ceremony began. Darryn patted her hand, as if he could read her thoughts and hoped to comfort her.

King Birron seemed bored as the couples approached. He opened a small pouch and dipped his finger inside. When he withdrew it, his finger was covered in a fine red powder. The king stuck the finger in his mouth, coating his gums with the substance. He closed his eyes and inhaled deeply as it took effect. When he looked around the room again, his eyes were almost black and his grin was malevolent.

No one seemed to notice. Linneya was stunned that everyone continued on as if this was expected or normal. She stole a glance at Darryn, who inclined his head and whispered. "Sluryn, that red powder, is said to unleash the user's inner demonic force. King Birron uses it both ceremonially and recreationally. Personally, I find him harmless even with the uncanny visage."

She nodded and tried to relax her shoulders. She doubted the destroyed bas-reliefs would think of the king as harmless. Linneya suspected he had little intention to be cruel, but the games he played would hurt many in Enthor. Possibly even in Aelor.

The ceremony was a quick affair. Names of the couples were read out loud as they were presented before the king. It ended with the head page announcing a feast in the great hall in honor of all of the couples. The revelry would go on all afternoon with many of the guests traveling to the amphitheatre for the games and back to the palace for another round of merrymaking.

Most quickly dispersed to the feast. Falryn and the other healers had slipped out before the ceremony had finished. Mariel and Straion nodded in Linneya's direction before making their way to the great hall. Linneya felt out of place and unsure of what their next steps should be. She rubbed her neck with her free hand, worrying whether she would face political backlash for hiding her elemental power or arriving unbetrothed. King Birron was immersed in conversation between his consort and his queen and had not as much as glanced her way.

Darryn finally cleared his throat and leaned down. "Princess, shall I escort you to the feast? Perhaps we can catch the king later." She nodded, relieved at having something to do. They began to turn to walk away, but the king stood and they stopped.

"Darryn, Linneya, wait. We must talk." King Birron motioned for them to come forward. Darryn placed his hand on Linneya's lower back and guided her toward the throne. They both bowed and murmured a greeting. The queen and King Birron's consort pushed past, headed toward the hall for the feast.

"Dear Linneya, I am happy to welcome you to Enthor. These circumstances are unusual, but I am glad to have you back." He stood up and walked toward a side room, motioning for them to follow. "The messenger relayed your note, Darryn, but I want to hear everything from the two of you. Come, we will talk further in my private stateroom."

As they fell in step behind the king, Darryn's hand returned to her lower back. Linneya was surprised how his nearness had become a comfort over the past few days. His hand radiated strength, a warm sensation flowing up her spine.

She entered the stateroom and marveled at the plush interior. The designs etched onto the walls complemented the wood paneling on various furnishings. There was a long table with several places to sit. Darryn motioned her to a seat as the king plopped into the armchair at the head of the table.

King Birron turned to Darryn, "Go ahead. I want the full report."

"Of course, sire." Darryn launched into his recounting of the past mooncycle. Linneya stared out the window, marveling at the massive gardens, full of maroon and butter yellow flowers on lavender colored vines.

As Darryn finished, King Birron stood up, beaming. "How marvelous! What an epic tale. Linneya, dear, what a predicament. The legendary flame-talker? If I was not already married I would have you for my own. What power. The godking's heirs and their inherited elemental affinities! True signs of a divine force." He threw his head back and laughed heartily.

Darryn clenched his fists while Linneya flinched at the king's enthusiasm. Nobles had died on their trip, Darryn had made that clear. Joking about claiming her power in the face of all the tragedy struck her as flippant, dismissive even.

The knight cleared his throat. "Sire, I have offered to train the princess in combat. Falryn has said they will oversee her training in elemental magic. She could be set up in my guesthouse and allowed to nurture her skill set." Linneya fought to keep her smile contained at the thought of being free.

King Birron shook his head and stared out the window, eyes unfocused. Confused, Linneya cut her gaze to Darryn and opened her mouth. He signaled her silence with his eyes, the gesture so slight she wondered if she imagined it, but she pursed her lips and waited.

After a few minutes the king jerked and turned back to them. "No, she must be married. This ridiculous treaty demands it and fate would have it no other way. Since you killed her betrothed, who do you suggest replaces Orrain?"

Darryn caught her gaze and studied her face. Her heart beat faster - would he honor her request to make an alliance and let her return home to protect Aelor?

He cleared his throat, never breaking eye contact with her. "His brother, Johann, seems like the natural solution." Linneya's stomach dropped and she dipped her head, looking to the floor to hide her disappointment.

King Birron nodded, "Of course." He clapped his hands twice, moving to the door. "Guard, have Johann brought to us. And bring plates from the feast whilst we wait." He grinned back at the two of them. "When the sluryn powder wears off, I always want something tasty."

They did not have to wait long for Johann to arrive. The kitchen maids delivered platters full of delicacies and he swaggered in right behind them with his own plate. He was broad and tanned, with eyes eerily similar to his brother's. His hair was long and it hung wild about his shoulders. She watched the man settle into a seat across from her and dig into the food. His smile suggested he had no cares, but Linneya wondered if it masked deep pain.

Johann bowed to the king and nodded to Darryn. His lopsided grin settled on Linneya and he nodded as if he knew her. She did not remember him from their previous trip to Rathen, but something about his countenance felt like an old friend.

She relaxed, a relieved breath escaping her lips. Although the man had some of Orrain's features, his demeanor suggested a more genuine care for those around him.

King Birron stood and gestured for Johann to take a seat. He flopped into a chair, twisting into a position that Linneya thought looked most uncomfortable.

They started to eat and the king began. "Johann, I know you have been made aware of Orrain's death. We are all devastated by his loss and we must decide what to do with his betrothed."

Johann sighed. "Orrain was always getting himself into some sort of scheme. I am mourning my brother, but I do not fault you for his death - either of you." He nodded to Linneya. "Consider yourself fortunate, dear. He was not kind to his women."

Linneya pressed her lips together and nodded.

Darryn busied himself with his goblet, but his hand tightened against the cup as King Birron continued. "The treaty requires Linneya to be wed. The simplest answer is for you to give her shelter in your house."

Johann shook his head and held his hands up, "I cannot agree to this. I am not going to marry to save Orrain's honor."

Darryn growled, "You must. The treaty requires each bride to be spoken for. You cannot leave the princess without a suitor. Your refusal puts her in a nightmarish situation. The nobles here would use it as an excuse to demand she be stripped of her titles and made a slave so they could control her flame-talking ability."

Her heart sank. She was surprised the king had not suggested this for himself. She bit back her protests, not wanting to tempt fate.

"If you have grown so fond of her, why do you not take over?" Johann smirked. King Birron settled back in his chair and grinned as if he were watching a play. Linneya ground her teeth and glared at the men who were deciding her fate.

Darryn would not look at her, his face turning red. "I cannot, I have taken oaths that forbid it. Not to mention, my family would never agree."

Johann scoffed. "This is ridiculous. I refuse to be forced into a marriage that I was never consulted on in the first place. I am not some broodmare sent to fulfill a contract." Linneya snorted and he turned to her. "What?"

"You are not the only one who was not consulted about this." Linneya crossed her arms "I would happily return home and never speak of the past mooncycle again. Diplomatic nightmare or not, I have more important things to do than marry and play housemaid." Darryn furrowed his brow and it was Linneya's turn to avoid his gaze.

Johann gestured toward her, smirking. "See, Darryn? You will not force this on us." Darryn made no reply, but his face went from red to almost purple.

King Birron barked a laugh. "If you boys cannot come to an agreement, perhaps a duel is in order. The games to honor the exchange are still going on. We can work you in for this afternoon. A multi-elemental fight has not been seen for ages."

Linneya raised her eyebrows. Was the king suggesting that both these men held affinities? Multiple affinities? Darryn's wicked smile told her the duel was welcome.

Johann was also grinning. "Alright. I will fight. If I win, you have to concede and I can walk away from this."

Darryn's jaw pulsed. "As you say. If I win, you will marry Linneya and give her a safe home."

Johann pursed his lips as if he was suppressing a laugh and turned to Linneya. He took her hand in his and brushed his lips across her knuckles. "I fight for you as much as for me, dear lady. Wish me luck as I go to win our freedom."

Linneya smiled. "Well, then best of luck, dear sir."

Darryn rolled his eyes, but clapped a hand on Johann's shoulder. "Let us go prepare for this duel. The sooner we get done, the sooner we can get into the ale." The two of them left together, laughing and joking as if headed to a friendly match with no dire consequences.

She stared after them, wondering why Darryn had never mentioned his elemental abilities. He did not owe her an explanation, but she thought they had become close the past few days. She rubbed her face. So much had happened on the journey that nothing should surprise her. Still, was his elemental power what drew her to him?

"We will leave for the amphitheatre after noonrest." The king was humming a tune and grinning.

She turned back to him and inclined her head. "Is there somewhere I can refresh myself?"

King Birron gestured to a servant. "Take the princess to the primary guest suite. Make sure she has refreshments and whatever else she might need to rest for the hour."

She bowed slightly and limped out the door, following the servant.

After noonrest, the king met Linneya in the front hallway. A maid had found a fresh outfit and cane for her. The skirts flared around her, cumbersome and ostentatious. The orange material rustled like trees in a sharp wind.

The king held out a hand. "Come, Linneya, my wife and consort will join us later. If we go now, I can show you more of the attractions before the duel." He motioned toward the carriage.

Once inside, King Birron pulled out his red powder and coated his gums. He closed his eyes and sighed as it took effect. "I despise all the preening and prancing that goes with tradition." He shook his head. "At least now that my people have accepted me as the reincarnation of Matu, I am able to play bored with court ritual and no one bats an eye."

Linneya raised her eyebrows at his confession. "Why did you disrupt things?"

He pursed his lips and peered out the window. "Declaring myself Matu was tricky. Early on, rebellions tried to declare me a heretic. My sister was killed in the ensuing uprising." His voice turned dark. "They quickly found out siding against the godking was a mistake."

Curiosity spurred her on, but she did not want to press too much and upset the king. She studied his expression. "It appears you have succeeded in establishing your own dynasty."

King Birron chuckled. "You cannot deny - it is one of the more clever ideas I've had. It has been easier to overhaul some of my father's poor planning and quickly make widespread changes. Now that the harvests are better, no one is questioning the transition. Whether luck or skill, this has solidified into what promises to be a fruitful reign."

She crossed her arms. His father had been a wise and careful king. She struggled to believe he had made poor decisions or that King Birron's new plans were leading to a bountiful harvest. "What happens when your luck runs out and the harvests are poor? When your people start to question your wisdom?"

He blinked, surprised at her snippy response. Then he threw his head back and belly laughed. "If things get messy, I am sure my cunning will help me find a way out of it."

Linneya inclined her head with a small smile, then affixed her eyes to what was happening outside the carriage window. The bustling capital was full of busy people, well kept buildings, and clean streets. There was a patchwork effect to the dwellings, some built from the ancient ruins of Tirathel while others sported newer designs. The more she saw of the city, the more she wondered how this prosperity was possible in the face of the droughts.

"Are you looking forward to the fights?" King Birron leaned in as if he was eager for her response.

She worried her lower lip. "What happens if one of them is gravely injured? This duel feels pointless and dangerous."

He waved his hand in dismissal of her concerns. "It is just a spot of fun. This gives the boys a chance to get out some of their pent up frustration. Johann and Darryn are evenly matched. No one will come to real harm."

Linneya gritted her teeth. King Birron's ideas were dangerous territory. The king was still playing with his loyal subjects as if they were *Hajut* pieces on a game board. He hid behind his self-proclaimed status and ignored long term consequences. Instead, he chose to escape with his powder and the stolen glory of a deity.

Still, she could not argue that some of his policies seemed to be bringing prosperity to the realm. As the carriage jostled down the streets, the lively residents made Linneya smile. Everyone looked well fed and content. Perhaps there was a wisdom to King Birron's plans. Her brain wanted to believe he was proving himself a fit ruler, but a niggling doubt remained in the back of her head.

The carriage turned down a final street and slowed. The square leading to the stadium was packed full of people and the front entrance to the amphitheatre loomed ahead. This feat of engineering had fascinated Linneya and Eleanor when they had visited as children. The entire trip home, they had emulated the announcers - driving their mother mad.

The booming voice of the master of ceremonies was the same one from her memories. The sound resonated so loudly that it was even heard from outside the structure. Jeering from the arena echoed through the streets and if she closed her eyes it was almost as if she was already inside. They exited the carriage and began wandering down the street. The royal guards stayed close and the crowds parted and bowed to their godking.

He pointed to some conical-shaped additions at the top of the building and yelled over the growing clamor. "Those devices were created to funnel the sound out into the streets. It draws more people in on game days. More people means more funds for researching how to keep our crops thriving...

and maybe some leftover funds for a few revelries." His lips curled up in a lazy grin, clearly pleased with himself.

Linneya's eyes widened as they made their way toward the royal entrance. Food and trinket vendors were crammed into the streets around the stadium. A few of the couples from the caravan, including Mariel and Straion, were browsing, enamored with the business of the market. The smell of warm, fresh baked goods wafted toward her. Bells sounded from different stalls as merchants tried to catch the attention of passersby.

Children romped freely throughout the square in front of the amphitheatre, their parents running after them. A group of men were drinking ale and singing a folk song that was sped up to sound like a jig. A gaggle of women tittered about, batting lashes at one handsome man or another. Elderly couples sat in chairs in front of a bakery, rocking and chatting. The celebration and joy found in the groups of people made Linneya wonder - perhaps declaring oneself a godking was a better decision than she thought.

King Birron walked up and stood beside her. "I have accomplished impressive feats within such a small time. Stick around and you will see the mighty changes I could bring over duodecades."

The private entrance made for quick access. The halls were empty and before Linneya knew it they were in the royal box. The wind whipped as she leaned over the edge, looking down into the fighting pit.

The arena was unlike anything Linneya had seen before. On one end there was a large pond surrounded by trees. The other end hosted a massive firepit, blue flames reaching taller than the trees.

King Birron followed her line of sight and chuckled. "We had to put the food vendors on that end since their ovens already heat the space. No one wants to sit near the flames, especially at the height of summer season."

"Why do you have such an elaborate setup?" Linneya asked.

"Our elementals are revered in Enthor. I know that there are fears around elemental hunters, but here harsher punishments exist for someone who tries to harm a person with affinities." He gestured to the arena. "We host lots of fights that include the elemental magic, but many of those with weaker affinities cannot conjure their elements without having them close by. Aether and ground are easy enough to come by, but to make things more interesting, we added water, wood, and fire for the others."

Linneya chewed on her bottom lip. The hum from the throng of spectators was exhilarating. She was so curious to see Darryn's elemental affinity, it almost overruled her worries around the outcome. "What are your rules for an elemental duel?"

"They can change based on the setup, but a duel such as this is relatively simple. We do not allow Creators-blessed powers to be used in the arena. Nothing psychic - it changes the dynamic too much. These matches are not fought to the death. Nobles and elementals only fight until one party yields or the master of ceremonies declares the victor."

She wrung her hands in her lap, barely hearing his words. Elemental or not, Linneya had seen enough tournament fights turn sour to know nothing was guaranteed. She feigned interest in the embroidery on her borrowed dress and tried to keep her mind off the tumbling in her stomach.

Chapter 12

The queen and King Birron's consort arrived shortly before the fight was due to start. The king busied himself with his consort, leaving Linneya to sit awkwardly by his wife. The queen smiled and leaned toward her.

"Linneya, I am Queen Rhylanna. I am glad to have you with us." The woman patted Linneya's hand and nodded.

"Thank you, Your Majesty." The knots in her stomach loosened.

"Yes, yes, enough you two. There will be time later to get acquainted. Now we must watch the fights!" King Birron stood and the crowd quieted for his announcement. The queen's lips pursed, an almost indecipherable movement, and the king continued. "Loyal subjects, these games have been commissioned to celebrate another success: the return of our nobles and their new wives!" His hands shot into the air and the crowd roared.

Linneya wondered if the people were actually excited for the nobles' return or if they would have cheered for anything he said.

King Birron lowered his arms and continued. "We are interrupting your expected tournament to bring two of our esteemed fighters into the arena."

The crowd murmured in anticipation. "They are here to fight for the legendary flame-talker's hand - Aelor's own Princess Linneya!"

Shocked silence created a vacuum. Linneya trembled, realizing that the king had placed a target on her back. Even with his assurances that it was safe in Enthor, she had not planned on making her unusual powers so widely known.

A rumbling of voices began to build as people realized what their king meant. As the noise level rose to a thundering pitch, Linneya tried to steady her breathing. Shouts of approval and welcome smashed against elated cries of relief. Her eyes widened as she drank in the response of Enthor's people. She had been unaware of how far the stories of her healing powers had traveled.

King Birron winked at her and raised his arms once again, this time the crowd going silent. "Let the match begin!" The crowd roared. Linneya laughed in shock and King Birron grinned as if he was pleased with his own theatrics.

Darryn and Johann swaggered into the arena through the fighter's entrance. Johann held an axe in each hand and rotated them with flourishes toward spectators. Darryn had opted for a single sword and seemed more focused on their starting mark than the mob of hysterical women yelling in his direction.

Another wave of bellowing excitement swallowed the amphitheatre as they gathered in the center of the circle. The two men lifted their weapons, inviting the crowd to cheer them on. Linneya's curiosity rose. "So they both have elemental affinities? What are they?"

King Birron nodded. "They both have more than one, but I do not want to ruin the surprise of your first duel by telling you which ones." He chuckled at her annoyed expression. "Darryn and Johann know this is as much about the entertainment as it is the actual duel. It is bound to be an unforgettable match."

Linneya smiled, but a twinge of discomfort shot through her. His decision to publicize her power meant she would not be allowed to leave, no matter the outcome. The arena, this duel, her presence... again, all of the pieces felt more like the king was playing a game for his own entertainment. She glanced toward the queen, but the woman was staring off into the distance and stroking her rounded stomach.

The master of ceremonies met the two fighters in the center of the field. He spoke to them, although no one could hear through the raucous cries from the crowd. Between the spectators' enthusiasm and the men's relaxed demeanor, Linneya suspected that Johann and Darryn were favorites and had done this many times before.

The men shook hands and made their way to their marked starting positions. Facing each other, Johann lifted his two axes and bared his teeth. Darryn's fingers curled around the hilt of his sword, a promise of violence in the gesture. The master of ceremonies signaled the beginning of the fight and Darryn began to circle. Johann matched him, step for step, as they sized each other up.

Darryn rotated his sword in one hand and Johann used the casual gesture as an opportunity to charge. Metal clanged and the men strained against each other's strength. Linneya steadied her breathing and tried to ignore the anticipation building in her chest.

The knight parried an attack from one of Johann's axes, but it threw him off balance and he fell face first into the dirt. Johann grinned and swung the other axe high. Darryn grunted and pointed toward Johann, flicking his fingers twice as he scrambled to right himself. Sky blue smoke billowed from his arms. A gust of wind caught Johann at the top of his movement, knocking away one of his axes and leaving him unable to complete the attack. Linneya gasped at the force of his aether.

The queen chuckled. "Darryn's aether-weaver skills are almost unparalleled. He always puts on a gripping show."

Linneya's head spun as she tried to take it all in. The crowd bellowed as Johann tossed the second axe down and raised his arms. Darryn dropped his sword with a flourish and gestured toward Johann. Both men panted as they wove around each other, blocking and throwing strikes in turn.

Johann whispered to the wind and Darryn charged. Johann grinned and flicked his wrist through the navy vapor emanating from his arms. A gust spiraled downward and knocked Darryn to the ground. The knight growled, threw a handful of dust at Johann, and slammed his hands into the dirt. A deep brown smoke curled around them, almost the color of the dust.

Johann cried out and stumbled backward. Vines as thick as tree trunks erupted from the ground and wrapped around Johann's legs, cementing him in place. Linneya's jaw dropped at the massive display of power. Darryn commanded the plants with unspoken edicts, demanding they twist and move without a single word.

Darryn jumped up and took advantage of Johann's predicament. Johann blocked Darryn's punch and waved his free hand toward the vines, a cloud of crimson radiating from his fingers. Steam began rising from the plants, an orange glow emanating from inside.

Flames burst forth, burning the tendrils away from Johann's legs. The man stumbled back, chanting and pointing toward Darryn. The wind whipped around them, blowing ash from the fire into Darryn's face.

Darryn conjured more vines, wrapping Johann's hands behind his back and stopping his aether attack. The crowd booed at the lull in action as Darryn lumbered toward his sword. The king's consort laughed and clapped his hands at the sight.

Linneya shivered as she watched Darryn call his affinities - more from excitement than fear. She wiped her sweaty palms on her skirt, then hugged herself. Her blood was singing, almost as if it wanted her to join him and stop Johann...

She blinked rapidly, clearing her head. Stop Johann? The man was trying to free her from this antiquated mess of a treaty.

The scent of charred plants coated Linneya's nostrils. Johann ripped his hands free and fell to his knees. Flames from the bonfire across the arena were rising into columns of rotating fire. He pointed at Darryn's back and the inferno followed suit. The crowd roared and King Birron leaned forward. Linneya's heart pounded a frantic rhythm as Darryn pointed at the sky. He did not turn around, just made a fist.

As fast as the flames had formed, they were gone. Linneya's jaw dropped at the display of power. Darryn slowly picked up his weapon, a swirling plume of blue and brown building around him. Chaos erupted from the spectators and Johann rushed to ambush Darryn. He turned at the last second, snatching up his axes and pivoting back in time to stop Darryn's sword. The sudden switch threw Darryn off, making it possible for Johann to knock his sword away. Darryn twisted his hand and roots popped up, tripping Johann. Johann cursed and drew aether and flame in the same movement, tendrils of navy and crimson smoke following his gestures.

The wind whipped so fast Linneya almost couldn't see the men. Terror wracked her body as she watched Darryn's silhouette crumple to the ground. His tunic was torn to shreds, cut by the ash and debris flying through the fiery whirlwind.

She glanced in panic toward the king. He was grinning and picking something from his teeth. Looking around, no one else seemed concerned. Would they let Johann kill Darryn?

She ground her teeth together. Darryn's power called to her, she had the urge to go to him and break up the fight before he was dangerously injured. Something snapped in her mind, a cord going taut, as Darryn stopped moving.

Just as her heart sank, he raised his arm and the ground began to rumble. A rust colored haze filled their box, as if the dust from the arena had wafted to them. The dirt split around Johann, swallowing him into a pit. The onlookers cheered and Darryn struggled to stand. He picked up his sword and pointed into the pit.

"What - he has ground affinities too?" The queen was staring slack jawed at the spot where Johann had disappeared.

King Birron laughed. "Our dear Darryn has been keeping secrets, I see!"

The master of ceremonies stepped toward them both, raising a banner. The crowd groaned and jeered as the men sat back. Johann flopped his arms in the air in protest.

King Birron turned to Linneya and motioned toward the man. "That is the signal that they must stop. He has determined Darryn to be the winner. Johann could not recover any advantage in his current position. Stuck in the ground is an almost certain demise in the arena. As I said, we do not tempt death with our nobles in the arena."

Linneya grimaced as Darryn leaned down and offered Johann a hand. Johann scrambled out of the pit and stomped toward the master of ceremonies. He began to scream, leaning into the man's face. Several in the crowd booed at his aggressive behavior, but Linneya's eyes were locked onto Darryn's frame as he stared up at her and the royals.

The expression on his face was possessive and victorious. He pointed at her, then raised his fist. Others might have thought he was saluting the king, but she knew. It was a silent declaration of his intention to protect her. Her cheeks burned at the gesture.

The master of ceremonies had ambled off in the direction of the next set of fighters. Johann was bellowing at Darryn and flapping his arms. Darryn ignored him and started to trudge back toward the fighters' entrance when a gasp shot through the crowd.

Johann charged him and tackled. Linneya jumped up, crying out. The queen stood and joined her, leaning as far out as she could.

The men were rolling on the ground, too weary to throw meaningful punches. The scene was no different than two schoolboys tussling. The mob of spectators began booing, egging on the fight. Someone threw a soft, squishy fruit and the jeers became louder. A crash came from the other side of the arena and a fight broke out in the crowd.

King Birron stood and nodded to some of his guards. "My dear, you must return to the palace with the queen. We will settle tempers and bring the men along shortly."

Linneya tore her eyes from the scene of the two exhausted fighters pummeling each other. Her stomach twisted at the thought of losing Darryn, but at least Johann seemed kind.

The ride back was a blur. Queen Rhylanna stayed silent, eyes closed. Linneya's head spun. The streets were as lively as they had been earlier, but everything felt too loud, too bright. Her future was sealed and she had no say in it.

Once they were in the palace, she was led back to the same stateroom and settled into the same chair as before. A maid brought tea and honeycakes. The floral and spicy scent from the warm drink helped to clear the remaining burnt stench from her nostrils.

Her thoughts drifted to Johann. The man seemed gracious enough, but so had Orrain before Linneya was forced into his arms. Would Johann agree to let her return to Aelor? He was a rule breaker, so perhaps he was more amenable to the deal Darryn turned down.

Darryn... his expression as he pointed at her was burned in her mind. She pressed a hand to her forehead, as if the gesture could contain and settle the maelstrom of thoughts whirling through her brain.

She jumped as the door burst open. King Birron was laughing and the two warriors followed, still arguing. Darryn was still in the torn tunic and Linneya struggled to keep her eyes from dragging across his exposed shoulder. The king plopped onto a chair and the men made their way to their seats.

Johann shook his head. "I never conceded the fight. I also never verbally agreed to your terms. You will not force this on me, Darryn. I am not here to fight your battles."

Darryn gritted his teeth. "What was the point of this if you were going to refuse anyway?"

Johann just smirked and stretched. King Birron grinned as Darryn stewed. The king leaned forward and gestured to Johann. "You are losing honor every time you mess with the expected traditions around these duels. I may applaud you for some of your bravado and caprice, yet I find myself losing patience for your chaotic whims."

Johann shrugged. "Sire, I beg your forgiveness for testing your patience, but my honor is my own concern." He pointed toward Linneya. "Send the girl home and use the gesture of goodwill to negotiate with Aelor. I am certain King Varilon would agree to send aid as soon as we know Serathor is going to attack. It is ridiculous to hold her hostage."

Linneya wanted to feel grateful, but instead she prickled at his flippant manner. These men were discussing her as if she was not there. The thought burned at the back of her throat until she shot up and slammed her hand on the table.

"I will remind you that I am the highest ranking noble in this room, besides the king. I should be consulted on my fate." Darryn smirked like he was proud of her outburst. Linneya continued, turning to King Birron. "Please, your majesty. I would like to return home. I am worried that Serathor's threat on my home country will lead to devastation and people will die because I will not be there to heal them."

King Birron drummed his fingers on his armchair. "I cannot send you home, especially now that I have announced your presence in front of so many of my subjects. Enthor cannot be seen as snubbing off our oldest ally's royal family members. We are in an important time for this realm and I cannot lose support over a technicality."

Linneya shook her head. "If that is the concern Sire, I promise I will return once the battle is over, but I am certain that Serathor is going to attack Aelor. Their scouts have been navigating the fjords without being seen, as if some power allows them to subvert our watch."

He dismissed the concerns with a wave. "Dear Linneya, for you I will send some of my best spies to do some counterintelligence. Serathor does not have the ability to survive an Aelorian winter, so we have a whole season before we even need to concern ourselves with an attack on your home realm."

She pressed her lips together and surveyed the room. Darryn had lost his look of pride and was seething in the corner. Johann watched the exchange with an amused expression. Linneya might have found the situation humorous if there was not so much at stake.

King Birron continued. "Due to these unusual circumstances, I believe I must step in. Johann, you and I will discuss a fitting punishment later, leave us."

Johann's shoulders dropped and he exhaled the breath he had been holding. Turning to Linneya, his eyes softened and he nodded. "I am sorry for the pain I have caused you. Please know it is no commentary on you, no matter what the rest of the court might claim."

Warmth flushed her cheeks and she clenched her jaw, giving him a slight nod. Darryn snorted but said nothing. With that, Johann stood and strode out of the room.

King Birron waited until the door shut and nodded to them, "Darryn, you and Linneya will wed. I will deal with the fallout. Who am I as godking if I cannot declare when I see fate at work? I will set it into a decree this evening. Your knightsmaster will not hold this against you, nor will anyone else. Other Falorian knights have been wed."

Darryn slumped forward, placing his head in his hands. A dizzy sensation swept Linneya into a panic and she was unable to hear the rest of the king's commands. She gripped the arms of her chair and struggled to breathe. She needed to go home, not be wed to the one man who did not want her. He would never hear her pleas to save her people. He would never be willing to love her like she desired.

Darryn's jaw pulsed and he ran his fingers through his hair. His anger was palpable and it broke something in her. Her tears were raindrops cascading down her cheeks. As she continued to cry, something wet dripped onto her head. Linneya looked up into the shocked face of the king as a torrent of water began to fall. It was raining inside. Darryn chuckled and King Birron gasped.

Her hands were pulsating a greenish vapor. She leapt up and her eyes met Darryn's. He grinned and leaned forward, just as another wave of water came crashing down. Instead of the hopeful excitement she dreamt of as a child, her forced marriage was her country's damnation.

The rain was so intense it separated them and the stateroom began to flood. Guards were shouting and busting down doors to protect their king. Linneya did not want this. No one would. The pull she felt toward the man was not worth the hurt of Darryn's rejection. Every day would be a reminder that he did not value her the way she wanted to be valued by a spouse.

King Birron was bellowing at Darryn. Darryn was roaring with laughter. The chaos was almost unbearable.

Linneya stood frozen in the middle of the deluge. Numbness washed over her as if the rain channeled, then released all of her emotion. She remained transfixed on how comfortable she was in that lack of feeling until the scent of citrus and cedar wafted to her.

"Come here, princess," Darryn rasped, stepping in front of her and holding out his arm. His tattered tunic was now soaked and clung to his chest. In her haze, she could not appreciate the view. He met her with a steady gaze and a small smile.

She stumbled back, tripping over the chair in her haste to move. Too much had happened since this man came into her life, too many ups and downs. He stepped toward her, but she was shaking.

Linneya was torn. She wanted to run into his arms. In the next breath, she wanted to get as far away as possible. How could she go through with marrying someone that made her feel so deeply and then ripped her heart in two?

Darryn stepped close, arms out like he was trying to soothe a cornered animal. Irritation jolted through her. Perhaps crouching and leaping to scratch his eyes out was the right answer. She was trapped, after all.

"Linneya, we will make this work. I swore to protect you and I will continue to do so. This is not the end of your freedom, I promise."

She blinked and her shoulders relaxed. He reached for her and she fell into his arms, shaking. "Breathe, just take a deep breath and allow the suns to come out."

She panted, focusing on the sound of trickling water running off the furniture and out the door. The rain stopped.

Chapter 13

Pride shone in Darryn's eyes. "I suspected you harbored more elemental affinities than you realized."

"I - I had no idea. I thought I was just a flame-talker. This is..." Linneya's voice trailed off as she tried to comprehend what had happened. She plopped back down into the chair, the cushion squishing from the rainwater.

Darryn's voice was rough as he laughed. He knelt in front of her and gently grasped her chin, lifting her face to meet his gaze. "Welcome to the world of multiple affinities, princess. I told you that you would be one of the most powerful warriors. I am glad to see your second element finally manifest."

Something seized in her chest. "You do not seem surprised that I have a mist affinity. You knew?"

Darryn shrugged. "Falryn and I talked about this after Orrain was swept downstream. We suspected that you may have held more than one elemental power then. The surge of water was so unusual and happened at such a critical moment, it seemed likely."

Linneya's eyes widened, her stomach twisting in knots. She felt bad enough for killing the bandit, but knowing that she had murdered one of their own made her nauseous. "So this means I killed Orrain?"

Darryn's eyes darkened and he brushed a stray lock of hair out of her face. "Your power saved me from being murdered. You saved us both. He would have easily killed you after I fell. Your power protected us - it was in self-defense."

Her stomach lurched and she chewed on her lip. Part of her felt horrid for destroying a life. The other part was excited to know she harbored such abilities.

He stood up and placed his hands on her shoulders. "You are extraordinary, Linneya. I would bet by the time you are done you will be one of the most intimidating elemental warriors. Falryn and I will train you and you can use your time in the capital to learn more of the healing arts. We will work to make you a fine fighter."

Her heart was split in two. The darkness called for her to step out of her hiding place and into the full, destructive force of her affinity. The light begged her to fear the aggressiveness and focus on what she had always done. On what made her most valuable.

She slowly shook her head. "My healing powers are where my talents lie. Even if I start training now, I will not be a strong enough soldier when Serathor attacks."

He smirked and leaned down, his lips hovering just above hers. "Too bad, princess. You start in three days' time. If nothing else, you need to learn how to control your affinities. We cannot have you flooding the royal palace anytime something happens you did not expect."

He ran a knuckle across her cheek and Linneya shivered. She wanted him, wanted this. His touch awakened something in her, something dark and feral. She wanted more.

Darryn's eyes fell to her lips. Her breath came fast and he growled, putting his forehead to hers. "Linneya, I -"

King Birron burst back into the room and Darryn straightened up, rearranging his features into a bored demeanor. The distance between them made her heart ache. How could someone go from eager to cold so fast? She hugged herself and stared at her feet.

The king was followed by several attendants who began cleaning up the remaining water. One person handed Linneya some linens and she did her best to dry off. Another handed Darryn a fresh shirt, which he slipped into a storeroom to put on.

Linneya cringed, worried that the king might be furious with her. Instead, King Birron clapped his hands together, beaming. The knight returned to the stateroom in an overly baggy shirt and the king addressed them both. "What a show! We already boast some of the most powerful elementals here in Enthor. I am excited to add you to our numbers. A carriage has been ordered and your luggage has been transferred. I beg the two of you, make the best of this. Fate demands it."

Darryn bowed and placed his hand on Linneya's lower back. The familiar strength of his warm touch pulsed to her core as he led her to the courtyard and into the carriage.

The ride to Darryn's house was filled with awkward silence. The suns were quickly slipping beneath the horizon, their evening glow lighting the streets. Darryn stared out of the carriage window, lost in thought. Numbness crept through Linneya once more, icing over any remaining panic. The king had decreed this union; she had no power left to change her destiny. The truth should have stung, but only a hollow ache remained.

Her thoughts wandered back to the arena. Darryn's affinities were commanding and unexpected. Linneya had already witnessed his willingness to be violent with the bandits, but seeing his elemental gifts in action made a primal part of her purr.

He shifted and crossed his arms. She drank in his muscular form, reliving the moment in the arena she realized how strongly his power beckoned to her. His brutality should have scared her, but instead excitement warmed her core.

He looked at her and crooked one side of his mouth into a half-smile. "What are you thinking, princess?"

Heat flooded her cheeks. She searched for a half-truth to hide her embarrassing reverie. "I did not know you had affinities."

Darryn playfully narrowed his eyes. "You did not ask. I would have gladly told you about my elemental power. At the bonfire, you called me friend. From that moment, I was prepared to be open and honest with you."

Linneya resisted rolling her eyes. His words would have been sweet if they were serious, but she was in no mood for jests. "I told you, I was terrified of what it meant to admit my elemental powers to anyone. And yet, if the child had not been burned, the next words out of my mouth were going to be my confession." The truths spilling out of her heated her blood in prickly irritation.

She gestured around the carriage. "Now here I am. Stuck in a loveless, arranged marriage with you after listening to all your protests about how I am not enough for the past mooncycle. You made no effort to stop me from being ripped from my home. I cannot trust your claims of loyalty." She hissed, hiding her disappointment behind a mask of anger.

The knight frowned at her change in tone. "You have not given me a chance to prove my loyalty to you." He leaned in. "I take my friendships seriously. My vows even more so. You are to be mine, Linneya. I will see you trained and safe, even if you think it is futile."

Her eyes burned, tears pooling. Darryn sighed and pulled out a cloth, offering it to her. "Enough about this for now. We cannot undo a king's edict. Dry your eyes. I will not have you blubbering when I present you as lady of the estate."

"How much farther do we have to go?" Linneya refused his handkerchief and blinked rapidly, trying to hide her tears. One slipped out into her cheek anyway and Darryn brushed it away with his knuckle.

"It's the house with the blue roof." He gestured to the structure looming at the end of the street. Linneya's eyes grew wide as she took in the scene. House was a misnomer - the massive home was nothing short of a mansion.

She studied his impassive demeanor. This man was practically orphaned. A position as a knight paid handsomely, but this home was well beyond his means. How had he managed to afford such an estate? The tall structure spoke of opulence and grandeur, with intricate carvings and gorgeous gardens.

The gardens... all other worries dissipated as she took in the beauty of the plants. Violet colored vines were artfully grown across the front of the house, a curated display of elegance. "The vines, they are beautiful." Linneya breathed.

Darryn chuckled softly. "I bought this house with the inheritance my mother left. The gardens were mostly barren until my sister became old enough to be interested in plants. Shailyn is responsible for the landscaping. Ask her for a tour, as I am sure she could give you more detail, but I am familiar with the vines. She has a fascination with *lunampe* and demanded we trellis it up the front of the home. The bright white flowers bloom under the height of the moon."

There was a flurry of movement from the servants as the carriage approached. The courtyard was smaller, as the gardens had been extended to cover every possible spare area. Linneya heartily approved of the setup.

Darryn offered his hand and helped her out of the carriage. She wandered to the nearest plot, leaning on his arm, and marveled at the array of herbs and flowers growing in a sort of ordered chaos. The bright colors and patterns called to her. While she recognized some of the plants, others were foreign and fascinated Linneya.

Darryn nudged her toward the steps. The household was arranged in a welcome party. All of the servants were lined up as if formal greetings were typical. They inclined their heads as one unit as Darryn cleared his throat.

"This is my betrothed, Linneya, Princess of Aelor."

Several of the maids gasped at the announcement. The footmen chuckled to each other. A small smile played across the housekeeper's face and the butler dipped his head to hide any reaction. Everyone scrambled to curtsy or bow, immediately deferential to the royal in their midst.

The next several minutes were a blur as Darryn introduced Linneya to the household. She was met with polite nods and reverent conversation. Everyone seemed welcoming and excited to have a lady of the house. Darryn stepped into a graceful authority as he spoke with each servant and exhibited interest in each person's wellbeing.

A shout from the side garden caused everyone to turn. "Darryn! You are back!" A young woman bounded forward, cheerful and beaming. Her excitement reminded Linneya of Eleanor, but that is where the similarities ended. Long, dark hair framed a heart-shaped face. She was willowy with warm umber skin.

The woman was covered in dirt and leaves, her manner jolly and full of warmth. She leapt into Darryn's arms and he spun her around, the two of them exchanging hectic greetings.

They settled down and the woman turned toward Linneya. Her mouth opened slightly. "Oh! Who is this? My brother has brought home a woman at last?" Shailyn reached for Linneya's hands and squeezed. Linneya tried to smile, but in her shock only managed a grimace.

Darryn flushed and stammered over introductions. "Ah, this is Linneya. She is to be my wife. Linneya, this is my sister, Shailyn."

Her heart hammered against her chest, waiting for Shailyn's response. Darryn had told Johann his family would never accept her. For a moment, Linneya worried that Shailyn would be furious and the situation would escalate into another dramatic scene.

Instead, his sister wrapped her up and squeezed. "I am so excited to have you here! You will have to tell me everything. How did you manage to get him to agree? He has always been so silly about women..."

Shailyn let go and grabbed her wrist. Relief washed through her and she allowed herself to be dragged into the house by the chattering woman. Linneya glanced back over her shoulder and gave Darryn a small smile. The man leaned forward as if he was considering interfering. She turned before he could say anything and followed Shailyn inside.

She sucked in a breath at the opulence. The massive entrance hall was covered in rich, warm wood. Intricate carvings of flowers and vines decorated almost every surface.

"... and over here is our study. My side stays covered over in drying herbs, but we can rearrange and give you a cleaner spot." Shailyn pointed toward the botanical chaos.

Linneya beamed at the enormous room. One side had dark, serious furniture with hefty books and organized piles of work. On the other, plant sketches littered every surface of the light-colored secretary and bookcase.

Some herbs had been hung in a shadowed corner and the curtains fluttered in the breeze from an open window.

In the center was a conversation area with several plush settees. The fireplace on the inside wall warmed both the study and the parlor next door. This was not a room that was decorated to display wealth or prove status - people lived here and enjoyed the space. Linneya could imagine the lively debates had with friends. The quiet evenings reading in front of the fire.

The study reminded her of the second floor nursery space back home that had been converted into a reading room for her and her siblings. A warmth spread in her chest as Shailyn chattered away with mindless details.

She finished and flopped down on one of the settees, looking back up at Linneya. "Do you prefer to be called Linneya? Linn?"

Linneya sat on the seat across from her. "My closest friends call me Lia."

Shailyn grinned. "Alright, Lia. Welcome to our home. Or I suppose welcome to *your* home now. Call me Shay."

Darryn cleared his throat. He was leaning in the doorway, watching their interaction. He had changed into an outfit that had been tailored to his frame. Linneya's eyes roamed over the white shirt and slacks he wore, surprised by their soft, rich design. His arms were crossed and his muscles bulged beneath the fabric.

In this light, relaxed in his own home, Darryn's nobility shone through. It was a marked difference from his demeanor during their travels. He could have easily been a royal, a prince surveying his kingdom.

"Stop lurking and join us." Shailyn rolled her eyes to Linneya. "He is always acting mysterious, like he is some tortured soul. Really, he is as goofy as the rest of us."

He lightly cuffed Shailyn's shoulder and strode toward Linneya, a tentative expression on his face. "What do you think, princess? Do you approve?"

She smiled and inclined her head. Linneya did not want him to know how much she approved. The house was beautiful. His sister was charming. It would be hard not to fall in love with this life.

A snarl came from underneath one of the loveseats. "Narruan, behave! We have company." Shailyn dropped to the floor and dragged a spitting orange fur ball out from under the settee. The adorable feline had his oversized ears pulled back and his feathered tail was poofed. His fangs were smaller than most. Still, Darryn groaned and ran his hands through his hair, taking a few steps back. Shailyn turned to Linneya giggling and thrust the angry feline at her.

Linneya fought to keep a straight face. "This must be your *hiduh*." She eased toward them, reaching one finger out for the creature to sniff. He eyed her warily, but curiosity won out and he stretched to rub his face on Linneya's proffered hand.

Pride shone in Shailyn's eyes. "Yes, this is Narruan. He is a sweetheart but gets scared easily. I am forever telling my brother that if he would move slowly and give Narry a chance, they would quickly be friends."

Linneya nodded, returning her attention to the *hiduh*. "Hello dear Narruan. I hope we can be the best of friends." A proud sensation bubbled up in her chest as the fluffy creature began to purr.

Darryn huffed. "That mini beast is purposefully winning the house over to make me look like a fool. He is a crotchety old thing that is determined to conquer the title of head of this household."

Shailyn snorted and lifted her nose in the air. "He is not crotchety. He is fierce." As if emphasizing her point, Narruan spit a hiss in Darryn's direction. The man took three more steps back as everyone laughed. The *hiduh* flicked its tail as if he was proud of himself, then jumped from Shailyn's arms and stalked out of the room.

Linneya turned to her. "Darryn tells me that you are responsible for the landscaping. I would love a tour sometime this week, if you have the time."

Shailyn beamed. "Yes, we must! But after your travels, I am sure you are ready to rest. I'll say goodnight." She inclined her head and wandered off in the same direction as Narruan.

At the suggestion of rest, a wave of fatigue washed over Linneya. The last mooncycle had been full of excitement and drama, but today alone was enough to make anyone exhausted. She swayed and her vision blurred a bit. Goosebumps trailed up her arm as Darryn stepped to her side and steadied her. He motioned to a housemaid, a plump woman with graying hair and blue eyes. "Kapeyni, please show Linneya to our suite."

The blood drained from Linneya's face. "*Our* suite?"

Darryn grinned wickedly and stepped toward her like a predator, eyes locked on his prey. "Why, yes. You are my betrothed, after all. We will be married within days. Do not fear, you will have your own bedroom. I will even install a lock on the door so you do not have to fear unwanted company."

Linneya rolled her eyes and studied the intricate crown moulding - avoiding his gaze as if he could read her thoughts from her expression. Part of her wanted his company. Touching her. Claiming her. Thoughts that ran a tingling sensation up her spine.

"Madam, if you will come with me I will show you to your suite." Linneya nodded and followed the maid out of the study. The exhaustion had set in faster than she expected. Walking up the stairs was a challenge, her ankle throbbing and feet dragging at each step as if she slogged through mud. At the landing, Kapeyni turned and opened a set of double doors.

She gestured for her to go through first and Linneya stepped into a sitting area that was larger than her father's private office. Two bedroom doors sat opposite each other, sandwiched in between rows and rows of beautiful tomes. A stone fireplace crackled on the back wall. Several loveseats and cushioned chairs were scattered across the room. Two tables held books and half written letters, as if someone had dropped what they were doing and abruptly left. Two of the fluffiest chairs flanked a small settee by the fireplace. Seeing such a comfortable setup caused Linneya's shoulders to relax and a sigh of contentment escaped her lips.

Kapeyni motioned for her to follow through a door at the back of the room. Linneya almost panicked as she stepped into the largest washroom she had ever seen. The other side of the massive stone fireplace opened into this room. Several shelves offered soaps, towels, and other supplies. Floral and citrus scents wafted throughout.

The sunken bath was the size of a small pool, large enough for four people to comfortably lounge. *Four people...* Her sharp intake of breath caught in her throat and she choked. Coughing, she tried to regain composure, but it was too late. Kapeyni came to her side and patted her arm. "Do not worry, Sir Darryn is kind. He will not demand anything from you."

She flushed red at the thought of the two of them enjoying the bath and rubbed her face. "I am sure you are right, Kapeyni. It is just... a lot has happened in the past mooncycle. Today alone was like being tossed to and fro on the waves."

Kapeyni smiled "Once the wedding is over, you will have plenty of time to acclimate. Please let me know what I can do to help you feel more at home."

Darryn knocked on the doorframe as he walked into the suite. Kapeyni curtsied to Linneya, then made her way out, leaving the two of them staring at each other awkwardly. Linneya shifted on her feet and Darryn rubbed the back of his neck.

She had seen another side of him tonight. A regalness she had only had glimpses of before. Now he stood before her, a nervous tilt to his head. It would have been perfect if she thought he wanted her, if perhaps one day he could love her. A lump formed in her throat and she blinked back tears at the bittersweet feeling of being at home with him.

He finally cleared his throat and raised his eyebrows. "What do you think of the suite? I sent word with my butler to have my things moved into the wing over this next week so that we would have a connected space."

Her lips twitched up at the corners, forming a shaky smile. "I did not expect to have my own private reading area. The book collection is amazing."

He walked to one wall and ran his hands along the spines. "Many on your side are my mother's old books. I can pack some up and move them to the library. We can make room for whatever manuscripts you want."

Embarrassment flooded Linneya's veins. "I do not want you to have to remove memories of your mother on my behalf. Besides, I love the smell of old parchment. There is something about the almost spicy sweet scent that feels like home. I spent hours in the palace library in Loraen."

Darryn shook his head and stepped closer to her. He placed his hand on the back of her neck, his thumb stroking the pulse point behind her ear. "They will still be available in the library. If I learned one thing from my mother, it is that we must make room and adjust for each other where we can. This is your home now and we will make space for you."

Another surge of fatigue washed over her and she swayed on the spot. He wrapped an arm around her waist and led her to one of the settees. "You must be hungry. Let me call for a tray to be brought up." Darryn cocked his head as if asking for permission and she nodded. He walked to the side of the fireplace and pulled a silk tassel. "I will leave you to it. Shay and I have much to discuss. If you need anything else, just ring for it. Your bedroom is through there." He gestured to the door. Without so much as a glance backward, he strode out of the common room and down the hall.

Kapeyni bustled in with some food and fussed over Linneya as she ate. After, she hobbled into the bedroom, barely able to change into a nightgown. She slipped into the sheets, surprised by their smoothness.

Linneya was accustomed to the rougher woolen throws that kept her warm in Aelor's frigid climate. The soft, inviting feel of the fabric was unusual, but welcome. Her muscles unwound and her body melted into the gentle bedding.

That night, she dreamt of Orrain being swept downstream. The insects hissed their condemnation once more: *murderessssss.*

Chapter 14

Escape felt unlikely. Too many people knew her face already. The city was busy and there were too few opportunities to disappear. Linneya cursed King Birron for making her an object of curiosity.

In one morning, she had been dragged from merchant to merchant as Mariel hurriedly prepared for her part in the mass wedding that would take place after noonrest. Linneya spent the time supporting her friend and scouting possible escape routes while avoiding the curious gazes and whispers of those around her. The realization that she was likely stuck until the winter season was over churned her stomach.

"Here, Lia, what about this outfit for you?" Mariel beamed from behind an eggplant colored top and flowy pants with intricate gold embroidery. Linneya shook off the dreary thoughts and managed a smile.

"How I wish we were being married at the same time! It would be so lovely to have the same anniversary. The same memories..." Mariel sighed, fingering the fine threads of the fabric.

Linneya patted her friend's arm. "Yes, but this way I get to stand in as your attendant. Then tomorrow you will be a witness at my wedding. It is close enough that we can still celebrate together." Mariel's lips quirked up in excitement. Linneya tried to mimic her enthusiasm, but the rock in her stomach was heavy.

First thing that morning, Darryn had gone to the palace and convinced King Birron to allow them a private ceremony in the Arduin chapel. He argued that between her status as a princess and her abilities as a flame-talker, a small affair was prudent. Linneya was grateful that she would not be paraded in front of masses of people, but she had hoped he could negotiate more time before their wedding. Being yoked to a man that still seemed hesitant to love her made her skin crawl.

Mariel interrupted her thoughts, pulling her out the door and across the street to the jeweler. There was a tinkling sound as they opened the door. A sweet scent filled the room, like a foreign spice tempered with cream. An intricate crystal chandelier hung from the ceiling, illuminating the room with soft candlelight.

"Ladies, welcome." A graying fae bowed slightly at the waist and gestured toward one wall. "I am guessing you are here for our wedding collection?"

The jewelry display shone with all the colors of the seasons. Mariel sighed happily as she tried on different sets. Linneya wandered about, letting the fae jeweler focus on Mariel's selection. One bracelet caught her eye, gold with brown gemstones. The coloring reminded her of Orrain's brooch and her stomach dropped.

There had been so little time to process his death, much less yesterday's revelation that she was at fault. She worried her bottom lip between her teeth and stared at the reminder of the destructive forces she possessed. Since leaving home, her power had only brought devastation.

Her trembling fingers trailed over the cool stones. She longed for her simple role of healer, of helper. Tapping into the darkness her affinities offered was almost an empowering thought, but she did not trust herself. Linneya picked up the bracelet, examining the metalwork. She took a deep breath and focused on the intricate designs woven through the gold.

The jeweler hobbled over as his assistant wrapped Mariel's selection. "Ah! My Lady has fine taste. Those brown gemstones are rare. Very few of the most bold dwarves mine for these beauties. The entrances to the mines can only be reached on the dwarven isles through caves on the rocky cliff front. Once inside, things are still precarious. Unpredictable storms threaten flash floods into the mines. It takes a balance of luck and skill to procure these gems. Shall I have it sent to your home?"

Mariel made her way to Linneya and peered over her shoulder at the bracelet. "Oh, Lia, I am not sure you should. He is in the past. I do not understand why you keep his brooch."

Linneya smiled sadly. She would explain her decision to Mariel some other time. For now, she nodded to the jeweler. "Yes, please put it on my account."

She also picked out a purple and blue set that mimicked some of her favorite plants and they walked back to the central thoroughfare. Linneya was content to watch as her friend soaked up the excitement of the day.

Mariel's eyes sparkled as she made decisions on the pattern of her bread loaf, her dress, and the wording of their vows.

When they parted ways, Linneya hugged Mariel. "You will make the most beautiful bride this evening. I believe you and Straion are lucky to have found each other."

Mariel blushed and squeezed Linneya's hand before walking away. Linneya could see her friend struggling a bit, spending the morning out and about must have hurt her foot. Straion was waiting by a carriage and swept Mariel up into his arms. She shrieked and laughed, turning red as he carried her.

Linneya went home and spent noonrest preparing for the mass wedding. The purple outfit and jewelry had been delivered and Kapcyni wasted no effort in arranging her hair into a braided style that would rival everyone's at the ceremony. The maid put the finishing touches on her just as a bell rang, signaling it was time to depart. She shooed Linneya out of the room and down the stairs.

Darryn was standing in the hallway, waiting. His lips parted with a sharp intake of breath as he laid eyes on her. "You look fantastic, princess."

She blushed. "Thank you. Do you have the sword?"

He grinned and held out his ceremonial blade. Its scabbard hung on a belt. "Let me help you."

Linneya nodded and held her arms up while he fitted the belt to her waist. His nearness left her breathless, his fingers lingering a bit too long. He may have been the source of all her problems, but she still ached for his touch.

Darryn finished, stood, and motioned for her to turn in a circle. She did and his intense gaze seemed to drink in her whole form. He grabbed her hips and squeezed. Leaning forward, his lips brushed her ear and he murmured. "My wife will be the fiercest swordswoman attending to a bride today."

She bit her lip, surprised at his choice of title. *Wife.* A warmth spread through her, followed by a twinge of anxiousness. So much was changing so fast.

He offered her his hand and they walked out the front door. The royal park was only a few blocks away, so they strode hand in hand toward the central lawn. As they got close, the conversation of the crowd of guests rumbled. Linneya's eyes grew wide as she realized how massive the crowd was. King Birron had spared no expense, decorating each of the chairs with flowers and gold ribbons. A temporary outdoor ballroom had been erected beside the ceremonial area.

Darryn squeezed her hand and let go. "I am going to find a seat near Mariel's section. I will save you a spot." She nodded and they wandered in opposite directions.

Linneya searched for the brides. She had not expected so many people and it took a bit before she realized they were hidden behind a stand of trees. The women lined up, their outfits an array of gold hues representing the first sun. Each woman carried a decorated loaf of bread and stood with their attendant.

Linneya wove through the throng of sunsbeams, barely making it to Mariel in time. The gong rang, signaling the start of the ceremony. Music began as they made their way to the crowd. They walked to the front, hand in hand, and found Mariel's designated spot. Quiet conversations created a constant hum from the crowd. Mariel hugged the wrapped loaf in her arm and Linneya could feel her shaking with excitement. She squeezed her friend's hand, hoping Mariel would find comfort in the sensation. They took their spots, facing the crowd.

A horn sounded and the men lined up in the back of the audience, the red and orange hues of their outfits matching the flames of the second sun. They found their places and began walking down the aisles. Friends and family cheered and threw colorful paper folded in the shape of birds.

Straion's face split into a grin as he saw Mariel. Linneya marveled at how his expression never wavered. He was so sure of their marriage. She was overjoyed for her friend.

He stopped in front of Linneya and raised his ceremonial sword. The symbolic duel would name Straion as worthy of his spouse. She stepped back into a fighting stance, drawing her sword to strike. One quick motion, above her head. Straion blocked, deflecting her blow to the side and laying his sword on her shoulder. He chuckled and Linneya beamed. Mariel deserved someone this lighthearted and fun.

The tradition complete, Linneya nodded to Straion and they both sheathed their weapons. She stepped aside and gestured her permission for him to proceed to Mariel. Her best friend radiated joy as he approached.

He knelt before her and she handed him the loaf of bread. Linneya took her seat beside Darryn and watched as Straion whispered something to Mariel. The bride blushed and giggled, just as the high priest called everyone to order.

The ceremony went quickly. Vows were exchanged. The breaking of bread, completed. King Birron walked down the line, laying his hands on each couple and dramatically reciting blessings. Tears were shed, the couples kissed, and everyone seemed thrilled with the outcome. Once the high priest dismissed them, Mariel and Straion rushed forward to see his family.

Straion craned his neck and motioned for Linneya and Darryn to join them. They walked up and were introduced to his brother and mother. His brother stood a head shorter, but had an almost identical smile. His mother was petite and plump with a boisterous laugh. She was making over Mariel, clearly pleased by the match.

"They came down from the Northern Isles just for this." Straion grinned. "I've been such a lone wolf, I think Mother worried I would never find a wife." His mother nodded exuberantly in jest. He laughed and continued, putting his arm around Mariel's waist and squeezing. "Now here I am with a wife who has more experience with women than I do."

Linneya's eyebrows raised in surprise and Mariel's cheeks turned red. "Dear, that was not something that I tell to others."

Straion sucked in a breath and rubbed his hand on the back of his neck. "Love, I am sorry. I did not mean to make you uncomfortable!" He looked back to the others, looking nervous. "I am terrible at knowing when to keep my mouth shut if I am excited."

Linneya was unsure whether to chuckle or cry from the awkwardness. Mariel had her lips pursed in an expression that suggested she was more flustered than uncomfortable. Linneya was certain they would all laugh about this later. Mariel grabbed Straion's hand. "We should be dancing, husband." He grinned and let her lead him to the ballroom floor.

Linneya watched them spinning. Mariel was glowing and Straion was glued to her, so enamored it was as if no one else was there. He held her up, keeping the weight off her foot, and it all seemed effortless.

A word she could not associate with her own upcoming nuptials. She started as Darryn laid a hand on her shoulder. "Shall we, princess?" Her stomach fluttered and she took his hand. At least this part was easy. He wrapped her into his arms and smiled down at her, a bit stilted but earnest.

They danced the afternoon away.

They stayed too late and were rushed once they arrived back at the mansion. She changed quickly in her room, the fast pace of the day helping keep her nerves at bay.

She inspected herself in the mirror, neither pleased nor upset by her appearance. Her silver dress cascaded off her frame. The jewelry Kapeyni chose was chunky and bold, carved silver with emeralds. The maid had fussed over her hair, allowing half to fall around her shoulders.

It was fine, but something about that verdict caused a tug in her chest. Linneya wanted things to feel more special than this.

She sighed and sat back down at the vanity and pulled open a drawer. A different set of jewelry would help to bring everything together. After all, a princess only gets one magnificent engagement feast at the palace.

The gold from Orrain's brooch and the bracelet she bought earlier sparkled in the candlelight. Linneya's fingers trembled as she picked them up. The man was horrid to her, but she was the reason he was dead. Her powers killed him. It felt right to honor him by wearing it - just this once. She was grateful he would not be her husband. Still, the thought of his life ending in such a tragic way because of her unchecked power left a bitter taste in her mouth.

Linneya turned to Kapeyni. "Do I have time to change? I would like to wear this set with my outfit tonight." She could not make eye contact as she handed Orrain's brooch to the woman. Kapeyni pursed her lips, as if she was suspicious of Linneya's demeanor, but nodded and walked out of the room.

She returned with a blue gown that had gold floral embroidery accenting the bodice. "This stitching would match your jewelry set, My Lady. The blue will highlight your eyes."

Linneya smiled and they hurried to get her changed. As they finished, Kapeyni turned her around and squeezed her shoulders. "I hope tonight and tomorrow are joyous occasions for you, madam. I look forward to getting to know you better as you grow into your role as lady of this house."

Lady of this house. Linneya's soul was split between the excitement of working by Darryn's side and being permanently torn from her people. She took hold of the woman's hands. "Thank you so much, Kapeyni. I am grateful for your help."

The woman nodded. "Of course. Now, we must get you downstairs. You will be late." She waved Linneya on and turned back to clean up the vanity.

Linneya rushed out of the room and down the stairs. Darryn was once again in the front hallway. He stopped pacing and his eyes dragged over her frame as she stepped off the bottom stair. Warmth pooled low in her belly and she tentatively turned one corner of her mouth up, but he clenched his jaw. "That brooch..."

She nodded as a flush crept up her neck. "I killed him. The least I could do is honor his memory."

Darryn sighed and held out his hand. "You are too generous with that knave."

She gave him a small smile and slid her hand into his. "At this point, it may be more for me than it is for him. I need to feel I have done the right thing by honoring his life, even if he was horrible at the end."

His jaw pulsed, but he remained silent as they climbed into the carriage. Darryn sat down next to her, closing the space between them. He ran a knuckle across the back of her arm. "What a surprising outcome. A week ago, I would have laughed if you told me I would be headed to our engagement feast. Are you excited for tomorrow?" His touch left goosebumps in its wake, betraying her body's cravings.

"You cannot expect me to be happy when all of this is forced. You have made it clear over and over again that you do not care for me. Marrying my captor was not my plan."

Darryn waggled his eyebrows. "Are you saying you do not find me attractive? That you do not want this union?"

Linneya sighed in defeat. "Of course I do, but I do not care to marry a man who does not want me. I do not care to marry someone who will not listen to my concerns. You say you will protect me, but you are choosing what that looks like without considering my needs. I wanted to marry someone who would be my partner, not my jailer."

He let out a long breath. "Princess, I am not your jailer. I am trying to make the best of a maddening situation."

"Maddening? For whom? You? You are not the one being claimed like chattel, sir." Linneya scoffed, feeling the heat rising in her veins. She subtly leaned away, pretending to stare out of the carriage, and Darryn growled. She jumped and her head swiveled at the feral noise.

He ran his fingers through her hair, twisting it into his fist at the base of her neck. Her core went molten as he forced her to hold his gaze and dropped his voice. "I would claim you right now if I thought it would help you see sense."

This. If he would show this level of passion, she could almost be convinced this would work. She gave him a wicked smile and traced his pulse with her pointer finger.

He pulled her hair, exposing her neck, and kissed down her jawline. Her heart raced as he whispered against her skin. "Make no mistake. I want you. I am thrilled that Birron ordered this. For the past mooncycle I have craved you. Your scent, your touch, all of you - *mine*."

He raised his head to look her in the eyes. Her lips tingled with his nearness and she struggled to breathe. The heat from his skin scorched her fingertips as she ran her hands up his arms.

"I want to be yours, Darryn."

He groaned and let go of her hair, pulling her onto his lap. Linneya gasped and clasped her hands behind his neck. He ran his thumb against her bottom lip as their breath mingled. Heat pooled in her apex, an aching sensation that whispered that she wanted to know all of him. His hand squeezed dangerously high on her thigh.

The carriage halted and Darryn blinked, shaking his head and dropping his hands as if the motion jolted him back to reality. He slid her off his lap and abruptly turned to leave.

"My apologies, princess. I forgot myself." He threw open the carriage door and stomped down the footboard.

"Wait, I -" Linneya panted.

"Come, your banquet awaits." His face was set in an unreadable expression. Her thoughts whirled, frustration bubbling to the surface. She forced herself to regain composure, patting her hair back into place before she exited the carriage.

The palace loomed. Inside the ballroom, the ceilings were so high she felt like she would float up if she looked too long. Everything was draped in the gold, orange, and red tones of traditional Enthorian weddings. Courtiers milled about, drinking and chattering. King Birron's booming laughter rang out, cutting through the revelry.

"Darryn!" A shorter man with shaggy blonde hair and a scar that trailed from the hinge of his jaw to his collarbone waved. A tall woman with brown hair and shock-green eyes stood beside him and inclined her head in their direction.

Shailyn was on the arm of a second man. He was rugged, with curly deep red hair and a beard. The man locked onto her, as if he absorbed every micromovement, but his smile seemed genuine. Linneya resisted the urge to wring her hands and held her head high.

Shailyn bounded forward and grabbed her arm. "Lia! How was the ceremony? Did your friend have a lovely wedding? The crew is excited to meet you."

Linneya glanced at Darryn, hoping he would answer. He beamed and placed a hand on her lower back. "Come, princess, and meet my friends."

He led her into the center of the group and gestured toward the man with the scar. "This is Graisor, one of my fellow Falorian knights." Graisor bowed his head and placed a hand over his heart. The man moved like a trained assassin, precise and with a deadly undertone. Even in this benign interaction, Linneya could tell he was a formidable warrior.

Darryn turned to the woman with the green eyes, but she stepped forward before he could introduce her. "Shay has been telling us of your exploits, princess." She curtsied and held a hand out to Linneya. "My name is Chrysa." Her accent was reminiscent of the southern islanders that lived alongside merfolk. Linneya took her hand and squeezed, smiling.

Shailyn pulled the man with the dark red hair forward. "This is Trotyn. He is also a Falorian knight." Trotyn bowed and held out his hand. His pointer finger was cut off at the second knuckle, and the remaining part was twisted at an odd angle. Linneya clasped his hand and he brushed his lips over her knuckles.

"It is wonderful to meet you all. I hope we get to know each other better." Linneya smiled and Darryn snaked an arm around her waist. Everyone stared at each other awkwardly. The silence was painful, but Linneya could not think of anything to say. She was surprised to find Darryn had one friend, much less three.

"I am just going to say it." Graisor cleared his throat, a crooked smile playing across his lips. "After everything, I think we are in complete shock that Darryn has taken a wife."

Chrysa folded her arms. "It's a bit difficult to refuse when the king orders you wed. Linneya, ignore him. We are pleased to have you. Tell us more about yourself. What do you do? Besides healing, I mean. We have all heard about your legendary flame element."

Trotyn chuckled. "And mist. We all cheered when we heard you flooded the royal stateroom. It is a fantastic day around here anytime someone can create a bit of chaos in the palace."

Heat crept up her neck. Darryn kissed the back of her hand, his eyes full of mischief. "It was glorious to watch her create such a deluge."

Chrysa walked up and grabbed Linneya's arm, waving Darryn off. "Shay and I need some girl time with your future wife. You three go find something else to do other than harass the poor woman."

Shay gripped her other arm and the two women began pulling her away from Darryn. Linneya caught sight of his face, his mouth agape as if he did not know whether to demand they bring her back. She laughed and let the women lead her toward a quiet alcove.

"Now that those beasts cannot interrupt, tell us. What do you like? I want to get to know you." Chrysa cocked her head, genuine curiosity in her voice.

"Well, besides my love of plants," she nodded to Shailyn, who beamed, "I also read a lot. I know my way around a sword if I have to fight, but I spend more time at the infirmary volunteering as a life-tender. What about the two of you?"

The women chattered, excitedly running over each other. Chrysa was an artist. She described an oracle deck she was designing that included the deities and legendary creatures from the islands of her birth. Shailyn interrupted with tales of a new instrument she was learning to play. They both loved botanical poisons and the conversation quickly turned gory with descriptions of the concoctions they wanted to try. Linneya occasionally piped up with antidotes or suggestions on how to make the poison absorb more quickly.

She settled into the rhythm of their newly formed trio, but found it hard to stay focused with Darryn in her line of sight. He was casually leaned against a pillar, animatedly talking with his men. Graisor was twisting his arms in the air, mimicking some fight. Darryn laughed and clapped Trotyn on the shoulder. His sleeves were partially rolled up and his forearms were strangely alluring.

She tensed when a hand snapped in her face. "Lia, we are over here. There will be plenty of time to ogle my brother later." Shailyn giggled as Linneya turned red.

Chrysa shook her head. "Leave the poor woman alone, Shay. At least she likes him and he is not stuck with that horrendous Alayne." She grabbed Shailyn's elbow and tugged. "Let us show Linneya where the king hides the *real* wine."

Shailyn started cackling as they headed for the refreshments and Linneya's lips turned up in a small grin. She did not only like Darryn, his friends seemed to be a lovely bunch as well.

The wine Chrysa was referencing was faewine. Through duocenturies of refining their fermentation process, the fae had created a libation that could spin the most seasoned drinker into a state of bliss. Some debated whether it was really the fermentation or if they had infused it with some clandestine magic. Less than one glass had Linneya floating. She hesitated as Shailyn handed her a second, but she was willing to do anything to help her forget her impending nuptials.

She tipped her head back and chugged the entire glass. As she lowered the goblet, a man stepped up. He was portly, bald, and sported a gray pointy beard and over-waxed moustache. His eyes raked over her and he sneered. "Sir Darryn has found himself quite a wild one, it would seem."

Chrysa crossed her arms as Shailyn seethed behind the man's back. Linneya was beginning to appreciate this little entourage. Their reactions mirrored what she felt inside as she sized up the newcomer.

A warm hand pressed into her lower back. "Sir Fyrain." Darryn nodded at the man. "This is my betrothed, Linneya, Princess of Aelor."

The man leered at her. "Yes, I have heard of your impressive catch, sir." Darryn's jaw pulsed and his arm possessively snaked around her waist. The man inclined his head and raised his eyebrows.

"He is quite lucky." Johann sidled up, grinning and nodding at the women. The air became stifling as Darryn pressed Linneya close.

Sir Fyrain motioned toward Linneya's chest and turned to Johann. "What a beautiful brooch. Your brother had a similar one, did he not?"

Linneya blanched. She would never have worn the jewelry if she thought Johann would be at the feast. "It is Orrain's. I meant only respect for the dead when I wore it." She was mortified.

Johann's eyes sparkled and he gave her a slight bow. "Thank you for honoring him." He grabbed Sir Fyrain's elbow and maneuvered him away. "Sir, we need to speak on the horses that you are housing for me."

Beads of sweat formed on her brow and her stomach turned. The room was sweltering. Chrysa and Shailyn excused themselves to chase another barrel of faewine. Darryn let go of her waist and she bent over slightly, hand on her chest. The knight raised his eyebrows and held out his hand. "Shall we dance? It might help distract you."

She nodded and he swept her onto the dance floor. The song was a faster jig and the faewine tilted her world. She stumbled a few times before he finally wrapped his arm around her waist and drew her close.

Darryn leaned forward and whispered, "Do you think we could sneak away for a bit? I have something I want you to see."

Linneya chewed the inside of her cheek, looking around. No one seemed to be watching them, so she nodded. "We might as well slip away. It will give everyone something to talk about."

Darryn grinned. "I knew I could count on you. Come on, it is not far." He took her hand and led her through a side door. They nodded to the guards and made their way down the hall. Once they turned and were certain no one was suspicious, he picked up the pace.

Linneya laughed at his eagerness. Her head spun, as much from excitement as the alcohol. "Where are we going?"

He pulled her close and chuckled, whispering in her ear. "The catacombs." Her jaw dropped open.

The catacombs were ancient, layer after layer of unusual architecture and styles. Throughout the duocenturies, different tunnels had been used for mining. Others were secret passageways for underground cults to worship forbidden gods. Many areas were converted into burial crypts.

No one knew how deep the tunnels went. Some of the earliest tunnels were said to hold remains of the deities themselves. Spirits of shadow demons were rumored to torment anyone who ventured too far alone. Linneya had heard of more than one person that got lost, turning up weeks later babbling and incoherent.

He laughed harder at her expression and stepped away. "Do not worry, princess. You are safe with me." He grabbed a torch from its holder and lit it at the next sconce.

She bumped into him as he ground to a halt in front of a painting. "Here we go. This latch is always finicky, give me a moment." He bit his bottom lip as he fiddled with the lock mechanism.

Linneya's heart raced and she glanced up and down the hallway, waiting for someone to catch them and demand to know what they were up to. The catacombs were revered by some as sacred, by others cursed. She worried what might happen if they were caught breaking in.

Darryn swore as the latch ground on something, making a loud screech. Linneya cringed and wrung her hands. He pressed a second time and the door clicked. "Ah, there it is."

Chapter 15

The painting swung forward and he grinned, beckoning for her to follow him. She blanched as the musty scent of a rarely-used corridor wafted up. They walked down the steep staircase, all light dissolving behind them. Their shoes precariously slid on the slick stone steps. The only other sounds were their breathing and something dripping in the distance.

At the bottom, the torch Darryn held barely lit up their path and Linneya stumbled. He reached out and pulled her close. "Be careful princess. That dress of yours looks too good on you to ruin it down here." He wrapped his arm around her waist as they continued.

The air was damp and smellt stale. Linneya's stomach churned, that second glass of faewine wrenching about in her gut.

They rounded a final corner and Darryn stopped in front of a rough-hewn oak door. "Since we are to be wed, I do not want secrets between us." He took a deep breath and nodded to the door. "This room holds all of the secrets of the Falorian knights. This vault is why we fight the way we do. The reason for all of the cryptic lore that we perpetuate."

He placed his hands on her shoulders. The oppressive air in the dank corridor melted away as he held her gaze. Her urge to press into him intensified and he spoke, his voice rough. "This is not a secret I share easily. No one else must know, not even my sister. If these secrets got out, people could be hurt. You could be killed. Please promise me this will stay between us."

She nodded. "Of course. I would not want anyone hurt."

He gave her a small smile and turned to open the doors. They walked into the largest wine cellar Linneya had ever seen. Bottles lined every wall, from floor to ceiling. She looked up at him, unsure if he was playing a joke.

"Follow me, princess." He slipped behind one wine rack, disappearing behind a false wall. She inched forward, her heart beating fast. The narrow passage was straight for a few paces, then turned to the left. Light illuminated Darryn's muscular silhouette as they neared the end of the corridor.

Linneya slipped into the lit space and gasped at the cavernous vault. On three sides there were ornate bookshelves with rolling ladders lining the wall from floor to ceiling. The other side had a large fireplace and rows of plush armchairs around small study tables. Two men looked up from their work and nodded at Darryn, then returned to their parchment.

He gestured toward the shelves "The Falorian knights do not kill at random. We are sworn to protect elementals from hunters who would steal their power. We have collected books, carvings, and parchment with all of the magic lore this world holds. All of the prophecies, all of the legends, anything that might help us understand more about the elemental powers we control."

"I thought the only collection like this was in the fae holy mountain, Varsha. It seems like it would be a safer place for all of this knowledge."

Darryn nodded. "Yes, we have debated whether or not to take it there several times. They have the means to better preserve this collection and the fae may have tomes we have never seen. However, our knightsmaster has decided to keep this a secret for now. If the wrong people found out we had these books, it could be a disaster. Precious knowledge would be lost if someone decided to attack whoever moved the manuscripts."

Linneya gaped at the rows upon rows of reading material. She drifted toward one of the shelves and reached for a tome, gasping as her hand entered a pocket of dry, warm air. "Why are they warm?"

Darryn chuckled and pointed to the red stones at the end of each shelf. "We use aether and mist conduits to keep the books and parchment better preserved. That is how we have ancient books that are still readable."

He pressed a flower in the moulding and a portion of the bookcase opened. He held it as she stepped through to the hidden room. Her heart pounded and she drew in a quick breath. The bookcase clicked shut behind them and she stood in the center of the room, speechless. Glittering stones in all colors were piled into glass cabinets. Linneya's eyes grew wide as she scanned all of the different shapes and sizes.

Darryn followed her gaze. "This room is even more important to keep secret. Each of these jewels represents at least one elemental whose powers were absorbed when they were murdered. We cannot send them back across the dimensional rift because they hold important magic for our realm. The head of our order believes the droughts may be a result of this magic being trapped. Until we can figure out how to release it back into the world, we keep the gemstones locked up here. The Falorian knights hope that the prophesied will be able to uncover the secrets to releasing this magic."

She slowly approached the largest case on the far wall, tears welling up in her eyes. There were more gemstones in this room than she had ever seen. Even Aelor's crown jewel collection was smaller. At least one life per stone - so many people gone for someone else's pursuit of power or longevity.

Darryn continued. "We keep this secret because this vault could be the downfall of the human realm as we know it. This power in the wrong hands could control everything - fae, dwarf, even faun. King Birron knows of the library, but he has not been told about these stones. King Shumor undoubtedly suspects its existence, but he is not yet bold enough to try to infiltrate in search of the stones."

What would happen if Serathor's king found out about this powerful store of elemental energy? She trembled and he stepped closer. "When we go into a city, we destroy everything related to the elemental hunter and their family. Most people do not know what happened, but the hunters fear being caught by us. Rumors make us seem like deranged, bloodthirsty murderers. No one looks too closely and it is easier to keep our true purpose hidden."

Linneya let the tears spill over and he placed a hand on her arm. "My work is dangerous. Graisor's wife was captured by a particularly brutal band of hunters. They killed her as we arrived to rescue her. I vowed never to put a woman in this position. Even if I did not have my oaths, I did not want to risk someone's life." He grabbed her hands and squeezed. "I will do everything I can to keep you safe. I know you are angry with me for forcing you here, and I do not deserve your forgiveness. Still, I would like to have the chance to be your friend, Linneya. Let me protect you."

Friends - was that even possible after everything? She chewed her bottom lip and he pulled her to his chest. The faewine was wearing off, but her head continued to spin with all the new shocks. A hidden vault, duocenturies of lore, and so many murdered elementals.

He brushed his hand through her hair, sending a tingling sensation down her spine. "It is dangerous and I want you to be as safe as possible. Let me train you, please. If nothing else, see it as an opportunity to find balance. Everyone should know how to fight, even life-tenders."

Even with his explanations, he was hiding something. Linneya had been around enough diplomats to know when someone was telling a partial truth. She struggled to reconcile the forces pulling them together with the logical facts. "I do not know. I prefer my way of healing and supporting life. I know you think poorly of my grandparents for not teaching their elementals to fight. After the bandit attack and Orrain's attempt to kill us, I may sound naive to you, but I am not ready to kill again."

He grasped her chin and lifted her gaze to his. "I will not force you to do anything you do not want, princess, but you will train somehow. Being my wife is dangerous and I want you to have the best chance of survival if anything happens." His dark eyes bored into her soul. The intensity of his stare stirred something inside her. Her eyes dropped to his lips, *citrus and cedar.*

The click of the bookcase door caused them both to start. Graisor stepped through and his eyes went wide. He coughed, red flushing his cheeks. "My apologies, but King Birron sent several courtiers to find you. It would be best to sneak out to the gardens so no one wonders where you have been. The less the king thinks you know, Linneya, the better."

Darryn nodded to him and squeezed Linneya's hand. "Ah, your first test as the intended of a Falorian knight. Come, let us get caught in a scandal." His eyes twinkled with mirth and she followed him out into the library. He led her out a different exit, this part of the catacombs took them back under the palace and into the main royal garden.

They emerged behind a tall waterfall that emptied into a pool. The slippery rocks made it difficult to maneuver back toward dry land. Linneya gripped Darryn's hand, struggling to stay balanced. The shallow pond was full of little yellow fish, darting to and fro. White lilies were clustered together along the shoreline. Darryn sat down on a rock and she stood in front of him.

Voices were headed toward them. Her heart beat faster as they grew louder. "What do we need to do?"

He pulled her onto his lap and grinned. "Princess, kiss me. It will be more convincing if you ruffle my hair or something."

She blinked, still trying to process everything. Darryn grunted impatiently. "Just do *something*, Linneya. Pretend if you have to. You look too serious for a pre-wedding tryst." He ran a hand under her skirt and placed it lightly above her knee. His touch made her go tense and loose all at the same time.

He looked over her shoulder, then leaned in close. "The king cannot be suspicious. He knows the tunnel is here and he will realize I took you to the vaults. He is drunk on faewine and may announce it to the wrong people. We still do not know who Serathor's spies are. Bite my neck or something, princess."

Linneya panicked, eyes darting. The voices were growing louder. He rolled his eyes and scoffed. "I thought you were made of sterner stuff."

Fury surged through her veins, or maybe it was the remnants of the faewine. She reached around to the back of his head, twisted handfuls of his hair in her fists, and crushed his mouth to hers. For a moment, he froze. She ran her tongue across his lips until he parted them. He tasted like sweet mint as he softly laughed into the kiss.

His citrus and cedar scent enveloped her as he squeezed higher up her leg and wrapped his other arm around her waist. Crushed against him, her breath quickened and their kiss became urgent. His strength held her in place and she almost forgot it was a ruse.

"Ha! Found them!" King Birron cackled as he pushed aside shoulder-length bluegrass. Linneya pulled back, panting. Darryn stared at her, his eyes dark with a predatory scrutiny.

Linneya leaned forward and breathed in his ear. "Do not question whether I can rise to the occasion ever again, sir." He growled as she pushed his hand away and slid off his lap. She smirked as he adjusted his pants and they both turned to face the king.

A small crowd had formed. The queen was there, her arms crossed. Graisor was off to one side, grinning. King Birron clapped his hands and motioned them forward. "You two are supposed to be inside enjoying this phenomenal feast! There will be plenty of time alone after your wedding tomorrow." The king nudged Darryn in the ribs. "Are you pleased I decided to give you our lovely Linneya? Feeling better about it today?" He laughed crassly and turned around before Darryn could reply.

The knight's jaw pulsed as the king waddled away, but he kept quiet and offered Linneya his hand. She stood a little taller as they walked back into the palace. There may be dangerous days ahead, but she was up to the task.

They danced the evening away with his friends, the faewine flowing freely. Darryn, Shailyn, and Linneya did not arrive back at the mansion until it was almost time for second sleep. Her room was already beginning to feel like a place of safety, like a second home. She fell in the bed fully clothed and dreamt of gemstones spinning and cool mint kisses.

The next morning was bright and Linneya woke to the sounds of Kapeyni opening the curtains. Her head pounded and her mouth was fuzzy, like she had swallowed a clump of Narruan's fur. The hangover was bad enough, but realizing she would be shackled to Darryn by the end of the day hurt worse. She sat up and groaned.

Kapeyni motioned toward the breakfast tray. "Raw eggs and fermented fish sauce. It will help perk you back up, My Lady."

Linneya grunted her gratitude and hobbled over, grabbing the goblet and gagging through the horrid combination. Kapeyni bustled about, pulling out garments and jewelry. The opulence was hollow in the face of what she had seen last night. The piles of gemstones, representative of people killed for their abilities, haunted her.

Once Linneya finished nursing her hangover, the maid hurried her into the bath. Lavender and rose petals sprinkled the surface of the water. The floral scents mixed with a grounding incense burning near the far end of the room. It was beautiful and if she was not being forced down the aisle to marry a man that would never love her, she would be glowing with excitement about the big day.

Linneya sighed as she sank into the water. The heat of the bath soothed the soreness in her muscles. She was tempted to have Kapeyni bring her some more faewine so she could drown out the critical voice blaming her for her predicament. Bile rose in her throat at the thought, and she coughed. No wine today. She would have to be clear headed and face her fate. She stood, grabbed a towel, and returned to the bedroom to get ready.

Kapeyni helped her into her wedding gown. It was a deep gold with sleeves that flowed down in a bell shape. A lighter metallic lace trim accented her curves in all the right places. The maid braided her hair, piling it on top of her head and adding more jewelry.

Linneya looked in the mirror and an ache radiated in her chest. She should have been getting ready with her mother. She wanted a royal wedding at home, surrounded by friends. She longed to be trading vows with a man she chose. Someone who chose her. A wave of homesickness washed over her as she made her way downstairs and into the courtyard. At least she would see Mariel at the chapel.

She had not tried hard enough to get away. Marriage would complicate everything. It would destroy her last hope of getting free and returning home. Her chest tightened as the carriage arrived and she swayed on the spot.

Darryn's challenge from last night rang in her ears. *'I thought you were made of sterner stuff.'* She set her jaw, held her head up, and stepped into the cabin. A brick wall was forming around her heart, the only promise of consistency she could offer herself. The carriage driver urged the horses on and she watched the city pass her by.

The streets were bustling with opportunities for escape. A merchant was loading pelts onto his wagon. She could pay him to take her north.

A woman was haggling with the baker. Linneya could entreat her to hide at her home until the guards stopped looking.

A side gate was unmanned. She could slip out and into the woods with no trace.

Linneya sighed. The reality was she could not leave without a plan and it was much too late to get out of this wedding. She could not even jump out of the carriage and run, as the chapel had come into view.

It had been built as a place to worship all Arduin. The smooth, dark stones were accented with white alabaster motifs. The constellations associated with the three Creators, Substantia, Libra, and Motus, were carved into the doors. Gilded statues depicting scythes and sheaves of grain had been added to the courtyard to emphasize Matu-reincarnated-Birron as the godking.

King Birron was outside and a small crowd had gathered. His ostentatious outfit was black with gold and burgundy embroidery. He waved her inside and Mariel met them at the door, beaming. She handed Linneya a round loaf of bread. "I made this for you."

"Thank you, Mari! I would have thought you would be too busy last night. What with your wedding and all the, um, aftermath."

"You mean the main course?" Mariel smirked, a red flush across her cheeks. They both giggled and Linneya unwrapped the loaf.

An intricate pattern was carved into the golden crust. Elyre flowers encircled the sigils of the storytellers. Linneya's throat tightened as tears of gratitude swam in her eyes.

"This is beautiful. Thank you so much." She hugged her friend tightly, grateful to have someone she was close to witness such an important day.

King Birron clapped his hands. "It is time, dear princess. Let us proceed." Mariel winked and slipped inside. The king offered his arm and pursed his lips.

She took a deep breath and wrapped her hand around his forearm. The music started and they made their way down the aisle. Musky incense filled the space with a heavy smoke. Guests began quieting down and finding their seat. Linneya stepped up to the platform and turned to face the crowd.

Her heart stuttered. The chapel was packed with people attending and the only familiar faces were lined up in a row near the front. Mariel and Straion sat beside Graisor. Trotyn and Chrysa had managed to squeeze in closer to the end. Linneya did not see Shailyn, but perhaps she was further down. Linneya ground her teeth, frustrated that King Birron had ignored their request for a smaller affair.

The music changed and Darryn appeared near the back in his crimson suit. His muscular form strained the fabric and she bit her lip. The homesick feeling that had plagued her chest dissipated and was replaced with a swelling warmth.

He began walking down the aisle, paper birds being tossed as the crowd celebrated. Linneya laughed as Graisor pelted one particularly hard and it clipped Darryn in the ear. The knight pointed at his friend and shook his head, a smile tugging at his lips.

The entire time, she waited for him to look at her. He never did. Darryn approached the king, sword at the ready. His lips were set in a line and his breathing was heavy. King Birron smirked and swung overhead.

Darryn swiftly blocked and tapped the king's shoulder with the blade. His expression darkened, as if he challenged the king to refuse him. King Birron grinned and gestured toward Linneya. Darryn's jaw pulsed and a possessive storm raged in his eyes. It left her breathless. Finally, they locked eyes and a warmth crept up her neck.

He sheathed his ceremonial blade and stepped up to the sacred space, standing beside Linneya. His gaze softened and he mouthed *'you look beautiful, princess.'*

She blushed. The knight inched closer and she dropped her head and stared at her feet. She was trembling so hard the white cloth covering the bread was shaking. Darryn kneeled before her and placed his hands over hers. He slightly squeezed and a calmness washed over her.

With a deep breath, Linneya presented the bread to him and the ceremony began. The vows were a blur. He squeezed her hands several more times and in each instance the sensation grounded her in the moment. They broke bread, the sweet taste of Mariel's creation reminding Linneya of home.

The ceremony was coming to a close and the high priest signaled for them to kiss. Darryn hesitated, his brows furrowed as if he was uncertain what to do. Heat flooded Linneya's cheeks. She leaned in, raising up on her toes, and kissed him on the cheek.

Darryn's jaw pulsed. She bit her lip, looking down in shame. He sighed and reached toward her. "No, princess. Let me do this right."

He wrapped one hand around her waist, pulling her to him. She stumbled forward and gripped the fabric of his tunic. His other hand went to her chin, angling her face.

Darryn brushed his lips across hers, an invitation. She wound her hands up his chest and around the back of his neck, kissing him back.

A sharp intake of breath and he crushed his mouth to hers. He held her there, tasting her, bruising her lips with an unexpected urgency. It was done. They were husband and wife. Something tightened in her chest even as her core went molten. Linneya was trapped, but it was a wonderful trap. They broke apart and she looked out into the cheering crowd.

Sounds were muffled and everything seemed farther away, as if she was looking at the crowd through the wrong end of a telescope. Mariel was smiling with her hands clasped beneath her chin. Shailyn had run to the front and looked ready to burst from excitement. Linneya pasted a smile on, hiding the numbness that threatened to overtake her. The only thing tethering her was the heat of Darryn's arm around her waist.

King Birron ambled back up and laid his hands on their heads. He prattled on about fertile soil and sunsbeams. He flourished his arms above them and pronounced them blessed.

Darryn offered her his arm and they strode back down the aisle, out of the chapel, and into the carriage.

Chapter 16

The ride back to the house was tense. Darryn sat next to Linneya, gripping her hand in his. He stared out the window the entire way, humming to himself. The only sign that he realized she was there was an occasional squeeze to her hand. Linneya did not know what to say, so she stewed in her fate until the carriage ground to a halt at the back gates of the mansion.

She stepped out and gasped. Shailyn had decorated the gardens in red and gold. She and Chrysa were directing caterers to set up rows upon rows of delicacies. Graisor and Trotyn were arranging tables for the partygoers. Elegant tunes came from a small group of musicians in the corner of a dais.

Guests began piling in, wishing Linneya and Darryn a lifetime of happiness before descending on the revelry. Mariel and Straion arrived and joined Darryn's friends in setting up more tables and food. Linneya was stuck in a long line of nobles who were mostly vying to win the favor of a foreign princess.

Darryn stayed close, stealing a caress here and there. He would occasionally lean down and whisper something about one of their guests. Some of the anecdotes were ridiculous. "Duke Ishvriel is rumored to have started his own cult, they meet in the catacombs and worship him as Matu's younger brother, Solon." Other tidbits seemed more important. "That is Lady Alayne's mother, Duchess Jenyce. The woman was a servant in her husband's parents' household. You can imagine the tales that go with her rise in rank."

Linneya finally turned to him, laughing at the stream of unusual stories. "How do you know all of this? You do not strike me as the type to care for gossip."

Darryn raised his eyebrows and placed a hand over his heart, a teasing gesture. "Me? Gossip? Never. It is important to listen and learn all you can about those around you, especially when you are working to stop hunters from murdering more elementals."

She leaned in to ask another question, but he pressed his lips together and nodded toward an approaching figure. Duchess Jenyce floated their direction, her eerie grace reminding Linneya of the woodland snakes back home. The woman towered over her, almost meeting Darryn's height. She curtsied as she stopped in front of Linneya.

Darryn cleared his throat. "Linneya, this is Lady Alayne's mother, Duchess Jenyce." Linneya nodded, partially expecting the woman to flick a forked tongue out into the air.

"I see you finally picked a bride, Sir Darryn." The woman pursed her lips. "I hope your family is pleased."

He narrowed his eyes. Linneya stepped up before the knight could respond. "Shailyn loves me and his friends seem happy enough I am here. Thank you for joining us in our celebrations, but we have other guests we must greet." She turned her head in a dismissive motion.

The woman smirked and inclined her head. "Of course, princess. It is just..." She stepped closer and lowered her voice. "I am an avid practitioner of celestial storytelling and the wandering stars suggest a family rift over your union."

Darryn rolled his eyes. "The duchess fancies herself a fortune teller, reading the skies for hints of the future. Enjoy our party, but stop trying to scare people with your soothsaying."

Duchess Jenyce grabbed Linneya's arm. "Please, you must speak with me about this. The crown is to pass to your head, it is unnerving to see it unfolding in the skies, but perhaps I can help." Linneya did a double take. The woman's face had contorted as if she was in pain. It was an unusual manipulative strategy, bordering on treason, to suggest that Aiden would die and Linneya would be forced to take the throne. She wanted to ask more, to attempt to discern the purpose of the woman's scheme.

Darryn stepped between them, forcing the woman to back away from Linneya. He glowered at the duchess, fists clenched. Mariel walked up and touched Linneya on the shoulder. "Lia, I am sorry to interrupt but we wanted to get you and Darryn to the front for the toasts."

Linneya kept a neutral face, but her shoulders relaxed. Darryn nodded toward the duchess, who sneered and curtsied. He offered Linneya his arm and they walked back toward the more open garden area. The duchess' warnings sat wrong in her stomach; there was more to it than just a poorly presented manipulation.

Linneya shook her head and tried to focus on the next part of their evening. Two silver and black upholstered armchairs had been hoisted onto the dais in front of a display of a few well-placed *lunampe* vines. They were seated together as servants began handing out goblets and pouring wine.

The toasts were long and tedious. Nobles lined up to wish them well, stumbling over flowery phrases and repeating unnecessary descriptors as if they would win the princess' favor with a few perfectly worded sentences. Darryn's eyes were glazed over as if the performative speeches lulled him into a stupor.

On the other hand, Linneya had spent hours with her family on display as her father, King Varilon, listened to the petitions of their people. She had perfected a pleasantly neutral expression. It was now coming in handy.

Once the formal toasts were finished, many of the nobles dispersed. Soon, only friends and some of Darryn's Falorian knights remained. The evening morphed into a more informal gathering. Someone found a few hidden caskets of the more potent faewine and things quickly devolved into celebratory chaos. The musicians swapped the sophisticated music for more rustic, spirited tunes. People cleared several tables away from a grassy area and started dancing.

Darryn was standing in the shadows, silently watching the merriment. Linneya walked up beside him and touched his arm. "Where did your crew go? They have not left already, have they?"

The knight placed an arm around Linneya and pointed toward some bushes. "Most of them went that way. I sent Graisor home. He and his wife had their reception here. With her passing so recently, I did not want him to suffer on our account. I hope you do not mind."

Linneya nodded. "Yes, you did the right thing. I would not wish that on him, either. I am going to go see what the rest of them are up to."

He squeezed her waist and motioned her on. She wandered in the direction he had indicated, following the raucous commotion. Chrysa, Trotyn, and Shailyn were seated in an alcove created by a purple hedge. They were cheerfully shouting and bickering in a way Linneya expected from siblings. She walked up in time to hear Shailyn shriek. "*Poisonshadow* root cannot be used with *mysticane* flowers. They counteract each other and no one is the wiser! Drink, you beast!"

Trotyn cackled and took a swig of his ale. "How do you even know that, little one? Been carousing with the merfolk again?" The islanders brought in all kinds of unusual plants, including *mysticane* and *artensian* - two plants known for their relaxing properties.

Shailyn socked him in the shoulder while Chrysa giggled into her drink. Linneya stepped around the hedge and all three straightened up. "*Poisonshadow* root cannot be mixed with *mysticane* flowers, but mix it with the root and you make a strong hallucinogen."

Trotyn cheered and lifted his goblet. "The missus knows her plants! Come, play with us."

Linneya grinned and sat beside Shailyn. "What are we doing?"

Chrysa hiccuped and slurred her explanation. "Trotyn has an uncanny knack to be able to determine an antidote for almost any poison. Shailyn has more knowledge on plants than anyone else we know." She pointed to herself. "And I can identify almost any poison, track down almost any source." She smirked.

Shailyn nodded enthusiastically. "Yes, so we get into these contests to see if we can trip each other up on identifying the underlying issues with poison mixes. Sometimes we come up with totally new horrors." She giggled.

Linneya was reminded of the strategic games she and Aiden would play in the caves around the palace. After the most recent shadowlands raids, he had told her that one of the things that saved the company was based on a particularly memorable round of their cave tactic competitions.

She settled in and grabbed a goblet. Chrysa filled it with the faewine and smirked, clearly pleased that Linneya was interested.

Trotyn piped up. "I know it's dark, but it can come in handy. Chrysa and I have both used ideas gleaned from these games in combat. She saved me from a poisoned weapon once just based on how my symptoms presented after the fight. Shailyn has been experimenting with some theoretical poisons to coat a blade. Things that do not have a quick antidote and that would cut through magical shields."

Her stomach fluttered and a warmth expanded in her chest. She was excited to find others that liked to talk plants, even if it was not about their healing qualities. "It sounds like a game I could win, then."

The others exploded into laughter and friendly jeering. She grinned and motioned toward Shailyn. "Start us off, dear sister."

Shailyn cackled. "Alright, so if we have *shadowbane* bark and mix it with powdered conch shells..." Linneya settled back and fell into a comfortable rhythm. Her family in Aelor was wonderful, but propriety had stood in the way of these kinds of bonds. Darryn's friends interacted with an easy flow. The back and forth of amiable debate and discovery was a soothing cadence.

Linneya wanted to stay hidden away all evening, but etiquette demanded she return to the other guests. After three rounds - two of which Linneya almost won - she set her goblet down and bid the others farewell. When she wandered back into the main area, Darryn was judging a drinking contest between several of the knights.

One of the men toppled over and the other men roared. He tried to stand back up and Darryn shook his head and pointed away from the kegs. "Trainstead, your knees hit the ground. You are done. Move over."

Trainstead stumbled toward Darryn, desperately trying to plead his case, but his words were unintelligible. Darryn clapped him on the back and chuckled, motioning for a couple of the others to drag him out of the way.

Linneya made her way to Darryn's side. He turned to face her and brushed a lock of hair out of her face. His voice was thick and rough. "You look like you have just about had enough of this party."

She hugged herself, the floaty feeling from the faewine was beginning to set in. "Yes, I believe I am ready to retire for the evening."

"Shall we give them a show, then?" He grinned and leaned down. The crowd cheered as he swept her up in his arms. Linneya gasped, but secretly felt satisfaction at being cradled against his chest. He turned and climbed the back stairs into the house.

As they shut the doors, the sounds of the ongoing party were muffled and a sense of dread washed over Linneya. Her stomach ached. The thought of bedding the man twisted her insides into knots, even as his citrus and cedar scent drew her further into his trap.

Darryn looked at her and waggled his eyebrows. "Well, shall we go to bed for the evening?"

Linneya flushed and pushed against his chest. "Put me down first." He chuckled, lowering her to the floor, then turned and began walking toward their rooms. The house felt like a haven, but in this moment it was turning into a prison. With every step, her freedom slipped further away. If they consummated, there was no turning back. She could not try to have the marriage annulled.

Even worse, she was torn. In her heart, she was already a traitor to her people in Aelor. This man had captivated her and she wanted him, body and soul. His friends were lovely and he seemed good. Vicious, yes. Dangerous, of course. But at the core of his actions seemed to be a person intent on doing the right thing. Too bad his idea of 'right' did not include protecting her home country. Her heart sank with the thought.

Her feet were lead and the furry *hiduh* kept winding around her ankles, causing her to stumble. Darryn caught her elbow and steadied her. He kept his grip on her arm, but did not say anything until they were at the door. "After you, princess." He gestured into their sitting room. Narruan pranced in ahead of them.

She made her way to what was becoming her favorite futon and plopped down on the middle cushion with a sigh. He followed, standing in front of her and rocking back and forth on his feet. The anticipation of their wedding night left butterflies in her stomach and his gaze hinted at a similar anxiousness.

The feline rolled on its back, showing off its fluffy belly. Darryn shifted and the furry creature scrambled to turn over, spitting and huffing as it ran under the settee. He rolled his eyes at Narruan for comedic effect and Linneya giggled, grateful for the lighthearted moment.

Darryn cleared his throat, almost looking nervous. "Shall I call for some tea?"

She nodded and pressed a hand to her stomach as it growled. He pulled the tassel and sat down across from her. He leaned forward as if to say something, but thinking better of it he closed his mouth and sat back on the seat. She bit her bottom lip and crossed her arms. Darryn marked the movement and began bouncing his leg up and down. They spent the next several minutes skillfully avoiding each other's gaze, unsure of what to do next. The sounds of their reception drifted up, an occasional loud cheer making Linneya wonder if it was still the drinking contest or if the partygoers had moved on to a different game.

They both jumped as the door to the hallway swung open. Kapeyni bustled in with a tray of drinks and teacake. The expected teapot was there, but a decanter of spirits was sitting next to it. Linneya couldn't help but grin and Darryn chuckled. The maid nodded to them both, smiling a bit at Linneya. She set the tray down, and left without a word.

They busied themselves with making their plates and spiking their tea. Linneya sipped on the warm drink, hoping the alcohol would settle her nerves. What would he expect from her? At the engagement feast last night, Darryn had said he wanted to be friends. Would he leave it at that or would he try to push her further?

After she had her fill, she cleared her throat and stood. He jumped up and clasped her hands. "Go ahead and change and we will retire to my room." Her eyes grew wide and his lips quirked up. "It is customary to spend our wedding night together, princess. We are married, after all."

She made a small noise and escaped to her room. Someone had brought in clothing that was more suitable for a warm climate. The wardrobe had several nightgowns that were low cut, fabric barely there, and looked uncomfortable. Groaning, she searched for her trunks. There was one tucked in a corner that still had some of her clothing. She ruffled through it and found a long sleeved summer dress that could pass as a nightgown. The evening was cool enough that she would not suffocate. It would do.

Linneya shook as she changed. There had been no time to come to terms with what had happened. She wondered if Orrain would be dead now if Darryn had just agreed to marry her to begin with. Was it better this way? She was a murderer now, but at least Eleanor was spared the misery of a violent, arrogant husband.

She tied her hair back, sighing. It was difficult to trust a man with her heart when all he had done was try to be rid of her. If being compelled by one's king to marry was the only reason he was being gentle now, she did not want it. She frantically gathered bricks around her heart.

A heavy weight settled on her shoulders, but she tucked a stray curl behind her ear and inspected her choice of outfit. Her reflection in the mirror was satisfactory. The only way forward was to make the best of the hand she had been dealt. She lifted her chin, smoothed her hair a bit, and walked back into the common room.

Darryn's lips curved upward as he saw her choice of outfit. "Are you sure you will be cool enough in that, princess?" She turned red and stalked toward his bedroom. He followed and she pushed his door open. Like his side of the downstairs study, the bedroom was sparse and covered in dark furniture. His bedspread was deep red with gray designs and silver stitching.

He walked inside and motioned toward his reading nook. "They will expect us to spend tonight together, so I will stay in this chair. After tonight, you will be able to return to sleeping in your room."

The armchair he referenced was piled in books and parchment. Even if it was cleaned off she suspected it would be too cramped. Linneya shook her head, "Darryn, you might as well lie down and sleep comfortably tonight. It is only one night. I trust you not to try anything untoward."

He quirked an eyebrow. "Is that so? It seems I have lost my edge." A wicked smile crossed his lips and he stalked toward her. She backed up, bumping into the bedding. His eyes narrowed and he looked her up and down with a predatory gaze.

Heat warmed Linneya's cheeks and her breath caught. Her legs turned to jelly and she sat back onto the bed. He leaned in, placing one hand on the bed, and gently took her chin in between his fingers. "You say it is only one night... I can think of a plethora of ways to convince you to keep sleeping in here with me." She melted as his lips brushed the sensitive pulse point on her neck.

She chewed on her lip, trying to keep her breath even. Every bone in her body cried out for her to pull him to her, to bring him into the bed and seal her fate. Instead, she drew away from him. "Fine, if you want the chair that badly, be my guest."

He threw his head back and laughed. "As long as I still inspire a bit of fear, I am satisfied."

Darryn pressed off the bed and walked toward his armchair. He reached up, grabbing the collar of his shirt and pulled it off in one smooth motion. Linneya's eyes widened as his back muscles rippled.

She could not contain her gasp as he turned. Burn scars decorated his left side, disappearing under the waistband of his pants.

His mouth twisted into a bitter smile and motioned to his side. "They add a bit of character, yes?"

Her heart hurt at his sharp tone. She was certain he hid pain beneath the rough mannerisms. "Do they hurt?"

"Not usually. My mother was a healer, like Shailyn. She had a salve that kept the scar tissue from seizing up and making my side stiff. They are harmless, but unsightly."

A flash of Darryn as a child filled her mind. He was crying from the burns as a dark haired woman gently tended to him. Warmth coursed through her chest and a lump rose in her throat.

She stood up and walked to him. Her right hand brushed across the scars and he stiffened in surprise. "Not unsightly. I was thinking more fierce than anything." She tilted her head up and smiled tentatively.

Darryn wrapped his arms around her, pulling her close. She mirrored him, squeezing him tight, and felt him take a deep breath. Perhaps she could find a way to be at peace with this arrangement. Perhaps he would even come to love her.

He kissed her forehead and backed away, dropping his arms. Prickly cold taunted her, mocking her for losing his touch. Her heart wilted a bit and she stacked the bricks higher.

"Goodnight, Linneya." His expression was unreadable as he turned to clear off his armchair. After a few moments, he flopped into the chair and looked back at her. His eyes were shadowed as he motioned for her to go to bed.

She climbed in, welcoming the silky sheets that matched hers, and curled away from him. Frustration in the face of his rejection stung, but she was too tired to ask him why. Her eyelids were heavy and she drifted into an uneasy sleep.

The assassin was hidden in a crowd. A local festival was in full swing and the islanders sang their praises for the firemountain that was fuming and glowing red in the distance. Drums beat, rhythmic yelps rose into the sky, and dancers reenacted the legends of their gods. The smoky scent from the bonfires mixed with the sweet and savory aromas of fruits and meats roasting.

Many wore masks, some had cloaks. The assassin moved freely through the celebrations, searching. Children were playing around a pond near a stand of palm trees, not far from the main celebrations. They were mimicking their elders, dancing and playing with toy drums.

The assassin moved closer, watching one particular child who kept making the water swell and shrink in time to the rhythm. Tendrils of smoke and light spurted from his fingers. His playmates cheered the mist-whisperer on, laughing every time the water spurted up and reached the palm trees swaying overhead.

The babe looked like he was barely an annum old, four and a half seasons at best. He looked up, as if he could sense the assassin watching. He picked up a large shell with water inside and waddled over. "Wanna see my mist? Here." The assassin took the shell and watched as the ripples in the water made simple designs in beat with the music.

"I like your mash." The boy pointed toward the assassin's *trillin* mask. The man just stared. The child continued. "Are you here for the firemountain celbation? Mama says the gods have awoken a new spirit to bring peace to our home."

The assassin took a deep breath. "No, child. I am here to sacrifice and heal the human races. Those on the continent need to be united." He stepped toward the brush and the child followed.

"My mama says the other humans do not unnerstand us. She says we might as well be merfolk without the fins. That we do not need to worry about the people on the contentent. Why are you healing everyone?"

The assassin inclined his head, his shoulders slightly shaking as if the child's mispronunciation caused a chuckle. "Because my king will use my power to restore balance and bring glory." He walked a few more steps, just out of view of the others, and the boy curiously stepped with him.

He lifted his hands, vapors trailing down his arms. No words were said, but vines began creeping out of the brush. The boy's eyes grew wide as they tried to wrap around his ankles. He pulled out a small knife and began slashing and yelling.

The assassin growled, grabbing at the boy. "Stand still, you brat! I must kill you - your sacrifice will heal the lands." He reached out, trying to pull the child into the brush.

The boy wrestled away and started back toward the celebration. She screamed, terrified the assassin would succeed with his threats. The world tilted sideways as the child began to run. The scent of citrus and cedar called to her.

"Lia, wake up!" A frantic voice pulled her back to her bed. Strong hands shook her and she realized she was still shrieking.

Linneya bolted upright, almost knocking Darryn in the nose with her forehead. "I am sorry, I-" she gasped, trying to catch her breath.

Chills ran up her spine as she recalled the dream. If it was real, the implications were devastating. The assassin had attacked a child. She hugged herself.

Darryn pulled her to him and began stroking through her hair. The temptation to tell him everything welled up in her throat, but she was wary.

The last time he found out one of her secrets he forced her to leave her family. Would he feel obliged to tell the king if she admitted the dreams?

A knock on the door interrupted her thoughts. Kapeyni bustled in along with one of the kitchen staff. They had trays filled with traditional wedding moonwake snacks. The fruit and cheese would have looked appetizing any other time, but tonight her stomach was twisted in knots. Darryn stood up and walked over to the tray, nodding to the maids as they left.

He made up two plates and brought one back to her. "Eat, princess. Then I can hold you until you are able to go back to sleep."

Linneya took hers and tears burned in her eyes. "Why are you treating me so kindly? All of this is a farce. You did not want this marriage any more than I did."

The knight plopped down next to her and pulled her back to his chest. "As I told you, I find you lovely. My aversion to marriage has never been about you. It is not safe for me to have a spouse and I swore an oath that prevented me from taking a wife. Only an order from Enthor's king would allow me to marry. " He ran his fingers up her arm and her skin heated in response.

"I like you, Linneya. I am serious about us being friends and I will do my best to help you be comfortable in my care. Now that I am required to be wed, I am grateful it is to you and not to some horrible screeching shrew. At least, if you are a shrew you have hid it well so far." He grinned and she shoved his chest, laughing.

She studied his face. He seemed genuine. How could he act so unsure and standoffish the entire way from Aelor and now seem willing to forget it all and plunge headfirst into this marriage?

"Get some rest, Linneya. No more nightmares. I will keep you safe. Tomorrow, you start training with both Falryn and me. The sooner you start learning how to hone your affinities, the stronger you will be if Serathor decides to attack."

She grimaced and he laughed again. "Come on, sleep. I can stay in the bed with you if that helps."

Linneya sighed, half pretending to be annoyed. "Alright then, but you have to stay on top of the covers."

He chuckled and flopped out on top of the blankets. "You can lay on me, princess." Butterflies fluttered in her stomach as she took in his muscular, bare chest. He raised an arm and patted his ribcage, an invitation. Her cheeks warmed as her eyes drank in his scars. Then she followed the trail of hair down his abdomen to where it disappeared, pointing to *that part*.

She rubbed her face and he rolled his eyes at her hesitation. "There is no point in you arguing. I promise not to do anything, how did you put it... *untoward*." His lips curled up at that last word.

Giggling, she laid her head on his chest. She was still a bit shaky with the fright from her nightmare. His body radiated heat, even with the blankets between them. Part of her wished she had worn one of the more revealing outfits and had demanded a real wedding night with the man, part of her scolded her boldness and desperately added more bricks to the wall around her heart.

Darryn squeezed his eyes shut. "I know this is not what you hoped, but now that you are here I promise I will keep you safe and see you trained."

Linneya's eyelids were heavy and she did not respond. The gentle rise and fall of his chest lulled her into second sleep. Her dreams transported her to peaceful forests and calm streams.

Chapter 17

The first sun peeked over the horizon as Linneya and Darryn made it to the field to train. He had demanded that she be up before dawn, insisting again that there was no time to lose. They had slipped out a side gate and walked only a few minutes to the land that was used by the Falorian knights. Some days the men practiced drills, other days were reserved for tactical war games. The head of the order had granted Darryn a small grassy area off to one side to allow Linneya the chance to learn to fight.

Linneya was still exhausted from the previous day's events. The assassin nightmare had not helped. Now, here she stood in a field full of blue and purple grasses, a slight dew spread across their blades. The fresh scent of the outdoors wafted around them on a light breeze.

Still, she was grumpy. "No other noble is put through their paces the morning after their wedding," she grumbled, hiding how anxious she was to be training.

He elbowed her lightly. "No other noble is married to me, princess. Between your position as my wife and your elemental affinities, you have multiple reasons to want to know how to fight. Now, show me what you know. You said you trained with your brother some, let me see what you remember."

She chewed on her lip as he watched her move. The fighting instructor she had as a child paid her little attention, which was fine by her. Later, Aiden had taught her some basic blocking and kicking strategies. Sometimes she could put them together into combinations, but rarely did they turn out smoothly. Having Darryn evaluating her meager fighting skills was embarrassing.

"Turn your hips forward, Lia." He placed his hands on her sides and nudged her into position.

She nodded and kicked again, a red flush of shame creeping up her neck. One would think a princess would be better trained, but she was always more interested in escaping to the woods than learning self defense.

The knight stopped her and cocked his head. "Pull a bit of weight forward. You are signaling your intention too much. Do it again and add the punch."

Her head spun, but she was determined to try whatever he suggested. "If I put my weight forward, then I lose my front kick."

Darryn smiled and moved behind her, sliding his hands around her waist. Something other than embarrassment heated her cheeks as he squeezed and adjusted her stance. "You need to be far enough forward that you do not stomp onto your front foot, but far enough back that you do not have to shift to kick either direction."

Linneya nodded, but the knight did not let go. Her breath caught as he pressed against her and ran his hands up her sides. She leaned into him, savoring the security of being in his arms. The brick wall she had so carefully built crumbled a bit.

She ground against him, breathless. "If you keep touching me like that, I am going to demand we have a *real* wedding night..."

He froze. Disappointment stacked the bricks back into place as he dropped his hands and stepped away. A shadow veiled his face, making it impossible to guess his emotion.

"I am sorry, wife. We need to focus on training."

She drew in a deep breath, shaking off the longing and schooling her face into an unattached smile. "What do you have for me next, husband?"

Darryn smiled sadly, but called the next exercise. Soon, they settled into a more comfortable pattern. He did not touch her again and they carried on like this until her arms were sore and her legs felt like jelly. Both suns were well into the sky before he suggested they take a break.

They wandered to a shady spot underneath a tree. Linneya pulled out the canteen from their supplies and they both sat on exposed roots, sipping on the water. They laughed about his friends' obsessions with poison. They talked about the wedding and Darryn gave her more details on several of the attendees. Inevitably, the conversation turned back to Serathor and the impending fights.

They stood back up and he handed her a practice sword. She bit her lip and eyed him carefully as she swung the weapon. "Could we consider going back to Aelor once the winter season is over?"

Darryn shook his head. "No, princess. I do not mind us going to visit but I cannot go and sit around hoping that a war will find its way that far North. I must be available to go wherever the Falorian knights are needed."

He signaled for her to change to a second set of cuts. She obliged, knitting her brows together before she continued. "Then convince your leader that you are needed in Aelor. There were already some scouts seen in the fjords. This could quickly become dangerous for my family."

He laughed, the sound cutting her. "You are fixated on the strangest details. It is ridiculous to think they would pass up our lands here in Enthor. Especially when many outside the capital would gladly turn on their godking for an extra loaf of bread. His removal of the traditional religious choices has not set well in some of the villages. King Shumor would be a fool not to take advantage of the unrest. I still think we will see the Serathanian military here long before they consider invading Aelor."

Her neck heated in shame. She was exhausted and had not had a chance to get deep rest since leaving home. Never mind wanting a powerful love. Being married to someone who did not respect her opinion made her stomach churn and she was out of patience.

Linneya tossed the practice weapon back to him and a lump rose in her throat. "If you are going to mock me for trying to find a way to help my people, then you can carry on without me. You want me to train with you, but you will not recognize my concerns as valid. How can you expect me to respect you when you refuse to acknowledge that I have more understanding of Serathor's motives than you?"

He reached out to her and she twisted away, letting the tears flow freely. "I am exhausted. There is nothing more to say if you will not hear me."

Linneya turned on her heel and left before he could respond. His gaze burned into her back, but he let her go. It was an easy walk back to the front gate. She stormed through into the city, not paying attention to where she was going. She wandered the city for awhile, scheming a way to escape. At noonrest, she returned to the mansion to change.

Beautiful weather held no comfort after such a row. She was still stewing as she marched into Falryn's garden that afternoon. The scent of familiar herbs wafted her way as she closed the gate behind her.

Falryn was kneeling in a patch of citrusbalm. The plant sprawled around them in a massive bush. Linneya crashed through the gate and stopped beside them.

The healer sat back and looked her up and down. Linneya's hair was disheveled and her face was still flushed. Falryn raised their eyebrows. "I take it this morning was less training and more... battle?"

Linneya grimaced. "I find it difficult to fully trust the person who took me from my home."

Falryn snorted and stood, dusting the dirt off their trousers. "Girl, you would be expected to leave at some point anyway. This is the fate of noblewomen. At least here you are given the freedom to train and do as you please."

Linneya scoffed. "Darryn has proven over and over that he will not let me do as I please. He is ignoring my concerns about the impending war. My opinion does not matter to him. If he really wanted to take care of me, he could have left me in Loraen or taken me back to Aelor when Orrain died."

"How would you have suggested he explain that to our king? Is it fair to expect him to defy a direct order on your whim?" Linneya grimaced and Falryn shook their head. "Never mind that now. We must focus. With war on the horizon, there is no time to bicker."

Linneya's stomach twisted in knots. The healer was right, no matter where Serathor chose to strike first, fighting amongst themselves would make things worse. Darryn was offering her a way to at least train and become stronger.

"Healing is only half of your ability. Here, we train all elementals to fight. Let me see what you can do with what you know now. Perk up, child. You learn to control this and you can at least use it to keep yourself safe as a healer on the battlefield."

Falryn's wisdom was sound. Learning how to fight with her affinities would allow her to defend herself. Maybe even defend others. She raised her chin. "What would you like me to do?"

Falryn turned to walk inside, motioning for Linneya to follow. "I have heard enough to know you possess strong healing abilities. Our focus will be on learning how to control your elements." They grabbed a candle from the kitchen table, lit it, and held it up. "Try drawing this flame to you."

Linneya lifted her shaking hand, palm facing up. *"Krehth aeki raewi."* The familiar rush of heat flooded her body and a small amount of red smoke sputtered from her fingers, but the flame stayed put. The flickering candle mocked her. She strained, willing the flame to come to her.

Falryn laid a hand on her arm. "Try *'Krehth aeki viodo'* and see what happens."

Linneya repeated the words. Smoke billowed and the flame instantly sprang into her hand, dancing playfully. Linneya beamed, her eyes widened, and she looked at Falryn. "What is this? I thought we only had summoning words and amplifying chants from the ancient texts."

Falrryn's mouth curved up on one side. "When you are as ancient as I am, girl, it is easier to uncover long lost spells. The fae in Mount Varsha let me spend a duodecade in the archives, dredging up old enchantments."

Linneya's eyes widened. Being granted access to the archives at the holy mountain was almost unheard of. Staying for an entire duodecade sounded like a dream come true. Falryn nodded at her hand. "Now, try sending it back."

The healer offered different enchantments and let Linneya experiment with the directional commands. Linneya could make the flame leap on command, disappear and reappear, and even be stored in an airtight container. After a while, Falryn grunted their approval and relit the candle. "All right, see if you can call the flame to you without speaking."

Linneya was already fatigued from tapping into a part of her affinity she had never used before. The mental energy alone was exhausting, but she was also unaccustomed to using her powers for anything but healing. The idea of silently commanding elements was daunting. She bit her lip. "Without speaking?"

"As it stands, you are barely tapping into your power. Most flame-talkers with your level of affinity can conjure fire without a source. They are also able to activate enchantments without speaking. Some people require hand movements. Others can control their elements with thought alone."

Linneya's eyes grew wide. "I did not realize there were so many ways to use flame."

Falryn nodded. "It is the same with every element. You saw Darryn and Johann in the arena. True masters of each affinity can hear that element's resonance. They can bend it to their will and tap into a small amount of their affinity's sister elements."

She cocked her head. "What are my sister elements?"

Falryn walked to the doorway, squatted, and began to draw a diagram in the dirt.

They gestured as they wrote. "The sister elements to Flame are Vine and Aether. Sister elements to Mist are Aether and Ground. As a flame-talker and mist-whisperer, you could harness limited power from all five elements." Falryn dismissed that thought with a wave of their hand. "Do not focus on this for now. That kind of skill takes duodecades, even duocenturies to master. We must focus on the tasks at hand. Your next step is to learn how to use these enchantments without speaking."

Linneya nodded. She raised her hand again, calling the flame to her without a verbal command. A fine vapor swirled around her and the flame shot to her palm. Falryn nodded and Linneya beamed. Being able to more accurately control her affinities could make a difference in her healing capabilities. Perhaps there were even ways to create new procedures that could help somcone who was dealing with internal issues.

The rest of the afternoon flew by, with Falryn giving her directions on where to send the flame. First, it was any candle. Then, they added a wooden hoop to send it through. Finally, Falryn directed her to loop it through the hoop twice and send it to a specific candle. Linneya was shaking and wobbly by the time they finished.

As the suns began to set, they stopped and picked leaves for tea. The two of them sat at the kitchen table, sipping on their herbal concoctions and debating different ways the affinities might make a difference in life-tending scenarios.

Shailyn poked her head in and knocked on the doorframe. "Helloooo! I am here for dinner, dear Falryn. Lia, the carriage is waiting for you." Linneya blinked, surprised by the interruption. Falryn waved Shailyn in and the woman bounded over and plopped down beside the healer.

Linneya stood and brushed off her outfit. "I do not mind the walk. I will tell the carriage driver to go ahead."

Shailyn shook her head. "No, you need to ride home. Darryn kicked me out so the two of you could have dinner together." She smirked at Linneya's expression. "I am certain he plans to win you over with a few evenings alone."

The heat that crept up Linneya's neck was equal parts embarrassment and anticipation. She nodded to Shailyn and turned to Falryn, clasping their hands in hers. "Thank you for today, this was enlightening to experience."

The healer patted her cheek and shooed her out the door. Linneya walked toward the carriage, but could still hear Shailyn cackling. The carriage driver nodded to her and helped her in. Her mind spun as they sped off. She was not ready to face the consequences of her morning outburst. Shailyn may have thought he was being romantic, but Linneya knew the knight had cleared the house in case the morning argument continued.

She walked in the front door, still fumbling over what she could say to make things right, and was startled by Darryn leaning in a doorway. "Princess, care to join me for dinner?"

She stiffened at his gruff tone, but nodded. There was no point in avoiding the inevitable fallout. Darryn gestured toward the dining room and she hesitated. "Should I not change first?"

He shook his head. "It is just us. If you want to change, you can, but if you are more comfortable in your current outfit, I say we just eat. Cook received a package from your mother with *carramon* and instructions on how to make a sauce you love, so she has tried it out."

Linneya's heart fluttered at the thought of a taste of home. "Alright, that sounds lovely." She stepped into the dining room and warmth flooded her chest. This was her first time seeing the expansive space. The deep blue color of the walls was accented with silver. The dark mahogany table was intricately carved with scenes from the legendary Arduin battles on each leg. The chairs were upholstered in a fabric that mimicked the color of the walls.

Two place settings had been laid out at one end of the table. Darryn strode toward the head seat. He motioned for her to sit to his right and poured her a glass of wine. She sank into the chair and sighed. Every room she saw in this house felt more like home than the palace in Loraen. Everything had a welcoming glow that seemed safe and inviting.

Servants brought out chicken drizzled in *carramon* sauce. Linneya's mouth watered as the savory and sweet spice aromas drifted into her nostrils. A stew of dried root vegetables was served as a side. A bit of home, combined with the warmth of her current residence, brought a lump to her throat.

She cleared the pressure and took a deep breath. "Thank you for this."

The knight flashed her a crooked smile and gestured for her to eat. For several minutes they sat in silence, savoring the food. The sauce was a harmonious blend of umami and sweet, the chicken was flavored exactly as she liked. Even the spread of stewed vegetables was delicious, albeit different than what they ate back home.

Darryn made no effort to bring up the morning's spat. Linneya decided to follow suit, avoiding the subject altogether. "How was your afternoon?"

He put down his utensils and grimaced. "I have been called away."

She gawked at him. "What? We just got back."

Darryn sighed. "Yes, but I have to go." He reached over and brushed a stray lock of hair out of her face. His eyes burned with a dark flame. She wanted to be drawn in and consumed by his fire.

But he had made things clear: they were to be friends and nothing more. She pasted a pleasant look on her face and focused on her plate. She took another bite of the chicken before sucking in a deep breath. "Where will you be? When can I expect you back?"

"Linneya, I..." His teeth gritted together. "I cannot say."

"What, your knightsmaster is sending you on a secret mission?"

He shook his head, a frown on his face.

She drained her goblet, poured another cupful, and hissed, "where could you possibly need to go, then? I thought you said we would have no secrets."

His eyes darkened, a cold fire growing as his pupils expanded. "Lia, sometimes I have to..." He inclined his head, searching for the words. "... do things to protect the people I love. I need you to trust me."

Linneya clenched her jaw. "Why should I trust you after everything? You swore to protect me but you handed me over to Orrain. You tried your best to pawn me off on anyone else before finally having to acquiesce to the king's orders. Now you leave and will not tell me where you are going nor how long you will be gone?"

Darryn studied her face, the shadows still obscuring his eyes. He sat back a bit and his shoulders dropped. "I was not thinking about how much you have endured these past few weeks. Spend your mornings resting for the next week. Hopefully I will be back by then to resume training. Would you like me to tell Falryn your afternoon lessons will wait too?"

Her stomach clenched at the change of subject, but she shook her head. "This afternoon was enlightening. I had no idea there was more my power could do. I even tried some silent enchantments." She managed a small upward curve to her lips. There was no point in fighting him.

He placed his hands on the table and balled them into fists. "I am sorry, Linneya. I want to do my best to set you up for success here. I know it is not easy being ripped from your home and I have not been conscientious."

"No, I also owe you an apology." She touched his fist and he relaxed a bit under her fingers. "You have duties as well and I am sorry I have ignored that."

He offered her a stiff smile and they went back to their dinner. Linneya's heart sank as she finished off the second glass of wine. She would have to find a way to come to terms with her situation.

Love was not in the cards, but maybe her training could lead to mutual respect. Perhaps Darryn would even allow her the freedom to return home to Aelor before Serathor attacked. She could try to convince him to come with her and bring some of the other knights.

They finished and he stood, offering her his hand. Linneya entwined her fingers with his and the two of them made their way to their suite. In the sitting room, he turned to her and smiled. The hope bubbling up was quickly squashed as he pressed a kiss to her forehead and slipped into his room without a word.

Two days of marriage and she was already alone.

He left before she was awake. No note, no goodbye.

The next week was a combination of peaceful moments and shocks of emotion. Some days she would be fine. Others, a crunch or a splash would throw her into a memory and force her to relive the kills she had made. Her brain would replay the sounds, the sensations, as if it was trying to demand an alternate ending. Her soul ached for Darryn's citrus and cedar scent to wipe it all away.

Her mornings were spent wandering. Sometimes Shailyn would join her, other times she was alone. Once, Shailyn took her into the woods to forage and they spent the better part of the morning giggling after ingesting hallucinogenic mushrooms. More often, Linneya used the strolls to familiarize herself with the city.

Her afternoons were full of elemental practice with Falryn. They had shown her several enchantments and worked with her to strengthen the ones that did not come as easily. They would work until Linneya was too exhausted to continue, then they would sit around and drink teas made from whatever they wanted in the garden. Falryn offered tales of other lands, firsthand accounts of legendary events, and unusual anecdotes from their studies at the fae's holy mountain.

Evenings, Linneya ate alone and retired to her bed early. Some nights she longed to tell Darryn about her day and his absence left her empty. Others, she focused on building her brick wall into a fortress, freezing out her heart and protecting herself from more pain.

Chapter 18

After the week was up, Linneya woke up early and dressed for training. She went into the common room and Darryn was nowhere to be found. She pushed his door open to find an untouched bed. A dull ache grew in her chest.

Was he even coming back?

She hugged herself. She turned to the books on Darryn's shelves, looking for his collection on military tactics. If there was no training, she could at least read about it.

A knock startled her. "Come in?"

Kapeyni stuck her head in, eyebrows raised. "Miss, you have a visitor. I tried to tell him it was too early, but he claims Sir Darryn sent him for you."

Her heart sank and her legs became heavy. She dipped her chin to Kapeyni and sighed. "Thank you. Please tell them I will be down in a moment."

The maid left and Linneya collapsed into an armchair. She placed her head in her hands and sat there for several minutes. Distance from Darryn had not helped her freeze him out. If anything, she wanted him more. Knowing he was not home yet weighed her down. The thought of getting up and facing whoever was waiting drained her of energy.

A surge of sheer willpower finally propelled her from the armchair. She marched downstairs, head held high. She stopped short in the hallway as a man turned to greet her.

"Graisor?"

He inclined his head and smiled, his scar stretching with the motion. "Princess Linneya, Darryn asked me to take over your training for a few weeks while he is gone. He thought you might like to get experience working with different knights and their techniques."

"A few weeks? Where is he?"

Graisor lifted a shoulder in a shrug. "Sometimes he leaves with no explanation." He glanced at her sideways. "He is rarely gone more than a mooncycle, though. He will be back to you soon."

She nodded, deciding not to push the subject. As frustrated as she was, learning from more than one Falorian knight would be useful. She kept her face impassive. "Thank you for taking the time to work with me."

He grinned. "Of course. Darryn says you already know some basics. I had hoped we could go over the drills today and then decide what might be most useful in conjunction with your affinities. I am also a mist-whisperer, so I can guide you through some techniques that I find practical in a fight. Maybe in a few sessions, once you have those basics down, we can move on and look at weapons and close quarter combat with elemental powers."

A smile crept across her face and excitement bloomed in her chest. They made their way out of the house and toward the side gate closest to the Falorian training grounds. Once they were in the woods, Graisor whistled to some of the birds. Her eyebrows raised in surprise, as the song was similar to Darryn's.

"You know birdspeak too?"

He looked at her, surprised, then burst into laughter. "Birdspeak? Who told you it is called birdspeak?"

She turned red. "No one, I just," Linneya flopped her hands in an awkward gesture. "Darryn never really called it a name so I made up something I liked." She let out a nervous chuckle.

Graisor shook his head. "It is as good a name as any, I am just surprised you know of it. We tend to be tight-lipped about its existence. The original language is extinct. It comes from the northern fae islands and we only know some of the leftover words. Not many are aware, but the birds have become a great source of information when enemy units are descending upon us."

Linneya looked into the trees. The birds were whistling and chirping toward them, as if they wanted to tell them more than the impending threats of bloody battles. She imagined that they hoped someday the knights would stop and listen to their tales of the beauty of untouched woods or the excitement of flying freely through the air.

They arrived at the training site and Graisor quickly put her through her paces. He seemed pleased with her basic understanding, though he made many of the same adjustments Darryn had suggested in their first session. He assigned repetitive exercises and they talked in between sets.

Linneya asked Graisor about the knights and why he chose to swear to the order. She was surprised to find out he was originally from a northern town in Aelor. They debated their home country's best foods. He lamented losing his northern accent in an effort to assimilate once he came to Rathen. Inevitably, the conversation turned toward the hunters and the threats that both countries now faced.

Graisor grunted, rotating the wooden sword in his hand. "My wife, Curynna, died at their hands. Every hunter I murder, I do so in her name."

Linneya stopped and turned to face him. "What happened? Do you mind talking about it?"

He shook his head. "She was captured by a group of hunters who thought she would be a valuable gift to King Shumor. She had strong vine affinity and they had seen her using it in the garden." He shuddered, but continued. "We went to rescue her, but they found us out and killed her in front of me. They tried to take off my head, but Trotyn charged the hunter attacking me and managed to get me to a life-tender before I bled out." He pointed to his scar and his eyes grew distant, as if he was back in the room with his wife dead in his arms.

"Darryn took the death of Curynna almost as hard as I did. She was like an aunt to Shailyn as the girl grew up. Darryn gave the order for us to attack and one of his signals gave us away. He could not have prevented it, but it was clear he blamed himself for her death."

Thorns twisted around her heart. The loss of a close friend was hard, but knowing Darryn held himself responsible for Curynna's murder was devastating. Darryn might try to present as a cruel, bloodthirsty knight when fighting, but he carried guilt for any innocent person who was harmed. "Her death affected so many. I am sorry you are dealing with that."

Graisor grunted and went back to their drills. By the end of the session, Linneya was shaking and weak from exertion. She was certain that if a frail, sickly person chose this moment to attack her, she would not be able to defend herself. Still, there was a satisfaction to burning off some of her frustration through the drills. Maybe even over time she would become proficient and able to protect other healers when they were on the battlefield.

Weeks passed with no word from Darryn. Most days Graisor met her for training for at least an hour. Occasionally, Trotyn would step in and work with her on unusual weapons choices. Both would sometimes lead her into the catacombs to search through the Falorian knights' vault for more information on the elemental affinities they all held. The sessions felt more like play than serious work. She wondered if all the Falorian knights had developed strategic, game-like training protocols or if it was just Darryn's crew.

Frustration built as Linneya had little time to study or practice her healing arts. A knot grew in the pit of her stomach, a sense that she would never be viewed as worthy. Mediocre fighting skills. Unused healing skills. No clearly defined duty. Her life had unraveled, like a torn stitch on a knitted sweater. The only escape from this reality was the hefty collection of myths and tales Darryn's mother had left.

One morning, she was devouring one of said tomes, a legendary adaptation of Luthin and Payera, when voices and a clunking sound in the hallway made her perk up. A gruff baritone barked something and the sound of scurrying servants suggested the master of the house had returned. Linneya bit her lip, her eyes darting as she debated whether or not to retreat to her bedroom.

Before she made up her mind, the door to their sitting room flew open. The blood drained from her face as Darryn's large frame filled the entryway. He wore a grimace and the dark bags under his eyes suggested he had not slept. A split across his cheekbone and newly scarred gash on his left arm made her eyes widen.

She left the book open on their table and sprung up, her heart beating out of her chest. Every muscle in her body wanted to run to him and jump in his arms, but she stayed glued to the spot. A wild mix of relief, frustration, and happiness coursed through her.

His chest rose and fell with his panting. The untamed heat in his gaze stirred a longing in her, knocking her carefully designed fortress to the ground. He stepped inside the sitting room and closed the door behind him.

"You are back."

"Of course I am." He slowly dragged his eyes over her frame. His hands flexed at his sides, as if it took every bit of his strength to stop from running to her. Something mad flickered in his eyes and her conflicting emotions boiled over.

"I missed you." She began shaking and took a hesitant step toward him. His restraint snapped. With a growl, Darryn covered the remaining distance between them and wrapped her into his arms.

"I am so glad you are safe," he muttered and buried his face in her neck, exhaling with relief.

"Of course I am." Linneya laughed softly at the absurd comment. Her body relaxed, safely entwined in his arms, where she belonged.

The feeling lasted only a few moments before worry settled in. She pushed against his chest, leaning back to meet his gaze.

"But you... What happened? Where did you go?" She traced the wound on his face and he winced.

The knight grabbed her hand and pressed a kiss to her wrist. He grimaced as if he was fighting with something inside himself, but then he shook his head and sighed. "I am sorry, Lia. I cannot tell you."

He promised no secrets, but now he was full of them. Her insides twisted at his turbulent behavior. She pursed her lips and dropped her arms to demand he explain himself, but he pulled a scroll out and waved it around. "This came for you. The page arrived as I was walking in."

Linneya raised an eyebrow. She held out her hand. "Well, it must be extremely important for you to be using it to get out of answering for your absence."

The knight gave the note to her and cocked his head. "It looks like a royal summons. It is the queen's seal. Another was delivered to me from King Birron. Do you want me to wait? I have a carriage ready to head that way."

Linneya broke the seal and scanned the invite from the queen. Noonrest tea. She put the book back in its spot on the shelf and pulled the ribbon to signal Kapeyni. "Yes, please give me a moment to change."

He dipped his head and sat down on the settee. A sigh escaped his lips and he pressed his palms to his eyes. Darryn stayed there looking defeated and an ache settled into her chest.

Her heart was raw. Caring for this man hurt. She was grateful he was back safe, but his vacillating emotions left her confused and unsure. He entranced her, but ripped her from her home. The knight refused to marry her, yet seemed thrilled when he was ordered to be with her... then disappeared for over a mooncycle.

Once, she and her siblings had built a small play shack near the edge of a bog. It took two days and numerous trips to the leftovers pile with the wheelbarrow. Aiden had stacked stones waist high, then she and Eleanor wove together the top into a thatched roof.

By the time they were done, no one could have told them it was not grand. All three could sit inside with room to splay out. They declared it would be their permanent hideaway spot when their instructors were threatening exams or strenuous recitation of banal facts.

But three days later a storm hit. Torrential rain forced them to stay in the palace. They spent the day in the library, trading favorite stories and pulling pranks on Lord Caelin when he came through looking for a historical account of the fawns' conquest of the Schloan Isles.

The next morning, they returned to their shack. It was half sunk in the ground, completely unusable. It had been built on unsteady ground, unable to weather its first and only storm.

Much like this marriage.

All she wanted was to feel secure and maybe have the chance to travel home to defend her people when it was time. She shook her arms as if it could clear the unsettled sensations from her body and slipped into her bedroom to put on something presentable.

The only sounds were the wheels of the carriage clattering while the horses' hooves clip-clopped. Linneya and Darryn watched out separate windows, the capital flying past as they headed to the palace. She heaved a sigh, trying to ignore the man across from her. She should be more curious about the Enthorian royals' fascination with her powers.

Instead, she mulled over how long the knight would keep her in the dark about his mysterious trip. Only crazy or dangerous people disappeared for weeks with no explanation. Her eyes burned with unshed tears.

"Linneya, look at me." Darryn placed a hand under her chin and forced her gaze to meet his. His brow furrowed as he saw her expression. "What is it?"

Her chin wobbled and her voice was rough from holding back the tears. "Do you really have to ask? You left without any sort of explanation. We have not spent a moment together since the day after we were wed."

His jaw pulsed. "I am so sorry. I knew I had behaved badly, leaving you with so little notice. I had to go, but then I was so ashamed that I could not figure out how to come back and ask your forgiveness."

She pulled away from his hand and dropped her gaze. His admission that he had stayed away longer than necessary twisted her gut. "I may not be who you wanted to marry, but we are wed now and should be a team."

Something rough coated the knight's voice. "I am happy to be married to you, but I am miserable knowing I will be your destruction. I do not know how to claim you as mine. I cannot see how to reconcile my role with our marriage."

Her voice shook. "Fight for it. That is how. You have been gone for weeks and left me to fend for myself."

He leaned forward, their foreheads almost touching. "You are right. You are my *wife*. I do not want to be separated like this. Even if it cannot be a full marriage, I want to be friends."

She reached out and touched his cheek. Linneya longed for his caress, his mouth on hers, their marriage complete in every way. She was desperate to be in his arms. Desperate to enjoy him without hesitation, but she did not know how to tell him. She was not even sure they could let their guards down with each other. Even if he did not offer these cryptic hints about how he would bring her to ruin, so many other things stood in their way. Still, the undeniable tug drew her to him. Their breath mingled, warmth brewing between them.

Linneya whispered, "I do not like this separation, either."

He slid over to sit right next to her and she was swallowed whole into his arms. Tears spilled down her face and he squeezed her close. His citrus and cedar scent enveloped her once more and she sniffled, smiling with relief. He stroked his fingers through her hair and down her arms, leaving goosebumps.

Darryn was sent down toward the king's stateroom and Linneya was whisked away to the queen's private wing. Queen Rhylanna had not spoken more than a few words to her in the past two mooncycles. She wondered why the queen could be calling for her now. The woman was an enigma and seemed to keep more to herself as her pregnancy wore on.

The sitting room was bedecked in red and orange, as if the designer had tried to emulate living inside the second sun. The patterns were overwhelming and aggressive. Only a faint scent of sweet and citrus spices whispered of a comforting presence.

Linneya sat in a chair that had been arranged with several others in a circle around a tea table. A servant brought the most ostentatious tea service set Linneya had ever seen and offered seven types of expensive, imported tea blends. She chose one and began sipping on the brew while waiting for the queen to appear.

The clicking sound of cork on stone told her the queen approached. Linneya stood and bowed her head as the woman made her way to the circle of chairs. The queen grabbed Linneya's hands and kissed her on the cheek before they both settled back into their seats.

Queen Rhylanna motioned around the room. "Awful, is it not? Birron had it redone when he brought me here, but took no notes on my preferences. Now I sit and suffer an overdone den of luxury while our people suffer sparse harvests and oppressive policies."

Linneya blinked, hesitant to respond. Was this a trick to see if Linneya would make treasonous statements against the Enthorian regime? The queen leaned forward expectantly. Linneya wiped her sweaty palms on her skirt and nodded. "It is important for you to find the balance between proving your divinity and your people's needs, Your Highness. I commend you on your awareness."

Queen Rhylanna chuckled. "Dear, you can speak freely here. I do not need diplomatic coddling. There are things happening with this land's magic that we do not understand and I will do my best to care for our people and keep my children safe." She laid a hand on her stomach, cradling her unborn child.

Linneya's shoulders relaxed a bit, but she kept a neutral expression. "How can I help you with that?"

The queen stared into the distance and stroked her belly. After a few moments she blinked and looked back at Linneya. "I would like to know more about your affinities. How we might could help you nurture your powers. Do you prefer healing or fighting? I believe that strong elementals help to keep the natural balance in our lands.

Linneya cocked her head to the side. "Thank you for being interested, madam. Darryn has assigned warriors to work with me on my fighting skills. Falryn is showing me a wide range of applications for my affinities."

Queen Rhylanna pursed her lips. "If I may, could I speak with you again soon about possibly going into the surrounding villages to help? I know you are a renowned healer and your presence would bolster the others. Perhaps you can even teach a workshop or two for the elementals who cannot come to the capital to train."

"Of course, whatever you need." Linneya studied the queen as she made herself a second cup of tea. Was it possible that this woman was behind many of the beneficial changes that had come with King Birron's reign? It would make more sense than the king being a child-like genius. Or an idiotic prodigy, if one wanted to be a bit more treasonous. Linneya chuckled to herself.

A loud bang caused her to jump. King Birron strode through the sitting room entryway, closely followed by Darryn. She blanched at her husband's strained features, but stood and curtsied in front of the king.

"Well done, my queen! Wonderful of you to have our dear princess over for a spot of noonrest tea. I have just finished with Darryn and thought I should send the two of you off together." The king grinned at the two of them, wild eyed. Queen Rhylanna inclined her head in acknowledgement.

Darryn walked to Linneya's side and offered her his arm. She took it, unable to meet his gaze. They both bowed to the royals, but the king was already standing over his wife and chattering about an addition to the gardens that would allow him to grow a new strand of the flowers that could be ground into his precious drug, sluryn. They made their exit, neither one willing to break the silence.

The knight was quiet as they stood in the entryway, waiting for the royal carriage to be brought to the front of the palace. She tried to slip her hand out from the crook of his arm, but he grabbed it and held her there. The sound of horses' hooves signaled the carriage was approaching and he guided her toward the courtyard.

He helped her in, before sitting opposite her. The conversation with the queen had been brief and odd. Something about it settled wrong in her gut, like she had eaten too much food. She wrung her hands in her lap, trying to divine the meanings behind the woman's requests.

"Why did the queen ask you to come?" Darryn leaned forward and placed a hand on hers, stilling them. A sense of calm tranquility flooded her body as his hand put pressure on her lap.

Linneya exhaled, her shoulders relaxing. "She seemed interested in understanding more about my affinities. It was a pleasant teatime, not much else. What about you? Why did the king summon you?"

Darryn sat back and folded his arms over his chest. "He asked much the same. Falryn had sent him reports on your progress, but he seems to think they are not disclosing everything about your abilities."

She chewed on her lip and nodded, pulling the rough carriage curtains back and peeking out the window. "It was an odd thing. She mentioned me going to villages and teaching."

"Do you want to teach?"

"Of course. I think it would be an enjoyable way for me to use my skills. It would help me feel useful."

He nodded. "Then when you are ready, I will help you make arrangements to do so."

Linneya gave him a small smile, then shifted the conversation. "I know you have only just arrived, but Mariel and Straion are having everyone to dinner this evening."

"Do you want me to come with you? I can stay home if it would make it easier on you, but I would love to escort you."

"Yes, please. Let us go together. I know it will be a good time."

Darryn nodded, a cautious glimmer in his eye. He reached for her hand again and squeezed. Her chest opened up and she sucked in the first comfortably deep breath in weeks.

Chapter 19

Linneya crept out the back door and quietly made her way toward the front courtyard just as the suns began to set. The smaller, red sun was beginning to hide behind the larger one, signaling the cooling of the winter season. This also meant sunset was faster and light lingered for only a few moments after they disappeared beneath the horizon.

She walked around the corner to the courtyard. Darryn was wringing his hands and looking up at the rapidly changing colors in the sky. His dark outfit complemented his hair. The relaxed tunic and slacks combination showed off his muscular frame, a sign of the damage he could do when threatened. Linneya shivered, her own darkness purring at the memories of his fighting skills. He was brutal when those he was sworn to protect were in harm's way. The last of her ire melted away as she snuck toward him, not wanting to break his contemplative mood.

Her shoe caught on a rock that jutted just high enough out of the ground and she stumbled forward with a grunt. Linneya managed to right herself before falling, but the noise caused Darryn to turn. His face lit up as he saw her. "Princess, I was beginning to wonder if you had changed your mind."

She straightened up, heat rising to her cheeks. "No, I was just taking my time getting ready." She walked to him and slipped her hand in his. He blinked and his mouth opened slightly, as if he was surprised by the ease of her simple gesture.

Quickly recovering, he grinned and ran a knuckle across her cheek. "Well, we will be fashionably late. At least we are still likely to beat Shailyn." Linneya laughed softly and they took off walking toward their friends' house.

Rathen at dusk was full of activity. People were bustling toward the taverns in groups, shouting and joking with one another. Others strode in the opposite direction with packages wrapped in paper, taking items for dinner toward residential areas. Bells at various chapels rang out, calling Matu's faithful to chanting and meditation.

The entire way, Darryn held her hand. His occasional squeeze felt like he was as grateful as her to be reconciled. Only to a friendship, she reminded herself. There was a tugging in Linneya's chest, a longing for more, but she suppressed it. They were finally falling into a comfortable rhythm.

They rounded a final corner and Linneya's heart swelled in excitement for her friend. The large home was built from the ruins of a previous house, creating an unusual presentation of partial stone and partial wood. Ancient carvings had been artfully propped throughout the front gardens, a nod to the previous city, Tirathel, and its residents. The patches of garden were full of bushy, herbaceous plants for the kitchen. As they walked by, a slight riverside breeze ruffled the herbs and the woodsy scent of green spices filled Linneya's lungs.

Mariel was beaming as she threw open the front door. Her hair was tied back and flour was smudged across one cheek. "Come in! Darryn, so good to see you again. Half the crew is here already. We were just about to open a cask of faewine. Straion should be back with the tap soon."

She bustled back toward the kitchen and Linneya and Darryn stepped over the threshold. Straion and Mariel's home was decorated in greens and light browns, clean lines framing designs that offered a more modern tone. Whatever Mariel was cooking coated the air, thick with pungent spice and oils. The laughter of Trotyn and Graisor filtered from one of the back rooms.

"You have made it! Come, meet my wife." Falryn ambled toward them, beckoning them toward a room that looked like a parlor. A petite woman with auburn hair was sitting in a chair, watching out the window. Falryn tapped her shoulder, waiting for her to turn, and then gestured as they spoke. "This is Harilyn, my spouse. She is deaf, so we use movement language to communicate everything. She helped to establish the first deaf school here in the capital."

The woman beamed at Linneya, nodding her head and motioning with her hands. Falryn translated. "Princess, it is an honor to meet you."

Linneya tapped her heart twice with her palm, a gesture for gratitude or to say thanks. Harilyn grinned and repeated the movement. Linneya sat beside the woman. "I am sorry we have not met sooner. I would love to know more about your teaching."

The woman leaned forward, her eyes wide with excitement and fingers flying faster than Linneya could fathom. "I will have to bring you some day! The children are from all over Enthor and they come to receive schooling that cannot be offered at home. I grew up with no education, no way to communicate. I have vowed that others will have the chance to read, write, learn the stories of our deities, even read the portents. We are grateful to King Birron for establishing the school as part of Matu's temple's work."

"That sounds amazing. I would love the opportunity to meet everyone." Linneya leaned forward, fascinated by this woman's energy and motivation. They spoke further on Harilyn's work while Darryn and Falryn interjected interesting tidbits. After a few minutes, Mariel came into the living room and requested Harilyn's help in the kitchen.

The woman nodded and stood up. She turned back to Linneya and Darryn and pointed them through to the dining room, motioning. "The rest of the boys are through there."

"Found it!" Cheers and a knocking noise from that direction suggested Straion had managed to procure a tap for the wine barrel. Linneya motioned her gratitude to Harilyn once more before standing. Darryn and Linneya made their way toward the commotion. Graisor and Trotyn were slapping Straion on the back and filling up goblets.

"Gentlemen." Darryn announced their presence and the men shouted their excitement at seeing him. Straion shoved goblets of the faewine into their hands and then took three more to the front rooms for Mariel and the others. Graisor and Trotyn stumbled forward, already tipsy from their host's generosity.

"Tell him we are pushing you with these training sessions." Graisor came to stand by her side.

Linneya grinned. "Only if you promise to tell him how brilliant I am at everything we practice."

"You are a fierce one with that dagger." Trotyn chuckled and draped an arm over her shoulders, ignoring how the gesture caused Darryn to clench his fists and offer a villainous glare. "But your footwork needs polishing if you plan on keeping away from fighters with vine affinity. I have seen how often you trip."

Linneya elbowed him as Graisor guffawed. "I will have you know I am the most graceful one of all my siblings." She raised her chin, pretending it was a matter of pride.

Trotyn clutched his chest in mock horror. "The Aelorian succession risks being brought down by a poorly placed rock in each of the siblings' path."

She laughed and a small pang went through her body. She and Aiden used to joke, but not nearly as freely. The family that Darryn had built here was bonded in a way she had never experienced before. A lightness enveloped her and she looked over at her husband. He was watching her with eyes that darkened as she met his gaze.

Linneya inclined her head, a subtle gesture meant for him alone. His lips curved slightly upward and they turned back to the others. Graisor and Trotyn had moved on to some form of drinking game that included puns and birdlanguage. Darryn brightened when he realized what the men were doing, so she left the three of them to it.

In the kitchen, Mariel sat on a stool, rubbing her ankle. She signaled to Harilyn, showing her what needed to be moved to the table. Linneya knocked on the doorframe. "Can I help with anything?" Mariel gestured a couple of the words and fingerspelled the rest.

She turned to Linneya and nodded, a bit breathless from the cooking. "Harilyn has invited me to help with the school. I am learning movement language so I can be of service. We sign everything so everyone is included, no matter how trivial the conversation. If you can wash dishes, that will be a big help"

Harilyn beamed at Mariel. Linneya squeezed her friend's hands and picked up a cloth to wash the dirty dishes in the sink. The women worked in comfortable silence, the occasional snap or hand wave keeping them out of each other's way.

As she washed and dried things, she could hear the four men yelling in excitement. It sounded like Straion was beating the Falorian knights at their own game. It made Linneya chuckle. Straion, with all his musical talent, probably saw it as an easy game of do-re-mi. Darryn would be furious if he had managed to figure out birdspeak that fast.

She was glad they had found a way to be friends again, but she wondered if there could be room for more. A lump rose in her throat. The only thing she wanted in this moment was to be close to Darryn, to breathe in his citrus and cedar scent.

She laid down her washrag and motioned to Mariel that she would be back soon. Linneya crept around the corner to check on him, but realized he was no longer in the dining area. Falryn had Darryn trapped in the corner of the parlor. His arms were crossed and the healer was talking through a tightened jaw. Darryn shook his head and rubbed the back of his neck, mumbling something to them. He looked like a child that had been chastised. Falryn patted his cheek and he nodded to them. He saw Linneya and gave her a curt smile before stalking off to join the other men.

Linneya made her way over to Falryn. "He sees you as a parent figure." She raised her eyebrows, curious and hoping the healer would elaborate.

Falryn obliged. "I helped take care of almost all of these boys since they were barely able to walk on their own two feet. When Darryn arrived with Shailyn, I took them in and guided him on establishing their home here. I have seen generations of Enthorians born and die. Some way or the other, the entire capital has become my extended family."

They grabbed Linneya's arm and led her to the couch. The healer did not let go, even after they sat down. "I have been fussing at that boy for mooncycles to embrace you. He has a deep seated shame that comes from having to grow up too fast. He became a parent at only twelve seasons to keep his sister safe and made plenty of mistakes along the way. Have patience with him. He will figure himself out eventually."

Linneya pursed her lips and dipped her head. "I believe you, but I worry that my family does not have much time." She twisted her hands together. "I wish I could convince him to come home with me so we could fight Serathor together."

Falryn sighed. "You both have much to learn. Yes, war will come to Aelor or Enthor. But tomorrow may never come for any of us. You must do what you can with the time you have been given."

Linneya nodded. In many ways, Falryn was right. They only had the moment they were experiencing right now. Yet, the niggling sense of dread pulled at the back of her mind. She needed to find a way to talk to him about returning to Aelor again, to beg him to come with her if she had to, so they could protect her people together.

Mariel signaled for everyone to move into the dining room. A couple of servants appeared to help set up the food, but then they left and all the dishes were informally handed from person to person. Everyone chattered and laughed as they passed around the food. Falryn translated and flailed their hands, keeping up with the conversation. Mariel did her best to gesture her comments and responses as well.

Trotyn and Graisor were quickly immersed in a tactical discussion with Darryn. Some of the units had been dispatched to the nearby isles when a volcano festival had been interrupted by an intruder. The event had descended into chaos and no one was sure who the culprit was. Most of the knights expected to spend more time helping the islanders rebuild homes that had been destroyed in the confusion.

Mariel and Straion whispered and giggled to each other, sharing lovers' secrets. At one point, he nipped her ear and she turned bright red. Straion took a swig of the faewine and smacked his lips. "My wife cooks almost better than our hired help. Do not let the cook hear me though. We will end up without someone!"

Mariel blushed a deeper shade and grinned. "I only have one or two meals up my sleeves. The rest of the things she cooks would be destroyed if I tried."

Straion shook his head and hiccupped. "Nonsense. You keep complaining about how much you miss Aelor. Maybe we should put you to work in the kitchen with her to give you something to do. Then maybe you would not be so homesick."

Everyone stopped. Mariel just rolled her eyes and kept eating. Straion threw his head back and emptied his goblet. It was only after he lowered it that he saw everyone staring. Linneya was fuming, but Mariel seemed more irked than hurt.

Straion looked around, his red rimmed eyes blinking fast. "What?"

Darryn stood up and walked to the head of the table. He picked Straion up by his collar. "Go. Outside." Straion's chair clattered over onto its side as Darryn dragged him from it. Linneya's heart began pounding in her chest from the thrill of seeing Darryn's darkness emerge in defense of her friend.

Mariel jumped up, protesting, but Falryn held her back. "Let them go, girl. It's better this way. They both could do with a fight tonight."

Mariel's face went pale and Graisor stood. "My Lady, Trotyn and I will go make sure no real harm is done." She nodded and the two men followed Darryn and Straion.

Everyone else just stared at each other. The awkward silence stretched as everyone strained to hear the sounds of a fight. The quiet lasted until Mariel started sniggering and Linneya cracked a smile. Soon, everyone was chuckling.

The laughter grew and tears came to Linneya's eyes. Mariel shook her head and belly laughed. "Straion is so ridiculous sometimes. He means no harm, he just has no filter. His mind is kind, but some of the stuff he spouts off is absurd. Remind me to keep him out of the faewine next time."

Everyone returned to their meal. Linneya cringed at the thought that Darryn might have overreacted. The front door opening made her sit up straighter, anticipating the knight's return. Her eyebrows raised in surprise as two women walked through to the dining area.

"Sorry we missed dinner, the show went longer than we expected." Shailyn walked in and plopped down on Graisor's empty seat, taking a glass of the faewine from Mariel and nodding her thanks. Chrysa stood in the doorway, arms crossed but a small smile on her face and Shailyn continued. "Where are the boys?"

Linneya raised her eyebrows. "Did you not see them as you came in?"

Shailyn shook her head and Falryn snorted. Mariel spoke up. "No matter. Here, let us make you some trays. You can bring them through if you like." The rest of them finished up their meal and made their way to the parlor.

Darryn and Straion stumbled back through, chuckling darkly at some joke one of them had made. Linneya sprung up, expecting to see blood or bruising on both men. Instead, they looked as if they had barely taken a stroll. Mariel ran to Straion's side and he wrapped her up into a tight embrace. Linneya hesitated in front of Darryn and he placed his hands on her waist. Graisor and Trotyn wandered in behind them, looking a bit bored.

Mariel was patting Straion down. "Are you hurt?" Her brow furrowed as she searched for signs of damage.

He laughed and grabbed her hands. "Only in spirit. I am sorry love. I do not mean to blurt out such stupid things."

Darryn pulled Linneya close. She stretched up and whispered, "you did not fight?" He shook his head and leaned down.

His breath tickled her ear. "I was tempted, but he mainly needed rescuing from himself. We went for a walk. I believe he really loves her. He just has no sense of when to shut up." Darryn ran a hand up her arm, leaving a trail of pleasant tingling sensations.

The after dinner lull hit the party and everyone settled in around the fire. Darryn wound his arm around Linneya and tugged her to his shoulder. Mariel's head was in Straion's lap and he was stroking her hair. The only sounds came from the card table where Graisor and Trotyn had challenged Shailyn and Chrysa to a round of games.

Harilyn broke the stillness. "Love, tell us the creation myth. We all know you are dying to share one of your stories."

Falryn chuckled and looked around. "Well? I can stay quiet if I need to." Everyone murmured their interest, so the healer continued. "Time devours our literal understanding of these myths, but in their retelling we are able to gain stronger access to ancient powers. My stay at Mount Varsha taught me that we can study these stories and find hidden truths that reconnect us with earlier knowledge. I share these tales as a sacred duty to pass on whatever I can."

Linneya sat up. The more Falryn spoke of the fae's sacred mountain, the more she was drawn to it. The myths fascinated her, but on a more primal level they sang to her blood the way Darryn's power called to her.

Falryn kept going. "Before this world existed, before the Arduin were breathed into being, there were three deities - our Creators: Substantia, Motus, and Libra. They formed our existence from their power. Substantia brought form, the shape of all things. Motus created movement, interaction. Libra offered balance and rhythm."

They went on to tell of the origins of the different beings: fae, merfolk, and more. The creation story spoke of balance and harmony. Of caring for all creatures with respect and sharing elemental gifts amongst the sentient species.

Falryn finished by telling of the dimension rifts, portals through which the gemstones were brought from the Other. "It is said that these fissures of realities were formed as the Creators walked in between our worlds. Whatever it may be, the deep magic we were given was abused and now elementals are suffering."

The card games had stopped earlier as everyone became enraptured by the creation story. Now, silence settled like a heavy condemnation. The suffocating sense of doom caused Linneya to shiver.

Darryn leaned into her, squeezing his arm around her waist. "Shall we?"

Linneya stifled a yawn and nodded. Perhaps a good night's sleep would help to reduce the aching terror that threatened to consume her. They stood and made the rounds, bidding everyone farewell and thanking Mariel and Straion for a great evening.

The cool night air washed away the dread. Linneya tried to remember Falryn's earlier words: do what you can with the time you are given. They made their way home, struggling to stay in a straight line. Darryn kept an arm wrapped around her waist, his strength giving her permission to be less on guard than usual.

They stumbled back to their suite. Linneya was giddy and light headed from the faewine. She felt Darryn's laugh rumbling in his chest as she leaned on him to climb the stairs.

They entered their rooms and he stopped them before she could pull away to go to her room. Something shone in his eyes, a hunger that made Linneya's breath come faster.

Her hands wound around his neck and through his hair. "Thank you for the evening, friend."

She gasped as he buried his face in her neck and groaned. "I know this cannot be more, princess, but please know I will always take care of you."

His words flooded through her veins like ice water. She chided herself for hoping for more. Linneya stepped back, unable to look him in the face. "Thank you for escorting me this evening." His fists opened and closed at his side, but she turned away. A click cut through the painful silence as he opened his door and retreated to his bedroom.

She wobbled to her door, then hesitated. It was ajar and she pushed it the rest of the way. Blood drained from her face. Clothing and jewels were scattered across the floor. Her secretary was open, parchment spewing out everywhere. Her mattress was sideways on the frame. She began shaking at the sight and backed out of the room.

"Darryn, can you come here?" Her voice cracked.

His door burst open and he bolted to her side. "Linneya, what is it? You sound -" He stopped short and clenched his jaw as he took in the haphazard mess.

Darryn crossed their sitting room in two strides and began yelling orders down the hallway. A guard rushed into the suite and began checking any possible hiding spots. Linneya was frozen. Her thoughts whirled, trying to figure out who might have broken in. Why they might have tried to get to her.

Darryn slammed the door shut and paced. The guard finished his search and quietly reported to Darryn before slipping out. Linneya barely registered the chaos around them. Several others came and went, Kapeyni brought tea, and eventually Graisor marched in, his mouth set in a grim line. "The guards are searching the house a second time. We have secured all entrances and sentries have been called to search the grounds. If the culprit is still here, he will be caught." He looked sideways at Linneya and grimaced at her pallid face. "Do you two need anything else?"

Darryn shook his head. "Thank you, brother. I will call you if we do." He waved a dismissal, but Graisor hesitated. Darryn's eyebrows raised. "What is it?"

Graisor cleared his throat. "With your permission, Trotyn and I will be posted outside the suite tonight. Until they are caught, we have to consider that this person may make a second attempt."

Darryn nodded. "Yes, thank you." Graisor left and he turned back to Linneya, frowning. The numbness of panic had her frozen in place. He stepped forward, brushed his hands down her arms, and grabbed her hands. "Linneya?"

His hesitant tone made her look up. Her body began to shake again and he pulled her close, wrapping her in his arms. Her body warmed as she sagged into him.

She basked in the safety of his strength, but tears still welled up in her eyes. She gasped and his arms tightened around her. "It's okay, princess. Graisor and Trotyn will make sure he is found."

She prickled as irritation at the intruder set in. Why would someone break into her home and destroy their peace? She pulled back and looked at Darryn. "This makes no sense. I hold no secrets in my room. What would they be looking for?"

He crossed his arms and stared into the distance. "I agree. It is odd..." His eyes focused on her again. "Would you be okay to go through your items right now? Maybe we can see what is missing."

Linneya nodded. Darryn walked with her into the ransacked room. Kapeyni bustled in with some tea and quickly joined them. Linneya cataloged each item as they went. Kapeyni busied herself with putting up items after Linneya noted them.

She pulled open a drawer and stopped. The brown and gold gemstone bracelet was untouched, but the brooch was gone. Linneya chewed on her lip and glanced back over the list. "The only thing that is missing is Orrain's brooch. It makes no sense, why would they want that?"

Darryn's eyes narrowed. "I do not know. I thought they might be after information on the Falorian knight's vault and we might find your diary or correspondence missing, but taking jewelry does not make sense."

"The jeweler that sold me the matching bracelet said those types of stones were rare. Is it possible there is more to the brooch?"

He ran his hands through his hair and sighed. "Someone has been feeding information to King Shumor. We have been worried for a while that Sir Fyrain is a spy for Serathor. It is possible that he saw it and thought it would make a fine offering for their king."

The color drained from Linneya's face. The ridiculous man had been fixated on her brooch at their engagement feast. "What if they did it to prove they could get close to me?"

Darryn's eyebrows shot up. "It is a possibility, but King Shumor would not have a reason to come after you, would he?"

Her stomach twisted into knots and she cringed. "The way Mother tells it, she and Father were close to King Shumor. They had agreed to marry their firstborn daughter to his firstborn son." A shadow passed over Darryn's face and his jaw pulsed, but she continued. "My parents rescinded the agreement when he destroyed my grandparents' kingdom, but King Shumor has never quite let it go."

He huffed a laugh. "Of course he has not let that go. You are quite the catch." Her cheeks burned at his words and she turned so he could not see. She pretended to be focused on putting away some final items.

After a moment, he shifted toward the hallway door and cleared his throat. "If you will excuse me, princess, I am going to check with Graisor and Trotyn and then prepare for bed. Are you alright in here by yourself?"

She nodded, feigning interest in a document on her desk. The door snapped shut and she let out a sigh. She flopped face down on the bed, exhausted from the whirlwind of emotions. This house had been a haven during her time in Rathen, her bedroom had turned into a sanctuary. Now, things felt more precarious than ever. Someone unwanted had been in her room. They had taken something from her. Their essence remained, as if the intruder was still watching her.

Linneya turned back over, so she could scan the room one more time. No one was there. She was safe. She took a deep breath, but the painful prickling at the base of her skull made her wary.

Scratching at her door told her that Narruan wanted in. She dragged herself up and let him in. The orange fluffball began purring and butting his head against her legs. He followed her back to the bed and poked her with his paw, demanding ear scritches.

His soft fur was a welcome comfort after such chaos. He stretched out, daring her to touch his tummy. She grinned. "Nice try, Narry." He chirped and curled into a ball.

Linneya sighed and laid back on her pillows. Even with the fierce little *hiduh* for company, her senses were on high alert. Her breath became shallow as the four walls began closing in. The room spun from a combination of anxiousness and faewine. She tensed when something thumped in the hallway. Her heart was racing as if it knew she would need to run at any moment.

The smallest noise outside the doors left her uneasy. The sound of Trotyn greeting a maid startled her and she jumped out of her skin, bumping into the feline. Narruan flicked his feathered tail at the disruption of his nap, looking up at her through narrowed eyes.

Sleeping on the couch would at least put her closer to Graisor and Trotyn if anything happened. The faewine was still coursing through her system, making it hard to react quickly. Being within a few paces of the warriors seemed like the right move. She grabbed a throw blanket and her pillow, padding out into the common space and plopped onto her favorite settee. She punched the pillow, trying to find an angle that felt comfortable. Once she was settled, she pulled the blanket tight, as if the pressure could squeeze out the dull ache of dread.

Someone had targeted her. They had stolen the brooch of a man who had died because of her affinity. It did not feel like a coincidence. Winter was wearing on, but she worried that perhaps Serathor would find a way to attack Aelor before the spring season. She shivered and drew the blanket even tighter across her body.

Fog clouded her mind and her eyes would not stay open. The fright was wearing off, leaving her with nothing but exhaustion and a bit of leftover drunkeness as company. She wanted to be alert, to be ready to fight if they returned for her. Instead, she began to doze off to dreams of orange fluffballs and dancing brooches.

A shuffling sound brought her back into her body. She sprang up into a seated position as the doorknob clicked. Her eyes widened as the door opened. Darryn walked in and stopped short, frowning. "What are you doing, princess?"

She drowned in the intensity of his gaze and hugged herself, trying to focus. Her breaths were shallow and she struggled to slow them. "After this burglary, I cannot bring myself to stay in that room. I am just going to sleep out here tonight."

He ground his teeth as his eyebrows knit together. "Linneya, I am not letting you spend the night on that lumpy couch. Come with me. You are welcome in my bed anytime." He stepped aside and motioned for her to enter his room.

She chewed on her lower lip, eyes darting between him and his bedroom. She wanted to join him, to feel safe in his arms. As if he could read the indecision on her face, he stepped forward and smiled darkly.

"Come, princess. If anyone tries to harm you tonight, they will have to get through me. I promise to make them suffer and bring you their head once I am done." He knelt in front of her, his eyes burned with an intense, threatening flame. Her body went taut and loose all at once as he ran one hand up her leg, settling it dangerously high on her thigh. "I can also help you forget this mess, if you prefer."

Warmth crept up into her cheeks, but she acquiesced. She grabbed the hand on her thigh and squeezed. "Alright, please protect me tonight. This was terrifying and I feel safer with you."

Darryn stood, helping her up from her makeshift bed. She padded into his room and crawled into the silky sheets, yawning. He watched her settle in, smirking as his eyes narrowed possessively.

He strode to his wardrobe and began to undress. His back muscles rippled as he pulled off his shirt. Linneya tried not to watch, but she was drawn to him like a flower straining to taste the morning sun. His burn scars twisted as he moved, a reminder that he had suffered but remained resilient. Forced into a caregiving role, orphaned, and starting over in a new city so young, he chose a path of strength and kindness.

He dropped his pants to the floor and she stifled a moan. The man was built like an Arduin deity. She ached to pull him to her, to whisper all the things she wanted from him into his ear. Wetness pooled between her legs and she rubbed her thighs together to relieve the throbbing sensation that was building.

He pulled on a pair of sleep pants and turned back to her. Darryn marked the flush of her chest, the foggy look in her eyes, and smirked. "Like what you see?"

Her mouth opened, too flustered to respond. He stalked toward her, a predator marking its next kill. She would gladly be his prey if it meant him touching her, relieving the longing that pulsed through her body.

Any thought of remaining just friends was pushed from her mind as he crawled under the covers, hovering over her. Citrus and cedar drifted around them and Linneya breathed his scent in deeply. His eyes darkened as he drank in her frame. "Beautiful," he growled.

The warmth of their bodies and the thrill of his voice made Linneya's head swim. Darryn ran his hand up her torso and her breath caught as he palmed her breast. She grabbed his hair and crushed her mouth to his.

Their tongues tangled and he lowered his body to hers. The safety of being caged in his arms helped her forget the intruder. Their hands wandered and became wilder, more insistent. His hardness pressed into her center, a longing coursing through her body. She arched her hips, desperate for sensation, and he hissed with pleasure.

She yawned and hiccuped slightly. The motion made him still and distance himself from her. Linneya moaned and tried to pull him back to her. "No, do not stop."

He sighed and shook his head. "You are exhausted and possibly still drunk. Get some sleep, princess. Ask me again tomorrow." He grinned, but there was a sad tone to his voice, and motioned for her to roll over. She grumbled, but was too tired to argue.

He fitted himself against her back and she melted into him, feeling the evidence of his arousal. The sensation sent more heat through her core and she ground against him. He groaned and pressed his hands to her hips. "No more, please Linneya, not tonight." She smiled in satisfaction, he was aching as much as her. With that knowledge, she drifted off to sleep.

Chapter 20

No one tried to break in and there was no news on why the brooch had been taken. Darryn forced her to have a guard every day. Sometimes they trained, other times he showed her different catacomb entrances to sneak into the vaults and research her elemental energies. At night, Linneya stayed in Darryn's room, although the insufferable man had retreated to his armchair after that first evening. In all fairness, she did not ask him to stay in the bed with her, either. She was embarrassed by her drunken moment of weakness and hoped to spare both of them the awkwardness of discussing it.

Instead, she focused on honing her elemental powers and training in combat with Darryn. As their training sessions progressed, Linneya became better at fighting with a weapon and using her affinities at the same time. Graisor sometimes joined them for lessons still, bringing his mist-whisperer ideas for her to try. Trotyn only showed up once, wielding a whip.

Her full blown nightmares were less frequent, but the assassin still popped into her sleep on occasion. She would only receive small flashes. Maybe an elemental taunting him and running away or his powers not working like he needed to while an elemental struggled to get free. These snippets were tinted with desperation. The assassin spoke more aggressive declarations, with wild eyes and gnashing teeth. Linneya woke up screaming after almost every encounter, his newfound madness terrifying her.

One night, after a particularly bad dream, she was stuck and could not pull out of the terror. Strength enveloped her, swallowed her whole and gently guided her out of the horror of the nightmare. She gasped for air as Darryn traced soothing circles on her back.

"This is the third time this week. Princess, I am not going to demand you tell me what is going on in your head, but I wish you would." He brushed the hair from her face and watched her intently.

He deserved to know. If someone was actually murdering elementals with a more sinister plan than taking the power for themselves, the Falorian knights needed to be made aware. Surely, he would keep this from the king if she asked. She rubbed her face and took a deep breath.

"I think I may be a dream-walker." Darryn kept his face neutral, so she continued. "I have these nightmares of a man in a *trillin* mask murdering elementals. Recently, he has been getting more reckless and less accurate. It seems that his recent failures have made him more furious and those he has killed have been brutally destroyed."

He took one of her hands in his and began making small circles on her palm. She took a deep breath. "I thought he was gathering elementals so he would have one of each affinity. He would slice their throats and bleed them out over a gemstone." Darryn's jaw pulsed and his expression housed a deadly threat.

"I am not even sure they are real. I have not said anything sooner because I do not want others to know." She placed a hand on his cheek. "Please, can we keep my dreams between the two of us for now?"

He closed his eyes and leaned into her touch. Linneya trembled a bit, worried that he would feel the need to tell King Birron or his knightsmaster. She sat with bated breath as he steadied himself.

Finally, he lifted his eyes back to her. "Linneya, I worry you may be witnessing King Shumor's lackey. We have intel that suggests that someone has been killing elementals in order to fulfill the prophecy. The king got tired of hunting for a natural-born wielder of all five elements and is making his own." He shook his head and his shoulders slumped. "I do not understand why you have this connection to the assassin, though. This feels dangerous."

She grabbed his hands. "I understand, but please, let us keep the dreams secret. At least for now. I worry what might happen if it gets out that the famed flame-talker is now dream-walking."

He nodded. "Yes, I think it is wise to keep it between us. Can you tell me more about these dreams? No detail is too small."

They spent the next several hours pouring over what she could remember. Locations, phrasing, even weather patterns. Anything Linneya could think of, Darryn noted it. He bandied about several theories that could explain the new patterns of behavior. It was sobering to realize that King Shumor was aiming to take control of a prophecy that might help him destroy the other human realms.

The nightmares made Linneya more determined than ever to learn what she could about her limited powers. She eagerly anticipated the training sessions with the Falorian knights. She devoured anything Falryn suggested on mythos and elemental abilities.

So one day, when Falryn unexpectedly summoned Linneya to the royal gardens, she ran straight there without a second thought. She knew Falryn would be on the far side of the lake, near a stand of everblue trees that included a couple of benches.

Mariel was slowly making her way off the lake bridge. Linneya waved and Mariel grinned. "So great to see you! When are you coming by our house again?"

Linneya wrapped her arms around her friend and squeezed. "What are you doing tomorrow? I could come visit in the morning."

Mariel beamed. "Yes! I am making bread. Cook lets me kick her out of the kitchen regularly, so it will be the perfect time for us to catch up."

Linneya nodded. "I will be there." The women said their goodbyes and she headed on over the bridge.

Falryn folded their arms over their chest as she walked up. "Your friend has many rare qualities. You are lucky to have each other."

"Yes, she has been a wonderful friend. Not many people know how to be as patient or as caring as Mariel."

Falryn pursed their lips and grunted, then gestured around the garden. "I have brought you here because today I want to try you on your sister elements. Technically, you should have potential to access to all five elements. You already have such a strong control over your mist and flame affinities, it seems likely that some day you will be able to tap into the other three."

Linneya nodded. "Please, tell me what to do."

Falryn tossed her a list of enchantments. "These are to call any sister elements into your blood. We shall start with vine." The healer pointed to a stand of trees. "Command one of them to grow a branch."

The next several hours were full of disappointment. She produced no light, no smoke, no signs of elemental affinity. They went down the entire list of enchantments, Linneya straining to feel a pull to any of the sister elements. Falyrn stoically commanded her to start from the beginning, the healer never indicating that they felt disappointed in her failure to produce any results.

After the second round of attempts, Falryn took the parchment back from Linneya. "Good. We will try them again another day."

Linneya bit her lip and hung her head, disappointed. She had been able to produce something on the first try for flame and mist. Falryn had said it could take annae, but she had held out hope that she might have a breakthrough without the wait.

As if they could read her thoughts, Falryn patted her shoulder. "It is not an easy task to pull elements that are not your natural affinities. You will eventually have some control over all five, I am certain, but our focus should remain on mist and flame for now. You and Darryn will need your powers before long. War is coming and you must be ready to step into your destiny."

Linneya bit back a scoff, unwilling to let the healer know how little she believed in fate. They began walking back through the gardens. Falryn stopped on the bridge and turned to face Linneya.

They tapped the iron railing and gazed into the distance "Confidence in your calling and a willingness to step forward and fight for what is right is a vital part of healing the world. Payera and Luthin remind us of that every day, right here on this bridge."

Linneya cocked her head to the side, "This is the second time you have mentioned them." She had read the book that Darryn's mother had left him, but Falryn almost always had more details than the fictionalized versions she found in any novel.

Falryn grinned. "Yes, you and Darryn remind me of the lost final chapter of Payera and Luthin's story. They were lovers from this area who were destined to save the humans from the *sharvach*. The wolf-like beings were recruited by the corrupt council to act as guard dogs. For annae, the *sharvach* served the council and kept dissenters in line.

"Payera and Luthin were demigods who were sent by the Arduin. They were meant to bond as mates and fight the council, exposing the malfeasance using their combined abilities. They loved each other, but lifetimes of trauma stopped them from fully accepting each other.

"Instead of defeating the council, their arguing and hesitation led to their exposure. The council tried to have them arrested. This bridge is where they met in order to run away. Payera and Luthin escaped execution and hid in the countryside, ignoring their destiny."

"The *sharvach* became popular servants to those in power. They bided their time until corrupt leaders everywhere had employed at least two of their kind. Then, one night, as if they had planned it for the height of the moon, *sharvach* across the human realms slit their masters' throats." Linneya shivered at the thought of these beastly creatures having free rein in the human world again.

Falryn coughed, cleared their throat, and continued. "Humans became their slaves. The *sharvach* removed humans from countryside homes that they wanted and forced the humans that resided there into servitude. Payera and Luthin were separated and sent to live out their final days in two different courts."

"A duocentury later, the pair was reincarnated. Payera had dreams of Luthin, Luthin visions of Payera. They eventually found each other in this new life. This time, they remembered the lessons from their past and did not resist the bond. They drove the *sharvach* back to the shadowlands and freed the humans from the nightmare of enslavement."

"Every time I am here, it reminds me that one should face their destiny with trust and confidence. Even if things feel chaotic and unsure, it is better to have faith in those whom you love and to work toward your fate together."

Linneya shook her head. "I was convinced I was going to be a healer. That I would stay with my people and save them from the horrors of being burned to death by Serathor's dragons."

One side of Falryn's mouth quirked up. "Now here you are, learning to fight alongside some of the most powerful Falorian knights. The Creators are calling you to a grander destiny than the one you had imagined for yourself. The lost, final chapter of Luthin and Payera's story tells of how they would someday return and find a way to bring the *sharvach* into a harmonious relationship with humans. Balance would be returned."

They snorted. "Of course, humans do not want to consider those wolf-like creatures as sentient or deserving of a peaceful life. Only snippets remain of the final story, most of it has been lost to time."

Linneya raised her eyebrows, but kept her gaze on the lake. Falryn's words brought a surge of power through her blood. The two of them started walking again, heading toward the exit that would put them near their homes.

What would Linneya's fate be? How were humans supposed to discern what they were meant to do? She thought she was meant to heal the world with her power, but instead she was stuck in a foreign land with no way to help her family.

If she could not find a way to help her people in Aelor, her work meant nothing. Her training meant nothing. Her dreams meant nothing. Her dreams...

Maybe Falryn would have some insight into what the dreams meant. Linneya pulled in a breath and turned back to her mentor. "Might I tell you something that I have kept secret?"

Falryn pursed their lips. "Go ahead, girl."

As she recounted the nightmares of the assassin and the elemental power being absorbed into stone, a weight melted off her shoulders. Falryn's brow furrowed in concentration. Linneya admitted to wondering if it was dream-walking or just an overactive imagination.

She finished and collapsed onto a bench in front of King Birron as Matu. Falryn rubbed their chin and stared into the distance. Linneya chewed on her bottom lip, waiting for their verdict.

Falryn finally turned back to her. "You say you have kept these dreams from everyone except Darryn. Why?"

Linneya shook her head. "I do not know. Somehow they felt private. Even after realizing that my father and Lord Caelin were discussing a man that had probably been in my dream, I could not bring myself to tell anyone."

Falryn narrowed their eyes. "What meaning do you think the dreams have?"

Linneya shrugged. "At first I believed them to be an overactive imagination combined with vicious rumors of elemental hunters. Now I am not sure. Sometimes they feel real. Other times they seem feverish. Darryn thinks they are probably me seeing one of King Shumor's minions at work." She shuddered at the thought that every brutal murder she witnessed was someone suffering immense pain and fear in their last moments.

Falryn nodded and kept walking. Linneya stood back up and followed. At the edge of the park, Falryn turned and patted her shoulder. "I will look further into this. Perhaps there is something in my books that will trigger a thought. I will let you know soon."

The next morning, Darryn knocked on her bedroom door, causing it to swing open. "Good morning, princess. Why are you still getting dressed?" His reflection in the vanity mirror was enough to stir a fluttering in her abdomen.

"Kapeyni is not feeling well, so I am wrestling with my own hair this morning." She sighed and pinched the bridge of her nose. "I have plans to visit Mariel and was trying to get to her house while she was baking.

Darryn chuckled and stepped behind her. He began stroking his fingers through her hair. "May I? I can at least plait it in a way that will look presentable."

Linneya raised her eyebrows. "You know how to braid?"

He nodded and took a few strands, twisting them together. "I learned when I was younger for Shailyn. Our mother died giving birth to her and we moved here soon after. Once she got old enough, I would braid her hair. Even after we got her proper staff, she would still ask me to do it on occasion. I do not expect to ever replace a lady's maid, but I can work a bit of magic when necessary."

She smiled and he began to pull strands of hair into the weave. His strong hands were gentle against her scalp. Linneya closed her eyes, allowing his rhythmic tugging to lull her into a meditative state. The warmth of his body radiated onto her back and her shoulders began to relax.

The normalcy of it was soothing. They were spending a quiet moment together without having to strategize for a fight or a new opponent. Longing tugged at her heart, a whisper of what they could have.

All too soon, he was done. He fastened the end and the tension of the braid settled into a comfortable line down the back of her scalp. She sighed and he placed his hands on her shoulders, running his thumbs along her neck. The sensation left goosebumps that trailed down her back.

She wanted to twist around, stand up, and claim his mouth. Claim all of him, madly and selfishly. His eyes burned with a similar want. They stared at each other in the reflection of the mirror, neither willing to break the silence and end the moment.

Narruan bolted into the room and headed straight for Darryn's legs. "By the shadowed void, you little beast!" He jumped backwards and Linneya laughed. The fur ball spat at Darryn, rubbed his head against Linneya's ankles, and pranced off as if the sneak attack had been successful.

She called her praise out after the *hiduh*. "What a fierce little warrior!"

Linneya giggled and Darryn shook his head. "That beast is going to be the death of me." He placed a kiss on the top of her head. "You had better head out if you want to make it to Mariel's and have any time to visit before noonrest. Linneya squeezed his hand and stood, leaving for her friend's house.

The view from Mariel's back porch was incredible. Being close to the water brought with it a wide variety of vegetation and wildlife. The birds were singing and riverside critters were scurrying about, chittering with one another.

The river was rushing by, a large rock in the center. Local legend said a dragon had fallen in the final battle for Tirathel and landed in the middle of the river. Over the duodecades, silt and clay had bunched up around its skull. Now, a black, smooth stone had formed as its tomb.

The yeasty smell of baking bread wafted through the open door. Her friend was humming and thumping dough. The quiet peace of Mariel's home brought a pleasant sense of tingling in Linneya's heart.

She knocked on the door and leaned in. "Mari? It's me. Sorry I am late."

"Lia!" Mariel bustled through the kitchen entryway. Her face was glowing from the heat of the stove. "Come in. I am just finishing up this bread. Have a seat."

Linneya followed her into the kitchen and plopped down at the table. Bright light streamed in through a window and the walls were a brown, sandy color that reflected the sunsrays throughout the room. Mariel's mother had sent some Loraian pottery and Mariel hung them in a functional, yet decorative, cascade on one wall.

Linneya smiled at the small reminder of their home city. "It looks like you are settling in well. The new decor is beginning to look more like you."

Mariel grunted her agreement, wrestling the last of the loaves into the primed oven. She stood back up and began gesturing around the space. "I am lucky our cook is not jealous about her space. She has let me hang up everything and has made room for all the gadgets I have bought since I arrived."

Linneya giggled. "You would run your cook out of her own kitchen."

Mariel grinned. "Having unfettered access to grain has turned me into a fiend. I cannot remember the last time I had such an easy time getting the different ingredients needed for my baking."

Linneya cocked her head. "Why do you think it is easier for Enthor to have bountiful harvests? It seems like the droughts would be making it more difficult here with the heat."

She sat down and brushed the strands of hair out of her face, leaving streaks of flour across her forehead. "Straion said Queen Rhylanna has acted on the theory that the elemental magic drying up in the land is fueling the droughts. She has convinced King Birron to nurture his elementals and tries to keep them safe and happy. Her plan seems to be working. I hear in the markets that grains are easier to come by now than two annae ago."

Linneya nodded. "That makes sense. I have seen similar actions from the queen. Mother always said food production has slowed down over the last few duodecades in all the human kingdoms. Perhaps it is a matter of balance."

Mariel waved her hand, dismissing the conversation. "It is not anything we are going to solve. I am glad you have come. Something has been on my mind recently. I keep having nightmares about the bandit attack that we endured on the way here."

Linneya steadied her breathing and chewed on her lip. She would rather think of anything other than that dreadful day, but her friend clearly needed to talk. "I remember it well."

Mariel crossed her arms and twisted her lips, looking thoughtful. "They were definitely mercenaries. King Birron has determined someone hired them specifically to attack us."

She studied her friend for a moment before responding. "Darryn did suggest that they were not your typical bandits. He said their willingness to fight to the death gave them away."

Mariel nodded. "Straion thinks they were sent to steal powers from one of the elementals. You and Darryn both may have been targets. After Orrain's brooch went missing, I wondered if the events were related."

Linneya pursed her lips. "It seems possible. The leader mentioned me as Darryn killed him and I have been worried that we would experience another attack. Darryn acted as if he was not going to let me out of the house after the burglary. But it has been so long that I no longer know what to think.

Mariel shrugged. "The threat is over. There is something else brewing. I suspect it is related, but not the same person."

Linneya's eyebrows knit together. "How do you know that?"

She drummed her fingers on the table. "If the person behind the attack was still around, something else would have happened by now. You would have experienced another attempt on your life. It seems most likely that they are dead."

Linneya's eyes widened and she hugged herself. "You think it was Orrain."

Mariel pursed her lips and nodded. "We all saw how he treated you. Then, think back on how he separated us. In the chaos of the attack, I was so panicked I did not think it through. But now I can see he had bad intentions. It was not safe to send me unarmed through a bunch of fighting men to find my betrothed. He needed you alone for a reason."

Linneya shivered and whispered. "A bandit was chasing us and he pushed me down."

Mariel raised her eyebrows. "He *what?*"

Linneya straightened her shoulders and looked her friend in the eyes. "He pushed me and kept running. Left me for dead. I thought he was just taking advantage of the moment to rid himself of an unwanted wife. However, if your theory is correct, there may be more to it."

Mariel's mouth was open "How did you escape? Those men were warriors."

Linneya grimaced. "It was mostly luck. The tremor during the battle shook a stone loose and I used that as a weapon."

Mariel raised her eyebrows. "A tremor?"

She nodded, her stomach twisting in knots from the memory. "Yes, it was not long after we got separated. It was strong, surely you felt it."

Mariel was silent for a moment. Her eyes were distant, lost in thought. Then she shook her head. "I do not think we did, but there was so much happening that perhaps I mistook it for losing my balance."

She shook her head as if she was clearing her thoughts. "Oh Lia, why did you not tell me about this sooner?" Mariel reached across the table and took Linneya's hands in her own.

Tears burned in Linneya's eyes, threatening to spill over. "So much has happened. I was not trying to keep it from you, it just seemed inconsequential in light of everything else."

Mariel stood up and hurried to her. She threw her arms around Linneya and squeezed. Wetness coated her cheeks and she collapsed into her friend's arms. They stayed silent for several minutes while Linneya cried. She had not had the time to mourn how she was forced to take a life. Now she was ready to do so again, if necessary, but snuffing out all of the potential that someone has was a difficult thing to process. Her chest seized and she sobbed. Mariel hugged her tighter.

When finally she sat back up, Mariel handed her a cloth to dry her eyes. The woman went to the window and stared outside. "Orrain is no longer a threat, but with his brooch being stolen... I wonder if there were more people involved in the plot."

She thought back to her conversation with Darryn and her stomach twisted. Sir Fyrain had not been seen since the brooch disappeared. Perhaps the man had taken off with it. Were there powers in the brooch that she did not recognize?

The sweet scent of bread that was finished baking bloomed in the air. "Ah, it is time to pull these out." Mariel stood and began preparing space on the counter for the loaves.

She watched her friend bustle about the kitchen, a sense of warmth and love washing over her. The thought of the two of them, lifelong friends, chatting in Mariel's kitchen - it made Linneya smile. "Enough about me, how are you and Straion?"

Mariel busied herself with the oven, balancing hot trays and pretending not to hear. Linneya's heart sank. Straion and Mariel had seemed so close on the journey from Aelor, but since they married, they had struggled a bit. Had the doldrums of everyday life destroyed their magic?

"Mari?"

She sighed and sat down. "We are doing alright." She began to bite at her nails, looking out the window.

Linneya shook her head. "Mari, I know you better than that. What is going on?"

Mariel fidgeted as she turned back to Linneya. "I wonder if I have made a mistake. Straion has a good mind. We love each other. But... it has been so hard trying to adjust to this life. He has moments where he blurts out private things to others and I walk away feeling so awkward. You have heard him. Even after that horrid dinner where Darryn pulled him outside to save us both from the embarrassment, he resolved to do better and nothing changed. He cannot distinguish when something is not for others to hear. He is also terrible about making jokes when I need him to be serious. Most of the frustration is little, but it builds and dredges up my insecurities. We end up fighting more than feels normal."

Linneya laid a hand on her friend's arm. Mariel smiled sadly. "I do not mean to sound ungrateful, but I wonder if he would be happier with someone else. I wonder if we both would. I feel as if I have failed as a wife and he seems to not understand how uncomfortable his jokes leave me."

Her stomach sank. "The man adores you. I hate that things have turned out to be harder than it seemed at first."

Mariel looked down at her hands. "I know there are cultural differences. Plus, the folks in the Northern Isles are more outspoken. He is thoughtful of my physical needs. His comments are never intentionally cruel. He has always been helpful with my disability. He is always careful to show love, but he reveals things that I do not want others to know. My interest in women, my severe homesickness, he just - is not careful.

Linneya nodded and patted her friend's hands. They sat for several minutes in silence before Mariel stood and began slicing into the fresh bread. "Stay for noonrest. I have some lovely raspberry jam. We need some time to talk about happier things."

Linneya smiled and stood up. "Show me how I can help, Mari." They spent the noon hour reminiscing about their childhood and recalling things about their homeland. Linneya was surprised how vivid certain details were and how much she had forgotten about some of their everyday experiences in Loraen. By the time she headed back to the mansion, bittersweet nostalgia had gripped her.

Chapter 21

Everyone was preparing for Meðon, the midwinter festival. The second sun had finally disappeared behind the larger sun, signaling the winter season was in full swing. The brighter hues of winterlight created a cool tone to the air.

After noonrest, Linneya met Shailyn at the back gate to the mansion. The woman bounded up and linked arms with Linneya. "Hello, sister. Are you excited to experience our world-famous festival?"

Linneya could not help but feel jubilant as they strolled toward the busiest part of the celebrations. Shailyn chattered the entire way, talking about her favorite artist booths, the traditional mulled ciders, and what foods to avoid to keep from ruining the evening with an upset stomach. Arm in arm, the women meandered toward the festivities.

Lightness bloomed in Linneya's chest. Shailyn had become like a trusted younger sister. They bantered and laughed, always allowing for each other's opinions. Shailyn, Graisor, Trotyn, and even Chrysa... The crew was fast turning into family. The ease with which they joked, the fierceness with which they loved, it was wonderful to be adopted in to such strong bonds.

Musicians lined the entrance to the festival. The scents of mulling spices and savory roasted meats filled the air. Crowds gathered around temporary stages, listening to poems or plays about the dark of the annum.

Shailyn dragged Linneya down a side path, toward the artists' corner. The colorful creations were wondrous to look at. Merchants from all over the kingdom, as well as some from other lands, had crafts that ranged from eccentric to practical. Some pieces were the expected, classical styles. Others held a unique twist. Linneya marveled at the wide array of expression.

A dark booth drew her attention. Several silver carved *trillin* masks were placed at the front. Trepidation crept up Linneya's spine as she approached. A woman with straight, jet black hair that fell to her waist was seated in the shadows.

Shailyn bounded forward. "Sharya! Creators, I did not know you would be here!" She threw her arms around the woman, who only raised one hand to pat Shailyn on the back.

She drew back and motioned toward Linneya. "This is my sister. Well, Darryn's wife. Close enough." Shailyn grinned and pulled Linneya into the tent.

Sharya cocked her head to one side. "I am pleased to meet you."

Linneya nodded and gestured toward the masks. "You have quite the collection of masks."

The artist lifted one side of her mouth. "Many find the power of the *trillin* alluring, although few wield it as they should."

Linneya's brows knit a bow, but they were interrupted before she could respond. "Could I walk with you a bit, princess?"

The voice was familiar but Linneya could not place it. She turned and hazel eyes met hers. She was face to face with Johann. Why would the brother of the man she had killed - albeit unintentionally - want to speak with her?

Shailyn waved them on. "Sharya and I have some catching up to do! You two go enjoy the festival."

Johann offered Linneya his arm with a warm smile. They began walking down the path, admiring different booths along the way. She tried to find something to say, even opening her mouth twice, but nothing seemed appropriate.

She studied the man's face. He had braided his honey blonde hair into a festive style and his lips were curved in excitement. His brown eyes twinkled with mischief, but she detected nothing sinister in his countenance.

After a few minutes, Johann broke the silence. "How have you found our darling capital? Is married life treating you well?"

She nodded. "Rathen has been lovely. I am as happy as can be expected, given the circumstances."

"Good, I am glad to hear it. And your family? They are well? Have you heard from Aiden recently?" He leaned toward her, a genuine look of curiosity on his face.

Linneya blinked. For this man to seem friendly toward her family felt odd. "Well, they seem to be alright. I have not heard from Aiden much, but our mother suggested he was going to be on a deadwinter hunt. Why? Have you heard differently?"

"I met your brother on a raid. We have stayed in touch through the annae, although I have not had a letter in the past few mooncycles."

She bit her lip. Her correspondence with Aiden had been sparse, but not odd. Her mother sent more detailed letters and everything seemed alright. She resolved to send him a note when she got home, just to check in.

Johann motioned for them to break off onto another path and she followed. The stalls down this alley were unusual. Some housed artwork, others appeared to be full of talismans or trinkets. A darkness shadowed the row of stalls. It sent a shiver spiraling up Linneya's spine, but Johann seemed unphased. He continued guiding her toward the far end of the path, back to the main festivities.

A gray haired, scraggly man stopped them and shoved an unusual bird statue in their faces. "Madam, sir, you look like you know rare art. Might I interest you in this phoenix statue? It is from the Other, a recent shipment I received."

Johann scoffed at the vendor's claims. "No trade has been allowed through the portals in the past duocentury. There is no way that is real."

The street vendor leered at them, his sharp teeth bared like a threat. "There are more ways to the Other than using monitored portals. I assure you, sir, this is a real artifact from beyond our world."

Linneya stared at the phoenix. It was painted with bright colors and the wingtips were iridescent. It looked as if it could come alive at any moment, rising from the ashes of whatever sacrifice had been made to create it.

Johann shook his head and maneuvered her away from the stall. Almost instantly, the spell was broken. Linneya stumbled and the allure of the statue fell away.

"Merfolk think we cannot recognize a siren song." Johann grunted. "Hawkers of such junk."

They made their way back to the livelier festival area. Darryn was standing by a wizened old man. Both of them had their arms crossed and their heads down. Linneya dropped her arm from Johann's and nodded toward Darryn. "Thank you for the escort, but I believe I need to meet my husband now."

Johann flashed a smile. "Please, let us keep in touch. Come to my house for tea when you have an afternoon free. I would like to get to know you better, as long as you are not offended by my refusal to wed you."

Linneya grunted a noncommittal answer. She was locked onto Darryn's frame. The festival seemed to fall away and she was drawn to him. She approached slowly, unsure if the conversation he was having was private.

Darryn looked up and furrowed his brow. "Were you just with Johann? What did he want?"

Linneya shook her head. "I think he is trying to mend fences for his part in refusing my hand." She shrugged and raised her eyebrows, motioning toward the old man by Darryn's side.

The ancient one had not moved. His gray eyes held dark specks in a starburst pattern and his shock white hair stuck out at all angles. He seemed deep in some sort of trance, his body frail and lanky.

Darryn laid his hand on the man's shoulder and he started. "What, oh, yes, yes." The man coughed and Darryn motioned Linneya forward.

"This is Noryo, the Falorian knightsmaster. We were debating the merits of a northbound training mission once the spring season returns."

Linneya greeted the man with a slight curtsy. She knitted her eyebrows toward Darryn and he seemed to nod in return. Hope swelled in her chest. Was he planning on sending Falorian knights toward Aelor just in case? Or was he teasing her?

Noryo kissed the back of Linneya's hand. "It is an honor to finally meet Darryn's wife. Northbound mission aside, perhaps you can talk some sense into the lad. He is refusing my request to name him successor to the Falorian knights."

She crossed her arms and looked at Darryn. "Oh? And why have you refused?"

Darryn's eyes darkened dangerously and he strode to her side. "I have told our esteemed leader that I will not leave your side. I cannot risk putting you in more danger by taking such a position."

She blushed, her blood heating under his possessive gaze. Linneya turned back to the wizened old man. "I am sorry, I cannot argue with my husband on that front."

Noryo nodded and smiled. "Young love. You must enjoy it whilst you can." He waved them off and went back to staring into the mists.

A group of children ran by, shouting and laughing as they tossed a ball. Two girls were clapping and reciting a traditional Meðon rhyme. Darryn offered her his arm and they walked toward the main celebrations. She waited until they were far enough away that the man could not hear her, but still she whispered. "What is he doing?"

Darryn grinned. "He is creature-walking. Old Noryo can slip into the mind of any creature within a day's journey and see what is happening around it."

Linneya gaped at the thought. The level of intelligence gathering that the knightsmaster was capable of was stunning. It was no wonder he was chosen to command them.

She studied her husband. His regal presence and easy care for his subordinates suggested he would make a fine leader. Did he only refuse because of her? She should not hold him back from such an important role. Linneya's chest constricted. "Darryn, do you want to lead the knights?"

He stopped and turned, cupping her face in his hands. "No, princess. You are my priority. I would not want the role even if I was unmarried, but you make it doubly unappealing." He pressed a kiss to her forehead and they stood in the middle of the path, staring at each other.

After a few minutes, a snapping sound shook her from his gaze. Harilyn was walking toward them with a little girl at her side. Falryn was close behind.

Harilyn waved to the two of them. The woman gestured to the child beside her, patting the side of her face - signaling the child was deaf as well. Falryn translated the rest of Harilyn's movement. "This is one of our students, Rhia. She comes from the Northern Isles. Rhia has mist affinity. She wanted to meet one of her heroes."

Linneya smiled and crouched down beside the girl, waving a greeting. "It is so nice to meet you!"

The child grinned. Rhia had wavy, light brown hair and a gap in her front teeth. She was thin, but seemed well cared for.

Rhia patted Falryn's arm and began motioning with her hands. "How do you heal with your mist? I want to help but all I can do is make splashes in the bath!"

Linneya grinned. "Lots and lots of practice. Listen to your teachers. Beg Falryn to show you which books can help. It takes time, but you can become a life-tender if you put your mind to it!"

The girl stared up at Linneya with the biggest eyes. She seemed in awe of the princess. Linneya's heart warmed as the child asked questions about her power. Darryn stood beside her, occasionally rubbing her back or squeezing her hand.

She did not notice when the sounds of the festival began to fade. Only once the fog crept in did the hair stand up on her arms. The sky quickly turned dark and the wind whipped about, cutting like sharp ice. Falryn motioned to Harilyn, a frown on both of their faces.

Everyone braced as a scream ripped through the dull roar of the festivities. Darryn grabbed Linneya's wrist and scanned the crowd. The momentary pause of activity thawed and people began running, the festival quickly devolving into complete chaos. Rhia began crying and Harilyn patted her head to soothe her. Shaking, Linneya motioned for the others to huddle close and then looked at Darryn for direction.

Noryo appeared at their side. "It is a rogue *sharvach*. I have sounded the alarms, but we need to go. Now."

Darryn's jaw pulsed and he turned to Linneya, brushing hair out of her face. Her head spun. How had such a shadow creature arrived in the capital? They were hard to miss. The wolf-like appearance and large antlers were creepy enough to make anyone's skin crawl.

There was no time to puzzle it out. "What do we do?"

Darryn pulled her close, hugging her tightly to his chest. "Take Falryn, Harilyn, and the girl and hide. If you run into the *sharvach*, use your fire."

She nodded and tore away from him. Linneya scooped up Rhia and grabbed Harilyn's hand, motioning for Falryn to do the same. Screams and alarm bells cut through the air. They ran deeper into the wooded areas, Linneya frantically searching for a hiding spot that would hold all of them.

It was slow going, trying to balance a hysterical child on her hip while not tripping on anything through the fog. Her heart pounded in her head and she gasped for breath. They needed to hide before the *sharvach* made its way toward them. They would never survive an attack in the open.

Falryn yelled for Linneya to stop. The healer was gesturing toward a small drop with an overhang. Linneya nodded and they made their way down the slope.

Relief flooded through her, warming her like sunsbeams on a cold day. There was heavy brush in front of the natural divot in the ground. It almost created a cave-like feel. Linneya motioned for everyone to crash through the brush and underneath the overhang.

They huddled together against the dirt. Falryn shushed Rhia, reminding her to stay still so things would be quieter. The loamy, grassy smell emanating from the ground helped soothe the worst of her fear. Linneya took deep breaths, her hand pressed into her chest. The frantic noises of the disrupted festival were fading. She hoped that Darryn and the other knights were safe.

They stayed there for what felt like hours. Rhia was becoming restless and there had been no clanging metal or fearful shouts for the past several minutes. Falryn soothed the child, pointing out unusual flowers and leaves nearby. Harilyn motioned to get Linneya's attention. "When do you think we can try to head back? Rhia needs to get home."

Linneya whispered back. "Let me see if I can sneak out and see what is happening."

She crept into the dense brush surrounding their natural divot. Linneya's legs shook as she broke through into the wooded area and looked around. Her shoulders relaxed. There was nothing in the area. Perhaps they could make a run for it, although she would prefer to stay a little while longer - just in case.

She turned to go back, but her body tensed. The woods became eerily silent. Out of the corner of her eye, a dark mist danced in the trees. She slowly turned, hoping that it was a trick of her vision.

The mist came closer and out stepped a six foot tall, gray, wolf-like creature. It stood on its hind legs, walking as if human. A sword was strapped to its back and the massive antlers that sprouted from its head looked deadly in their own right. Its eyes were pure white. A damp, mildewy scent radiated from it.

Linneya gagged and shivered as a spark of dread crept up her spine. Her skin crawled, as if her body wanted to reject the creature's presence. She tried to slowly crouch to the ground, hoping the brush would hide her.

Instead, the *sharvach* pointed directly at her.

Blood drained from her face. It unsheathed its sword and charged. She ran, leading the beast away from the hiding spot of her friends. Brush ripped at her face and clothes. Her lungs burned, but the wild energy of survival surged and she kept pressing forward.

Wheezing and growling told her it was gaining on her. The enchantments of mist and flame stuttered from her mouth. Darryn had told her to focus on flame, so she brought that forth first, a red smoke creeping from her hands.

Turning, she directed her flame at its face. It screamed as the inferno engulfed it, but only for a moment. The fire abated and it hunched down, creeping forward.

Linneya's jaw dropped. The fire had only created momentary pain. There was no charred fur, no writhing that might indicate the beast had been attacked. She swiveled to run, hoping to at least lead it further from Falryn and the others.

She was stopped, yanked to the ground. Linneya spluttered, face down in the dirt. A tree root had caught her ankle. She scrambled to turn over and laid her eyes on the monster as it raised its sword for the killing blow.

A red haze billowed around her. She shot fire out of her hands, desperate to stop it long enough to get away. As the flames cleared a second time, the *sharvach's* eyes turned a bright blue and it looked at her, wrinkling its forehead in confusion. The expression was almost human. For a split second, she thought her fire had done something to buy her a chance to escape.

Instead, its head rolled to one side and its body collapsed in front of her, blood pulsing from its neck. Darryn was standing behind the corpse, panting. She groaned in relief and he ran toward her.

"Darryn, Falryn and Harilyn, they are still -" He shushed her and wrapped her into his arms. Her shaking became severe and he stroked her hair.

"Graisor will tend to the others. You and I are going home right now." His eyes darted wildly over her body, checking her for any injuries as if he thought she would collapse at any moment.

He picked her up and strode forward. She buried her head into his neck, too spun up to think straight. Shouts from other knights reached her ears as they exited the forested area. She faintly heard Darryn giving commands and assuring everyone that the *sharvach* had been defeated.

At the mansion, he instructed Kapeyni to bathe Linneya and then disappeared. She barely felt the warmth of the water, barely smellt the luscious floral soap. After a long soak, she dressed in loose, flowing clothes and returned to the common room.

Darryn had returned, but he said nothing. He gruffly acknowledged her with a grunt, then made his way to the bathroom, stripping off blood-soaked clothing. He shut the door with a sharp click and Linneya meandered to the bookcase in search of an escape.

She settled in with a book in front of the fireplace, but struggled to focus on the words. Johann's face kept coming into her mind. It was odd, so much had happened at the festival but his curiosity around her family was what stuck. She sat down and began writing a letter to Aiden, updating him on the rogue shadowlands creature, among other things.

Darryn sauntered out of the bathroom with only a towel wrapped around his waist. He walked up to her and leaned over. "What are you writing?"

She sighed. "A letter to my brother. I will probably try Eleanor again as well, even though she has never written."

He pulled her wet hair away from her neck and kissed behind her ear. "I am glad you are okay. When I saw your flame affinity, I was so proud. Then, I was horrified when I realized the monster was not phased."

She chuckled. "I was horrified as well." She laid down her pen and turned to him, placing a hand on his stubbled cheek. "It worries me. Why was a *sharvach* on Enthorian lands? Who brought it here?"

He shook his head and sighed. "I do not know. It does not bode well that we had no idea it was a possibility."

She put away the letter and stood, facing him. "Thank you for saving me. I would have been dead."

He shuddered and brushed his hands over her hips. "That is exactly why I want you training as much as possible. I know your family values peace and the healing light of the elements above all else, but that got your grandparents in trouble against King Shumor and I do not want you to suffer the same fate.

Her eyes narrowed and she stared at the crackling fire. "Why would you even bring that up? My family is ready to fight when necessary. It is you and King Birron that will not offer aid."

He huffed a laugh and ran his fingers through his hair. "I have no power here. No real power, anyway, and the king will not risk weakening his defenses on a whim. Rathen is so much closer to Serathor's borders. You need to trust that I know what I am talking about, Linneya."

Her lips pursed together and she ground out, "What happens when King Shumor brings both dragons and those beasts?"

"Shumor will attack here first. He has no treaty with the *sharvach*. It will just be a few dragons and King Birron has the forces to hold him back."

"Then why did you suggest a northward training mission to Noryo?"

"There is cult activity increasing in the North. We would be going toward the shadowlands, not Aelor."

She clenched her jaw. "Aelor is my home. The least you can do is help me to get them support. Or go home with me. We can surely do some good together."

He smirked, stalking her like a predator as she backed up to the wall. "No, princess. Your home is here, with me. You seem to have forgotten the vows we took. We are family now. Just because you wish it was different does not mean you can change your mind."

The heat of his body muddled her mind. His citrus and cedar scent melted her resolve. Her breathing became shallow as he stepped so close that a deep breath would cause them to touch.

He leaned in and his voice tickled her ear. "Admit it. This marriage is not as bad as you had hoped it would be. My power sings to you, like yours sings to me. You may want to hate me, but your body is begging for my touch."

"Your power may call to me, but it does not make up for that tongue of yours, sir," she spat.

Growling, he placed one hand on the wall beside her head and the other around her waist. He drew her body close and pressed against her, their hips aligning and his lips brushing against her ear. "Do not underestimate what my tongue can do, Linneya."

Her core went molten and she moaned before she could control herself. Darryn hissed at the sound, wrapping both arms around her waist and burying his head against her neck. He moved down, kissing and nipping his way to her collarbone.

She shivered and he trailed his fingers underneath her top. They circled up her abdomen, his thumbs brushing the underside of her breasts. His breathing was ragged and she grasped at his arms, her nails digging into his muscles as his mouth explored. He ground his hips against her, evidence of his arousal pressing through the towel and adding friction to her sensitive areas. Linneya's knees went weak. He tightened his arms around her, keeping her from collapsing to the floor.

Just as she thought she would explode, he pulled back. "I would have you beg for me, Linneya," he panted. In one motion, he licked up her collarbone and neck, retracing his earlier steps with his tongue.

"Oh, Darryn," She gasped and he froze.

Linneya ached at his stillness. She tapped his shoulder with her palm. "What is it?"

He lifted his face to look her in the eyes and his voice lowered dangerously. "Say my name again - just like that."

Linneya shuddered, running her fingers into his hair. "Darryn..."

He devoured her with a bruising kiss. Her lips parted and he swept his tongue inside of her mouth. She moaned and he swallowed it, smiling through their kisses.

Between her legs ached with the urge to press against him. She rubbed her thighs together, desperate for any sensation to relieve the throbbing. His hands inched higher on her torso, one hand claiming her breast and the other pressing her to him.

She nudged at his towel, signaling for him to let it drop to the floor. The motion made him back away, panting. Frown lines formed between his eyebrows and he gave her a sad smile.

She grasped at his arms, pulling him to her, but he resisted. The lust had cleared from his eyes and he gently untangled himself from her.

"No, please..."

"I am sorry. You are going to be my undoing, Linneya." Darryn leaned down and planted a kiss on her forehead.

The excitement churning in her gut shifted from anticipation to hurt. Hurt became anger. She was upset with herself for being drawn in. He had made it clear that even though they were stuck in this marriage, he would not give in to these moments of frenzy.

She stepped away without another word. As she shut the door to her bedroom, she desperately tried to stack bricks around her heart again.

After all, they were just friends.

Linneya settled into a peaceful routine over the next few mooncycles. It was too cold to do much in the harsh conditions of midwinter, so they spent hours in the study with their friends. Some days were debates over plants and poisons. Other times they played charades or *Hajut*.

Falryn and Harilyn visited on occasion. Harilyn delighted in teaching them dirty phrases in the movement language. Falryn, Shailyn, and Linneya would hunch over old materia medicas, Linneya making notes on the healing properties Falryn mentioned that were not included in the texts.

Darryn left twice more on his mysterious trips. He only stayed gone a few days, but it left an aching vacuum in her chest each time. When he was home, he kept a respectful, albeit maddening, distance. On occasion, she would catch herself thinking the knight was looking at her with that gleam of wanting, but it was more likely the fireplace reflecting in his eyes.

Linneya frequently broached the subject of a spring trip to Aelor to await the battle with Serathor. Darryn mostly avoided the conversation, but on the occasions she cornered him, he dismissed her concerns with assurances that King Shumor would come to Enthor first. The rejection stung worse than his insistence that they only be good friends.

Her dreams became more vivid. One night, the assassin was under a bridge close to the entrance of a village. The musty smell of mildew and damp suggested *sharvach* were nearby. The town seemed to be on the border of the shadowlands. Clanging noises came from the watchtower, as if the bell had been damaged but no one wanted to - or could afford to - replace it.

A man stumbled out of the front gates, humming a jaunty tune. He had a bald head and rotund belly. His face held a pleasant expression, but that might have been from the ale. He staggered across the bridge and stopped in the road. The assassin crept forward, watching.

The man pivoted and tottered back before collapsing into a heap near the center of the bridge. The assassin groaned and peeked out from underneath the bridge. One of the town watchmen shouted at the drunkard, but the man was already asleep. The assassin slid down one of the supports and plopped to the ground.

For hours, the assassin sat, waiting. The rhythmic snores of the drunk man could have lulled a less vigilant person to sleep. The man stirred twice, but both times proved to be false alarms. He slept on the bridge as if it was a bed in a palace.

The musty stench grew stronger and the assassin sat up straighter, looking for the source. A *sharvach* approached the sleeping man and growled. It was a guttural sound that rattled anything living within several paces.

The man started awake, eyes wide. The *sharvach* crept forward as the man tried to scramble to his feet. The drunk began screeching for help, but the watchtower was silent. He lurched down the bridge and into the woods.

The wolf-like monster began to follow, but a howl stopped it in its tracks. The *sharvach* sniffed the air, its head swiveling around. The assassin dared to peek out at it, observing its movements. The *sharvach* dropped to all fours and ran into the opposite side of the treeline, away from the path of the drunk man. The rustling of the creature crashing through brush grew fainter until it dissolved into the background noise of night.

The assassin stood and stretched. He lumbered toward where the drunken man had disappeared into the forest. The loud whimpering of the portly fellow made it easy to locate him. The assassin stepped into the clearing where the man sat, trembling.

"Please, help me. The wolfman is coming to devour my soul! I am an elemental, I will give you anything - anything!"

The assassin leered. "Judgment has come, flame-talker. The *sharvach* is gone. I need your power to save the humans from the coming destruction."

He pulled out his knife and the drunk man vomited. The sour smell of ale and half digested bread burned through the clearing. The assassin slapped his head. "Is this any way to go out? You said you would give me anything. Kneel before me and allow your power to become part of a greater story."

"*Krehth* -hic- *aeki rae- rae-*" the man heaved again, spilling the contents of his stomach a second time.

The assassin rolled his eyes and slit the man's throat. Then he turned to look directly at her.

She sat up, disoriented and gasping for breath. The room was still dark and she could barely see to get out of bed. Linneya stood, needing to pace and burn off some of the urge to run outside and down the street. After a few moments, her breathing slowed. She grabbed a shawl and crept into the sitting area.

The fire was burning low, but still warm. She flopped into her favorite settee and stared at the embers. This dream had felt more personal. Her flame affinity had been part of her life as long as she could remember. Watching another flame-talker as their life was drained from their body left a pit in her stomach.

A click told her Darryn was emerging from his room. He was already fully dressed, a grim look on his face. He nodded when he saw her. "Princess, good morning. I have been summoned to Noryo's home. We are being dispatched for an assignment."

"You are leaving?" Her heart rate sped up.

He nodded. "Yes, tomorrow. I will lead the expedition. We are to meet with some of our fae allies as we move north. I must meet with the knightsmaster today in order to finalize details."

"So soon? How long will you be gone?"

Darryn grinned and playfully leaned toward her. "Why? Are you afraid you will be lonely without me?"

Linneya smiled sweetly, matching his jest and hiding the sinking feeling in her heart. "Not at all, sir. I am wondering how long I will have to enjoy the peace and quiet of the house before you return and disrupt everything again."

He threw his head back and laughed. "For you, Linneya, I hope it is sooner rather than later."

She stood, hugging herself. The thought of him leaving left an ache in her chest. It felt safe to have him close, but there was something more brewing underneath that she did not want to explore. She tried not to think of Falryn's admonitions to trust each other and live in the moment. "Where will you go?"

He ran his hands through his hair as he inspected his bookshelf, pulling out a couple of hefty titles. "We have to go into the shadowlands. My proposed training mission is now a reality. We received confirmation that a certain cult that worships the *sharvach* has recently appointed a notorious hunter as its head. They are moving toward the shadowlands in search of *sharvach* to join them. The fear is that they will begin harvesting elemental power under the ruse of a sacrifice to the creatures, but more likely the new head of the group will be keeping the gemstones for himself."

He stepped toward her and grasped the back of her neck to kiss her forehead. "Please be safe. I will return as soon as I can. Try to keep Shailyn out of any shenanigans and do not let Narruan think he has finally run me out of the house."

She nodded. Her smile could not quite reach her eyes as he finished pulling books off the shelf. As distant as he had been, at least having him close was a comfort. She dreaded him being away.

Kapeyni bustled in with a breakfast tray and a letter. Darryn dipped his chin to the maid and wished them both a pleasant day before slipping out, lugging a pile of tomes.

Linneya thanked Kapeyni and poured herself some tea while inspecting the memo. She turned it over to find Aiden's stamped signet and perked up. Her brother had not written in a couple of mooncycles, only gracing her with one letter after the deadwinter hunt.

The wax seal broke easily enough and she devoured his words. Her face fell as she read his account of the raid that destroyed some of the surrounding farmland. King Shumor had sent some scouts and a dragon. Half the fields would be unusable this coming spring.

His final request tore at her heart. *"Serathor is coming, though we are unsure as to how quickly the king will strike with his full force. Speak to Darryn and see what support he can rally. Father said not to bother you, but I hope we can see you both with an army at your back within a mooncycle."*

Linneya chewed on her lip and her shoulders sagged. Darryn would never let her go. He most certainly had no interest in rallying troops to the cause. He would forbid her to leave if she admitted this to him.

But, with him leaving, perhaps she could get away before anyone could raise the alarm. It might not be the same as having a full blown army, but her powers had grown and she might even be able to help with more than healing.

She rubbed her face and sighed. She had studied the maps and was confident in her escape route. As long as her knight was gone more than two weeks, she could be close enough to Loraen to stop him from catching her. Once she was in the caves at home, there would be no way he would find her.

Linneya sucked in a shaky breath. It is not as if she planned on abandoning him forever. She would return once the battle was over. Hopefully, he would find it in himself to forgive her.

This was it. She would betray her husband, but it would mean being in Aelor to heal those burned by Shumor's dragons.

She chose her path. Aelor needed her.

Chapter 22

Her stomach roiled from anxiety. The moment Darryn walked through that gate, she had a chance to get out. If he was not willing to take her back to Aelor, she would do it herself. Escaping would not be hard; it would be traveling undetected back to her home that would prove tricky.

The farewell party gathered near the front gates. King Birron was waving his arms around, talking animatedly with the knightmaster's inner circle. Darryn made eye contact with her and his lips quirked up, but the king said something else and he turned back to the meeting.

Graisor was huddled with Mariel and Straion. Mariel was handing Graisor some bakery items wrapped in brown paper. Straion was absentmindedly playing with one of her curls as she talked.

Trotyn and Shailyn were sniggering at some inside joke. Chrysa stood beside them, whispering to Trotyn's horse. The horse seemed to understand and nickered at her.

Darryn broke away from the knightmaster's circle, walked over, and said his goodbyes to their friend group. As he reached Linneya, he opened his mouth for a moment. Then, he shut it and wrapped his arms around her. She circled her hands around his waist, holding him close.

He leaned down, softly kissing her forehead. As he lingered there, she took a deep breath. The memory of his citrus and cedar scent would have to last her, possibly forever. Her heart shattered into a million pieces at the thought of leaving him - of turning her back on this home and all of their friends. Her tears spilled over.

Darryn brushed the wetness from her cheeks. Then he pressed his fingers gently under her chin, tilting her head to look into his eyes. "Linneya, I will be back before you know it."

She nodded and managed a quivering smile. He would never forgive her for this betrayal - but she could not think of that now. She had wanted to do this with him, but it was better this way.

He stepped away from her, grinning. "I will see you soon, princess." He strode back over to his horse, mounting him in one smooth motion. Darryn did not look back as the knights fell into formation. She stared after his fading figure as the group made their way through the gates.

As the last of the convoy disappeared around the bend, Linneya took a deep breath. Shailyn bounded up and grabbed her hand. "Chrysa and I are thinking about going to The Drowned Dragon for the afternoon. Incognito. Want to come?"

Chrysa groaned, clearly an unwilling participant in this scheme. Linneya chuckled. "I am not feeling up to it, but maybe Mariel and Straion will go with you?"

Straion nodded excitedly and Shailyn started debating him on the best ales. Mariel gave Linneya a long look, but did not comment. Linneya nodded, almost imperceptibly, and turned to walk home.

Once back in her room, Linneya locked her door. She placed a hand on her chest, willing her heart to slow to a more steady pace. All that she needed was enough to get to Aelor and get a message to Aiden that she would be hiding in the caves.

Linneya threw open her wardrobe and reached toward the back for her leather satchel. Now that the season was shifting from winter to spring, the nights were less harsh and she would not need as many furs. She tucked the dagger Darryn gave her into some clothing. She would take a few cooking supplies, but hunting and foraging on the way meant she could travel light.

The mooncycle-long journey home would be arduous, but she was confident this was her chance. With any luck, she would arrive before the battle. Her elemental powers had grown so strong that she was certain she could heal anyone who needed it. She might even use some of her training with Darryn to protect other life-tenders. Linneya chuckled at the thought.

A knock on the door caused her to jump. She darted around the bed, stuffing the satchel underneath a pile of pillows. "Come in."

Shailyn slipped into the room, her eyes scanning the wardrobe mess. Her shoulders slumped as she took in Linneya's disheveled appearance and heavy breathing. "You are leaving. You thought you could get away while we were out drinking." It was a statement, not a question.

Linneya pushed the stray strands of hair out of her eyes and sighed. "I have to. My family is in danger."

Shailyn sat on the bed and stared at the floor. "I thought you were beginning to see us as family."

The sting of shame twisted around Linneya's heart. She plopped down next to Shailyn, wrapping her into a hug. Then she pulled back, studying her sister-in-law's face. "You know I see you as part of my family, but your brother refuses to help me protect my Aelorian family. I have to escape while I have the chance. Once the battle is over, I will come home and beg forgiveness from Darryn."

Tears welled up in Shailyn's eyes, shimmering like broken glass. "Do you love him?"

Linneya inclined her head, ignoring the heat of her blush. "We are friends. We have made vows. I will always do my best for him, but he took me from my people when they needed me the most. It is hard to fall in love with someone who does not respect your duties."

Shailyn shook her head. "How can you say that you are just friends? I have seen how he looks at you, how you look at each other. Are you telling me that is not love?"

Linneya took a deep breath and looked out the window. "Your brother is a good man, but this is much more complicated. Imagine if someone forced you to leave him, knowing you were the only person who could save him. Then refused to let you go back, all because of an archaic law. No treaty or legal loophole should ever be so powerful it stops someone from doing the right thing."

"But surely there is time to talk to him."

"No, I am done talking. I wanted him to come with me. This would not be such an ordeal if he had just listened." She grabbed Aiden's letter and handed it to the woman.

Shailyn was quiet for several minutes, reading. Linneya resumed packing, hoping she would at least let her go without raising the alarm. To her surprise, her sister-in-law folded the letter and sighed in defeat. "Okay, let me smuggle you some food. I will be back in ten minutes and then we can sneak you out of the side gate."

Linneya blinked. "You are going to help me?"

She grinned and skipped to the door. She opened it and leaned back toward Linneya. "If my brother needed saving, I would expect the same support from you. You rummaging in the kitchens so soon after Darryn's departure might raise alarm. I go and grab snacks all the time. Cook will not notice me. Lock the door until I return so no one else stumbles in on you packing."

The door clicked shut behind Shailyn and Linneya turned the key. A small smile tugged at the edges of her mouth. She hoped that Darryn could forgive her after all of this. Maybe Shailyn would be an ally in that fight. For now, Linneya was grateful that his sister seemed to understand.

A quiet knock signaled she was back. Linneya rotated the lock, letting her back in. Shailyn grinned and held out a satchel. "Here, take this and let us get dressed to go out. We will leave through the front door."

"The front?" Linneya's stomach churned at the thought of being caught by Darryn's guards.

Shailyn nodded. "Again, the two of us walking out with a couple of knapsacks will not be as suspicious as you sneaking out the back of the house loaded in supplies. Leave a note for Kapeyni. Tell her we are going out drinking and you are not sure when we will be back. I will spend the night with Mariel and Straion and buy you some more time."

Linneya would have been impressed by this level of scheming if she was not apprehensive about getting caught. Still, it seemed like the best plan so far. Being with Shailyn would lower anyone's suspicions. She went to the desk to scribble a note for her maid. Once she was done she straightened up and grabbed her knapsack.

Shailyn hoisted the food bag over her shoulder. "Okay, time to go."

They peeked into the hallway. No one was around. Linneya's heart was pounding again, but this time it felt more exciting than anxious. Shailyn looked back at her and grinned, motioning for Linneya to follow. They made it down the steps and into the front hallway.

"My Lady, where are you going?" Linneya froze as Kapeyni scurried toward them, her arms full of linens.

"Oh, Kapeyni, so glad we caught you." Shailyn's voice was smooth and her facial expression innocent. "We are headed to Mariel and Straion's for the night. There's a tavern near their home that stays open well past moonwake. Thought we would take a change of clothes and spend the night in their guestroom. Lia left you a note in her room."

Linneya tried to maintain an innocent expression as Kapeyni narrowed her eyes and inspected her. Dread crawled through her chest, but she did her best to keep her body language neutral. She did not want to risk losing this opportunity to return to Aelor.

The maid pursed her lips and sighed. "All right. Well, if you are going together then you can keep each other out of trouble." She wagged her finger at Shailyn. "Do whatever My Lady tells you and remember who you represent! Do not cause more trouble for Sir Darryn!"

Shailyn and Linneya nodded and strolled out the front door as if they had no cares in the world. Linneya's breath came faster. Shailyn started giggling but clamped her mouth shut. Linneya's lips turned up and she did not dare to look at Shailyn until they were out of sight of the mansion.

They rounded the corner and collapsed in a pile of mirth. Linneya gasped and Shailyn wiped tears from her eyes. A man walking his dog eyed them suspiciously and hurried past. His wariness kept them laughing for several more minutes.

They finally picked up and continued on, one or the other chuckling randomly as they went. Shailyn motioned them down an alley and across a private patio. Linneya did not recognize any of the nearby buildings. "Where are we headed? I do not think I have been over to this area."

Shailyn gestured to the west. "I know of a side gate that is rarely used. No one guards it because it leads into a cemetery. Luckily, I know a way out through one of the crypts. I picked a lock one time and found a secret passageway into the fields around the capital. It's how I stayed sane during that last annum before I became an adult and could get my own place. Of course, then he made me move into the guest house." She smirked. "Darryn is fond of playing the overprotective big brother."

Linneya's eyes bulged in shock. There was no way Darryn knew how much exploring Shailyn had done. He would be beside himself if he knew she had been sneaking out of the city. Still, it was impressive. Shailyn was resourceful, if not slightly insane.

Afternoon revelries were already in full swing. The smell of roasting dinner meat wafted through the air. Laughter and jolly music spilled out of a tavern. Merchant stalls were selling the last of their daily goods and closing up.

They passed by a hedge on the main thoroughfare, blocking an alley from view. Linneya caught a whiff of something unsavory that tugged at a memory. She almost stopped, but Shailyn grabbed her and pulled. "We have to keep going. The side gate is up ahead. You will want to be out of the city before nightfall." They turned down a narrower street and the sounds of merriment faded.

They both jumped at the sound of a gruff voice. "Who goes there?"

The women exchanged a wide-eyed look. Straion. Shailyn motioned for Linneya to hide. "If he sees you, our plan is ruined. Go!"

Linneya climbed into a wooden crate and shut the lid. The fishy scent embedded in the slats caused her to immediately regret the hiding place, but at least she could watch the interaction.

"Straion! Why are you here? I thought you all decided to do a night in."

The man chuckled and held up a cut of lamb in wax paper. "Mariel was craving a special dinner tonight, but Cook was busy preparing for Mariel's baking day, so I obliged. What are you doing headed in this direction?"

Shailyn rocked back on her heels and looked at the sky. "I was just out appreciating the returning warmth. Chrysa canceled on me but I was not ready to go home yet."

Straion waved her on. "Well, do not let me hold you up. I know you are happy to have a bit more freedom with Darryn away."

She groaned. "Please do not tell him you caught me out alone like this. I will never hear the end of it." He laughed and nodded, already heading in the direction of his house.

Shailyn watched him round the corner and ran over to where Linneya was hiding. "Hurry! If we leave now you will have a bit of daylight and can get further out before you have to make camp."

They got to the gate leading to the cemetery and Shailyn pushed it open. "See? Nothing. It's rusted and no one cares about this ancient site. The crypt is back here."

Rows upon rows of worn down, round stones marked the final resting place of so many. Purple vines crawled up tired looking obelisks. Linneya followed Shailyn through the eerily quiet plot.

They stopped at a stone building with a solid door. Shailyn unfastened a hairpin and began wiggling it into the lock. She bit the inside of her cheek as she fiddled with the mechanism. Eventually it clicked, the door ground open, and they stepped inside.

A dank stench filled Linneya's nostrils. Shailyn beckoned to her and turned the head of a carved animal. With a rumble, one of the walls slid back and revealed a gaping, dark entrance in the corner.

"Keep a hand on each wall and you will be able to walk straight. Follow the tunnel and then turn east once you are in the fields. It will take you back to the route that leads to Aelor. I will stall anyone who asks questions, but know it might not take long for them to realize you are missing." Shailyn yanked her into a hug "Just promise me you will come back! You are part of our family now."

Linneya squeezed her, then pulled back to grab her hands and look her in the eyes. "As soon as I know my family is safe, I will return. I have no intention of creating shame for Darryn or causing a rift between our nations. It's just, with Serathor threatening to attack, they need me there."

Shailyn nodded. "I understand. Please be careful. This is only one battle. I fear there will be many more and we will need you, sister."

Linneya's eyes burned with tears. She nodded and hugged Shailyn one more time before setting off down the passageway. Linneya did not dare look back; the thought of what she was leaving behind was too painful.

She descended into the darkness, a rumbling sound behind her indicating that Shailyn had closed the entrance. The crunch of her footsteps echoed in the silence of the tunnel. Inky black pressed down on her eyes and she stumbled forward. Her hands reached out to touch the walls, the cool dirt soft beneath her fingers.

Her stomach dropped as she thought about what Darryn's reaction would be when he discovered her missing. Would he rage? Would he vow to never speak to her again? She began shaking, the stress of everything adding to the suffocating void. Her steps stuttered in fear and the whirlwind of her mind conjured all manner of terrible possibilities.

Linneya groped blindly, straining to hear any sound over her now pounding heart. The damp ground and still air mixed into a dank, musty scent of old stone and mildewing leaves. Just as she began to feel she could go no further in the oppressive veil of pitch black, the tunnel sloped upward.

The suns were still high enough that a bit of light broke through as she neared the end of the passageway. A weight was lifted from her shoulders as she crawled through the thick brush hiding the tunnel entrance. She gasped as she crashed through and fell onto the forest floor. Turning away from the suns, she set off toward the main road.

Once she was on the thoroughfare, she pulled her cloak's hood up to shield her face. The city was faded in the distance and only a few travelers were heading into the capital. Her breath caught every time one passed, but no one paused long enough to recognize her.

She made it over the river bridge and breathed a sigh of relief, quickening her pace to get as far away as possible. After some time she slipped off the path, and entered a dense part of the forest. It took little time to find a clearing that felt hidden enough that she could camp without unwanted company. The trees were beginning to show small blue buds on their branches. The promise of renewed life and spring was in the air.

Linneya opened the satchel of food and chuckled. Shailyn had packed fresh vegetables and cake. There were a few loaves of crusty bread, some jerky, and some dried fruit that would be useful later in the journey, but the vegetables would have to be used soon.

Linneya chewed on her lip. If she could catch a hare, she could make stew. How hard could it be? After all, she had seen Aiden do it several times.

She reached into her largest satchel and rummaged for some twine. Her fingers brushed against the rough string and she grinned. She pulled it out and got to work, twisting and tying the string into a workable trap.

As it turned out, it was not a simple task. She grunted as she tried to tie knots into the precise order needed. After a couple of tries, her face lit up as she got the string into a shape that resembled Aiden's snares. Her heart fluttered at the thought of seeing her brother again soon.

She stood and began exploring the clearing. To set the trap, she needed a branch low to the ground but still far enough up that it would trigger when the hare stepped into it. Most trees in her direct line of view had no branches that fit the description.

Her brow furrowed and she continued to stalk around the area. She stopped short and grinned as she found a worlnutt tree with low-hanging branches. Some tracks and tufts of fur indicated a hare frequented the area. She set the trap and returned to her supplies.

Linneya sat down, facing the tree. She settled into complete stillness as she watched for the hare. A warm breeze brushed against her cheek, caressing her like a lover.

She sighed, remembering the brush of Darryn's lips on her forehead as he said farewell. Her stomach twisted in knots, thinking about how hurt he would be when he discovered her betrayal. She tilted her face toward the setting suns and leaned back, willing their warmth to burn away the thought. After all, if he had just listened to her to begin with, none of this would be necessary.

A rustling sound reminded her of her prey. Linneya sat up straight as she caught a flurry of movement in the corner of her eye. Her heart thundered in her ears as she watched a hare shuffling forward. She leaned in as if her movement could coax the animal into her trap.

It scurried around, nibbling on stalks of blue and purple grasses. Anticipation swelled in Linneya's chest as it bounded straight into the snare. The twine did not move.

Linneya groaned and the hare sat up, ears twitching at the sound. Her prey scurried back toward its den. She stood up and plodded forward, grumbling about tricky fastenings and frustrating traps.

Linneya retied the knots, double-checking as she went along. Her stomach growled in protest of her poor hunting skills. If it did not work this time, she would dig into the jerky and figure out some other stew tomorrow.

Almost as soon as she sat back down, the hare was back. It seemed hesitant to retrace its steps under the worlnutt branches. "Come on, come on," she muttered under her breath.

The insects had begun singing. *Murderessss.* Their hissing condemnations no longer shamed her. Instead, she was irritated. Angry, even.

She had killed and would kill again in defense of her family. Of her friends. Of... Darryn.

The thought of someone harming him made her blood boil. She would gladly kill to see him safe. An ache in her chest whispered its protest of her leaving him. She sighed and tried to focus on catching her dinner.

Finally, the hare skittered forward, catching itself in the trap. Its screams pierced the quiet of the forest and Linneya hurried to finish the job and silence it.

Pride welled up into her throat as she took the hare and cleaned it. Aiden would be pleased to know she had caught and prepared her dinner.

She gathered some sticks and kindling to make a fire, only taking enough to cook the hare and heat the stew. The small pieces were dry enough that they would burn clean. She grimaced at the thought of being caught by a search team because of the smoke.

The fire barely lasted long enough to get dinner ready. Darkness settled around her and Linneya became lost in the chorus of insects chirping their lullabies. Her eyelids drooped as the excitement of her escape began to wear off. Settling onto a patch of soft moss, she slipped into a dreamless sleep.

Chapter 23

She startled awake to the sound of something shuffling around her. Her breath caught and she stilled, trying to ascertain the danger.

A male voice barked, "She's awake!"

She sat up, brushing the hair out of her eyes. Linneya pushed back onto her knees, her eyes darting as she looked for a way out. A dozen armored men surrounded her campsite. Her stomach twisted into knots and her shoulders slumped.

The largest of them appeared to be in charge. He stepped forward, leering at her. "Well, well. Dinner may have been bland, but it looks like we have a tasty dessert, boys!" The men roared their approval.

The ringleader grabbed her wrist and wrenched her onto her feet. Linneya stumbled, falling headfirst into his armor. He wrapped his arm around her and pulled her close. Her eyes watered as his rancid breath bloomed on her face. Linneya struggled against him, but his arms tightened around her and held her in place. She broke out in a cold sweat as he made a show of sniffing her neck.

"Yes, this is a sweet little morsel. What luck!" The men jeered and the sound spurred their ringleader on. He picked her up and carried her back to where she had been sleeping. He tossed her on the moss and started wrestling with her pants. Her heart began beating wildly, all her training memories dried up, and she longed for the safety of the sparring ring.

She tucked her legs in, then kicked into his stomach. He hissed, doubling over. Several of those watching cackled at their companion's misfortune. He caught Linneya's ankle as she lashed out the second time. "I guess the bitch has some fight in her." The ringleader cackled as his men roared. Then he grabbed her hair, pulling her into a kneeling position. She was shaking, eyes darting around as if she would find someone to help. The man began to work the laces on his trousers with his free hand, the evidence of what he wanted to do to her staring her hard in the face.

Panic clouded her thoughts. She twisted away from him and began crawling toward her doused campfire. She reached the cold embers and plunged her hand into the ashes. Relief flooded her as she wiggled her hand deeper and felt the sting of still-hot cinders.

Her magic stirred at the closeness of the element and a crimson vapor wafted from her body. Grabbing a handful of ash, she flung the hot pieces into her attacker's face. Linneya's eyes widened as flames shot from her fingers.

The man screamed, swatting at the fire lapping at his face. Some of his friends jeered. Others shouted obscenities. No one seemed to care if the ringleader was alright.

Darkness stirred within her and purred its approval. Even in the midst of the danger, she stood a little taller. She raised her hands, the red smoke billowing. "That was your last and only warning. Leave now before I incinerate all of you."

A voice cut through the chaos "What is going on here?" A man stepped forward and the others fell silent. His drawling, almost dwarven accent suggested he was from the far edges of the Southern continent. The others went quiet, whispering to each other.

Linneya dropped her hand and gasped for air. The newcomer eyed her curiously and she lifted her chin to meet his gaze. The man was short and lean with olive skin and jet black hair. His bright red eyes nearly gleamed in the darkness. He had a hand on one hip and cocked his head, waiting for an answer. The edges of a tattoo peeked out from his shirt collar.

"I was attacked by these men, sir." The newcomer raised his eyebrows and looked at the ringleader. The other men began to back away, distancing themselves as if they were not responsible for her frightened state. He turned, eyeing the burned man. The ringleader glared back, still bent over from the pain emanating from his charred skin.

"You assaulted this woman?" The newcomer grabbed the ringleader by the hair. "Well?"

The ringleader groaned. "No, she attacked me! I was defending myself."

The man huffed a laugh and turned to Linneya. "I will not demand that you heal your assailant, but you will remain in our custody."

Chills danced up her spine. Escaping from these men might prove impossible and there was no time to lose. "Where are you taking me?"

"You are a flame-talker." He reached out his hand and she spat on it, scrambling backward for more ashes.

He smirked and wiped his hand on his trousers. "Fine, let us get down to business." He shoved the burned ringleader aside and lifted his hand *"Kwaesh aeki raewi."* Smoke crept from his fingers and the embers hissed angrily as water poured into the firepit. Her stomach dropped as he drowned her only weapon within reach.

"You have elemental power. No one will harm you, but you must come with us back to Serathor." He crouched beside her, brushing a strand of hair out of her eyes. "Our assignment is almost done, we will return to our home country soon. In the meantime, you will remain with us."

The blood drained from her face and she jerked back. These men were Serathanian scouts. "Why are you in Enthor? I do not believe King Birron would approve of your presence here."

The scouts roared with laughter. The mist-whisperer smirked. "What your king does not know will not hurt him. We are not here to interfere with his rule - yet. However, we are under orders from our king to bring any elementals we encounter back to our capital."

She shook her head and tried to arrange her features into a mask of innocence. "I do not have any elemental affinities. Please, sir, I am traveling to visit family.

He cocked an eyebrow at her ridiculous lie. "What do you call that display of flame-talking you just showed us?"

She was certain that if they determined she was a princess, their promises of safety would be rescinded. Her eyes darted around, trying to find an escape. "Flame-talking? No, that was just luck."

He smirked and unsheathed his sword. "Most with a flame affinity train for decades and cannot throw fire from smoldering, nearly dead embers. You are harboring some form of powerful magic. Elemental or not, you are coming with us. King Shumor can decide your fate."

Linneya opened her mouth to protest, but the mist-whisperer drew back his sword. A *thunk* reverberated through her skull as he struck her with the hilt. The man doubled, converged, and doubled again before Linneya's vision faded.

Sometime later, she awoke draped over a horse. The swaying motion of the horse's trot jostled her, adding to the dizzying effect of her head wound. Her stomach roiled and she clamped her mouth shut to keep from emptying her stomach.

The scouts were chattering. "The prophecy is simple enough. He said the seer told him that he who claims the power of the five elements will determine the fate of the dragon riders, and thus all humankind. The man has taken all five powers. He is the prophesied."

Linneya steadied her breathing and tried to remain still. If she escaped, maybe she could take important details to her father. Another piped up. "How can you be so sure? The prophecy also says the prophesied will be born of ash and flame. Aelor's rumored flame-talker is more powerful than our prophesied. What if they are the true heir to the five elements and we are doomed?"

"There is no point in debating it. It is a rumor. Aelor has never produced their fabled elemental. Besides, it was a single affinity. Not nearly the all powerful claim to the five. The Aelorians do not stand a chance. The dragons are ready and the prophesied has completed the Claiming. In another two mooncycles, their country will be a memory."

"You do not think he will want to experiment further with offering power to the dragons?"

Linneya wanted to cry out and curse the men for their threats against her people. Thin bile filled her mouth. No longer able to stop it, she emptied the contents of her stomach onto the ground.

The man behind her grunted. "She is awake, boys. Next subject." She heaved again and her consciousness faded as the scouts grumbled.

The next time Linneya woke up, someone had unceremoniously dumped her in the corner of a tent. The heat from the midday suns cooked the shelter, scorching her skin. Her lips were cracked and covered in sick. Her tongue stuck to the roof of her mouth. The sour stench of her sweat mixed with the stale, humid air and made her stomach turn like she had eaten spoiled meat.

She tried to brush her hair out of her face, but could not. She gasped in pain as she realized rope had her hands tied behind her back. It cut into her wrists, sending throbbing pain up her arms.

Her breath came in short pants and her vision constricted. The panic heated her further, making the situation feel even more dire. The scouts were taking her into the heart of danger and Aelor was doomed. Darryn would never know what had happened. Tears burned in her eyes and spilled over.

She heard voices outside the tent. They laughed as they passed by, jesting about some ongoing bet. These men would not think twice about destroying entire kingdoms. It made her shiver. The tent flap opened and Linneya sat up straighter.

A guard ducked into the space. He was tall with salt and pepper hair. His beard had not been trimmed in several weeks and it stuck out in all directions. The wild look in his eyes matched his unkempt appearance.

He was carrying a bowl and cup. "Eat," he grunted and untied her hands.

She grabbed the bowl, a soupy gruel, and slurped. The man stared at her chest and she decided to pry while he was distracted. Perhaps he could give details that would help if she could escape. "So, your king has declared he found the prophesied."

The man smirked. "Yes, the prophesied completed the Claiming a few days ago. He will lead us in the fight to unite the human realms. The lands will heal and all will be stronger once all humans submit to King Shumor's rule."

She scoffed and wiped her mouth. "You actually believe that? You believe that he will take care of you and allow all humans to thrive?"

He showed her the gemstones sewn into his gauntlets. "King Shumor sees our worth. We are scouts first, but he gave us free rein to hunt down any elementals we encounter. He kills them, encases their power in these stones, and awards them to us depending on our rank and achievements."

The blood drained from her face. Would this be her fate? Murdered on the spot and bled dry for some lecherous fool of a guard? Or would the king keep her alive for his wretched experiments?

She stuttered, wanting to keep him talking. "Well, but... There cannot be that many stones left. No new stones have been brought to our world for over five duocenturies."

The guard shook his head. "New stones are being transported through the dimensional rifts. Our prophesied is a world-walker. He brings us new vessels to hold the ever increasing amounts of power we offer him. King Shumor uses the stones for us, but he also trains his dragons to use the elemental forces."

Linneya's heart sank. If the prophesied was bringing in new gemstones, how would the murder of elementals ever be stopped? Even more so if Shumor was trying to arm his dragons with their magic. "World-walkers have not been seen on this planet for duocenturies. They are legends."

He leered. "The prophesied is legendary. Now hurry up with your meal. I need to get back to my post."

She sipped the water, racking her brain for a way to keep him here longer. How to keep him talking. "I - I need to relieve myself before you tie me back up."

The guard narrowed his eyes. "Hold it. You can go before we head out this evening."

She shook her head. "No, I need to go. I get terrible infections when I hold it too long. It could be deadly without the right medicine. Do you want to explain to your king how you lost a possible power source?"

The man grunted and stood. "Fine." He drew his sword. "Come with me and make it quick. Up. Move."

Linneya struggled to stand. Her head spun and she stumbled as the guard pushed her outside. She squinted in the light of the suns and strained to adjust to the bright outdoors.

She kept her head down, but made note of anything she could see. The layout of the camp, which way was east or west, the trees that looked thicker and might be growing near water. She noted where guards were posted and who seemed to be paying attention.

The guard prodded her in the back and pointed. "Go behind that bush. Quickly. I will join you if you are not back fast enough for my taste." He grinned and licked his lips, a not-so-subtle suggestion of what would happen.

Linneya cringed and hurried to go. As she came back around the bush, she quickly took in anything she could about the camp. When the guard turned back to her, she ducked her head and marched back to her confinement.

As he tied her back up, she took a deep breath. "Are we headed back to Serathor now?"

The guard chuckled. "No, we have one more mission. King Shumor wants us to take out a group of warriors who think that they are going to stop us from getting what we are owed. We have been dispatched to take out a company of Falorian knights who are meeting with their fae allies. Then you will meet your fate."

A company of Falorian knights meeting fae... Linneya trembled. Darryn was in danger. The shaking became uncontrollable. The guard stopped wrestling with the ropes around her wrist and looked her in the face. "Why do you care?"

She bit the inside of her cheek, willing her body to focus on stilling itself. "I do not. I just feel more nausea coming on. My head wound..." To sell the lie, she started heaving and the guard backed up.

He sneered and left her. Once she was alone, she allowed the tears to flow. The day progressed slowly. No one else entered the tent. She was alone until the suns began setting.

At that point, the mist-whisperer lifted the flap and walked inside. He had a bowl in one hand and Darryn's dagger in the other. He tossed the blade at her feet and squatted down in front of her. "Explain how you have Darryn Stormbringer's weapon."

She clamped her mouth shut and his scarlet eyes flashed with fiery anger. He leaned in close, fury coating his rough tone. "How do you have this dagger? Who are you?"

She met his glare with defiant energy. He sighed and set the bowl in front of her before untying her hands. "Fine, do not explain how you ended up here, Princess Linneya. Darryn will be furious to return home and find his wife missing."

She narrowed her eyes and busied herself by sipping on the gruel. Slimy lumps slid down her throat and she almost gagged. How did this man have knowledge of her relationship with Darryn? Why did he name him Stormbringer? The title stirred something, a tug in her mind.

As if he could read her thoughts, the mist-whisperer sighed. "I am Raithor. You must not tell anyone, but I have sworn fealty to Darryn. Therefore, I am oath-bound to serve you as well." He placed his hand on her forearm. "If you tell me what your plan is, maybe I can help you."

Linneya pursed her lips. The guard seemed genuine, but Darryn had never mentioned this man. Was it a ruse? His gauntlets glistened with more stones than any other scout she had seen so far.

Raithor shook his head and lowered his voice to a whisper. "I understand your hesitation. Listen closely. I have ordered us to stall for another day and a half under the ruse that it will be easier to attack Darryn's company close to the Raelin crags. Tonight, during second sleep, you will have a chance to escape. The guards are always lackadaisical after moonrest. Dig out the back of your tent and run straight west." He pointed to the side of the tent. "That direction. It will take you back to the road. Follow it back toward Rathen. Hopefully you can warn Darryn before it is too late."

She just stared. Even if she could get free, she had already lost a day of travel back to Aelor. Darryn and his company would be with powerful fae. They would not need her warning. At least, she hoped they would not. Her stomach twisted at the impossible dilemma.

Raithor tied her back up, not quite as tight as before. "Remember, My Lady, you are no ordinary human. Use your powers." He winked and left her alone with her thoughts.

The suns set. Linneya was determined to leave sooner than Raithor had suggested. She listened for the shuffling sounds of the guards on duty. A pair of the scouts passed by at regular intervals. She steadied her breathing and counted how many times she would take a breath in between hearing their footsteps. It stayed consistent.

Finally, the murmurs of conversation and the crackling of the fire died down. First sleep meant at least some of the scouts would be getting rest. Once their bonfire was smothered, she began her escape.

She focused her power, honing in on the sensation of the rope cutting into her wrists. As much as she wanted to practice bringing forth her elements without speaking, time was of the essence and fear was diluting her effectiveness. Given the circumstances, surely Falryn would forgive her.

"Krehth aeki raewi." She murmured the enchantment, calling flame to her. Slowly, her fingertips began to tingle with warmth and a thin line of red vapor curled around her waist. The smell of burning rope scorched her nostrils.

Her hands broke free and she grinned, panting with the effort of concentrating her affinity through the thick fear. The tent flap rustled and she shut her eyes, trying to regulate her breathing. She snored lightly, hoping she would appear asleep.

The guard shuffled toward her, grunting. He knelt down in front of her, breath stinking of rot and ale. The man grabbed at her front and she snapped her eyes open. "Let go of me!"

She pushed back at him and he laughed. "Hold still, you bitch." He snarled and ripped her tunic. She clawed at his face and he wrapped his hands around her throat. Her vision blurred as he squeezed, cutting off her airway. A surge of wild energy coursed through her veins and everything became crystal clear.

Linneya locked her gaze on the man and grinned wickedly, calling on her mist affinity to fill his lungs with water. The guard's eyes went wide and he began to gurgle, clawing at his neck. She sucked in a breath as he released her. Her lungs burned, but she concentrated on the silent enchantments that would bring forth her mist element.

Green smoke billowed and water began spewing out of his mouth and nose. His lips turned blue and his eyes bloodshot. He convulsed against the internal tide before collapsing. She checked his heartbeat. He was gone.

No time was left. She could not count breaths in between guards and try to strategically escape. Someone was likely to realize the man was missing, sooner than later. Crouching down, she began to dig into the soil at the back of the tent.

The dirt moved out of her way, almost as if it was digging itself. Within moments, a hole opened up large enough for her to fit through. Belly first, she pulled herself underneath the tent's canvas and scrambled to her feet. She stumbled toward the woods, but heard two men coming. One was laughing as if their actions were not threatening most of the human realms.

Linneya saw red. She picked up a rock and whirled around. She jumped back into the path as Raithor and another guard stepped near her tent to inspect the hole.

The two men stopped. Raithor was grinning at her, as if he was proud. The other man snarled and reached for his sword. Before he could draw the weapon, she charged and bashed his head with a rock. He crumpled and she turned to Raithor.

The man chuckled. "Well done, princess. Go before someone else finds us. I will finish him off for you and stall any search."

She panted, staring at him wild eyed for a few moments before running. Brambles tore at her tunic. Sharp stones sliced through her shoes. More than once, a tree root tripped her. The mossy, resinous scent of the forest did little to soothe the panic.

Linneya ran until the surge of wild energy drained from her body. Then she collapsed, shaking and crying. Her legs burned, her wrists ached, and the only comfort she had was that she had managed to fight her way out. The world spun.

As the wave of emotions settled, she stilled and listened for any signs of pursuit. No one seemed to be following. Perhaps Raithor was on their side after all.

She could not tell which direction she was going. She took some deep breaths and looked up into the night's sky, searching for Zhaifa, the Arduin goddess of war. She always pointed north. With her direction, Linneya could head west, toward Aelor.

She oriented to the stars and turned, planting her feet toward her parent's country. Something tugged in her head and she hesitated. Darryn needed her. All of Serathor's scouts had gemstones on their gauntlets - they would be a formidable foe. Graisor, Trotyn, all of the Falorian knights deserved to be warned.

Her husband would likely lock her up and throw away the key once he found out what she had done.

The decision to choose him would almost certainly doom her family. It might possibly doom all of Aelor.

But the tug was too strong. She turned around and set her path back toward home. Toward Darryn.

Chapter 24

Pink dawnlight broke through the trees. Linneya had found the road, gotten a bit of sleep, then traveled parallel to the path while hidden in the brush. The pattering sound of hooves and rumbling of muffled conversation suggested she was close. She dashed toward the road, preparing to jump out, stop the convoy, and demand to speak to Darryn.

Her breath caught as the first of the soldiers came into sight. The banner was not the Falorian knights' insignia. *What if it is the scouts again?* The hair on her arms raised at the thought. She scrambled to move into the brush, hiding from the passersby.

As they drew close, she shivered from nervousness. Their glimmering uniforms and pointed ears told her all she needed to know: these soldiers were fae. Most had straight platinum hair, as white as the winter snow. A few hailed from further west and had rich brown curls from merfolk ancestors.

The curves of their swords reminded Linneya of a harvesting scythe. Their armor was lighter and less clunky compared to humans. As a child,

Aiden had been obsessed by their metallurgy. He spent hours reciting random facts about fae weaponry and protective gear. The fae blacksmiths dusted powdered dragonglass onto their armor as it began to cool. Their rituals guaranteed that the dragonglass protected against Creators-blessed powers. It also made for an impressive sight.

She hesitated. Unless the Falorian banners were being flown, she did not want to make her presence known. The first group of soldiers passed, but more came into view. Her heart leapt into her throat as the gold and red colors of the Knights of Falorian came into view.

Then they were passing by. Graisor. Trotyn. This was Darryn's unit. She stumbled into the road, flailing her arms. "Stop, please! I need to speak with Sir Darryn! Help!"

A few startled shouts came from the knights and she was encircled by steel and hooves. She held her hands up and tried to control her breathing. "Please- I just- Darryn, I need to talk with him."

A voice barked something and the men parted as her knight rode up. "Who is calling for me?" He looked down and his eyes grew wide, "Linneya?"

Relief flooded her. Panting, she stepped forward, grabbing the reins and mane of his mount. "Darryn, they are coming. They are going to ambush you as you begin to pass between the Raelin crags. They have stones! They all have stones."

His eyebrows knitted together as she spoke. "Who, love?" He slid off his horse and eased toward her. The other knights began murmuring to each other, their horses growing restless from sensing their masters' unease.

"Serathor has scouts that are headed this way. They captured me and were bragging about the ambush they have planned. They all have stolen elemental power and have orders to target your unit."

Darryn clenched his jaw and looked her up and down. The familiarity of his intense gaze settled something in her. Then, she realized she was standing in the midst of a group of soldiers, the shreds of her tunic barely holding together. The scouts' attempts to touch her, to violate her came flooding back. She blushed and tried to cover herself with her arms. He turned and rummaged through his saddlebags.

"They captured you?" He ground out while pulling out a cape. "What do you mean they captured you? Has the city been attacked? Is Shailyn alright?" He draped the light cape over her shoulders and she pulled it close.

Linneya gaped, flushing. "The city is fine, Shailyn is fine, it was just me. That is not important right now. You and your men are in danger of an attack. Darryn, all of these men had elemental powers. I think most of them were hunters. It's too dangerous. You must avoid this fight."

He ran his hand through his hair and his brow furrowed. "The Raelin crags, you say?" She nodded, chewing on her lip.

The sound of approaching hooves caused Darryn to turn. Some of the fae had made their way back toward the Falorian unit. One of them dismounted and stepped forward, two attendants flanking him. "Darryn, what is the meaning of this?"

Darryn clapped his hand on the fae's shoulder. "Linneya, this is Tiuthan, Prince of Bachael. He has been working with us to track down this shadow cult. Tiuthan, this is my wife, Princess Linneya."

She looked up at the newcomer. His tall, slender frame was muscular but he moved with the grace of a dancer. Even in his armor, he exuded an aethereal quality that suggested his immortality. His hair was unusual for the fae. It reminded her of Eleanor's, icy blonde with curls. The only sign of his age was in his eyes. They were dark gray and held the secrets of dozens of lifetimes.

The fae bowed and kissed her hand. "Princess, it is wonderful to finally meet the woman who has tamed this beast." He grinned. Linneya managed a forced smile that probably looked more like a grimace.

Darryn cuffed Tiuthan's shoulder. "She has been telling me there is a chance of an ambush up ahead." Linneya watched them, hopeful that the fae would take her warning seriously.

Tiuthan narrowed his eyes and looked toward the crags. "It is a notorious spot, but we have received no warnings from the other unit." He motioned to his attendants. "Syrtho, Jcanor send scouts ahead and let us see what we are riding into." They bowed and turned to leave.

Linneya's eyes followed the scouts, but a burning sensation told her Darryn was still eyeing her. He placed a hand on her lower back. "Linneya, come with me. We need to talk." He motioned for her to follow as he trudged into the woods.

They walked a few paces off the road. Darryn stopped in a clearing, He crossed his arms. "Why are you here and not back in Rathen? You look like you have been tied up for days, but we have barely left the city. What happened?"

She chewed on her lip. Her focus had been on warning him and she did not know how to explain her escape attempt. Heat crept up her cheeks and she looked up at a bird that was fussing in a tree.

Darryn stepped toward her and his eyes darkened. "I need to know. Who did this to you? How did they get you out of the city?" His voice was rough with the threat of violence. "I will hunt them down."

She hugged herself and shook her head. "I - I left of my own accord. The scouts came across me after I made camp."

His eyes went wide and he studied her with a hard stare. The dread gathered in Linneya's stomach. The sky darkened as first the second sun, then the main sun vanished behind clouds. Wind whipped around them both and the scent of an incoming storm permeated the air.

Darryn snarled and gripped her upper arm, squeezing tight. "You cannot leave. You are too important. I will not allow it."

Linneya braced against his words. His hand kept a vice grip on her arm, she was certain she would bruise. Of course he saw her as important, a prized fighter in the upcoming war against Serathor. He would never allow her to leave Rathen.

She sucked in a deep breath. She knew this would happen when she chose to return. It was time to face the consequences.

Rumbling sounds signaled thunder was growing closer. The birds overhead began screeching as if the tension between the two of them was unsettling the entire forest. She stepped toward him and he stiffened.

"Linneya, I need you to -" Darryn stopped mid sentence and raised his eyes to the trees. Linneya began listening to the avian cries. The tones were odd. They were reminiscent of the song Darryn whistled in the Loraen woods the first time she spoke with him.

She tugged on his arm. "Are the birds - " she glanced back at the covey growing nearby. "Are they talking to us?"

He grabbed her wrist. "Yes. Your scouts are here. The storm hid their advance. We have to get back to the others. Now." He started pulling her back through the brush.

Her eyes widened as they staggered through the forest. Shouting from the road suggested they were too late. He whipped around and pressed a kiss to her forehead. Leaning down, he brought his hand to her cheek and hissed through his teeth. "Hide, Linneya. I will come find you once things are safe."

Without waiting for her reply, he took off toward the sound of clanging metal and war cries. Once he was out of sight, Linneya crept toward the edge of the woods. A heavy rain began falling. She found a place under some brush where she could see some of the soldiers fighting against the Serathanian scouts.

The scouts were almost hidden from the amount of elemental smoke they produced. Most of them wielded more than one affinity and a rainbow of colors billowed across the field. Linneya wondered how many elementals they had murdered to create such a show of force.

The Falorian knights and the fae soldiers fought against the onslaught of power. Many of Darryn's men harbored more than one affinity themselves. All five elements swirled, the thunderstorm adding a chaotic element to the fight.

Graisor funneled the rain into bursts of water, aiming them at the scouts' faces to disorient them as he struck them down. Trotyn was conjuring flame into the rain and superheating it into steam, burning any scout that came within a few paces. Linneya struggled to understand what the fae prince, Tiuthan, was doing to make the scouts' weapons disappear. His dark smoke was formless, almost as if shadows devoured the light around him.

A tangy metallic stench from shed blood clashed with the petrichor. Singed tunics and flesh added an acrid note. Linneya's head spun as she witnessed a taste of the violence King Shumor threatened to release on the rest of the human realms. She pulled the cloak tight and steadied her breathing.

Darryn struck with such force, it made her blood heat. He called the trees to grow branches and wrap them around the scouts' torsos, holding the men in place while he swiftly sliced through their necks. Occasionally he closed his fist toward a charging scout, removing all air from their lungs, and they would drop dead within seconds.

A crack blasted nearby, lightning illuminating the fight with an aethereal glow. A scout turned the ground into a pitted graveyard, opening up holes and trapping his opponents up to the waist. Others were less creative, using their powers to shoot elements as they attacked. Spurts of emerald, crimson, ochre... the elemental vapors spiraled across the field.

One scout blocked Darryn's vine affinity and advanced forward. With a flick of the scout's wrist, a gust of wind knocked Darryn's sword out of his hand. Linneya gritted her teeth, terrified. Darryn charged forward, seemingly unaffected, and grabbed a fistful of the man's hair.

The scout cackled and threw an uppercut to Darryn's jaw. Linneya screamed, but the sound was lost amidst the thunder and shouting. Darryn recovered and grabbed the man's head, pressing his thumbs in the bottom of the scout's eye sockets. The scout fell to the ground.

Her stomach turned and her heart beat faster as the scout's eyes began to bulge outward. Darryn grinned, a bloodthirsty leer, as his arms strained to keep the man from standing. The scout's arms flailed until her knight called vines to wrap around him and hold him in place. The man's face was contorted in pain and Linneya held her breath. With a final scooping motion, Darryn forced the eyes out of their sockets. Then, he picked up his sword and decapitated the man.

Linneya released her breath and grinned. Darryn's brutal nature awakened something feral in her. She only wished he would bring that bloodlust with her to face Serathor with her family.

The rest of the battle was looking grim. The scouts outnumbered Darryn's fighters and boasted far more elemental power. A howling screech came from Trotyn as a scout burned his face. He collapsed to the ground, but was saved by a fae who tossed a small axe in the back of the scout. Other fae and Falorian knights were falling under the overwhelming force of stolen elemental affinity wielded by Serathor's scouts.

Linneya clenched her fists and let out a shaky breath. Her tongue was stuck to the roof of her dry mouth. A pit in her stomach urged her to jump into the battle, but she had no weapons and no armor. Maybe she could at least use her powers from here to disorient a few scouts.

She called flame to her through silent enchantments, focusing on the warmth of fire it would bring. Tendrils of her brick red smoke wove through her fingers. Tiuthan was fighting three scouts that were re-conjuring their weapons every time he made them disappear. The fae prince was breathing heavy, cringing every time he failed to block a blow. His armor was failing at the seams and a crack in the breastplate gaped open as if it was screaming he would be the next to die.

She pointed her hand at the most aggressive scout attacking Tiuthan. His tunic began to smoulder and he twisted in surprise. Tiuthan struck him down and Linneya refocused on the second scout. This time, she funneled the flame element into his sword handle. It glowed molten red and, after taking a moment to realize what was happening, the scout bellowed and dropped his weapon. Tiuthan dispatched that scout and quickly finished off the third. Once they were slain, he twisted about as if he was confused by the turn of events. Linneya smiled to herself and moved on to the next soldier in trouble.

A few minutes later, Graisor shouted as a scout with shock-white hair opened up a hole in the ground underneath Darryn, trapping his legs into the soil. Graisor charged forward, but another scout caught him with vines, growing manacles around his ankles and wrists. A few other scouts encircled the area, stopping others from approaching.

The man with white hair pressed his sword into an open spot of Darryn's armor. He cut into his back, torturing him by slowly slicing through muscle and sinew. Darryn's face drained of color and his breathing became labored. His eyes flicked to the spot where Linneya was hiding and a small smile crept across his lips, as if he could feel her watching. Then his entire body went limp.

Linneya began shaking and her vision went blurry. Without thinking, she crawled out from under the brush, yanking the cloak when it got stuck on a branch. She faced the battlefield and started to recite the amplification enchantment Falryn taught her. *"Krehth pfee."* The wind whipped around her and white-hot lava swept through her veins. Crimson smoke billowed. She raised her arms and focused on the scout that was torturing Darryn, imagining his mind boiling in its own juices.

The man began to convulse. His knees hit the ground and he fell forward, knocking his head on a rock. Linneya breathed a sigh of relief, refocusing on the other scouts to determine who would be next.

Her breath was knocked out of her as she was tackled by a scout and thrown into a boulder. The man began choking her and she scratched at his eyes, willing her flame element to burn his skin. But, the shock of being hit had severed her connection to her powers and nothing happened.

The scout leaned in close and chuckled, his breath a cloying stench. As the edges of her vision went black, the hilt of a sword thunked into the man's skull. He fell to the side, revealing the fae prince standing behind him. The scout made an odd squelching noise as Tiuthan stabbed him. Linneya doubled over, gasping for air.

The prince patted her on the shoulder once, then ran back toward Darryn. Other scouts had surrounded him and were kicking or slashing at his body. The rain had slowed, leaving bloody mud all around him.

She screamed in fury at the sight of his lifeless form. Nothing could stop it now. Lightning cracked through the sky and she reached up, willing the flame of the gods to empower her and end this. A burst of red light blinded her and the rushing in her ears grew so loud that it drowned out the sounds of battle.

A shockwave of heat blasted from her core. Fire spewed forth and consumed the entire area in the inferno. The force of her power knocked Linneya breathless and she surrendered to its strength. The final tendrils of her power shot forth and she collapsed, gasping for air.

A hush fell. The smell of ash and seared flesh singed her nostrils. She regained enough strength to lift her head and her jaw dropped.

Fae soldiers and Falorian knights stood amongst piles of incinerated corpses. The entirety of the Serathanian scouting force was gone. She was frozen and the men stared at her, gaping.

Graisor was the first to move. He ran to Darryn and began digging around his body. Linneya raced to his side. She dropped to her knees beside Darryn, clawing at his chest. "No, no, you cannot leave me here. Wake up!"

Darryn groaned and squinted. She threw her arms around his neck and sobbed with relief. He huffed a weak laugh. "Princess, I am fine. Just a little beat up."

Trotyn stumbled up, one side of his face blistered and peeling down to the bone. He and Graisor grabbed Darryn under the arms and pulled him out of the hole. Linneya followed the three of them toward the fae life-tenders. Some of the Falorian knights were ripping bejeweled gauntlets and belts from the bodies of the incinerated scouts and shoving the pieces into sacks. Others were pulling comrades out of rubble and tending to their wounds.

The healers were working as fast as they could, a soft glow of their combined light pulsing around their setup. Graisor and Trotyn deposited Darryn near one of the healers and started to walk off. Linneya ran after them. "Trotyn, wait. Let me see to your burn."

The man shook his head and tried to wave her off. The sickening wound sent a sympathetic pang down her spine. She ran up to him and grabbed his arm. "Stop. It is still fresh enough that it may not even scar."

Graisor raised his eyebrows, scrutinizing her. Trotyn scoffed and cringed through the pain, struggling to speak. "It will scar, My Lady. There is no way you can heal this severe of an injury."

Linneya did not answer him. Instead, she raised her hand and hovered above his face. A glowing light emanated from her palm. After a few seconds, the energy shifted. His skin knitted together and the blisters disappeared.

Graisor's jaw dropped. She removed her hand and nodded to Trotyn. Before either of the men could respond, she turned on her heel and went back to Darryn.

His wounds were bandaged and he was busy removing the saddle from Doshar. Tiuthan was standing beside him, fussing. "We have just started out on this journey. If our reports are true, the *sharvach* worshippers may have already secured an alliance with the leader."

Darryn clapped the fae prince's shoulder with his hand and nodded to the bags of armor and gems. "I must accompany my wife home. It will also give me a chance to secure these stones before someone else attempts to use them."

Tiuthan pursed his lips as he spied Linneya approaching. "We need to discuss this development further. Meet me at Mount Varsha when you are able."

Darryn grunted his agreement as the prince walked away. Linneya stepped around Doshar and touched Darryn's elbow. "You are taking me back to Rathen?"

He wrapped his arms around her, squeezing tight. "I cannot believe how close I came to losing you just now."

Linneya chuckled. "Losing me? You were the one halfway in the ground and passed out like a gravedigger quit halfway through your burial."

His laugh rumbled in his chest. "True. Still, I was worried when I realized how close to danger you were. From what the men have said, you proved your mettle on the battlefield today."

She sighed, pursing her lips. "Do not worry. Your prize fighter cannot find it in herself to leave for good. Your strategy is still in play and now you can brag to King Birron about how powerful my magic is."

He pulled back, just far enough to gently lift her chin and gaze into her eyes. "You know that is not what I meant, Linneya."

She could not meet his stare. "Yet, you keep me prisoner here. I want to help Enthor, but I also need to get to my family. King Shumor is finally making good on his threats. My people are in grave danger and you are risking their lives for your own sake."

He dropped his arms, clenching his jaw. "Your family is here." He growled and gestured toward the soldiers. "Your people are here. We can discuss this after you are safely back in Rathen."

Despite his dark tone, his movements were tender when he clasped his hands around her waist and helped her onto his horse. Her breath caught as his hand pressed into a sore spot on her side, but she managed to not cry out. He brought around a second horse with the jewels attached to the pack on its back. He kept its lead in one hand as he mounted behind her. With a click of his tongue, they turned and headed south, toward Enthor's capital.

As they settled into the journey, the fatigue began to set in. She leaned back on his armor. Even against the hard metal, Linneya felt safe. He pressed her close and occasionally squeezed her tighter.

The entire trip back to the capital, Darryn was silent. Despite their impending argument, Linneya struggled to ignore the shivers his touch sent down her spine. Somehow, in choosing to return to him, their connection had deepened.

Nonetheless, she dreaded the upcoming fight. Would he listen now that she had explicitly heard the scouts boast about conquering Aelor? Would he read Aiden's letter if she showed it to him? He might not even give her the time of day. Escaping the way she did might be a betrayal that ran too deep. Perhaps she chose him too late.

Her breaths came fast and shallow. Tears welled in her eyes. She blamed the bruise that bloomed on her side, unwilling to face the possibility that she had forever ruined her friendship with this man.

Darkness had fallen as they reached the bridge and the light of the capital city came into view. The warm glow illuminated the patchwork architecture of the city. Its ancient reminders of resilience and rebuilding sparked hope in Linneya's chest. Surely there was a way to defeat Serathor and keep everyone she held dear safe. Surely there was hope for her and Darryn.

Linneya's shoulders relaxed at the sight of the front gates. The last bit of her energy wore off and she slumped back onto his chest. She was barely aware of making it into the city. She jolted awake for a few moments when they stopped at Noryo's hut to deliver the jewels, but drifted off again until they made it to the mansion.

In the courtyard, Shailyn ran up to them. "Creators, I am so grateful to see the two of you!" She panted, one hand on her chest.

Darryn slid off Doshar and helped Linneya down. He turned to his sister, stone-faced. "My wife needs rest. We will discuss this later."

Linneya and Shailyn exchanged a glance. Linneya shook her head, hoping it would signal to Shailyn that she had not told Darryn of his sister's involvement in her escape. Shailyn seemed to understand and gave the most subtle nod.

Chapter 25

As they entered their home, Linneya stumbled. Darryn caught her, sweeping her up into his arms. She faintly heard the exclamations of the staff and his rumbling of orders to prepare food and draw a bath.

He carried her upstairs to their suite, then set her down on the futon and dragged over their favorite table. "Wait here." The room was spinning. Linneya groaned, closed her eyes, and drifted into a twilight.

The sound of knocking jolted her awake. Kapeyni entered with a couple of maids. The maids went to fill the bath and Kapeyni waved around a tray of soup and crusty bread. She plopped it down in front of Linneya, her jaw set as if she disapproved. Perhaps she suspected Linneya had escaped or maybe it was just seeing her lady in such disarray. The maid curtsied and left without a word.

Darryn returned, carrying a stack of parchment. He sat the papers down on his desk and spun to face her. Linneya cringed, waiting for his wrath.

Instead, he let out a long sigh and motioned for her to eat. Her stomach growled and she dug in, but she kept glancing at him and studying his reactions. He maintained his silence as he took off his armor, tossing the pieces into the armchair closest to the door.

Once the last gauntlet clunked onto the pile, Darryn pivoted toward her. He clenched and unclenched his fists and eyed her as if he did not know what to do next. Linneya set down her spoon and cleared her throat. "Will you eat something?"

He shook his head. "I will have food later. Eat."

"Nonsense, we fought a battle and then rode all afternoon. You need sustenance." She placed a slice of bread on a plate and motioned toward the soup tureen. He stepped toward the table and stood across from her. She reached out to set the bread in front of him, but winced in pain. The plate clattered as she dropped it back onto the table.

His face went pale and he darted to her side. "Are you injured?" He tried to lift her arm and she flinched again.

"I bruised my side when the scout tried to choke me and riding on a horse made it worse. It hurts, but I will be alright within a day or two."

His arms enveloped her in a warm, strong embrace. "I could never forgive myself if something happened to you."

Tears filled her eyes. He was supposed to be angry. She could handle wrath, but this cut her deeper. "Are you not upset with me?"

Darryn chuckled, his voice rough with emotion. "Oh, I am furious, but tonight you need rest. Do not worry, we will fight later." He stood and stepped toward his door. "I will be right back, I need to change." He ambled off to his room.

She nearly spit out her soup as he returned. He was rolling up the long sleeves of his v-necked shirt, laces undone. He cuffed them just below his elbow and ran his hands through his hair. As tired as she was, a warm sensation still grew between her legs. Lusting after her husband would be fine, except she was certain he would never want her now. She placed her spoon back in the bowl and rubbed her eyes. Being torn between him and her family was more work than she bargained for.

Darryn stepped in front of her. "We need to get you cleaned up so you can go to bed." He held out his hand and she took it, but wobbled as she stood. He caught her around the waist, carefully avoiding her bruise.

Linneya leaned into his strength, sighing as he walked her into the bathroom. The scent of rose and lavender with undertones of grounding incense struck her, reminiscent of the bath she had the morning of her wedding. It made her chuckle; Kapeyni knew she had run and was trying to remind her of her duties.

"Let me stay with you, you are exhausted and I do not want you to injure yourself more." He stroked her arm, leaving goosebumps behind.

She chewed on her bottom lip, eyes darting from him to the bath. She was fatigued, true, but she would be fine without him. Her knight kissed the top of her head and pulled back to meet her gaze.

He almost seemed to be asking for an invitation. As if he could sense her longing and matched it with his own. Surely not, her betrayal was still fresh.

After a moment, she took a deep breath. "Alright, I do not mind."

He grinned and pressed another kiss to her forehead, sending butterflies into her stomach. "Good. Shall I undress you, princess?" He leaned and whispered in her ear, his voice hoarse. "Your injured side may be my best friend this evening."

She bit back a smile and sighed, pretending to be defeated. "Yes, you will need to help me."

Darryn hummed his approval and set her down in a chair that had been placed beside the tub. He began working her laces loose, tugging gently at the knots. The ragged tunic was stiff, caked with blood and mud. Her body ached, but his touch muted the pain coursing through her.

He slowly lifted the tunic and let it drop to the ground. Her nipples pebbled in the cool air, but his eyes were trained on her injured stomach. He placed a hand gently on the bruise, sending a shiver across her abdomen. She wanted him to run his hands all over her, devouring her under his touch.

Instead, he drew back and unlaced her pants, helping her stand, and pulling them down over her hips. She had never been fully bared in front of a lover before. The urge to cover herself in shame was strong, but his eyes burned with an expression that empowered her.

He offered her his hand and led her to the tub. He helped her step down into the bath before taking off his shirt. Her eyes widened at the rippling of his muscles as he moved. His burn scars twisted as he turned to put his shirt on the chair. Somehow, they made him look all the more formidable.

She licked her lips as her eyes trailed lower to the straining evidence of his arousal. Half clothed, he stepped into the tub and settled on the opposite ledge. His eyes never left her frame; something like desire glimmered in the darkness of his pupils.

She sank further into the warm water as her muscles relaxed. "Thank you. This is perfect."

"After the day you have had, you deserve anything that can help you rest." He lathered up a small cloth before sliding into the seat next to her. Gently pulling her hair away from her back, he began running the rag across her shoulders.

She reached for the washcloth. "I can do it myself, Darryn."

His grip tightened, refusing to let go. "Let me do this. You are exhausted." She leaned back against him, sighing. His strength enveloped her as she drifted in and out of consciousness. His hands drifted over her curves, gently washing away the grime and stress of the past two days.

He poured warm water over her head and lathered shampoo. Heat dripped lower and the sensation made her rub her thighs together as his fingers massaged her scalp. Even fatigued, her body responded to his touch. Her knight awakened something within her. What had once smoldered now burned.

"Mmm, Darryn." She sighed. He growled as he pulled her close, his lips brushing her neck. Her core went molten and she let out a small moan, arching her back into the warmth of his chest. His arms tightened around her and his fingers traced circles on her arms. His responsiveness emboldened her.

She twisted to kiss his lips, but he placed his fingers on her mouth and shook his head. He stood up and offered her his hand.

"You are exhausted, Linneya. Let me get you to bed."

She blinked the tired from her eyes and the heat of embarrassment flooded her cheeks. Why did she keep falling into his arms? This man talked a big game about protecting her, but he had refused to help her protect her family. Even though she had chosen to save him, he did not want to save the people that she loved.

Harsh reality jolted her back to her senses. Throwing herself at this man would not change that she tried to escape. It could not erase nearly twelve mooncycles of distrust between them. She stood and ignored his proffered hand, stepping out of the tub.

A splash told her he followed. She reached for a towel, but he snatched it out of her hand. "Hold still," he muttered, rubbing her with the towel. The rough cloth sent tingles through her body.

She was too exhausted to maintain her anger, but tomorrow... tomorrow she would tell him why they were doomed...

The last thing she remembered was sinking into the cool sheets. Dreams of a silver mask and bloodshed enveloped her. She slept through the rest of the night and well past dawn.

The next morning, Linneya awoke with a start. She squinted against the disorienting, blinding light streaming in through the windows. The events of the past two days came flooding back and she jumped out of bed, gasping.

Her mind raced as she paced the floor. Her body was stiff from fighting, a dull ache begging her to get back in bed. She rubbed her face and looked around for the water pitcher Kapeyni usually left. She poured a glass and swirled some spicymint into it.

As that steeped, she stared out the window. She was glad she saved Darryn and the others, but what would this mean for Aelor?

If he could convince the Falorian knights to stand with her family, that would at least be something. Her shoulders sagged. It would be better if he would take her side and go directly to King Birron. Perhaps Aiden's plea would stir him to action.

Sipping on her tepid tea, her thoughts turned to Darryn's touch. Heat flooded her cheeks as she thought about the bath. Now she would have to apologize for throwing herself at him as well as running away. She cringed, irritation building and tamping down her embarrassment.

A cough from the common area told Linneya that Darryn would be at his desk. Last night he had been tender, but he was also angry and said they would fight later. Her darkness roared, ready to confront him. She balled her hands into fists, grabbed Aiden's letter, and stalked into their sitting room.

Darryn was already at their table, reading. Her darkness settled, even purred, as she observed him. She moved to put Aiden's note on a shelf, but could not help noticing the way her knight's shirt stretched over his muscles, straining against the cloth.

His brow furrowed and Linneya resisted the urge to walk to him and smooth out the lines. She smiled to herself. Last night almost did not feel real, and yet...

He looked up, closing his book and nodding to her. "Did you sleep well?"

"Yes, thank you."

He stood up and walked to the bookshelf, putting his book away and studying the other titles on the shelf. He stayed that way for too long, awkwardly avoiding making eye contact. "Good. To address your escape attempt, I will assign you a Falorian guard to make sure you are safe. You will still be allowed to go to Falryn's to train, stop by Mariel's place for a visit, and wander throughout the city as you please, but any efforts to go beyond the city walls will be immediately stopped." He picked another book out and stalked back to their table.

Linneya's stomach twisted as her jaw dropped and her anger came roaring back. "I will not be watched like a criminal, Darryn!"

He rounded on her, hissing through gritted teeth. "Then you should not have snuck out like one! Do you know how dangerous that was? It is a miracle you were not killed by those scouts!"

"I would suggest, after the way that ambush ended, I can hold my own against them."

"Fine. Maybe you can. But, what were you going to do when Enthor declared war on your home? Aelor would have had to answer for breaking the treaty."

A flush crept up Linneya's cheeks and she crossed her arms. "There is a cave system close to the palace. I am familiar with its layout and planned on hiding there. No one would know I was there until it was necessary."

Darryn huffed a laugh and stepped closer. "Even if that worked, you could not guarantee that King Birron would believe you were not being helped by your family. He does not take well to a noble defying the godking. He would have fought your family first, asked questions later."

She knew he was right, but she could not admit it to him. "I feel certain I could hold my own against the so-called *godking* if need be."

His lips curled into a snarl. "I thought we were a team. Did you even consider the consequences to me if my wife, the flame-talker who was under my care, was to disappear? If she was to defy King Birron and threaten him?" He ran his hands through his hair and studied her response.

Her shoulders sagged and she inspected the carpet, unable to look at him. "I know. I wrestled with it. I could not leave, not really. I came back the moment I heard you were in danger. My family needs me, though, and I am devastated. You talk about us being a team, but why are we not heading to help them together?"

He let out a long breath and wrapped his arms around her. "You saw what your powers did to those scouts. The best thing you can do is to continue training. Become unstoppable. Avenge any victims of Serathor by coming into your own."

She shivered. "What if he razes Aelor to the ground and there is nothing left to save? It would not be the first time."

Darryn shook his head. "King Birron will send troops to Aelor if it comes to that. For now, we must watch our Southern bays for signs of the Serathanian ships."

Tears burned in her eyes, threatening to betray her fury. "You do not understand. I need to speak with King Birron, he must send troops! Everyone keeps dismissing this, but I finally have confirmation." She thrust

Aiden's letter into his hands. "The scouts said their focus was to gather intelligence on Aelor. They will attack there first. They have trained dragons to use elemental powers. Aiden confirms it. A war will come to my family within two mooncycles."

Darryn's jaw dropped as he scanned Aiden's plea for support. "This makes no sense. Why would they target Aelor directly?"

Linneya's mouth was dry and she stepped away from him. "I already told you. Before I was born, my parents promised me to King Shumor's son. They rescinded the agreement when he destroyed my grandparent's kingdom. His pride was wounded and now his anger has festered into something more sinister. We must act before it is too late."

He shook his head. "They would have to march through Enthor to get to your parents' realm."

She crossed her arms and huffed. "No, Creators, do you ever listen? I told you, they have found a way through the fjords."

"The fjords are nearly impassable. Your father's soldiers would track anyone who was traveling that way uninvited. It would take dark magic that we have not seen in duocenturies..."

She nearly rolled her eyes. "What, like the kind of dark magic that the *sharvach* are rumored to hold?" The creatures would certainly have enchantments that could help hide invaders from the posted guards throughout the fjords.

Darryn sucked in a deep breath. "Of course. This is horrible." He placed Aiden's letter on their table and clenched his fists. "I am sorry I did not believe you sooner. I will go to our knightsmaster this afternoon and see what I can find out from him. King Birron will not act, but perhaps there are other options."

Linneya scoffed and hugged herself, angling her body away from him to hide her pain. "Thank you. Aelor may not be powerful, but my father will reward you for your loyalty."

He grimaced, then stepped toward her. "I do not do it for him or for the reward he might offer. I do it for you." He snaked his arms around her and pulled her to him. His citrus and cedar scent engulfed her and a familiar longing grew in her core. "Can you not feel what is between us, Lia?"

"After last night I thought there was something, but you rejected me." Linneya no longer cared if she sounded like she was pouting. Her heart beat a rhythm of urgency; she was unsure if it was from craving or despising him.

Darryn cupped her cheek with his hand and pressed his lips to her forehead. "Last night you were exhausted and needed sleep. Could you not see how desperate I was for your touch? I am so wrapped up in you. I do not know what I would do if you were gone."

She placed a hand on his chest and pushed, forcing him to take a step back. "I am tired of being your leftover baggage. We both know you are only making the best of your king's orders."

He shook his head and closed the distance again, her face in his hands. "How do you not understand this? I am sick of dancing around it. Whatever I do, I do it to protect you. The rest of the world is irrelevant. "

The knight growled and brushed his nose down her neck, causing her breath to catch. "King Birron's order gave me permission to pursue what I have wanted from the moment I first saw you in that courtyard."

"I want to keep you safe because you are *mine*, Linneya. Yesterday when you stumbled onto the road, bloodied and covered in dirt, I wanted to murder the person who did that to you. Can you find it within yourself to be on my side too?"

His breath became ragged as he searched her eyes for an answer. Linneya's hands ached with the urge to touch him, to soothe his worries. This man frustrated her with his stubbornness, but his devotion and care melted the ice she tried to keep around her heart. His power made her blood sing. His touch set her on fire, the flames turning her core molten.

She conceded to the feeling, stepping forward and running her fingers through his hair. His pupils flared and he crushed his lips to hers. She wrapped her arms around his neck, leaning into his warmth. His thumb slid over her mouth, nudging her to part her lips so he could taste her. Linneya obliged and he claimed her, his tongue expertly dipping in and out until she moaned from pleasure.

Darryn kissed down her neck, teasing and licking each spot. Her arms tingled as his hands brushed up to her shoulders. Linneya had never felt this strong of a connection to any lover. He tugged on the straps of her gown, pulling them down and leaving her chest bare. He pulled back, gazing at her like she was a gift sent from the Creators.

"I wanted to do this the first moment we were alone in the woods." His mouth grazed lower and she shivered.

"I would have let you." Linneya gripped Darryn's shirt, scrambling to touch bare skin. His growl vibrated through her chest as her nails grazed over his abs and she arched into him.

He dipped his head down and took one of her breasts into his mouth. Linneya gasped as he sucked and licked the peak of her nipple. Pulsing sensations radiated throughout her body with each caress. She snaked one hand around the back of his neck, holding him to her. Her touch spurred him on. He kneaded one breast as he expertly traced around her hip and squeezed low, where her upper thigh met her buttock.

Darryn picked her up and carried her to her bed. He set her on the edge of the mattress and she winced. He stepped back, panting. "Shit, Linneya, I am sorry. Do you want me to stop?"

She shook her head and bit her lip. "It's that muscle I bruised yesterday. Please, come back." She reached for him and he returned to her, gingerly gliding his fingertips over her arms. She shivered at his touch and leaned forward to kiss him.

He began again, dragging his eyes slowly over her bared curves and brushing his fingers through her hair. "I have thought of little else than your body against mine since the day I first saw you."

Linneya pulled his face to hers, nibbling on his bottom lip, and he groaned. She kissed across his cheek and brushed her lips against his ear. "Then do something about it, warrior."

His self control snapped and he growled his approval. He bruised her lips as if he was starved and her kiss could save him. They met each other with a longing that turned to flame and his fire scorched her everywhere they touched. He twisted her hair into his firm grasp and gently pulled, exposing her neck.

She pressed her thighs together to relieve the throbbing ache growing between her legs. Darryn marked the movement and slid one hand up her gown, squeezing just above her knee. She let her legs fall open in invitation.

He had once warned her he was dangerous for her. If he was her destruction, she would greet the realm of spirits with open arms. She laughed breathlessly and he pulled back. "What is it, love?"

"If this is the devastation you have kept threatening, I am angry at you for not following through sooner."

Darryn laughed and nuzzled her neck. His hand traced along the inside of her thighs, occasionally brushing higher. Each demanding stroke left a trail of warmth that spiraled up and coiled in her core. Her center ached, begging for him to relieve the pulsing sensation.

As if he read her mind, his hand slid up her thigh and rested over the area where she wanted him most. "Can I touch you, Linneya?"

She nodded and he buried his face into her neck. A shockwave of pleasure shot through her as he pressed his palm to her center. She moaned and he smiled against her. "Mmm, yes, this is where I belong." His mouth moved against her neck and her hips involuntarily bucked.

Linneya reached for his pants, eager to reciprocate, eager to feel him in her palms. He grabbed her hand and placed it against his chest while his other hand stroked the inside of her thighs, teasing. "We will have plenty of time for that later. I want you to understand how badly I have wanted you."

This man. They should have been fighting about how she betrayed him. She left, risking the king's ire against him and leaving no explanation. He could have tossed her aside for this. Instead, he was worshipping her. It made her tremble.

His hand trailed back up her thigh and around to her apex. Her entire body focused on the sensation of his fingers lazily tracing along the edge of her sensitive area. He ran one finger along her swollen, aching slit and chuckled.

"You are soaked, princess." He purred in her ear. Linneya went taut and weak, all at once. Slowly, he stroked up her center, each time stopping just short of where she needed him most. Waves of heat pulsed through her with each pass and she whimpered.

"What is it, Linneya? Tell me what you want." A wicked grin spread across his face as he watched her arch against him. All thoughts had flown from her head. She could not respond, so she pressed closer, physically urging him on.

He stopped all movement. She groaned in disappointment and tried to kiss his neck, but he pulled back. His voice darkened dangerously. "Tell me, *wife*. What. Do. You. Want."

"You, Darryn." Linneya gasped his name as if it was her tether to life itself.

"That's my girl." He dipped his head back down to worship her jawline as his thumb began making lazy circles against her sensitive bundle of nerves. She cried out, crumpling fistfuls of his shirt in her hands as her back arched.

He smiled against her neck and slipped one finger into her. A sensation of warmth spread through her core and she moaned, her hips bucking.

Darryn grunted his approval, nipping at her earlobe. His thumb continued to circle, his finger pumping in rhythm with her movements.

His mouth made its way down to her breasts. Her entire body tensed in pleasure as he bit down on her nipple and eased a second finger into her center. He pulled back to look at her as his fingers stretched her, adding to the building sensation. She clawed at him, desperate to have her body touch any part of him,

"Darryn, I -" Her inner muscles pulsed and she panted in rhythm with his hand. A tightening told her she was close. Her breath came in gasps. Her knight wrapped his arm around her and held her securely against him.

"Come for me, Linneya." His growl reverberated through her body and she exploded. He crushed his mouth to hers, swallowing her cries. He kept gentle pressure between her legs as she rode the waves of her pleasure.

She fell back onto the sheets, panting. One thing was for certain, she was ruined. This man had dug his way to her very soul. She would follow him to the ends of the known world.

He laid down and reached for her, gesturing for her to lay down on his chest. "Come here, love." She rolled over and propped her chin up on his arm, breathless. Small tingles of satisfaction still fluttered in her lower abdomen.

"Well, I am glad you finally decided to take me on." She smiled at him, glowing from the release.

He stroked her hair. "For you, dear Linneya, I would take on an entire army."

She sighed, resting her head on his shoulder. "I am not asking you to take on an entire army, dear warrior. I am begging you to convince King Birron to provide aid to Aelor. We should go back and help. Together. A team."

He kissed the top of her head and let out a breath. Linneya snuggled close, trying to not let the worries of the world ruin the moment. Darryn stayed silent for so long that she finally sat back up and turned to face him.

He was glaring at the ceiling and a muscle ticked in his jaw. "You are right. It is time to go see the king."

Chapter 26

The throne room was almost empty when they arrived. Incense still spilled from the censers, sunsbeams sparkled against the sandstone, but few people were in sight. The cavernous space seemed sparse without attendants and priests flocking about.

King Birron sat on his throne, his gigantic Matu sculpture looming behind him. He was dressed in a plain tunic and his beard was not braided, as if he had been in a hurry. The king looked up as Darryn and Linneya entered. He grinned and eagerly rubbed his hands together.

Queen Rhylanna stood beside the king, their baby in her arms. She was dressed in full regalia, as if this meeting was a state event. She inclined her head slightly as she made eye contact with Linneya.

She and Darryn reached the foot of the dais and bowed. King Birron shifted in his chair, curiously eyeing them. "Why have you called for an urgent meeting so early?" He frowned. "Darryn, should you not be with the Falorian knight units that left? Noryo indicated you all would be in the shadowlands for weeks."

Darryn launched into an explanation. Linneya added detail only as needed. The king seemed enraptured as they told of her capture and the fight with the scouts.

He growled and hopped up as Darryn finished explaining yesterday's events. "Those foul men were trespassing on our land. They got what they deserved. King Shumor has overstepped and we will answer in kind."

Hope surged through Linneya as King Birron paced in front of the throne. He seemed furious. Perhaps this time he would understand the need to act, to send aid to Aelor.

Linneya clasped her hands together, silently beseeching the Creators to sway the king to her side. The queen handed her child to an attendant and resumed her stoic mannerisms. Her eyes were unfocused as if she would rather be anywhere else.

King Birron stopped and let out a chuckle. Linneya and Darryn glanced at each other, bemused. It built into a laugh, a deep rumbling from his belly, and he wiped tears from his eyes. Linneya held her breath, anticipating chaos in his response.

"Dear princess, I knew you would be a delight. You took out an entire battalion of Serathor's scouts? Your powers are amazing. We must train you for the arena." He beamed and Darryn let out a low growl.

Linneya raised her chin. "I am glad that the work I have been doing with Falryn and the Falorian knights has paid off. I would kill more men if it meant keeping our people safe. However, fights at the amphitheater are not why we have come. The scouts made direct threats toward my home country."

King Birron turned to her, frowning. "You heard specific details about Serathor bypassing our shores and targeting Aelor directly?"

Linneya nodded. "The scouts were discussing an imminent attack on Aelor. I would request that you send units to my parents' realm immediately to help with the battle. Darryn and I hope to leave as soon as the other Falorian knights return from their mission."

The king shook his head. "Linneya, dear, I worry that this was an attempt to feed you bad information. My spies have not reported such a plan. Besides, the fjords that grant sea access to your father's territory are difficult to maneuver. Tactically, bringing his armies through those narrow passageways is not something King Shumor is likely to attempt. It makes little sense."

She shrugged. "He has done it before. We do not know how, but my father has had to stop entire brigades of soldiers disguised as merchants. Upon inspection, it was discovered they were coming through the fjords undetected. My father's advisor hypothesized there were Creators-blessed illusions at play or some darker spell from the *sharvach*."

Darryn raised his eyebrows at her, surprised she revealed so much, but she ignored him. Divulging secret intelligence that she should not have heard in the first place was not her finest moment, but Linneya was desperate. How could King Birron hear all of this and continue to withhold support?

The king grinned and offered an indifferent gesture as if her word were no more than a game of make-believe. "How do you know they were not making those comments to throw you off their real intentions? What happens if I act on this, instead of my spies' reports? Shall I send our armies to Aelor and leave my throne defenseless as King Shumor destroys our realm?"

Queen Rhylanna crossed her arms and set her jaw. Linneya resisted the urge to mimic the queen's body language. She understood King Birron's hesitation, but at this point his refusal to take her seriously burned white-hot anger through her body.

Linneya gritted her teeth. "It sounds like you need better spies. This was no ruse. The scouts knocked me out and draped me over a horse. Once they realized I had woken up, they quickly stopped talking and said nothing else about Aelor. If they had continued discussing the attack, I would share your concerns."

King Birron shrugged his shoulders and reached for his tin, coating his finger in the red *sluryn* powder. He spoke around his finger, coating his gums. "Perhaps. Perhaps not. I cannot agree to risk my troops or people with so little information. Without an official request from your father, I will not entertain this further. I will dispatch emissaries to Aelor to see if there is any reason to pursue this matter." He rolled his neck and sighed contentedly as the *sluryn* took effect. The darkness came back to his eyes and the wild grin painted across his face.

Steam was building in her head and Linneya took a shaky breath, fighting the urge to snap back. By the time the emissaries saw any sign of Serathor's armies, it would be too late. If Serathor took Aelor, Enthor would be surrounded on both sides by the evil king's territories. King Birron continued his games of *Hajut*, unbothered by the long term consequences of his decisions.

Darryn placed his hand on her shoulder and squeezed. The gesture cleared her thoughts, her entire being focusing on the comfortable current flowing between them. After this morning, they finally felt in sync. If nothing else, Darryn would stand with her. Her tense body posture relaxed at the thought.

He stepped up, offering a small bow of his head toward the king. "It is gracious of you to pursue this matter. With respect, there is no time to wait on a reply from King Varilon. My wife has received word from her brother detailing the imminent threat.

"The spring season approaches and King Shumor will move his armies quickly, especially now that his scouts have been decimated. He will not risk losing the advantage and will be certain to strike swiftly. If Aelor falls, Enthor loses its strongest ally and access to the fae battalions of the North. We might not even have the full two mooncycles once King Shumor discovers the fate of his scouts."

Linneya's eyes burned as tears of relief welled. Darryn choosing to press the king surprised her. He could have easily shrugged his shoulders and escorted her away. She looked up at his face. His expression was serious and a coal black fire of intensity burned in his eyes as he defended her position.

King Birron studied Darryn as well. Then, he shook his head and stared toward one of the incense burners, eyes unfocused. Linneya suppressed a smile. She was certain he meant to seem aethereal, but the act came across as absurd.

After a moment, he coughed and turned back to them. His mouth was set in a grim line. "I cannot determine what fate has in store. My decision stands. I will send emissaries to your father, dear Linneya."

Linneya dipped her head and stared at the floor. A crack through one of the tiles leered at her, a misshapen grin that mocked her defeat. The pressure from Darryn's hand on her back sent pin pricks up her spine.

Queen Rhylanna stepped forward and laid a hand on King Birron's arm. "My King, I believe it would be prudent to send support. A gesture of goodwill. Fate would have allies intercede for each other. We have auxiliary units that could go without depleting our main forces." She spoke to her husband, but her eyes flickered to Linneya.

The king pursed his lips and shifted on his feet. "Yes, I suppose you have a point my dear." His cheek sank in as if he was chewing on it and he stared into the distance, contemplating. Linneya wondered why he saw the need to maintain this facade in front of her and Darryn. Perhaps the king had pretended to be someone he was not for so long that he was beginning to believe it.

He jumped as if he had been startled and turned back to them. "I shall send three of our largest auxiliary units. No one will miss them." He motioned to one of the few men in the room with them. "Send word that one should depart first thing tomorrow. The other two can leave in three days' time." The man nodded and stalked off.

A jolt shot through Linneya, followed by relief. This was finally happening. War was coming, but she would be home to see it through. She was grateful for the queen's intervention, and rather surprised it worked.

She slipped her hand into Darryn's and he squeezed. They bowed to the king and queen and began retreating. No matter what horrors they would face in the next few mooncycles, Linneya was emboldened by this man's presence. Before, she would have begged to stay with the life-tenders, healing anyone who survived severe burns from the dragons. Now, she would stand beside Darryn and fight for everyone and then use her healing skills once the battle was won.

Before they made it to the doors of the throne room, King Birron called out. Linneya and Darryn stopped, turning back toward the dais. The king was stumbling forward, as if the *sluryn* made him unsteady on his feet. He raised his hands. "You must let me bless your mission! You go to protect the free realms from future threats and the Arduin would see you consecrated. Kneel, dear ones."

Linneya and Darryn complied. She nearly gagged as the king stopped in front of them. He smelled sickly sweet with an undertone of burnt plant material. Linneya wondered if he had been out all night, carousing with other nobles in one of the nearby taverns.

The king placed his sweaty palms on their foreheads and began reciting a blessing from the Book of Harvests, mixing up every few phrases. "Thy bountiful nature is brought forth from this blessing... uh... bringing all... all the seeded blossoms to fruit."

Linneya pressed her lips together, desperately trying not to laugh as King Birron rambled. Then he removed his hands and stood there. Everyone was frozen in awkward silence for a few moments.

He cleared his throat, forgoing the typical final benediction that would cue the end of the blessing. "Rise, my children."

Linneya and Darryn stood. She stared at the floor, hoping the red in her cheeks and her downcast stare would be read as an overwhelm instead of amusement. Within a few moments, she was able to look up with a straight face. King Birron was beaming at her and she dipped her chin, relieved he had not noticed.

Darryn turned to the king and bowed slightly at the waist. "Thank you, Your Majesty. We are grateful for your wisdom and amenability to send troops. Linneya and I must be on our way. I must stop to speak with Noryo and see how many knights can join us."

King Birron nodded to them both. "Give me a few moments and allow me to write a missive proclaiming my support. Noryo will be more willing to divert from the usual missions with his king's blessing."

Darryn turned to the king and bowed slightly at the waist. "We would be honored to take your letter to the knightsmaster. I have no doubt he will be more congenial toward our cause with this note. The princess and I are grateful."

The king waved, dismissing them from the throne room. An attendant motioned for them to follow. Linneya's hands shook; she could not tell if it was from excitement or anxiousness. Darryn's eyes were narrowed in determination, as if the battle itself was about to start.

The attendant deposited them in the grand entrance of the palace. Linneya flopped down on a bench and wiped her sweaty hands on her skirt. Darryn ran his fingers through his hair and paced in front of her. For several minutes they waited in charged silence. Courtiers and ambassadors whisked by, murmuring and laughing, blissfully unaware of the gravitas.

Everything had a slightly dream-like quality to it. The designs on the walls were warped, as if Linneya was looking through carefully polished, curved glass. Even the sounds of passing officials and nobles were muddled.

This outcome was better than she could have imagined. Instead of only being available as a healer, Linneya would be bringing battalions to fight for her people. Her flame-talker affinity was now complemented with her mist element. Yet, she was out of her depth. Raising military support and preparing to march home to fight did not match her deep set desire to heal, to mend.

She drew in a shaky breath. The scent of warm spices flooded her lungs, remnants from whatever the royal kitchens were baking. Her mind spun, not wanting to face the truth. The reality was that Linneya felt more powerful embracing the darkness and fighting for her people than she ever had by staying in the light and focusing on healing.

Her family had spent annae instilling the idea that repairing wounds, physical and emotional, were of utmost importance. The prevailing belief was that this could only be achieved through nurturing the light side of one's elemental abilities. They lauded her grandparents, Queen Altheia's parents, for shielding their elementals from the horrors of battle - even to their death. Linneya had desperately tried to prove her worth with her flame-talking abilities through healing as many as she could, but she never felt whole.

Now those two sides warred. Her light clashed with her darkness. Shame of abandoning the ideals she had been taught wrestled with the growing sense of completeness that came from using her elemental abilities for both healing and fighting.

A squeaky door made her look up. Queen Rhylanna stepped out of the throne room and marched toward them. Linneya sprung to her feet and Darryn stiffened. Up close, the queen's eyes were sunken in and bloodshot. Her expression was almost vacant, a haggard look. A pang of sympathy for the woman shot through Linneya.

The queen beckoned them into a side room barely larger than a coat closet. They piled inside and she shut the door. A single candle illuminated the tight space. A musty, loamy scent suggested the room was rarely used.

Queen Rhylanna leaned forward to whisper, "the king continues to descend into madness. He is infuriated that his first child is a girl. For all our progress in Enthor, women are still ineligible to rule." She chewed on her thumbnail before continuing. "I expect you to remember I was on your side if I ever need support."

Darryn balled his hands into fists and tensed, as if he imagined the queen's words to be a threat. Linneya placed a soothing hand on his arm and stepped toward the woman. "Of course, your majesty. I do not know how we could be of help, but I will not forget the aid you have secured for Aelor today. Is there something you need from us right now?"

The queen set her mouth into a hard line. "The king believes himself well loved, but I have seen the unsettled glances of his courtiers. I have seen the way the common folk sneer when his back is turned. There may come a day where my daughter needs protection until she is able to claim her throne." The woman pressed a hand to her stomach. "There may come a day when all my daughters need protection."

Linneya glanced at Darryn, whose eyes were narrowed. He was right to be suspicious, but this woman was responsible for most of the changes that benefited Enthor's people. Linneya was certain that the queen was the only reason King Birron had not been overthrown. Whether she did it from a sense of self-preservation or love for the people, it was hard to tell. Still, Queen Rhylanna appeared to be a useful ally and Linneya was not going to push her away.

Darryn hissed under his breath, then leaned in and glowered. "Why should we believe you? You still have plenty of time to give the king a son. What do you gain from this?"

The queen pulled one of her sleeves up, revealing a serpent subduing a *sharvach* on the inside of her elbow. "My father was King Chruno. After his kingdom, Khomor, fell to Serathor, my mother hid me in Bachael with her people. She was furious when I had the symbol of Father's realm inked into my skin." She smiled at the bittersweet memory. "At the time I was proud of my rebellion and how angry it made her. Now I realize she was terrified the wrong person would see it and try to harm me. I know the devastation that can be wrought by King Shumor. Worse can happen when a king is as fickle as my husband."

Linneya's stomach twisted at the queen's admissions. This woman understood how to play her role while maneuvering alliances toward mutually beneficial agreements. She wondered if Enthor would be better off with the queen as sole ruler. Treasonous thoughts, but one might argue that King Birron's neglect of his commonfolk was even more so.

Queen Rhylanna let her sleeve drop and crossed her arms. "Speaking of, I must go before he realizes we are all missing. I wish you both luck in the upcoming battle." She turned and pressed a piece of moulding on the wall. A latch clicked and she entered a hidden servant's corridor.

The queen looked back at both of them and nodded. Linneya laced her fingers through Darryn's and gave Queen Rhylanna a small smile. Darryn was stilted, but bowed slightly at the waist as the woman left.

The hidden door clicked shut and he turned to Linneya, taking her face in his hands and touching his forehead to hers. "I do not like this, Lia. Why is she trying to force this clandestine alliance on you? Demanding an agreement from you because she made something beneficial happen this one time is suspicious."

Linneya covered his hands in hers and smiled. "Mariel has told me about several things the queen has done to make the Enthorian people's lives easier. I believe she is the influence behind the nurturing of the elementals here. We women must use unorthodox methods in the face of adversity to make things work in our favor."

He sighed and closed his eyes. "Still, I cannot stand seeing you coerced into alliances. The queen overstepped."

She reached up and kissed his forehead before pulling back. "Do not worry about me. I am learning to be devious when I need to be." She grinned wickedly and Darryn huffed a laugh.

Linneya motioned toward the door. "We need to go back before anyone gets suspicious."

Darryn pulled her to him, aligning her hips with his. She gasped as his hand spread across her lower back and pressed her closer. He leaned down, sweeping his lips against the shell of her ear. "We are married, love. Sneaking into a hidden room for a few moments alone is more or less required." His fingers wound through her hair, holding her in place as his lips brushed over hers.

The heat danced between them. "Alright, warrior. As long as you require it."

Linneya wound her arms around his neck, her body melting into his as they kissed. Darryn groaned when she bit his bottom lip, tightening his hold on her hair until it was almost painful.

She would never tire of this. Linneya laughed into their kiss and he pulled back, cocking his head to one side. "What is it, princess?"

She beamed, stroking her hands through his hair. "I am pleased we have finally given in to this longing." She ground her hips into his for emphasis on *longing* and he hissed. She giggled again and stepped back. "But perhaps we should save it until we get home. King Birron will not take much longer to write this missive, if he has not already finished it."

Darryn pressed a kiss to her forehead. "Alright, but say the word and we will sneak back in here and finish what we started." He ran a knuckle across her cheek and tucked a stray strand of her hair behind her ear. She grinned and pulled him back into the hallway.

He shut the door and Linneya tried to fix her hair. Someone cleared their throat and she jumped. An aide was making a beeline for them, a bored look on his face. Darryn leaned down and whispered, "See? Totally expected."

She stifled a smile as the aide stopped and bowed to them. "King Birron has sent me to give you his missive and send you on your way. A carriage awaits to take you home." The man handed Darryn the letter and gestured to the door, as if their tryst had offended him and he wanted them out of his liege's palace.

Darryn nodded to the aide and offered Linneya his arm. She took it, but dared not meet his gaze. Any hint of humor in his eyes might cause her to burst out in laughter.

He led her into the courtyard and into the carriage. Linneya felt his shift from amusement to yearning as the door shut. Darryn's warm stare was burning through her with a passion that she had not felt before. He reached to clasp her hand, rubbing circles on the back of it.

They rode in silence, the heat between them palpable. Linneya leaned into him, placing her head on his shoulder. His warm strength enveloped her, his steady presence anchoring her in the hope that all would work out the way it needed to.

His power sang to hers, their fates intertwining in a way she had not expected. Her eyes closed and she sighed, contented. He pulled her closer to him and pressed a kiss to the top of her head.

A sudden jolt brought her back. The carriage had stopped. She yawned and rubbed her eyes, preparing to step out and greet Noryo. Instead, she huffed as she slid out and looked up. They were home.

She turned to look back at the carriage. Darryn had not moved. Linneya's brows sketched a bow. "Are we not going to speak with the Falorian knight's leader?"

He shook his head. "I wanted to drop you off first. Rest. It has been an eventful few days. I will join you for supper, princess." He waved the king's letter. "The concerns about the movements of this cult in the shadowlands are significant and Noryo will not be pleased to see that I have abandoned my assignment. Hopefully this missive will sway him to support us anyway."

She stepped back into the carriage, her heart warming at his thoughtfulness. "Let me come with you. This is my fight. I am witness to the scouts' threats. Noryo will want to hear exact details from me."

Darryn stopped and frowned. "I worry he may not be in the mood for details. I have returned without completing our mission. He is likely to be furious with me and I do not want you subjected to his wrath."

Linneya was unfazed by the thought. She might have even had a twinge of amusement at the thought of Noryo telling him off. She crossed her arms and plopped down on the bench. "After everything we have been through this past season, you are worried that Noryo's fury might be the thing that finally breaks me?" She huffed a laugh. "No, sir. I will be coming with you. I am made of sterner stuff."

He shook his head in defeat and banged his fist on the carriage wall, signaling for the driver to go. "Then I acquiesce to you, princess."

Chapter 27

Noryo's hut was smaller than it looked the other night when they had stopped to leave the confiscated Serathanian scout's jewels. The walls were made of a primitive looking clay, the thatched roof patched together with odd layers of plant matter. The leader was standing in the doorway, his white hair cascading around his shoulders. Unlike the time Linneya had met him at the Meðon festival, Noryo was piercing her with a gaze that suggested he had full control of his faculties.

As they approached, the wizened old man crossed his arms. "You wait an entire day to report in after abandoning your mission and showing up here with the largest cache of elemental jewels I have seen in duodecades. Barely a word." He gestured toward Linneya, "and that one looked half dead."

Darryn dipped his head. "Yes, sir. Might we come in? There is much to explain."

Noryo grunted in response and ducked back into the hut. Linneya looked to Darryn, more nervous than she wanted to admit. He smiled and followed his leader inside. She took a steadying breath before stalking into the dwelling herself.

There was a single window, casting everything in an eerie shadow. The burnt smoke of overcooked meat lingered in the air, the smell searing her nostrils. She shivered and wrapped her arms around her. The very resonance of the hut was unwelcoming.

Her eyes adjusted to the darkness and she realized the space was a single room. A bed was on one wall. The stove and a bucket sat opposite. The table with four straight backed chairs were placed in the center. The hut offered no comfort, nowhere to enjoy life.

A small box sat in the corner, covered with an ornately designed blue and gold cloth. Otherwise, the room had no decoration. No signs of Noryo's personality or his interests.

Linneya was unsure what to make of the head of such an infamous warrior group living in the cramped, sparse space. She had heard of orders that required their adherents to live unattached to worldly goods, but the Knights of Falorian made no such demand of the members.

Noryo gestured to the table. "Sit. Explain."

Darryn cleared his throat, rubbing the back of his head as they all sat. She was surprised at how well built the chairs were. The seat was more comfortable than Linneya had expected, and she settled in to hear Darryn tell their story for the second time that day.

Noryo listened intently, asking the occasional question and making Linneya clarify anytime he was unhappy with Darryn's explanation. He seemed unsurprised by the scouts' movements. He scowled as Darryn described the battle and his decision to return with Linneya.

Darryn wrapped up the story and splayed his hands out, palms up on the table. "So there you have it. I want to make a formal request to dispatch some of our men alongside the Enthorian auxiliary units."

Noryo grunted and his frown deepened. "This is not our purpose, Darryn. We must stay focused on the bigger picture. I sent you north for a reason. Whatever this cult is up to, it must be addressed before it threatens the human realms."

Linneya's heart sank and her shoulders dropped. They needed every ally possible. Noryo's reluctance stirred acid in her gut, creating a painful twisting sensation.

Darryn crossed his arms. "There will be no human realms to threaten by the time King Shumor is done with his conquests. Whatever nightmare you are imagining will not come to pass if Serathor is allowed to continue."

Noryo raised his eyebrows. "There will always be conquerors. Nations rise and fall. The crucial piece is knowing when to fight and when to turn to more important matters. I tell you, whatever is happening with the *sharvachs* and this cult is more vital to the wellbeing of our people than King Shumor's posturing."

Darryn surged from his chair. The table clattered as he slammed his hands on it. Heat rose in Linneya, along with a tug in her chest, as she watched her husband stand up for her people.

He hissed. "That man is not posturing. He is going to kill us all. We will all be damned to the shadowed void if something is not done to stop this."

Noryo slowly stood and set his jaw. His eyes turned pitch black and his breathing became insistent. "You will learn your place and stop demanding things of me that you know I cannot give. First you want to take the archives to Mount Varsha, giving away our secrets like some *fool*. Now you demand I move men from their posts to entertain the possibility that Serathor will kill us all with fabled amounts of harvested elemental power." He waved his withered hands around in a sarcastic gesture.

Darryn's nostrils flared and he leaned in. "You know what King Shumor will do. You and I have seen it." Shadows began gathering by Noryo's hands and Darryn flexed his fingers, blue and brown smoke emanating from his arms. Linneya gritted her teeth.

Nothing would be accomplished if they began fighting. She was not sure that the hut they were in could withstand the warriors' powers. The air turned frigid with a sharp, icy edge. Both of the men were breathing heavily, watching each other with unreadable expressions.

She shivered and stood up, preparing to call on her own affinities to stop them if necessary. "Please, no more. We have enough fights going on without harming each other. Darryn, show Noryo the missive from King Birron."

Her voice shattered the tension in the room. The air warmed and Noryo's shadows dissipated. Linneya worried her bottom lip, curious to the man's powers but rather afraid to voice her questions. Her knight glanced toward her before reaching into his tunic and retrieving the letter.

Noryo read the missive, his face becoming more pale with each sentence. He sat down, halfway through. Linneya and Darryn mirrored the movement, Darryn subtly scooting his chair to be closer to her. His hand pressed into her thigh, a reassuring gesture.

Noryo finished and they sat in silence. His face slowly contorted into a trance-like expression. Linneya wondered if King Birron modeled his theatrics after this man's. After a few moments, he coughed and rubbed his chin.

A shudder coursed through his body and he fixed his stare on Linneya. "King Birron insists that we band together on this. You have put me in a rather unfortunate political situation, Your Highness."

She inclined her head slightly, hoping the gesture conveyed an apology without wavering from her original needs.

Noryo huffed. "The man swore he would not interfere with our mission. I will not hold it against you that our king is fickle. In any case, I can see that fate has solidified in your favor."

Darryn smirked, watching the leader as if he was not so secretly pleased at the acquiescence. "So, what will it be? Will the Falorian knights stand on the right side of this battle?"

The old man waved his hand dismissively. "Yes, yes, you win this one, pup. We will mimic King Birron's orders. I will announce that some units will go in the morning with the first wave of troops. The rest will depart with you."

Linneya's face split into a grin she could not contain. "Thank you, sir. I am grateful that you are joining with us to protect my home country."

He shrugged, motioning for them to begin walking outside. "I believe we are both after the same thing, my dear one. Somehow this battle appears to be tied to our mission. Perhaps we will find something important. If nothing else, you all can harvest the elemental jewels off the dead Serathanian soldiers and bring them here for safekeeping."

Darryn raised his eyebrows and the two men exchanged a meaningful look. Linneya did not have time to wonder at their expressions as Darryn grabbed her hand and pulled her back toward their carriage. He helped her to climb inside before turning to wave to Noryo. The man had resumed the same position as when they arrived, staring daggers through them from the doorway.

The next couple of days passed in a blur. Darryn was busy sending missives and strategizing with the leaders of his order. Many held concerns about the rumors that Serathanian dragons were being armed with elemental powers. Linneya spent time in the catacomb archives, reading and absorbing any information that might help them against the creatures.

One evening was particularly warm and the spring plants were beginning to emerge. Linneya sent out invitations to Chrysa, Mariel, and Straion to join them for dinner. She enlisted Shailyn to help set up a table in the back garden and Kapeyni saw to it that the cook made something that each person would enjoy.

Darryn strolled through the back gates and Shailyn bounced over to him. "You are just in time to help me set the table!" Linneya grinned as her husband raised his eyebrows at his sister.

Shailyn stuck out her tongue, to which he responded in kind and then laughed as she pummeled his arm with her fist. "Alright! Alright! I surrender. Point me to the flatware."

Linneya's chest warmed at the sight. Darryn caught her watching and made his way over to kiss her. "I have been conscripted by my sister, but know that all I wish to do right now is take you upstairs and lock us away. Our tub needs a proper christening."

The wicked glint in his eye made her blush. She giggled and swatted at his arm. "Agreed, but for now we have guests arriving. Go, my warrior. See to your sister before she has a conniption." Linneya inclined her head toward Shailyn.

Sure enough, the woman looked ready to throttle them both. Darryn gave her one final kiss before making his way toward the kitchens to retrieve the flatware. For a brief moment, watching him teasing his sister and preparing for their friends, Linneya forgot about her foreboding thoughts. She sucked in a deep breath, tasting the light floral scents of early blooms celebrating the arrival of warmer days. Narruan watched nearby, his tail flickering in judgment of all the activity.

A shout caused her to turn back toward the back gate. Mariel and Straion were arriving, arm in arm. He was carrying a bottle of faewine and Mariel had a basket of her freshly baked bread. Shailyn skipped toward them, squealing with delight at the libations. The three of them began chattering animatedly about the vintage and Shailyn led them toward the almost completed dinner spread.

Chrysa slunk in behind them, a frown on her face. Linneya made her way to the woman, ready to inquire about what was bothering her. As she reached her, Chrysa smiled sadly, her green eyes a muddled, mossy color. Linneya's brows quirked up, but Chrysa shook her head. "Not here." Linneya nodded, curious but unwilling to probe in front of so many others.

Shailyn signaled dinner was ready and everyone made their way to the table. Conversation ebbed and flowed as they dug into the meal. A pang throbbed in her chest as she wondered if this would be the last full meal they would have together.

At the end of the main course, Darryn stood. "I know that you have all heard some of what is happening with Serathor. The threats they have made toward Aelor cannot be ignored." He looked at Linneya, the intensity of his gaze warming her. "Lia and I will be leaving for Loraen within a few days."

Chrysa twirled a piece of hair between her fingers. "I take it you have been able to raise support?"

Darryn nodded. "King Birron is sending some auxiliary units and Noryo has agreed to allow some of the knights to come. A wave of soldiers has already left and sent word to Linneya's family. We will leave as soon as my company has returned. I want Graisor and Trotyn to be with us. Chrysa, I know you will join us."

Chrysa nodded once. Darryn cleared his throat and continued. "Mariel, Straion, I want to offer for you to be a part of this. Please know we will not think less of you if you choose to stay here, but the invitation is open." He set his mouth in a hard line and sat down.

Linneya placed a hand over his and squeezed. The thought of sending their friends into a dangerous, almost impossible fight was heart wrenching. She wished there was a way to resolve things without the violence. Or, rather, without those she loved being subjected to the violence.

Others asked questions and Darryn detailed some of their upcoming plans. Memories of him fighting spoke to a part of her that she had fought to keep hidden. His skill with the blade, the dark fire in his eyes as he struck down their enemies... he was most at home with a weapon and a deadly mission. The thought tugged at her heart, a sense of pride swelling throughout her body. Now she was prepared to let the darkness consume her in order to keep her family - their families - safe.

Shailyn put her goblet down and turned to face her brother. "What about me? I want to come with you. I have been training with Falryn for annae."

Darryn shook his head. "No, I cannot risk putting you in harm's way, Shay. You know the dangers of the Serathanian soldiers finding out about any family I may have. They would capture you. Torture you for information about me or the knights. There is no benefit to dragging you into the midst of this fight."

Shailyn crossed her arms. "I do not have to stand with you. I can be in another battalion and no one has to know. I can easily make myself useful without being captured."

A muscle pulsed in Darryn's jaw. "I said no. You will not come with us."

His sister stared down at her plate, a deep frown etched onto her face. Linneya grimaced at the sight. Shailyn's personality did not allow her to be out of the loop. Linneya worried that there might be consequences to leaving Darryn's sister behind.

Chrysa squeezed Shailyn's forearm. "You will not be missing much. These battles usually end before they begin, with the leaders making a show of force and then drawing to a stalemate. When King Shumor sees the number of allies that have arrived, he is likely to change his mind and leave without a single drop of blood spilled. We spend all that time roughing it and come out on the other end with nothing but boring diplomacy talks. At least here you can continue to work with Falryn and train for future battles."

Shailyn attempted a smile, patting Chrysa's arm and turning back to her dinner. Linneya tried to put the worries of the upcoming battle out of her mind and focus on savoring this meal with her friends. Everyone seemed distracted. Mariel was chasing the same green vegetable around and around on her plate. Straion swirled his goblet, set it down, and picked it up to swirl again. Darryn's eyes had darkened at Shailyn's request and he was still glaring at an unmarked target in the distance.

Even shifting to the dessert course did little to change the heaviness that had fallen across the crew. The meal ended with a bittersweet, roasted seed drizzled with cream. Shailyn informed them that the delicacy hailed from south of Serathor, a favorite of dwarves and fauns alike.

Everyone crammed their portion down and began making to leave. The discussion of the impending fights seemed to add an urgency for their friends to hurry home and make plans. Linneya and Darryn walked to the back gate, preparing to tell everyone farewell.

Straion snaked his arm around Mariel's waist as they approached. He clapped Darryn on the shoulder. "I guess you already know we will be coming with you all."

Darryn grinned and cuffed him back. "We figured it would be impossible to leave you behind."

While Straion and Darryn discussed details of their departure, Linneya grabbed Mariel's hands. She was worried about her friend being anywhere close to a battle. As if Mariel read her mind, she shook her head. "I plan on staying back with the life-tenders. I know there is no reason to think I could hold my own against seasoned soldiers. I will be handling the supply cart and assisting when needed."

Linneya smiled, a bit of tension leaving her shoulders at her friend's admission. "No doubt, you would be fierce, but I would feel better knowing that you are out of harm's way."

Straion squeezed Mariel's waist. "I will be with her, protecting her. We want to help, especially with Mariel's family being in Loraen." Mariel grinned up at her husband and they both said their goodbyes.

Chrysa and Shailyn hugged them and made their exit toward Shailyn's cottage. The two would undoubtedly end up at a tavern before the night was over. Their giggling and chatter faded, leaving Darryn and Linneya surveying the aftermath of a well-enjoyed party.

Cups and platters were scattered across the table, as corpses on a battlefield. A napkin fluttered like dragon's wings. Linneya shivered and hugged herself, unwilling to look too deep at the unsettled feeling growing around the upcoming fight.

Her knight stepped behind her, running his hands down her arms. Her shivering turned from fear to desire and she leaned back into him. He wrapped his arms around her and squeezed. "Shall we clean up and head upstairs?"

She smiled and nodded. When two servants came to help, they made quick work of the mess. Cleaning up after friends and working to reset the garden had a mundane rhythm that helped ground Linneya into a sense of peace. If only they could be promised more nights like this. More dinners with friends laughing and planning for the future.

The servants shooed them away after the table was cleared, insisting they would be a bother if they stayed. Darryn and Linneya made their way upstairs and settled into their evening routine. Within a few minutes, Darryn was at a table, pouring over some parchment with what looked like battle plans. Linneya settled into her favorite settee with one of his mother's novels.

She had just been pulled into the legend of the burning star that struck Mount Varsha when a knock on the door made her jump. Kapeyni poked her head in. "My Lady, might I speak with you? Alone?"

Darryn stood up and nodded to them both, gathering his papers and walking into their bedroom. Linneya smiled toward her maid and gestured for her to sit in the chair by the fireplace. "Please, what is on your mind?"

Kapeyni sank into the seat and wrung her hands. "I overheard some of the conversation this evening. I knew that you and Sir Darryn would be leaving to defend Aelor, but I did not realize how dire the situation is."

Linneya inclined her head. "It is unnerving to know that my home country is under attack."

Kapeyni straightened up and looked Linneya in the eyes. "Should I plan to come with you? I have a mean throwing arm and an arsenal of daggers."

Linneya grinned at the thought of this tiny woman dropping Serathanian soldiers with her weapon of choice. "You are wonderful, Kapeyni, but this is not the place for you."

A fire lit in the maid's eyes, a fervor that Linneya had not seen from the woman. "If nothing else, you will need someone to attend to you. I want to come. I want to be useful."

Linneya grabbed her hands and squeezed. "No, but thank you. My parents will have people to attend to us. I would rather know you are here and safe. There are so many ways this trip could go wrong. We are already having to involve more people than I would like. Please, stay here."

The woman's shoulders sagged, as if the rejection was deeper than Linneya realized. There was another knock on the door and this time the butler made an announcement, indicating they should make their way downstairs. Linneya called for Darryn to join her as she and Kapeyni stood.

The remaining Falorian knights had returned.

Chapter 28

Graisor and Trotyn were standing in the hallway, flanked by Shailyn and Chrysa. They were still in their armor, dirty and rugged from being on the road for the past several days. Linneya's breath caught at the powerful sight of Darryn's inner circle, sparks of fury radiating from the entire crew.

Trotyn leaned forward, crossing his arms. "We hear there is a fight to be had up North." Darryn nodded and motioned toward the study without a word.

When Darryn finished updating them, the men were infuriated. Trotyn paced back and forth while Graisor stood deadly still. Chrysa held the same deep frown from earlier and Shailyn glowered. Linneya's heart squeezed at the sight of everyone's response to the threat on her family's kingdom. The group was prepared to fight for each other, to die to protect each other, and she was now part of it.

Graisor grimaced. "My cousins live near Loraen. If Serathor's armies attack and Aelor's capital falls, their village will be next."

Trotyn hissed. "King Shumor needs to be put in his place. This cannot continue. Nowhere will be safe."

Darryn clenched his fists, agreeing with his brothers in arms. While the men were huddled together, fuming about Serathor's newfound boldness, Shailyn grabbed Linneya's arm and pulled her into the hallway. She leaned in and whispered, "can we go somewhere and talk while they are distracted?"

Linneya pursed her lips. Shailyn was being sneaky and she was unsure if she wanted to be pulled into whatever scheme her sister-in-law was brewing. Still, her past sneakiness had never been cruel or vicious, so Linneya shrugged in agreement and followed her.

They slipped into a practically unused sitting room and Shailyn rounded on her. "You have to help me. I want to come to Aelor and fight." She wrung her hands and took a steadying breath. "I know Darryn thinks he is doing the right thing, but he cannot keep stifling me like this."

Linneya nodded and crossed her arms. "He wants to have you stay here to keep you out of harm's way. I am not sure he is wrong."

Shailyn huffed. "It is not about my safety. Darryn refuses to see me as a capable adult because he raised me. He will always see me as a child, as someone to protect. If he lets me fight, he has to admit I am not a child anymore. I want to come with the two of you. I am ready. Falryn has trained me well."

Linneya squinted, mulling over the idea. "I agree you should come. Your healing skills would be helpful."

Shailyn stepped back and shook her head in disagreement. Without a word, she lifted her hands and a rainbow of smoky tendrils crawled out. The air began to stir, quickly building into a whirlwind around them. She balled her raised hands into fists and the wind instantly stopped. Linneya's eyebrows raised at Shailyn's mastery of her affinity.

Then the woman held both hands straight out in front of her, palms up. A white hot flame formed and Shailyn held it without flinching. "I have multiple affinities. This is part of why Falryn has been training me. My powers rival Darryn's. I am ready to fight."

Linneya twisted her lips, trying not to smile at the woman's eagerness. Shailyn's eyes had a similar cold fire to her brother's. She willingly embraced the dark side of her powers, abandoning the healing light to go to war. Part of Linneya swelled with jealousy, but the other part worried Shailyn would be harmed.

Still, she was old enough to make her own decisions without her brother's interference. Her combined aether and flame affinities would undoubtedly be helpful on the battlefield. But, like Darryn, Linneya did not want to see her placed in harm's way.

As if she could see Linneya's brewing rejection, Shailyn stepped forward. "Please, you must understand. I cannot sit idly by. I want to come with you and help in whatever way I can. Your family is my family now. Do not deny me this. I helped you escape. Repay the favor and let me be a part of your fight."

Linneya smiled. Shailyn was determined and she did not want to snuff out her enthusiasm. "Alright, but you must let me bring it up at the right time. I will speak with Darryn and try to convince him that you have a place on the battlefield."

Shailyn squealed in excitement. The protectiveness Linneya felt surprised her. It was as if this woman was as precious to her as Eleanor.

Linneya continued. "You must promise me one thing: if you come you will do whatever Darryn requires. No sneaking around or being sly. In a battle, following orders will mean life or death. Do not jeopardize your safety or my husband's."

Shailyn was still grinning and nodding along, but Linneya worried she had not listened carefully. She grabbed her sister-in-law, squeezing her upper arms. "Please, Shay, promise me that. I cannot live without the two of you."

Shailyn wrapped her arms around Linneya. "Absolutely. I will listen and do what is needed. I am grateful you are on my side."

Linneya let out a worried sigh and squeezed her back. There would be time to figure out how to approach Darryn later. For now, she wanted to hear more of the plans being formed. "Let us go back before Darryn becomes suspicious."

Shailyn let go. Linneya was surprised to see unshed tears glistening in her eyes. The woman turned away and pushed the door open, gesturing for Linneya to follow her back to the study.

They walked into the hallway and Linneya spied Chrysa's retreating form. The woman's head was bowed and she was hugging herself as she stalked away. Shailyn squeezed Linneya's arm and ran after her friend.

Something was bothering the woman. Linneya's stomach flipped, a momentary twitch she shook off. Shailyn intertwined her arm with Chrysa's and they walked out of the mansion together. Linneya would not pry. The woman would share when she was ready.

She entered the study as Darryn turned to Graisor. "Return to our mission's rendezvous point. If all has gone to plan, Tiuthan will still be there. He may also come to our aid. Tell him to gather any support he can and meet us within a mooncycle."

Graisor's jaw pulsed, his scar going pale under the tension, and he nodded. Darryn clapped his hand on Graisor's shoulder. "Travel light and ride fast, brother. We will see you soon."

Graisor headed for the door, pausing to bow his head toward Linneya. She gave him a trembling smile and he turned to leave. Linneya stared after the man's retreating form. He crept along with the grace of a trained assassin. Her heart welled at the thought of this man fighting to protect her family. Even after losing his wife, he persisted for the sake of his friends.

Trotyn turned back to Darryn, fury coating his features. "What do you need from me?"

Darryn nodded toward his desk. "I have some enchantments I was researching. You are a faster reader than any of us. Can you dig in the archives further and see what you can discover over the next couple of days? Then ride out to meet us. I would have you catch up with us before we are too far into the journey."

Trotyn bowed his head, loose waves of red hair cascading around his face. "Consider it done." Darryn strode over and picked up a pile of parchment. Trotyn studied them for a moment, bouncing on the balls of his feet while Darryn found a leather holder to keep the documents safe. The man's uncanny knack at catching patterns combined with his sharp memory meant he would be the one to find whatever was needed. Darryn handed him the bound files and the intense fighter turned and left without another word.

The resulting silence caused Linneya's mind to roar to life with worry. Her stomach twisted into knots. They had three auxiliary units from the king and nearly half of the Falorian knights. If Graisor succeeded in getting Tiuthan to send a few units of fae soldiers, would it be enough against Serathor's sprawling armies?

Aelor was smaller in population compared to both Enthor and Serathor. The harsh, cold climate kept settlements tiny. This translated to less men to join the military. She shivered and hugged herself. Her parents' kingdom had enjoyed one of the longest unbroken lines of succession and relative peace through the duocenturies, but that had more to do with their geographical location than military strength.

Maybe they could hold out. She took a deep breath, feeling her body settle as she exhaled. Darryn's decision to support her and rally whatever help they could find gave her home country a fighting chance.

Linneya turned to find him watching her, his brows knitted in concern. He crossed the room and ran the back of his knuckles across her cheek. "Love, what is the matter?"

She smiled and pressed her body into his warmth. Entwining her fingers with his, she laid her head on his shoulder. "Nothing, warrior. I am grateful we are seeing this through. I was just thinking this is the best chance my family will have of protecting their people. I am glad to have you on my side."

He kissed the top of her head and squeezed her hand. They stood there, staring into the dwindling fire. Linneya wanted to remain forever in this liminal space, the vacuum of peace before a sweeping wind cuts through and brings chaos.

After a long silence, Darryn hummed a tune. The lullaby she had first heard him whistle in the forests of Aelor. Her knight nudged her to dance, twisting her into his arms and slowly swaying back and forth.

She settled her head on his chest and closed her eyes. The soothing rhythm of his heart combined with their rocking lulled Linneya into a meditative trance. Still, the foreboding sense that this battle would destroy everything lingered. She was desperate to hold onto as much of this peace as possible. Their time together had been too short and she was not ready for anything to change. Tears pricked her eyes and she blinked them back, trying to stay grounded in the moment.

He finished the song and they stilled. He snaked his arms around her, holding her to his chest, and kissed the top of her head. "Shall we go to bed, wife?" She mumbled her consent and they made their way back up the stairs to their suite.

The fire crackled in the large inglenook. The scent of wood smoke lightly coated the space with the smell of home. Without a second thought, she turned into his bedroom - their bedroom now. They finally felt like a married couple, bonded like husband and wife.

She was fast becoming irrevocably attached to this dark, broody man. Linneya was fond of his laughter, rare as it might be. She was fond of his presence. That sense of someone who would burn it all for the ones he loved.

Darryn pulled off his shirt and stretched. She was fond of his body. She watched him move, her hands tingling with the urge to explore his torso, the rippling muscles that spoke of strength and agility. She was fond of his touch, exploring, dipping deeper and bringing her to the edge...

Linneya's core heated at the thought. All of a week ago, she was running toward Aelor. Away from him. Now she was lusting after his body... aching for his hands on her, whipping her into a frenzy. She wrapped her arms around her waist, chuckling.

She could not outrun fate, and she no longer cared to. The last couple of days they had worked so well as a team. Their single-minded purpose had moved mountains that she had previously thought would never budge.

Darryn turned around and stepped toward her, signaling for her to turn around. He lifted her hair over her shoulder and began undoing her laces. Goosebumps emerged as his fingers brushed across her back. She stepped out of the skirts, reaching for a diaphanous nightgown.

He chuckled and helped her into the evening wear. "I am glad to see you have upgraded from the first time you slept in here."

Her ears burned and she swiveled around, popping him lightly on the chest. "As I recall, dear warrior, that dress was perfect for the chilly night."

He laughed and pulled her close. "At least I finally found a way to convince you to keep sleeping in here with me." He slowly kissed her neck and murmured, "although now I have you where I want you and we will be traveling again tomorrow morning."

She stilled under his touch. Linneya had almost forgotten Shailyn's request to join them on the trip to Aelor. If they were leaving first thing, there was no time left to discuss it. She shook off the lusty haze and looked up at him.

He leaned in. "What are you thinking, love?"

Linneya threw her arms around his neck and he grabbed her waist, pulling her close. She melted into him and stroked her fingers through his hair. "Shailyn dragged me into your sitting room to discuss going to Aelor with us. I think you should reconsider. It would be strategic to have her, even if we make her stay back with the healers."

He groaned, nuzzling into her neck. "Did you not get enough talk of strategy earlier? Nothing about this conversation is headed the way I want it to."

She placed her hands on his cheeks and shifted back to look him in the eyes, annoyed at his dodging. "We cannot avoid this conversation, sir. Shailyn deserves to fight with us. She is not a child anymore, Darryn. She is capable of defending herself."

Darryn sighed and looked out their window. "Yes, but I would prefer that Serathor's troops not find out I have a sister. It could be used against me. You see how Graisor has suffered from his wife being targeted by our enemies. She will not stay with the life-tenders and I dread what could happen to her if the soldiers realize who she is."

Linneya cocked her head. His worry seemed rooted in something else - something he would not share with her. Everyone in Rathen knew Shailyn was his sister. Darryn was hiding important information again, but she was not going to pry. "If your concern is her anonymity, we can have her stay with Eleanor during battle. That way she is with family, but not directly connected to you."

Darryn turned back to meet her gaze, his lips twisted as if he was straining to contain a snarl. "Alright, if you have taken her side on this, she wins. I cannot resist both of you. Shailyn can come with us, but I expect her to stay away from the fighting. Too much is at stake for me to be worried she will be discovered while we are in battle."

Linneya's mouth split into a grin. "Thank you, Darryn. She will be thrilled."

"Yes, yes, now can I touch my wife?" He smirked and she laughed in agreement. He pulled her to bed and they tangled together, a safe space that Linneya hoped would never be ripped from her. With the journey they would embark on the next morning, sleep eluded them both and they stayed up talking until the wee hours of the morning.

Both of the suns were up by the time Darryn and Linneya made their way to the palace courtyard. Organized chaos reigned and Darryn kissed her forehead before strolling toward some of the knights. King Birron was lumbering about, bragging to anyone who would listen that the entire expedition was his idea. Soldiers milled around, packing weapons and armor into the carts that would be pulled by *bluris*, cattle with three horns that were bred to drag heavy loads over long distances.

Shailyn was bouncing between groups, helping however she could. Her face was glowing and she chattered animatedly. Pride swelled in Linneya as she watched the woman working. Darryn had sent permission to his sister as soon as they woke up, but with her arriving before them, Linneya wondered if she had planned on trying to come anyway.

Shailyn made her way over to Johann. Linneya's eyebrows raised as she watched the man gesture toward one of the carts. Shailyn linked her arm in his and they walked over to speak with one of the soldiers who had been loading it with weapons.

Nearby, Mariel and Straion were packing a cart filled with life-tender supplies. Tinctures, woven bandages, and a variety of metal instruments were neatly stacked inside. Straion was wrestling to secure everything under the canvas top and Mariel was hissing instructions through gritted teeth. Linneya watched as her friend grew increasingly frustrated.

Mariel's face grew a deeper red, almost purple, when he looked her in the eyes and let go of the cloth, causing it to spring back and the ties to unravel. He threw his head back and laughed, as if he thought she would think it a grand joke. When Straion saw her infuriated expression, he sombered. Apologizing, he started over and made quick work of the packing.

Mariel stalked off toward the paddock of horses, running her hands through her hair. Linneya's chest tightened for her friend. Mariel was naturally lighthearted. It was devastating to see her flustered by her husband's poor attempts at humor.

She began heading the same direction, but a sniffling sound caused her to stop and turn. Chrysa stood by one of the chestnut horses, stroking its mane and leaning in toward its head as if they were having a heart to heart. When she realized Linneya was watching, she wiped her face and inclined her head in greeting.

Linneya stepped closer and asked softly, "What is wrong, Chrysa?"

Chrysa blinked rapidly, looking up toward the suns. "It may sound silly, but I dread this trip. I harbor unpleasant memories of your home country, Lia. My parents immigrated to Aelor when I was a child and tried to set up a business in the capital. They had been serfs and my father's business acumen pulled them out of the muck. He became one of the most powerful merchants on the islands and believed a fresh start in Loraen would mean we could grow up without the heavy cloud of our past."

Linneya placed a hand on Chrysa's upper arm and the woman took a deep breath before continuing. "We did not receive a warm welcome. The other merchants sent guild members to destroy the storefront. Overnight, we lost half of our valuables and all of the business. I can still remember the smell of the burning leather as my mother sobbed at the cruelty." She shuddered and Linneya's heart squeezed painfully tight.

She leaned toward her friend. "Did they know who did it? Why?"

Chrysa shook her head and resumed petting the horse. "Da figured someone must have found out about his upward mobility. Ma saw it as the merchants looking to shutter any new competition. Within the mooncycle, we packed up what little we had left and set our sights to the Northern Isles of Enthor. We managed to cobble together an existence there, but no one ever accepted us as part of the merchant class. We were foreigners with weird ways and barely enough means to keep up appearances."

Linneya ground her teeth at the thought. Aelor was backwards because of its isolated geography, so it was easy to believe Chrysa. It was devastating to realize how much suffering Chrysa and her family had experienced from the hostility of her people. Her parents had fought to bring more acceptance of foreigners and others who were marginalized, but change was slow in a scattered realm.

Linneya opened her mouth to ask Chrysa if she might share her story with Aiden, but Shailyn skipped over to them. "Chryssie, come check out this powder that the knights have created! It can be loaded into pots with a small amount of salt and the mixture explodes on impact!"

Chrysa raised her eyebrows. "I worry at how excited you are for this, Shay." Linneya giggled but Shailyn was undeterred. She pulled on Chrysa's arm, dragging her away from the horses and toward Johann and the cart of explosive powder. Chrysa looked back over her shoulder, her face arranged in an apologetic expression and Linneya managed a small smile.

A shadow darkened the sunslight. Startled, Linneya turned and came face to face with Darryn holding the reins of a beautiful black horse as well as his mount. He grinned at her. "Love, I brought you the gentlest beast I could find. She will be yours for this journey."

Linneya's mouth fell open as she took in the gorgeous horse's coat. She was completely black, like a night with a hidden moon. Her mane had been braided, a cascade of dark waves down one side.

Darryn marked her gaping stare and leaned in. "If she is not to your liking, we could always ride together." He patted his horse. "But Doshar might object to what I will do to you if you stay between my legs for an entire mooncycle."

As if the horse understood, he snorted and stomped his foot. Blood rushed to Linneya's face and she turned to the black beauty. "While that is tempting, I look forward to making friends with this doll. What is her name?"

Darryn's mouth quirked up on one side. "Thefa."

Linneya smiled. "Midnight? What an accurate description." She turned to the horse. "Hello, Thefa." The horse whickered and stepped toward Linneya. Darryn offered her the reins and she took them, excitement building in her chest.

This was really happening. She had raised aid and would be home to heal anyone who was burned by Serathor's dragons. Darryn had been a big part of bringing this together. She beamed at her husband, earning her a bemused look.

He motioned her forward to their spot in the caravan. The *bluris* cattle were being hooked up to the carts and families were saying goodbye. She took a deep breath, preparing to mount the horse, when a shout made her turn.

Falryn and Harilyn were elbowing their way through the throng, waving and trying to get her attention. Darryn whipped around, his eyebrows raising as Falryn squawked. Harilyn was gesturing animatedly and pointing to a scroll in Falryn's hand.

As the couple made it to Darryn and Linneya, they both had to stop and catch their breath. Falryn finally spoke up, translating for Harilyn. "We found this in our archives. It is the full retelling of the prophecy of Luthin and Payera's return. We needed to bring it to you before you left."

Darryn tried to take the scroll and Falryn snatched it back. "No, Linneya needs to read this. It tells of the circumstances of the *sharvach*'s renewed threat and what can be done to restore harmony. Only the flame-talker will have answers."

He looked perturbed at the healer's rejection, but Falryn set their jaw and turned to Linneya. "Keep this safe."

She nodded. Harilyn threw her arms around both Linneya and Darryn, smiling through tears. Falryn nodded brusquely, a slight tremble to their jaw. "Do not lose that scroll, girl."

And with that, the command to move out came rippling down the line. She and Darryn hurried to mount their horses and move. Linneya's stomach twisted as they made their way through the palace gates. She was going home.

Chapter 29

King Birron's auxiliary units were better prepared than Linneya expected. She had steeled herself for a ragtag group of men that had no business wielding a sword. Instead, she found a group of people who behaved as if they were part of the main army.

They traveled in a boisterous pack, laughing and joking with each other. At noonrest, they trained in drills as one unit. They invited Shailyn and Chrysa to join them at times, a genuine gesture of friendship. The sense of camaraderie was comforting.

She was grateful for their presence. The Falorian knights were less talkative. They rode as if the upcoming battle spelled their doom. Linneya had heard several of them trading rumors around dragons with elemental powers and the allies Serathor might procure with the tribes in the East.

Johann rode with the auxiliary. Occasionally, he would fall back and talk with Darryn. Linneya caught him watching her several times, his gaze making her uncomfortable. He seemed to be working up the nerve for a conversation, but she was not interested and kept her distance.

Linneya mostly rode alone. Many of the knights demanded to speak with Darryn, making it almost impossible for them to spend time together during the day. At noonrest, he was always surrounded by three or four knights, strategizing or debating something. Occasionally, Darryn would send one riding from camp with a message to the fae or back to Enthor.

He never seemed flustered by the incessant stream of questions and ideas. Linneya was fascinated by his ability to consider everyone's suggestions, even though she imagined half of them were too asinine to be helpful. It reminded her of her father, sitting in the throne room and hearing petitions from everyone - no matter how small or seemingly insignificant.

Mariel and Straion had once again taken to riding together and trading blushes and soft murmurs. Even with the occasional hiccup, they seemed to finally be enjoying the relationship the way both of them deserved. With her best friend enamored with her husband and Darryn brooding over strategy and maps, this trip was beginning to feel very much like the last.

At least the tents were less obnoxious. Noryo had allowed Darryn to tap into the Falorian knights' supplies and gather more practical accommodations for this journey. They were much simpler in design, easier to put up and take down. The hope was they could travel longer each day and arrive faster than the last trip.

This strategy was why both suns had set before they stopped to make camp that night. Everyone quickly went to work, pitching tents and preparing dinners. The *bluris* cattle were fed and tied into a makeshift paddock. Darryn and Linneya made their way throughout the regiments, making sure everything was in order for the night.

Once things were settled, they found their way back to the campfire where their friends had gathered. Mariel and Straion were huddled together, whispering and laughing. Chrysa and Shailyn were breaking down some of the noonrest training session. Darryn plopped on a log next to his sister and stretched his legs, groaning.

Linneya settled between him and Mariel, the latter of which leaned over and nudged her. "We have been discussing your semi-successful escape attempt."

Linneya raised her eyebrows. "Oh? What brought that up?" She ignored the warning glare Darryn sent.

Straion put his hands behind his head and yawned. "I am still impressed you got away with it. Kapeyni can be a force to be reckoned with. I would have thought she would keep you under lock and key with Darryn gone."

Linneya schooled her face into a mask of innocence. "The woman was suspicious, but she knew better than to try to lock me up. Although I am surprised she does not hate me for it."

Darryn grunted and reached for her hand, obviously unsettled by the topic. "I think Kapeyni was more worried when she realized you had been captured by scouts and forced through that battle."

Chrysa nodded. "She will never forgive herself for letting you out of her sight."

Straion shook his head and looked at Linneya. "I could not believe you had left. Mariel told me and I was convinced she was trying to pull a prank. You were back so fast, it did not seem real."

A mischievous grin danced across Shailyn's face. "Straion, you nearly caught us as you were leaving the market! After I helped Linneya escape, I was certain you or Kapeyni or someone would figure it out and I would be in so much trouble."

"You what?!" Darryn leapt to his feet, seething at Shailyn's admission.

Shailyn blinked in surprise, then turned to Linneya and laughed. "You did not tell him I helped you get out? I am impressed."

Linneya chewed on her lip. "I saw no reason for you to be in trouble. After all, I came back, did I not?"

Darryn growled at Shailyn. "So *you* are how it was so easy for her to leave."

Linneya stood and placed a hand on his arm, schooling her face to hide the giddiness rising from her chest. She fought the urge to tease him, instead adopting a soothing tone. "Darryn, she was just trying to help."

"Exactly!" He rounded on his sister. "I am going to lock you up until I can find a nobleman who will take you on. You are too wild for your own good."

Shailyn cackled. "You will do no such thing." She waved him off and smirked to Linneya. "He is all bark and no bite when it comes to family. Admit it, Darryn, you are just mad we bested you."

Darryn sat back down and buried his face in his hands. "The two of you are going to be the death of me. I cannot believe my wife almost successfully ran away - with my sister's help." Linneya let her grin crack through, settled beside him, and rubbed a hand across his back in soothing circles.

Straion chuckled. "You are outnumbered, sir. These women will win every time. Crafty, the lot of them." Mariel hushed him with an elbow, but even she was beaming.

Shailyn looked pleased at her brother's defeat. "Dear brother, I would have never let my new sister go if I did not believe she would return to us. After all, where would we be if you went back to the surly mess you were before she arrived?"

The others chuckled and murmured their agreement while Darryn grumbled at their teasing. Warmth bloomed through Linneya, as if sunsbeams gently heated her to her core. Darryn was only a part of the reason she turned back to Enthor. Every person around this campfire was needling their way into her heart. Their relationships were open and effortless. Lighthearted and impactful, all at once.

Mariel had always been a friend, but now they were thick as thieves. Straion knew how to lift everyone's spirits with his quirky bits of knowledge and happy go lucky demeanor. Even Chrysa, who still spent more time cooking up schemes with Shailyn than she did anything else, was becoming an important part of Linneya's circle.

Even though they were not with them, Graisor and Trotyn were also on this list. Graisor held a special place in her heart for how serious he was about making sure she had the best warrior training possible. Trotyn had an eclectic variety of taste: his bookworm nature and love of unusual weapons was bizarre, but Linneya loved the odd bits of knowledge he could share.

She shifted, looking around the campfire. Shailyn's frequent and open declaration of "sister" was especially potent. A pang went through Linneya's chest as she was reminded of her biological sister and their division. Eleanor had neither written nor sent word through anyone else. Their mother had skirted around the topic in her letters with vague comments around her health. Linneya missed her younger sister severely and worried that it might take more than an apology to convince Eleanor to repair this breach.

A warmth on her neck caused her to turn back toward her husband. Darryn was watching her, blazing heat in his gaze. The one good thing about their days being spent separate, their coming together again in the evening was that much more powerful.

She gave him a small smile and his eyes darkened. "I think it is time for my wife and I to retire." He stood and held out a hand to her. She took it, her fingers tingling at his touch.

The others said their goodnights, but Linneya barely heard them. He pulled her toward their tent, setting an insistent pace. Once inside, they worked in silence, setting up their sleep pallet and adjusting their packs so they could fit comfortably in the tent.

Linneya tried not to make eye contact with Darryn, worried that he was fuming in light of his sister's revelation. He made no effort to break their quiet reverie, so she bit back the myriad of things she wished to say to try to make him less angry.

Finally, their pallet was ready. She laid down next to her knight, their arms barely touching. Her body ached from all of the riding, but a deep satisfaction that they were on the right path kept the soreness from being overwhelming. Finally, Linneya looked over, studying his face.

"What are you thinking?" she asked.

"I cannot believe you did not tell me that Shailyn helped you." His tone was teasing and he nudged her with his elbow.

She giggled in relief and curled into him. "So much has happened. I did not mean to keep it from you, but the past several days have been a whirlwind." Linneya placed a hand on his chest and propped her chin on the back of it. "If it helps, my dear warrior, your sister drilled me about my intentions before letting me go. Then, she demanded I return as soon as I could. She is loyal to you, Darryn."

He brushed hair back from her face, studying her expression. "I know. She believes the best in everyone, especially me." He huffed a laugh. "She gives me more credit than I deserve, so I owe her whatever grace I can muster. I am stunned she thought letting you go alone into the wilderness for a mooncycle was the best course of action. She knows how valuable you are."

Valuable was an odd choice of words, but Linneya hummed her agreement. "Well, it is not as if she could come with me. I was desperate to go and she was a good friend for what she did."

His arms tightened around her. "Still, I am going to struggle to let it go. The thought of you in those woods, alone. Knowing what could have happened if you had not been able to escape..." He shuddered and she lifted her head.

"But I did escape. We are here now. Safe for this moment." Linneya kissed his jawline and he gave her a tight smile before she settled her head on his chest. They laid in comfortable silence, his fingers making gentle strokes across her back. Linneya thought back to the bandits, choosing Darryn over her family, and the subsequent ambush. She wondered if she would have been able to get to Darryn if Raithor had not stalled anyone who tried to follow.

She jolted upright. Raithor. The mysterious mist-whisperer in Serathor's camp. She had not thought of the man since, but did not remember seeing him when the scouts attacked. She ran her fingers through her hair and huffed. He claimed to be sworn to Darryn and helped her escape, but how did her knight know a scout from Serathor?

Darryn pushed himself into a half reclining position, stroking her leg. "What is it, love?"

"Who is Raithor?"

Darryn's hand stilled. He cocked his head and sat upright. "Who did you just say?"

Linneya sucked in a breath. "Raithor. He was with the scouts. The man indicated he was loyal to you and I want to know more."

"What did he tell you?"

"Only that he had sworn his fealty to you. He knew who I was and tried to offer a way of escape. Why? Who is he to you?"

Darryn hissed through his teeth. "He is a spy. I cannot believe he risked blowing his cover just to have a chat. He is so impulsive it is miraculous he has never been caught."

She shook her head. "He was not just chatting, Darryn. The man helped me escape. I would not have made it to you if he had not been stalling the others." She crossed her arms and narrowed her eyes. "I did not see him at the ambush."

He nodded at her. "That is because he was not there. He is adept at keeping out of battles that might create an awkward situation for him. He is loyal to me, but he should have never revealed himself to you. Raithor knows nothing beyond the fact I am married. You could have been hurt - or killed - if the two of you were caught discussing me." His eyes darkened at the thought.

Linneya studied his face, as if she could search hard enough and figure out what he was hiding. A spy on a mission for her husband. What was more, Darryn did not try to play it off smoothly. Raithor's actions disturbed him. They tapped into a primal fear.

Raithor had called Darryn something. Stormbringer. She had never heard anyone else use that title. Darryn had set his jaw and his expression was stone. He was already avoiding something and she knew he was unlikely to answer her query.

She pursed her lips and tried anyway. "He called you Stormbringer. Why?"

Darryn's jaw pulsed and a line formed between his eyebrows. "He should not have done that." The threatening tone told Linneya that he would not entertain her questions any longer.

She crossed her arms. "Fine, keep your secrets, sir. Just hope there never comes a day where it affects me to be out of the loop."

He sighed and pulled her close. She tried to relax into him, but her thoughts were whirling. A spy, placed in a Serathanian scouting party, was sworn to her husband. Linneya had always known that there was more to Darryn than he would admit, but this felt sinister. Dangerous.

She closed her eyes. The exhaustion from the day's ride finally won out and she drifted into a dreamless sleep. There would be time to fight about his spy friend later.

The next morning, Darryn and Linneya carefully packed the tent and made their way through the camp, checking on everyone and helping wherever they were needed. At the *bluris* cattle paddock, Linneya wrestled with the harnesses and Darryn helped pull out the stakes.

Approaching hoofbeats made them both straighten up. A few shouts of welcome sounded as the galloping horse made its way toward them. The dark red hair of its rider brought a grin to Linneya's face and she waved.

Trotyn slid off his horse before the creature had even managed to stop. He was holding up a couple of scrolls, wide-eyed and breathless.

Darryn stiffened at the sight and charged forward, snatching one of the papers from Trotyn's hand.

Trotyn's eyes sparkled and he lifted his chin, proud of his handiwork. "That was easier than I expected. Brother, have you ever learned how we catalogue the scrolls?"

Linneya laughed but Darryn waved him off, scouring the parchment as if it held life and death answers. She wandered over, peering around his arm at the scroll. Written in the ancient human tongue, *Hougoutian*, she could only decipher a few words. She bit her lip, wishing she had spent less time with the ancient fae and merfolk dialects and more time studying a more practical classical language.

Darryn read with narrowed eyes. Linneya became more antsy with each passing moment. Finally, he looked up and nodded at Trotyn. "Yes, well done. This is the final bit."

Trotyn grinned and Linneya cocked her head. "What are you two on about?"

Darryn rolled up the scroll and pulled her tight. "Just some enchantments that Falryn and I discussed. They are for my aether-weaver affinity." He kissed her forehead. "I was researching two: one will hopefully fortify the shields around the city to stop dragons from entering. The other will possibly slow death and give life-tenders more time to heal critically wounded soldiers."

Trotyn cocked his head with a bemused expression, but Linneya's eyes grew wide. If Darryn could slow death, anyone with a fatal dragon burn could be held in stasis while she healed them. This could save so many lives. Again, she swelled with pride at the thought of everything they were bringing back to her home country.

As they got closer to Aelor, tensions rose. The once animated auxiliary units turned somber. The Falorian knights stopped debating strategy with Darryn, as if they had finally come to terms with whatever final decisions had been issued.

One night, they stopped near a stream. Linneya remembered it as her one-week landmark from their trip out of Aelor. She smiled to herself, thinking of all that had changed over the past season.

Darryn had gone to check on the paddock setup and Straion was helping to build the fire, so Linneya was working with Mariel to erect their tents. They were laughing about an ongoing prank war between Shailyn and Straion when a rider emerged from the woods.

Linneya gasped and stepped in front of Mariel, preparing to fight the newcomer, until his shaggy blonde hair came into view. Relief flooded her body. She and Mariel both cried out in excitement and ran toward the man.

Graisor dismounted and bowed his head toward Linneya. "Your Highness, Tiuthan has returned to Bachael to his father's court. He has pledged to send the fae units to Loraen within a duosnight." She nodded, thanking him.

Mariel grabbed his arm and tugged. "Straion is going to be thrilled you have made it back to us." She started pulling him toward the center of camp, where her husband was stacking wood.

He threw his head back and laughed. "Calm down, fierceness! I just arrived." She grinned, but did not relent. Graisor let her lead him toward Straion. The man looked up from his fire and shouted in greeting as Graisor and Mariel walked toward him.

Linneya did not have the same cheerfulness. She wrung her hands, mulling over the news. Two weeks before the fae would arrive to Aelor's capital. Would that be enough time?

Chrysa stepped out of the woods carrying water buckets. Her eyes glowed chartreuse in the height of the moon's light. She stopped as she saw Linneya, studying her face. "Are you alright, princess?"

Linneya hugged herself, sucking in a deep breath. The woodsy, musky scent of their chosen camping spot was soothing. If she closed her eyes and stood here long enough, she could get lost in the sounds of the birds whistling their lullabies. The woodland creatures chirping their goodnights.

Chrysa set the buckets of water down and came to Linneya's side. She placed a hand on Linneya's forearm and squeezed. "Lia?"

Linneya grabbed her friend's hands and squeezed. "I am sorry. The journey has exhausted me. I am worried for what this means for my people." Chrysa nodded as if she understood, but Linneya suspected this trip was even harder on her.

"How are you feeling? Coming back to Loraen must be so difficult."

It was Chrysa's turn to hug herself, her green eyes becoming glassy with tears. "It's been so long that I did not expect it to feel as vivid as it does." She gestured around them. "I remember these woods. I can almost hear my mother softly weeping as we stopped to camp. Even the smell of the icy ground brings back the horror I felt."

A bitter pang coursed through Linneya at the thought. She reached for Chrysa and placed her hands on the woman's shoulders. "If it becomes too much, please let me know. I will do whatever is necessary to get you out of here if you need."

The woman blinked back tears, a watery smile forming on her face. "Thank you." She reached for her buckets and nodded a farewell toward Linneya.

Linneya sighed, turning back toward the tent to finish setting the final pegs in place. The dread in her stomach was quickly solidifying into something more sinister. This battle was going to be anything but easily won, and even then a victory might not mean relief.

Chapter 30

The assassin was hiding in the dark purple brush. He had eyes on a cave to his left, but was camouflaged well enough he could not be spotted from the village across the river. The sound of flowing water nearby drowned out the bustle of the town's dock and attached market. Musty odors of fish and mildewy mud spoke to the shallow river's lowering water levels. The sunslight danced across the rippling currents, unbothered by how fast the river was drying up.

The occasional raft or fishing boat floated past, pushing downstream toward the capital. Once or twice someone would shout they were stuck and a few dockworkers would scramble with poles to help. So far, they had all managed to break free and continue.

The assassin adjusted his *trillin* mask and stretched as if he had been waiting for hours. Finally, a weather-worn rowboat stopped at the small dock. Two men got out, lugging barrels, and a third remained behind to secure the rickety little skiff.

The man was limping, an inconsistent stride that seemed more for show than out of necessity. His jet black hair had a single white streak at the temple. After tying the boat to the dock, he slung a bag over his shoulder, turned, and made his way to the bridge. The assassin slipped into the mouth of the cave, squatting into an attack position behind some rocks.

The cave had a metallic, wet gravel smell. Something deep inside dripped, the noise growing louder as it reverberated off the walls. The assassin pulled out his shell and a red stone, setting them on top of a smaller rock to one side. A few minutes later, sounds of shuffling grew and the man with the jet black hair darkened the entrance to the cave. He huffed a bit, adjusting his bag, and shambled forward.

The harbinger of death sprang out just as the man lumbered past. The man jumped back, grinning and drawing a small blade from a hidden sheath in his tunic. "You have been following me, dark one. What do you want?"

The assassin stepped away from the blade and hissed. "You are needed. Offer yourself for the good of the human realms. Accept your place as a sacrifice."

The man barked a laugh. "Accept my place?" He snorted. "We all know the rumors of the false prophesied and what he is trying to accomplish. You will never succeed."

The harbinger leaned in. "What gives you the right to accuse me of this falsehood? I have worked hard to claim my title." He smacked his chest with one hand. "Me! No one else."

"*Gokaw aeki raewi.*" The ground-tamer ignored the assassin's question and the walls of the cave began to shake as reddish smoke billowed from his body. The ground split open, forcing them apart. The assassin fell back, grunting and the ground-tamer waved his arms as if he was directing his element. "The only way forward is peace! You must stop!"

The soil welled up, building a circular wall around the harbinger of death. His eyes grew wide and he scrambled to find purchase on the walls, to haul himself up, but the structure kept growing.

"*Krebth boshog.*" The assassin twisted his wrist and immediately all movement stopped. Another whisper and he lifted out of the pit. He leered as the ground-tamer's mouth gaped.

He touched down and leaned over the man, smirking. "You are incorrect. The only way to survive is to live for war and vengeance. Our king has demanded that we fulfill the prophecy and reunite the human realms. You must surrender. Be a willing sacrifice and leave this world for a place of honor with Rasha!"

The ground-tamer scoffed, but was unable to hide his trembling. "Your king plays dangerous games. You cannot cheat fate. The true prophesied will rise and you will never rule."

The assassin growled, baring his teeth. "You know nothing of fate. I have worked too hard, done too much to fail."

The man raised his eyebrows. "Worked too hard?" He shook his head. "Fate does not care how strenuously you thrash against the goads. It plows ahead, unburdened by your futility."

The ground shook again, a small pit opening up and swallowing the assassin. He crumpled into the soil, still. The ground-tamer sucked in a few breaths and ran his hands through his hair.

Before the harbinger could come to, the ground-tamer stood and dusted off his tunic. He heaved his bag back over his shoulder and walked out of the cave. A groan from behind made him stiffen. The man began to run, the pretense of his limp forgotten. He disappeared over the embankment, down toward the river.

The pit was not deep, not difficult to traverse. Hands appeared over the side, one by one. The assassin pulled himself out of the spot, his navy blue cloak streaked in mud. He ran after the ground-tamer, raising his hands.

The ground began to shake. Linneya fell through pitch black. Darryn's hands were on her shoulders, his voice strained. "Lia, wake up. Wake up!"

She gasped as she came back to. Blood had drained from Darryn's face and his eyes were wide. "What was that? What did you see?" She grabbed his biceps, hanging on as if it would keep her from being flung back into the nightmare.

Linneya took a deep breath and rubbed her eyes. "I..." Everything was spinning so fast she could not gain her bearings. She squinted, trying to bring his face back into focus. "The assassin..." Darryn's jaw pulsed and he ran a knuckle across her cheek. She hung her head and ran her hands over her face.

Rustling outside their tent indicated others were awake. Murmuring voices caused Linneya to sit up. "Why is everyone outside?"

A shadow passed over his face. "The ground shook right as you began screaming. Your flame element seemed to activate. It was quick but violent, and -"

He was interrupted by the sound of someone coming in. The tent flap rustled and Mariel poked her head through. "Is everything okay? Lia, you sounded terrified."

Linneya motioned for her friend to come in and sit. "I am fine, I just have horrendous nightmares sometimes." She took a deep breath and looked at Darryn, a question on her face. He seemed to understand and slowly nodded back. It was time to tell the others.

Mariel sat cross-legged at the edge of the pallet and watched their exchange. "What is it?"

Linneya chewed on her lip and ran her hands through her hair. "I think I see things in my dreams. Real events."

Mariel's eyes narrowed and her eyebrows scrunched, a worried look. "Dream-walking?"

Darryn put his arm around Linneya's shoulders, holding her protectively. Linneya smiled at her friend. "Yes, it seems so. I keep having dreams around an assassin who is hunting elementals for their power."

Linneya retold the events of her dreams from the past few mooncycles. Mariel bit at her thumbnail, occasionally interrupting with questions. Linneya answered them the best she could, letting Darryn fill in any Creators-blessed lore he knew from the archives. By the time they were done, Linneya's thoughts were muddled. Like a wet cloth that had been completely wrung out, she had nothing left.

Mariel folded her arms. "I think you should tell the others. If this assassin is connected to the impending threat from Serathor, the more trusted friends you have to discuss this with, the better."

Darryn grunted his agreement. Linneya nodded, anticipation knotting her stomach. "I would love to understand the purpose of my seeing these things. It seems odd for a dream-walker to be receiving only this particular set of events."

Mariel crawled to her and hugged her. "Whatever it is, we will figure it out. Get some more sleep. I will let everyone know we will meet in the morning." She smiled and made her way back outside.

Linneya settled back onto their pallet, staring blankly at the tent canopy. Beside her, Darryn's breathing steadied, the consistent sound of his sleep a welcome rhythm. Worry passed through her body, a whispering shiver. The ground-tamer had escaped, hopefully, and made his way back to his friends. She closed her eyes, petitioning the Creators for a peaceful second sleep. They did not grant her request.

The next morning, once the suns were up and the supply wagons were repacked, Darryn gathered their friends. She was struggling from the insomnia, her eyelids were heavy from the lack of sleep. Everyone piled around the doused campfire, settling onto logs and larger stones as he and Linneya explained the groundquake from the previous night and the possibility of Linneya's dream-walking.

Chrysa busied herself braiding Shailyn's hair, as if she wanted no part in the conversation. Mariel leaned into Straion and he played with a loose curl in her hair. Graisor and Trotyn shared a large boulder, acting the most intrigued out of the crew by grunting and tutting at certain details.

As they finished, Mariel sat up. "But this is not everything. Whether Linneya is a dream-walker or not, she almost certainly holds another affinity."

The question earned a rumble through the group. Linneya's eyebrows knitted together at the thought and Graisor scoffed, "Oh, sure, and grass is green." Others chimed in, incredulous at Mariel's comment.

Mariel chewed on her thumbnail and weathered the comments. Once the crew settled, she turned to Darryn. "Tell me, do you have hidden ground-tamer abilities?"

He grumbled. "No, I would gain nothing by hiding such a talent. Can you imagine how useful it would be for me to have triple elements as a Falorian knight?" Graisor and Trotyn huffed their agreement.

She leaned forward and nodded to him. "Then who dropped Johann into the pit during your duel?"

Everyone got deathly still except Chrysa, who continued braiding Shailyn's hair. Mariel continued, gesturing excitedly. "Lia, you mentioned the quake that happened when you killed the bandit. Last night, was it similar? I think there is reason to believe you hold ground affinity."

Linneya's stomach dropped and she clenched her jaw. It was true, she was only able to kill the bandit because the ground shook and a rock rolled to her. She had felt something at the duel, right before the ground opened up. And last night - could it be that the dream and her related emotions provoked a response from a power she suppressed?

Chrysa turned her head slightly and talked through the comb she had secured in her mouth."If you hold ground affinity, that would be highly unusual. Three affinities out of the five... Do you think it is possible you could be the prophesied?"

Linneya pressed her lips together to keep from laughing. The idea was absurd. She was a princess, sure, but her talents were in healing. She was proud of the skills she had learned over the past season, but her moderate combat abilities would not translate into anything more.

It was then that she realized everyone was scrutinizing her response. Linneya blinked rapidly, her eyes wide. "None of you actually believe this, do you?" She shook her head and huffed a laugh. "No, there is no way. I am grateful to have learned more about fighting, but I have no real skills in that arena."

Darryn had a gleam in his eye that she had never seen before. Almost greedy, almost murderous. His features shifted slightly, as if the idea of Linneya holding power over all five elements excited him.

The others were in varying stages of thoughtfulness. Chrysa had finished braiding Shailyn's hair and plopped down next to her. Mariel leaned into Straion and he wrapped his arm around her waist. Graisor and Trotyn stared at her as if she had morphed into a *sharvach*.

The silence was uncomfortable. Linneya shifted on her feet. "Look, if my dreams are real, then this assassin is the prophesied and it has nothing to do with me. There is no reason to waste time on false hope."

Trotyn spoke first, cocking his head to the side. "What little we have been able to glean about the prophesied does not match with your dreams. The person will not be able to force the powers, like the ground-tamer suggested in your most recent dream. The true prophesied will only come forth in ash and flame." He shrugged. "Of course, no one is completely sure what that means."

Mariel cleared her throat. "Even though affinities manifest slower now than they did a couple of generations ago, I imagine Lia would feel it if she had connections to the other elements." She turned toward Linneya. "You have always had an attraction to flame. I would guess you would have a longing to be around the other elements as well."

Linneya nodded vigorously. She had never felt a direct calling to other elements. Unless she counted her urge to spend time in nature. Her breath hitched and she wrung her hands. Had she misinterpreted her entire childhood? Is it possible this love of wilderness meant she had a destiny she could have never imagined?

She hugged herself and took a deep breath. No, she knew from the other life-tenders that many healers felt the calling to the woods, to the freedom of knowing how to harness nature for healing. Her ability to help others was her value. She was bringing help to her people, not coming home to claim her place as the prophesied. "I agree with Mari. I only feel that connection with flame and mist."

Graisor spoke slowly, weighing his words. "The person would not necessarily know they have the affinities. It is possible that the prophesied would not know until the moment that it is needed. Fate is an odd thing."

Straion piped up. "Yes, but Falryn is a phenomenal teacher and has an uncanny sense of a person's abilities. How would they not have realized Linneya's potential?"

Linneya shook her head. "Falryn never tested me for the other elements. We only did sister element enchantments."

Shailyn fidgeted with the ends of her braids. "Why do you think Falryn never tested you on the other affinities?"

Linneya shrugged. "I do not know. We never discussed it. It seems ridiculous to think I would be some special case with a legendary combination of power."

Chrysa crossed her arms. "Why? Why is that so farfetched? You are dream-walking and watching this assassin murder elementals. It is possible that you have a larger part to play."

Trotyn murmured his assent. Linneya's heart pounded wildly in her chest. The others chimed in with their agreement and her hands began to shake at the prospect. She could not shoulder that kind of burden, could not imagine herself embracing the warrior's darkness. It must be someone else.

Darryn stepped to her side and placed his hand on her lower back, the familiar warmth anchoring her. "I can test you, Linneya. At least we can see whether you have ground-tamer abilities. It could come in handy for the battle."

The thought of wielding another affinity left a sour taste in her mouth. She was unsure if she wanted to face the implications of controlling three elements. She sighed and shook her head. "Would it matter? There is no time for me to train."

Her knight smiled and brushed a lock of hair out of her face. "Yes, I can at least teach you some basics. Ground is a sister element to mist, so you are already partially there. It should be easy to tap into it if you are manifesting the affinity."

Linneya hugged herself and scrunched her face, considering. Fatigue muddled her brain and a sense of heaviness settled over her. His words from earlier in the trip crossed through her mind. She was valuable. An asset to his cause. Her heart sank.

No doubt, if they survived this battle and returned to Enthor, King Birron would demand her service upon learning that she wielded a third element. She doubted he would be satisfied with her in the arena, either. He would require her to join a special unit and wield her affinity for his gain. A knot of dread formed in her stomach. She had no interest in fighting more than was necessary.

Darryn ran his hand up her back, squeezing once at the base of her neck. "Love, it would be better to have all tools at your disposal against Serathor. Even one more person knowing how to call and suppress using ground could make a difference in how well we stand against their stolen elemental power."

Several in the circle murmured their agreement. Shailyn had leaned forward and raised her eyebrows in excitement. Mariel was chewing on her thumbnail again while Straion's leg bounced up and down in anticipation. Graisor and Trotyn had the same fire in their eyes. Chrysa was the only one schooling her face into boredom, but a twitch in her cheek indicated she was also invested in the outcome of this conversation.

Everyone here had sacrificed. They had dropped everything on her word that Serathor's scouts had threatened her home country. No one had complained, no one had guilted her for the inconvenience. They just showed up and prepared to fight. She owed them the same.

Linneya dropped her hands to her side. "Alright. We might as well see."

The tension broke and everyone began chattering. Darryn nodded his approval, his eyes bunching at the corners with a suppressed smile. She slipped her hand into his and squeezed, hoping he would mistake her anxious trembling for excitement.

Darryn angled away from her and addressed their friends. "Linneya and I will stay here and test her for all three elements. The caravan should continue as normal. We will catch up this evening."

Everyone scattered, packing the remaining tents and smothering any lingering campfires. Darryn went with Trotyn and Graisor to inform the auxiliary leaders of the change in plans. Linneya busied herself with helping Mariel, focusing on anything except the upcoming tests.

Before she was ready, the regiments were on the road. The knot in her stomach twisted tighter as the sounds of the caravan dwindled. The fog of sleepiness amplified her anxiety. Too soon, it was quiet, the only sounds coming from the wildlife that was re-emerging now that the bulk of the people were gone.

Linneya stood there, staring after where the last of the infantry had disappeared. It was as if the moment she turned, everything would change. She chuckled at how odd the thought was. Things had already changed.

Chillbumps formed as Darryn brushed his fingers along her neck and shoulder. If anyone could be a safe harbor in all of this chaos, it was him. She finally turned, locking her gaze with his. The dark depths of his eyes held her captive and the world fell away. She wanted to stay like this, with him, in the quiet spaces of the woods.

But nothing lasts forever. The new hunger in his gaze unsettled her. Almost as if her affinities meant more than their relationship.

"What is it, love?"

Linneya took a deep breath. "It is nothing. Nerves, mostly." She shook her arms and hands, trying to fling off the anxiousness like a creature removing water from its fur. "What do we need to do? What are these tests?"

Darryn motioned deeper into the woods. "We will find a clearing and you will use the elemental enchantments and see what happens. I figured you would not want an audience, which is why I sent everyone on." He stepped closer, his eyes shining playfully. "Of course, there are a few other things we could do without an audience."

She blushed and grinned, grateful for the deflection. "Let us see where the day takes us, warrior. Lead the way."

He offered her his arm and they wandered into the forest. The blue and purple of the tree leaves filtered the sunlight into a soothing tone. Linneya brushed her hands through a citrusbalm bush, distributing the tangy scent of its leaves. A chittering creature fussed at its friend and the two chased each other, winding up a trunk of a worlnutt tree.

For a moment, she could almost imagine they were on a morning stroll. Maybe they had taken the long way from the mansion to avoid the piles of paperwork that awaited them at home. She leaned closer in to Darryn as he motioned for her to look at a bird. In a different life, they could have had such peace. True happiness.

But reality was so different. Exhaustion washed over her. They were a team, sure, but he could not love her. Not when his first love was his vow to the Falorian knights. If King Birron had not demanded they marry, the man would have never followed through on his attraction to her. Linneya sucked in a breath, ignoring the ache settling into her chest. The best thing she could do for both of them was figure out how to wield the other elements.

Maybe being the prophesied would not be terrible. Maybe Darryn would see her as an equal. Or at least as someone who could be of use to him, could fight alongside him and his all-important knights.

She startled as she tripped over a tree root, stumbling into a large clearing. Darryn steadied her and grinned. "Whoa, princess."

Linneya huffed in embarrassment and dropped her arm. "You and your horses."

He threw his head back and laughed. She gave him a pinched smile and looked around. "At least it seems like we found a good spot for these tests."

The clearing had a large boulder and several smaller rocks scattered throughout. Standing puddles of water created a strange musty scent and invited gnats to play. Linneya picked her way across, avoiding mushier areas, and settled onto a rock with a hollowed out place perfect for her hips.

She kicked her legs out in front of her and cocked her head, ignoring the whirling dread that spun inside of her. "So, tell me, how does this work?"

Darryn stopped in front of her, hands on his hips. She struggled to ignore how his messy hair and half wrinkled tunic brought the fluttering of butterflies to her stomach. He was gorgeous, he was hers. At least, as much as he would allow.

He smirked and leaned in, as if he could read her thoughts through the expression on her face. "I need you to stand up and focus on the ground element. Find a way to connect as you use the enchantments. *Gokaw aeki raewi*. Try it."

Linneya matched his energy, leaning closer. For a moment, their gazes locked. She touched his neck with her fingers and his pulse beat an urgent rhythm. She whispered, "You will have to move back so I can stand."

Darryn's jaw pulsed as he stepped away. A sense of satisfaction rose in her gut. Linneya may have wanted a fierce, all-encompassing love, but she could work with what she was given. He might be hungry for her to gain more power and become a force on the battlefield, but she could see he was just as affected by this physical pull as she was.

She raised her hands and dug deep, trying to feel the visceral connection with the ground. "*Gokaw aeki raewi*." A reddist, rust-colored smoke pulsed from her hands. Immediately the rocks around them rumbled, several rattling or tumbling on the ground.

Her mouth fell open. It was an instant connection, a sense of deeper understanding. She could feel the dirt beneath her, the roots of the plants communicating fate through the soil, even the bugs and worms digging their way through. Creatures burrowed and the planet breathed.

She was drawn deeper, to a molten marriage of flame and ground.

She gasped and dropped her arms. Darryn let out a sound of victory and rushed to her side. She doubled over, panting.

"What - What was that?" she gasped.

He knelt beside her. "What do you mean?"

Linneya shook her head, unable to speak. Her heart pounded in her chest, beating as if it was the drums at the entrance of the shadowed void. She had *connected*. It was more profound than the first times she had tapped into flame or mist. It was sudden and extensive. Was this what it meant to wield all the elements? She shuddered, a mix of excitement and terror at the thought of being named the prophesied.

Darryn waited patiently until she straightened back up. The dark flame in his eyes danced. "You felt something."

She nodded. "It was like I was bonding. Instantaneous resonance." Linneya did not dare voice her thoughts around being the prophesied.

The expression on Darryn's face turned impassive. "We should move ahead with vine. Once we know what you are working with, we can devise a training plan. *Raegow aeki rawi.*" He motioned for her to repeat the words.

Her fatigue was wearing her down already, but she raised her arms. "*Raegow aeki raewi.*" Her voice caught on the last word. She coughed, cleared her throat, and tried again.

A branch shook and Linneya's eyes widened. It was not the same kind of powerful force as ground, but what if this was it? What if she could be the person who healed the lands? Even if it was through the brutality of war, perhaps the result would make it worth it.

The branch rustled again and her heart rose in her throat. She was not ready for this responsibility. This was not who she wanted to be. There was no way -

Her thoughts were interrupted as a chittering creature dropped off the branch and to the ground. She dropped her hands, simultaneously relieved and disappointed. A small chuckle bubbled up at her mistaking the animal's movement for a whisper of vine affinity.

If she had been the prophesied, this fight would be easier. Maybe she could have been the surefire advantage Aelor needed to win against Serathor. Maybe Darryn would have kept looking at her with that stare that melted her core. She cut her eyes to her husband.

Instead, Darryn's face remained neutral. He showed no signs of disappointment at her failure. "Now, aether. *Raeshio aeki raewi.*"

She bit her lip, not wanting to continue. "Is this really necessary? I have no vine affinity. It seems ridiculous to think I have aether."

Darryn shrugged. "We need to cover all of our bases. What kind of knight would I be if I did not make sure that our most powerful weapon was able to use anything. Aether, Lia."

His most powerful weapon. Her heart sank. The closer they got to her parent's capital, the more she had been reminded of their early conversations. An image flashed through her memory of the play hut, destroyed by a single storm.

She shook her head, trying to clear the thoughts of a weary mind. No matter what, he was taking her home. He rallied his own order to fight her battles. Even if it was for selfish reasons, they were going to be together. They would win. The rest could be figured out later.

It was no surprise to her when the aether enchantments offered her no power. Darryn was unusually quiet as they walked back to their horses. She hugged Thefa's neck and steadied herself before mounting. Exhaustion ate away at her confidence the entire time they rode to catch up with their friends.

Chapter 31

At dusk, they came upon the camp. Darryn took their horses to graze and brought back Graisor and Trotyn. The others gathered around and Linneya's heart sank as he explained the news.

Everyone else seemed to take it better. She found comfort in the chaos of their overlapping opinions. Trotyn chuckled. "If nothing else, the two of you have all of the powers combined."

Shailyn sighed. "Well, at least we do not have to worry about you dying in some heroic display as you fight their false prophesied."

Mariel just smiled until Straion cracked some joke under his breath and she elbowed him. Chrysa stood nearby, her bright green eyes narrowed in thought. Graisor leaned on a tree trunk beside Darryn, mirroring his closed off body language.

Linneya nodded along with the conversation, but she barely heard anything through the fog of fatigue. The knot in her stomach had solidified into a stone. Its heavy weight sank her emotions, but she pasted a smile on her face.

Her value was in her ability to heal, not fight. She had always nurtured the light side of her affinities. Only in the past season had she paid attention to the dark, destructive forces she could wield.

Linneya studied Darryn's expression. Why had he become so distant when she could not call all of the elements? Was his attraction to her because of her power? His love and honor was wrapped up in his Falorian knight oaths. He had said it over and over. Maybe she needed to recognize a losing battle when she saw it.

She yawned and he strode to her side. "Are you ready for bed? Graisor set us up beside Mariel and Straion."

She nodded and they said their goodnights to the crew. As they made their way inside the tent, she finally broke. "I will be okay if you need to leave me in Aelor once this is over."

He blinked rapidly and his brows knit together as he secured the tent flap. "Why would you say that?"

Linneya shifted away from him, shame flooding her veins. The heavy sensation of disappointment settled between her shoulders. "I am not as powerful as you had hoped. If this makes me a burden, I understand if you want to annul our marriage once this battle is over."

He grabbed her hand and shook his head. "Linneya, it is too late for second thoughts. I will not let you regret this."

She smiled sadly. "You will not *let* me? Darryn, how can you stop me? Our lives were upended. This is not where you wanted to be..."

He interrupted, wrapping his hand onto the back of her neck and drawing her close. "Stop. You did not sleep well last night and the tests today have depleted you. These are the thoughts of exhaustion, not reality."

She gave him a small smile and laid a hand on his chest. He was right, but the feelings did not dissipate with a single comment.

The glint in his eyes told her that he was still worried. "What is it, Lia? What happened to send you down this path?"

She dropped her head in embarrassment, staring at the ground. "I know how valuable I could have been to you if I had been the prophesied."

He stroked her hair. "Why do you think that matters?"

"You froze me out today."

"I tried to not seem excited or disappointed. You already work so hard, I did not want my reaction making things worse."

"Ah, I see."

"I am with you, no matter what. What do I have to say to get you to believe me? How many times will I need to worship your body?" He leaned forward and pressed a slow kiss on her cheek. He dragged his lips down, landing beneath her ear. His breathing became ragged, the sound sending a warm pulse spiraling to her center. She pressed her legs together to try to relieve the ache and hummed her approval.

"Hear me, wife." He grabbed her chin and lifted her face to his. "Your value lies in being here, being a part of my life. I only want you to have more power because it will keep you *safe*. I promise you, I am yours - body and spirit."

Linneya flushed under his gaze, but managed a wobbly smile. His understanding in this moment was welcome, the distraction of his body pressed against hers was a relief. "I want to trust this, trust us."

Darryn huffed, his voice turning husky. "I will make you come every night until you see it. Until you feel it in your soul."

He crushed his mouth to hers as his hand slipped between her thighs. He swallowed her moan and pressed her back onto their pallet. Linneya went molten under his touch, her hips bucking to meet his rhythm.

For the rest of their journey, he would keep his promise.

Linneya woke to the sound of Darryn rustling through his bag. She rubbed the sleep from her eyes and turned to watch him work. A flush warmed her as the memory surfaced of his hands between her legs. His muscles rippled as he dug through the knapsack. Somehow, even his burn scars made him look more powerful.

A relief flooded through her body. It finally felt like they were on the same page, completely on board. She reached out, stroking down his back. He startled at her touch and turned around, ears turning red. "Lia, I did not mean to disturb you." He brushed her hair out of her face.

Linneya's lips turned up at the corners. "It is okay. I am just happy to wake up to you." She sat up, running her hands over his bare torso.

He sighed. "I will never tire of your touch, of the way your hands stir something in me." Her knight pulled her to him, tucking a stray curl behind her ear.

She traced the rough skin of his burns, the texture like a bas relief, a hidden story of pain and resilience. "Will you ever tell me how you got these?"

Darryn wrinkled his nose. "It is not that impressive, really. Stupid childhood bravado. Mother took me to see dragon hatchlings after the last firemountain eruption in the North Isles. I snuck away in the evening to go back to the nest. I was convinced a dragon would bond with me if I was the first human it saw."

Linneya's eyes went wide. Witnessing the birth of dragons was an amazing experience. Her brother had gone once and came back with grand tales of the hatchlings glowing like the superheated rocks around them. She had always dreamt of one day watching the dragon hatchlings riding the flowing molten lava. Secretly, she thought one would sense her flame affinity and bond with her.

He laid back on their pallet and continued. "I arrived just as the hatchlings emerged, humming their birthing song. They were scrawny little things, barely reaching my waist. One coughed embers and I laughed. The sound startled them and the whole nest flew up in a defensive spiral pattern, as if they had practiced the maneuver in another lifetime. After that, I was obsessed. They were beautiful. I wanted to know everything I could."

She spread her hand on his abdomen and he murmured in contentment before continuing. "Mother enlisted Noryo to teach me more about becoming a dragon rider. The man was relentless. He made everything a fascinating adventure, but it was also a lot of hard work. I trained alongside some of the Falorian knights. They all treated me like an apprentice and I learned how to be cleverly brutal. I stoked my bloodlust, defining my fate with my well-honed cruelty. At least, my child-self thought I did." He smiled at the memory.

Something protective and proud boiled up in her at the thought of a young Darryn trying to be fierce. She wanted to wrap her arms around the little one and hug him close, but she imagined he would have squirmed away and demanded independence. Laughter tugged at her lips. "How did that lead to stupid childhood bravado?"

He let out a long breath, a look of regret shadowing his features. "I was only a few mooncycles into training when I overheard some of the knights talking about a hunter who had trapped a dragon and forced it to serve. My child-brain imagined one of those tiny hatchlings turning vicious and hurting our people. I was furious and wanted to fight the hunter and his beast. One of the knights mentioned they expected him to show up in a town close by, and I decided to try to find the hunter myself."

"I snuck out during second sleep and managed to make it to the river just in time to see the hunter descend. The suns' rays rising behind him made him seem like a god. His dragon towered over me and I realized I was no match for the creature, much less the man riding it. But, I could see there was something wrong." Darryn grimaced, as if the memory caused him pain. "The beast was stumbling, its head lolling about like it was sick. Its eyes glowed orange and its wings twitched in a frenzied manner. The hunter did not seem to care that this magnificent creature was in so much distress."

Linneya's hands clenched into fists at the thought. Warriors that abused their creatures were of the worst sort. She did not know how anyone could subdue a dragon in such a way. They were meant to fly free, to be a little wild. She watched him, trying to stay silent so he would continue.

Darryn sighed and placed an arm over his face. "So there I was, a lanky preteen, convinced I could take down this elemental hunter and his dragon. When I saw that poor thing suffering, it became more of a rescue mission. I was devastated to see such a creature trapped in its own mind, tormented. I got burned in the process, but I did manage to put the rabid beast out of its misery. Noryo discovered me before the hunter could destroy me."

"My mother was furious. She had never been so quiet as when Noryo walked back into our home with me half burnt and barely conscious. She set to work cleaning and dressing my wounds, but she hissed curses at me under her breath." He chuckled darkly. "I do not think she knew I heard her. We never spoke of it, there was never time. She died giving birth to Shailyn within the next season."

Linneya shivered and snuggled into his side. This man had always used violence to protect those he loved. Even as a child, he tried to do the right thing at any cost.

He shook off the memories and pressed a kiss to her forehead. "There is a lake nearby. With as warm as it is tonight, I was thinking we should go for a swim." He rubbed the back of his neck, blushing as if he was an anxious schoolboy.

She raised her eyebrow at his expression. "You are acting jittery. What is wrong?"

He cocked his head and sat up. "Nothing, I just thought we might not have another chance to be alone before the battle. I would like to make one more lovely memory with my wife before we face King Shumor and his dragons."

Linneya narrowed her eyes and poked his side. "As long as you promise you are not playing some prank, I will go."

He grinned, caught her hand, and kissed her fingers. "I have no pranks planned at the moment, but I refuse to swear to something that could change."

"That is not reassuring." She joked, returning his smile and moving to stand. "I will absolutely sic Narruan on you when we get home if you give me any grief."

He gave her a look of mock horror and rolled off the pallet, holding out his hand to help her up. She laughed softly and followed. They quickly dressed and made their way outside. Others were up, rising for moonwake, and Darryn gestured for her to stay silent as they passed through the campsite and into the forest.

Something about the setting felt like they were rebelling, sneaking away when it was not allowed. Linneya clung to Darryn's arm, suppressing her laughter as they picked their way through the overgrown trail. Mists rose around them like spirits beckoning, enticing them to wander from the path.

She gasped as they crested a knoll and the water came into view. The moon cast an orange glow on the lake, the water rippling with gentle movement. Some insects were emerging from their winterslumber, but Linneya no longer heard condemnation in their song. Instead, it was replaced with a sense of awakening. Celebration.

"What do you think?"

"This is beautiful. I am glad you suggested it." She let go of Darryn and took off, darting down the slope. Her knight was close behind and caught her around the waist at the water's edge. Linneya burst into giggles and turned around, kissing him.

Yesterday had been so heavy, so exhausting. Rest had lifted much of the melancholy and given her enough energy to suppress the remaining bit. She sucked in a deep breath and pressed her body against her husband.

"Warrior, I want you naked. Now."

Darryn grabbed her waist and squeezed before stepping back and smirking. "Patience, love."

Maintaining eye contact, he reached a hand up and pulled his tunic off in one swift motion. His muscles tensed in anticipation as she stroked across his abdomen.

Darryn gently slid his hands under her clothes and caressed her skin. The rough pads of his fingers sent her heart into a frenzied rhythm and her breathing became ragged.

"You caution patience and then touch me like that."

He grinned. "I want you begging me before we are done tonight."

She shivered at his tone and raised her arms so he could lift the tunic over her head. She did not want to think, did not want to strategize or figure out what would happen during the battle.

For tonight, she just wanted a good memory with him.

She kicked off her pants, grabbed his wrist, and began backing into the lake. His eyes wandered greedily over her curves. Goosebumps raised on her thighs as they trudged deeper. She began shivering and finally let go of him, raising her arms out wide and falling backwards into the water.

The warbling sound of being submerged enveloped her. Linneya always found a sense of tranquility when underwater. A momentary reset, cut off from the world, weightless. She could rest in this mysterious manifestation of the mist element forever.

But, as always, the moment ended too soon. Her body began pushing upward and her head broke above the lake. She sucked in the cool night air and wiped the water out of her eyes.

Darryn had made it a few more paces out, the water up to his chest. When they made eye contact, he motioned for her to join him. She pushed off the lake bottom and swam to meet him.

He pulled her to him, wrapping her legs around his waist. Darryn brushed wet hair away from her face and placed his hand on the back of her neck. Shivers traveled down to her core as he brushed his thumb over her pulse point. "I will never forget arriving at your home palace. I got off my horse, caught sight of you, and the world fell away. My purpose snapped into place. I wanted to protect you with my entire being. You are *mine*, Linneya. Your laugh, your spark... I have valued you from the very beginning."

She buried her head in the crook of his neck. "About yesterday, I am sorry, I - "

He twisted her hair into his hand, holding it at the base of her neck and angling her head. Linneya's breath hitched and his lips brushed the shell of her ear. "No apologies, love. It is to be expected after the chaos we have been through." His tongue dragged heat down her neck. "Now, tell me where you want me to touch you."

Linneya ran her hands up his chest and over his shoulders, interlocking her fingers at the back of his neck. She could feel his hardness rubbing against her through his trousers, the rough fabric amplifying the sensation and teasing the pleasure his thickness could bring. Her hips bucked against him and her breasts ached for his touch.

One palm dragged down her spine, pressing her closer as his other hand explored her hips and wandered to her breast. She moaned and he nipped her ear. "Words, princess. Where do you want me?"

"Everywhere. Anywhere. Just touch me, warrior."

He brought her lips back to his and devoured her. There was nothing gentle in Darryn's movement, as if he craved her and was being driven to madness. Her nipples pebbled in the cold and he ran a palm over one, causing her to cry out. Throbbing need built as he squeezed her closer. Linneya arched her hips into his and swallowed his groan with her tongue.

She was his. There was no denying it. His touch set her on fire. Creators, he could give her that *look* and she would melt.

Their bodies found a rhythm and Darryn dragged his hand up the inside of her thigh, pressing it into her apex. His warm hand against the cold water was a shock of ecstasy. Waves of anticipation radiated up her body. Linneya buried her head into his neck, humming her pleasure.

His responding laugh rumbled through her. "Come on, love. We should get out before we freeze. I brought blankets so we could enjoy ourselves." His voice dripped with meaning and Linneya shivered, more from eagerness than the cold.

They made it back to the bank and he wrapped a woolen blanket around her. She watched him pull out two quilts from his satchel and arrange them in the grass. He finally turned to her, smiling, and motioned for her to lie down on the makeshift pallet.

Linneya had other plans. "No, you stay there." Darryn needed to know how much she cared for him, how much she wanted his body every time they touched. She licked her lips and stared pointedly at his erection.

She slowly made her way to him and knelt down, unlacing his soaked trousers. Her body shivered as the woolen blanket fell away, but her focus was on the man in front of her. His length strained against the material, a clear indication of his desire. Linneya hooked her fingers around the waist and began peeling them off. The wet pants stuck to his thighs and he had to help her, but after several breaths of less than exciting wrenching and curses, he was finally bared to her.

He offered a sound of triumph and reached down to grab her hands. "We can continue this on the blankets."

She shook her head and grabbed his thighs, pulling him closer. "It's your turn, Darryn. I want you to understand how badly *I* have wanted *you*."

His responding chuckle turned into a groan as she wrapped her fingers around his length. The warmth of his soft skin was a welcome feeling after the cool night air. She gently squeezed and his hardness made her breath catch. Her apex ached, desperate for his touch.

Instead, she wrapped her lips around the tip and licked in slow circles. His legs tensed, as if he was trying to stop himself from thrusting. "Lia -" he gasped and she slipped him in further.

Linneya's core began to throb at the sight of this man standing in front of her, responding to her every touch with enthusiastic vulnerability. So different from the face he showed the rest of the world. *Hers.*

She pulled him out and pressed her lips against his thick head. Darryn looked down and met her gaze, his eyes glazed over and mouth slightly open. Without breaking his stare, she sucked him back in. He wound his fingers into her hair, twisting a handful to the base of her neck, and arched his hips. She moaned, signaling her approval, and began to move with him.

He hissed and she clasped his waist, bringing him to her. His tip bumped the back of her throat. She relaxed into it, greedily taking as much of him as she could. Stroke after stroke, harder and harder, she urged him on. Something about him coming undone thrilled her. It brought a new level of want to her core.

Darryn gasped her name, and she pulled back. His breathing was hard, feral, and he looked down at her wide-eyed and confused. A lusty haze had settled over both of them, but she knew she wanted it to last longer than this.

She pointed to the quilts. "Lie down."

His eyes flashed and his chest rose and fell with his panting. A grin cracked across his face and he bowed his head in acquiescence. Linneya took a deep breath, her arms tingling, aching to touch him again.

He settled onto the blankets and she leveraged her body over Darryn's, kissing and nipping her way across his collarbone. His hips bucked, grinding his hardness against her entrance. Need burned down her spine, settling low in her abdomen as a tight sensation.

But this was about him. He needed to know. So she pulled back, settling in between his legs. She licked from base to tip, circling her tongue around the crown of his length. Darryn threw his head back and groaned. She moaned in response, taking him in and massaging the parts of him that would not fit in her mouth.

"Lia, I want to touch you." The breathless request stirred a powerful wave of heat. She sat up and crawled perpendicular to his side, making her body available but keeping the apex of her thighs out of reach. She went back to work, pumping him in and out of her mouth, savoring the taste.

His movement became more insistent. An occasional gasp as she licked or sucked. She shuddered as his hands began running over her back, over her legs. Darryn grabbed the back of her thigh and pulled. "Come here so I can touch you."

Her core ached at the thought, her entrance slick and ready for him. She smirked. "Now who is begging for whom?"

He sat up and growled. Linneya squeaked in surprise as Darryn wrapped his hands around her hips, pulling her ass closer to him, and grunted with each movement, "I. Said. Come. Here."

Her knight laid back and brushed his fingers between her thighs before laying his palm on her aching center. She pressed into the sensation, every nerve in her body locking onto it. He slid a finger in and she cried out, losing all thought.

She took him again and he bucked further into her mouth, threading his fingers through her hair again. Linneya groaned her approval and grabbed his hips, working him as his muscles tensed and his grip on her hair became painfully tight. Darryn's length seemed to throb with their movements. He slid a second finger into her, stretching and pumping hard. It was pain and pleasure, wrapped into one delicious moment, as the great warrior came undone.

Her knight gasped her name like a petition to the deities. She met him stroke for stroke, humming encouragement. His final thrust spilled into her mouth and she slowed down, allowing him to ride the climax of his pleasure.

Once he finished, she pressed back up to her knees and made eye contact as she swallowed. She licked her lips and Darryn growled. He sat up and reached for her, gathering her to him. He snaked his hands down, one arm across her back as his hand cupped her ass.

The other hand hovered close to her slicked entrance and he whispered in her ear, "Now, be a good girl and come for me." She whimpered his name as his breath tickled her neck and he thrust his fingers back inside, setting a vicious pace.

The pressure of release gathered low in her core, trembling on the edge. All at once, he curled his fingers up and pressed his thumb into her sensitive bundle of nerves. Linneya writhed and he murmured his encouragement. She bucked once, twice, and a scream ripped from her throat as she shattered.

He circled his thumb over her swollen apex as the waves of sensation broke again and again. As they slowed, warm contentment washed over Linneya and she buried her head in Darryn's neck.

He slowly lowered them back to the pallet, covering them with the blanket. She snuggled in close, small shivers of her satisfaction still radiating through her body. He trailed his fingers up across her back, leaving goosebumps.

"That was..." He was still breathing hard and seemed to struggle for words. His arms tightened around her as if he would never let go.

Linneya ran her fingers through his hair, beaming. "Agreed." She would never get enough of this. Their bodies fit together perfectly. The intensity of his gaze could make her melt with one look. There would never be enough time to sate her desire toward this dark warrior.

She placed her hands on his chest and propped her chin on the back of them. "Are you going to tell me now why you were acting so suspicious earlier?"

He took a deep breath and brushed a knuckle across her cheekbone. "I know we took vows before the creators and our friends, but it was not the romantic experience you deserve."

She grinned, stroking his chest. "Maybe, or maybe not. That kiss was rather memorable."

Darryn tried to smile, but it was more a pained grimace. His hands shook as he pulled out a small pouch and handed it to her. "Still, it was not ideal. It was not the right way to do things. I wish I had started by showing you that you were cherished from the beginning. I hope this gesture begins to make up for that."

Linneya sat up, her forehead wrinkling in confusion. Darryn sucked in a breath. "This was my mother's ring. She wore it as a conduit for her aether. She would have loved you and I know she would be proud for you to wear it."

She raised her eyebrows. This was the stuff of legend. His mother must have been powerful. The stones could store energy, transforming it into another element or allowing the elemental to tap into the power later. Most people with affinities never had the level of precision or amount of power to successfully siphon anything into a secondary container, much less a small stone. The only other conduits she had seen were the larger stones in the Falorian knights' vaults.

He stroked a knuckle across her cheek. "With this, I vow to never leave your side, always protect you, and cherish you no matter what comes."

She opened the pouch and pulled out a silver ring with a pink teardrop stone. Inky black veins ran through the pink, creating a delicate web. On each side were intricately carved leaves, cascading down the band. Linneya's mouth dropped open. "Darryn, it is beautiful."

He looked out over the lake. "My mother wore it every day. She said the pink reminds us that we are called to nurture those around us, no matter how insignificant we feel. For even the diluted, soft rays from our smaller sun offer life."

Linneya slid the ring on her middle finger and studied it. "Do the black veins represent anything?"

Darryn took her hand and ran his thumb over the stone, a faraway look in his eyes. "She always said the black lines were whispers of the dark things you must embrace to protect those you love."

Her vision blurred with tears and she looked to the sky, trying to blink them back. "Thank you. This is lovely." Lovely did not cover it. The ring was a powerful piece of his past, a reminder of the mother he lost so young.

Linneya silently swore she would never take it off. Maybe she could even learn to wield it.

She turned to him. "Can you teach me how to use it as my own conduit?"

He narrowed his eyes and studied her face. Linneya could see some deeper battle raging, but stayed quiet. Finally, he nodded. "I think we can try. It might be worth letting Falryn talk you through it when we get back home."

She grinned and grabbed his arm, placing her head on his shoulder. "Yes, when we get home."

Darryn kissed the top of her head. "I think we should return to camp. It is past time for second sleep."

She murmured her assent and they began packing up. The ring kept catching the dwindling moonlight and she smiled every time it sparkled. The tangible reminder of his vow made heat creep up her cheeks. It was a side only she saw: the softness of his heart when he told her of the meaning behind the stone, the way he spoke of cherishing her. She breathed a sigh of contentment.

By the time they left, the moon had set and it was more difficult trying to traverse through the woods. Linneya jumped at more than one odd cracking noise. A giggle followed by someone crunching through the brush made Darryn pull her behind a boulder. She peeked around and grinned.

Straion and Mariel were sneaking through the brush. Mariel was clinging to his arm and he was whispering something in her ear. Straion grabbed her chin and wrapped his arm around her waist, pulling her close for a kiss. Mariel squeaked in surprise as he picked her up and they continued on.

Linneya ducked back down and stifled a laugh. Darryn raised his eyebrows and she pressed her lips together, shaking her head. He lifted up slightly, sneaking a look. He dropped back down, light dancing in his dark eyes. Linneya grinned and he grabbed her hand.

Mariel was finally getting her happily ever after and Linneya was thrilled. It had taken some time, but the harmony between Mariel and Straion was exciting. She could only hope that she and Darryn would follow suit.

Chapter 32

Returning to Loraen felt strange. After being gone for an entire season, Linneya found the woods around Aelor's capital mesmerizing. It was disorienting, as if things had slightly shifted in her absence. Colors were more vivid than she remembered. Details that had been ignored out of habit now struck her as unusual and fascinating. She hoped there would be time to explore and become reacquainted with the land once the battle had been won.

Anticipation formed, a clenching in her chest, as they approached the city gates. Yelling and loud pops startled her. Linneya's horse flinched at the sudden influx of sound. She reached down to soothe Thefa, then turned back toward their destination.

A crowd was forming, with more people running through the city's entrance. Her eyes grew wide at the sight of the multitude of citizens that had gathered to welcome them. The cracking of fireworks brought even more. Elated shouts rose as more of the residents recognized Linneya.

She and Darryn rode through the gates and into the throngs of people. Crowds lined every street, every alley, every balcony. A shower of flowers and leaves were tossed in their direction, one bundle flying over her head and nearly smacking Darryn.

Linneya looked at him. He was watching her, marking her every move. She smiled at him, her jaw a bit wobbly. His lips curved up and he nodded, almost in a deferential manner. A lump rose in her throat and she brushed away a few tears before anyone else could notice. She had spent annae hiding her affinity, fearful of what could happen if she was exposed.

But instead of a wave of elemental hunters chasing her down for her powers, she was met with this. Her heart leapt into her throat as she realized their return brought with it hope.

Hope of survival in the face of the most powerful army in the human realms.

Hope that this was not the end.

Hope for a future.

Someone threw a handful of red petals at their horses. A dark headed child sat on her father's shoulders, waving excitedly with both hands. Linneya's eyes burned with tears of relief. These people were not concerned with whether she stayed in the light and healed or gave into the darkness to fight and hurt their enemies. They wanted protection, in whatever form.

The cacophony followed their procession the entire way to the palace. More residents lined the streets, jostling to see the knights and soldiers. The market avenues were quieter than Enthor's. A few merchants had begun opening their stalls for the spring season, but it was still too cold for most.

Nonetheless, several women crowded around the booths, turning to shout their excitement as Linneya and Darryn passed.

The smells of freshly baked bread wafted from her favorite baker. The warmth of carramon spice drifted from a street vendor that made the most delicious tea. Linneya inhaled, sighing deeply as nostalgia washed over her. Serathor's threat felt distant, less viable when she was surrounded by safe memories of her childhood.

Still, the grounding sensation of her home was not as strong as the pull to the man beside her. A stoic warrior, Darryn showed little reaction to the crowds. His dark tunic and half pulled back hair made him look like a prince. Linneya sat a little straighter, proud to have this man at her side.

The palace walls came into view. They were dark gray stone, carved with the depictions of the forests around the capital. Although her family's home did not reach toward the sky like the grand towers of Enthor's palace, many sturdy annexes sprawled out from the main palace.

The wild celebration energy outside the palace did not carry through the gates. King Varilon and Queen Altheia stood on the steps in their traditional place, a smattering of courtiers behind them. The king was in full military attire, his dark green suit laden with hard earned medals. The queen had a dress that matched and her salt and pepper hair had been swept up in intricate braids. Aiden was beside the king, looking as regal as their father in a navy blue dress tunic. All had smiles plastered on their faces that did not quite reach their eyes.

Linneya raked her eyes over those attending. Lord Caelin was there, even Lady Alayne and her husband. A bitter pang coursed through Linneya when she realized Eleanor had not joined the welcome party. She had suspected it would be an uphill battle to reconcile with her sister, but had held out hope that Eleanor would not still be so angry.

They stopped in front of her family. Darryn slid off his horse and helped her down from hers. She slipped her hand in his and squeezed. He grinned down at her. "What a welcome, eh?" She tried to conjure up a laugh, but nerves made it fall flat. The somber mood left Linneya uneasy. A sense of being out of step. Could a single season away make such a difference?

With a shaky breath, she turned and faced her family. Darryn stepped forward and the two of them went through the protocols of greeting royals. King Varilon's eyebrows were slightly scrunched, as if he was in pain. Queen Altheia was paying them little attention, instead beaming at Darryn's friends.

Aiden broke the decorum first and grabbed Linneya into his arms, spinning her as she shrieked. He threw his head back and laughed. "Multiple affinities?! What a wild reveal. We must discuss things soon. In private."

Aiden set her down and Darryn was quick to snake a protective arm around her waist. Her brother eyed the movement, studying the two of them. Linneya gave him an encouraging smile, but Aiden narrowed his eyes, unconvinced.

Darryn cleared his throat and motioned back toward the palace grounds' entrance. "It would seem the princess is loved by her people."

King Varilon inclined his head. "Many rumors of King Shumor's soldiers breaching the fjords have circulated this past winter. The palace could not contradict them, as we knew something was brewing. With our small forces and the flame-talker in Enthor, everyone knew the outlook was bleak. When the first wave of Enthorian soldiers arrived, word spread quickly that our very own princess would be returning."

Queen Altheia beamed at Linneya. "The mood has lifted considerably, as you can see."

Linneya stepped forward, again interlocking her fingers with Darryn's. "I can see that, but my family's mood still appears to be dismal." She cocked her head, looking for an explanation.

Her father cleared his throat. "There are still many concerns about what King Shumor may be sending our way. Rumors suggest he has forced dragons from their natural sleep cycles in order to serve and produce new hatchlings faster than ever before. We can only do so much about a dozen, much less an entire horde."

Linneya's stomach sank, but before she could say anything, Darryn spoke up. "I may have a solution for that." He motioned for Graisor and Trotyn to step forward and turned to Aiden. "These are my brothers in arms. Graisor, Trotyn. You may remember them from the raids."

Aiden nodded, his countenance lifting considerably as he strode toward the men. "I could never forget." He strode to the men, clapping them each on one shoulder. They grinned and greeted him.

Darryn angled toward the king, gesturing to them as he spoke. "Your Majesty, Graisor has summoned Prince Tiuthan and his armies. Trotyn has recovered some ancient enchantments for shielding. I believe I will be able to solve the dragon concerns with Tiuthan's help."

King Varilon stroked his beard, assessing the warrior as if he was seeing him for the first time. "So, after all that argument, you went and married my daughter anyway."

Linneya blanched at the complete subject change. Her father had a slight twinkle in his eye, but she was unsure if it was because he was jesting or if he was enjoying seeing her husband squirm.

Darryn bowed his head, red creeping up his neck. "I did, Your Majesty. I apologize for my hesitations. It was not your daughter that caused me to hold back."

Her father narrowed his eyes. "Know this boy, I may not be your king but I am Lia's father and I will hunt you down if you ever turn your back on her."

He cleared his throat. "Let us go to my study. We have things to discuss. Hopefully the conversation will be more civilized than last time. Then, I will hear your plan for the shields."

Everyone got quiet, watching the exchange. King Varilon motioned for Darryn to join him. His hand went stiff in hers as he hesitated. She squeezed once and released him. "Go. He is not going to hurt you." She rubbed her hand across his lower back.

"If he kills me, remember me fondly, love." He sighed, kissed her cheek, and stalked off toward the king. Her father clapped his hand on Darryn's shoulder and her husband flinched.

They began to walk away, but Aiden hollered toward the retreating figures. "Father, if he acts up, I call first dibs at a duel!" King Varilon looked up toward the skies as if he was beseeching the Creators for help. Trotyn whooped, Darryn flashed a crude gesture over his shoulder, and the men collapsed in a fit of raucous laughter.

Graisor snorted. "I thought he was only afraid of his sister's feline menace. It would appear we can add his father-in-law to that list." Trotyn cackled.

Shailyn huffed under her breath, just loud enough for Linneya to hear, "He is not a menace. He is fierce." Linneya secretly agreed, a twinge of homesickness coming with the thought.

Aiden shook his head in amusement and turned back to Graisor and Trotyn, but gesturing toward Johann. "I see you two brought more of our comrades."

Johann stepped forward and bowed. "I was able to come with the auxiliary, Your Highness."

Aiden ambled over to him and held out his arm. They clasped forearms and the prince turned to Graisor and Trotyn. "Come, let me show you to your rooms. Then, I will give you a tour of the barracks."

He motioned for members of the palace guard to hand out orders for the knights and the auxiliary to be housed. Other courtiers began bustling about, returning to the palace or shuffling toward the newcomers. Linneya's heart sang as she watched her brother step into his role as leader. Aiden made quick work of splitting up tasks and led his friends inside.

A soft hand landed on her back. Linneya smiled and turned toward her mother. The queen watched Aiden as the men made their way into the palace and then took a deep breath. "I am glad you are here, daughter. Shall we see your friends to their rooms?"

Linneya nodded, motioning for Mariel and Straion to stand with her "Mother, you remember Straion? Mariel's husband?"

The two bowed and the queen inclined her head before sweeping them both up into a hug. "Of course! I am so glad you have found each other." She pulled back and looked them both over like a proud matriarch.

Mariel beamed and leaned into him. Straion brushed her hair off her neck and snuck in a kiss before addressing the queen. "I am grateful Mariel has chosen me."

Queen Altheia smiled, seeming pleased with the match. "Can we take you to your rooms?" She raised her arm, summoning one of the head maids.

Mariel stepped forward and bowed her head. "Your Highness, we are grateful for your hospitality, but we would like to stay with my parents. Give them an opportunity to get to know Straion."

The queen lowered her arm and clapped. "Of course! Give our love to your parents and you must come for dinner one day this week. I want to hear all about your new home."

Mariel blushed and Straion snaked his hand around her waist, nodding enthusiastically toward the queen.

Linneya piped up. "You must invite them one day when Straion can play with Father. He has a strong interest in the sacred thamu harps."

"Oh, of course! Varilon will be thrilled! You must join us and play to your heart's content."

Straion gaped at the queen, starstruck. Linneya grabbed her friend's hand and squeezed, quietly wishing her the best. Mariel murmured to her,

"If I do not see you before Serathor's armies arrive, know I love you and you have been an amazing friend."

Linneya's eyes burned with tears as she watched her friend say her goodbyes and amble back to the horses. A familiar tightness formed in her chest, dread building over the upcoming battles. She blinked away the worst of the feelings and turned back to her other friends.

Queen Altheia made her way to Chrysa and Shailyn. She was telling an animated story, her hands flying about more than usual. The women were laughing together and Linneya's heart warmed at the scene.

She stepped toward them as the queen summoned her head maid. "Please, take Chrysa and Shailyn to their rooms." Queen Altheia looped her arm with Linneya's. "You must excuse us, ladies, we have state matters to discuss."

Linneya stiffened as her mother's tone sharpened. The queen patted Linneya's arm and nudged her forward. They made their way toward the palace steps and an uncomfortable silence settled between them. Linneya twisted her hands together, worrying over what might be the next piece of bad news. "Is Eleanor alright?"

Her mother pressed her lips in a tight line. "She is still mourning Orrain. I wanted her to be there to greet you all, but she refused. I admit, she seems just as betrayed that no one told her you are our flame-talker."

Linneya frowned. "I must talk with her soon. I hate that she still thinks I conspired against her."

The queen hummed a non-committal response and nodded to the guards as they walked inside. A piece of Linneya settled into a happy, soft relaxation at the sight of the entrance hall. Dark wood paneling and rich, deep colors decorated nearly everything. Art depicting the isolated wilderness in the north sprawled across the walls. Carramon and boiled apples scented the space. Linneya breathed deeply, a flood of childhood memories washing over her.

The queen nudged her toward her study, picking up the pace. They strolled into the brighter office and Queen Altheia shut the door. Smoke tinged with sweet spice and grounding incense lingered. The windows were larger in this room, creating a sense of more space.

The queen settled behind her desk, the light wood carved with scenes from her home country, Rynor. Dragons flew across the skies, a winged beast with a long mane charged toward a statue, and a man crawled through an unending desert. Linneya's favorite was in the smallest corner. A single candle, the flame turned sideways as if a puff of wind was blowing it out, yet it was still burning.

"How are things with Darryn?"

Linneya blinked, startled by her mother's willingness to tackle the conversation head-on. The queen folded her hands together on the desk and pursed her lips, waiting for a response. Linneya thought back over the past season, the chaos of their forced marriage, the mooncycles where he stayed gone, her escape...

She turned red and Queen Altheia let out a sigh. "As I said before, I believe he is a good man. I knew his mother when we were young. He had a good upbringing, at least."

Linneya chewed on her lip and nodded, unable to find words for the tumultuous way things had unfolded. She was not sure she could explain it to herself, much less her mother.

Queen Altheia shifted in her chair and continued. "Your father and I struggled after the fall of my parents' kingdom. I felt we should have stayed and fought. Varilon knew that it was futile and forced me to leave with him before the final battle began." Her eyes filled with tears at the memories and Linneya's heart squeezed in sadness.

Her mother drew a shaky breath. "I took too long to forgive him, wasted so much time, even though his choices kept us alive."

Linneya nodded, but wondered why they were having this conversation now. She knew the stories about how her grandparents perished. Her family had always said that King Shumor's descent into madness was due to his obsessive use of the dark elemental energies. The things that tore down and destroyed.

She leaned forward. "What does this have to do with me and Darryn?"

The queen stared at her hands. A chill crept down Linneya's spine. She had only ever seen her mother like this before doling out punishment. The last time was when she and Aiden had nearly burned down the gardener's shed because he had dared her to juggle torches and a servant was hurt in the process of putting out the resulting blaze.

The servant was fine after Linneya snuck in and healed the burns, but she and Aiden were made to work alongside the gardener for weeks. Not the fun kind of work, no. They dug trenches, hauled stones from the woods, anything that was uncomfortable. It left an impression.

So to see her mother in that position, glaring through her hands... Linneya steeled herself. "Mother?"

The queen inhaled as she looked up. "We are not going to win this battle, Lia."

Linneya's stomach dropped. "What do you mean?"

She cleared her throat. "I appreciate Darryn sending for the fae prince, but the armies from Bachael will not be coming. Tiuthan's father made that clear mooncycles ago when Varilon asked for aid."

The blood left Linneya's face. Without the fae, there was little chance they could hold their own against Serathor's hordes. She bit her lip and twisted the ring on her finger as her mother continued.

"I tell you all of this because when we found out you were enroute, your father immediately said you were marching to your doom." Her knuckles were turning white and Linneya's blood ran ice cold at the intensity of her mother's admission. "You, Aiden, and Eleanor are the future of our realm, no matter what happens in this battle."

The queen pierced Linneya with the gaze only a parent can master. "If Darryn drags you away from this place, you are not to hold him responsible. Your father is giving him instructions as we speak. You must go if the battle cannot be won. Leave and find a place to study your healing arts, Lia. Only the light powers can save us."

Her head spun. She did not want to leave. She wanted to stay, to embrace all of her power, and fight. Surely Darryn would not make her walk away after all they did to get reinforcements.

Her mother's instructions and dismissal barely registered, a muffled sound against the roaring of Linneya's thoughts. She stumbled into the hallway, unable to get her bearings. All of a sudden, the somberness of her family's greeting made sense. Of course they had already tried to mobilize Aelor's allies. But if they had, why did King Birron not get a summons?

"You are wandering the wrong way." Her brother's voice startled her. Just like last time they talked, Aiden was leaning in a doorway. She tried to muster up a smile, but numbness was creeping in.

"What do you mean?" Her voice was hollow, but she could not rally anything more.

He crossed his arms and stalked toward her. "I mean, if you are trying to make it to the welcome banquet in time, you are going the wrong way."

"Ah." She turned and began walking with him in the direction he indicated. She wondered how much he knew. Were their parents making escape plans for him as well? Would he be responsible for getting Eleanor out?

She was so wrapped up in the news that she jumped when he addressed her. "I am glad you brought Johann. We grew close during the last raids. It was good to see him willing to stand for Aelor."

Linneya shook her head and hugged herself. "Johann came of his own accord. We did not invite him." The hallways grew a bit brighter as they made their way toward the dining hall. The shock had settled into her bones, an unwelcome addition to the tightness living in her chest.

Aiden studied her for a moment before changing the subject. "Do you love him?"

Linneya stopped and dropped her arms, blinking. Did she love Darryn? It was no secret that she was enamored. She could hardly keep her hands off him and every time his eyes roamed her body, she heated under his gaze.

But was that love? Had they chosen each other in such a way? Could she even bring herself to trust him like that? "I am not sure."

Her brother's eyebrows knitted together. "It is a simple question, Lia. You either do or you do not."

She squared her shoulders, staring him in the eye. "I do not know what I feel yet. We have hardly had time to get to know one another. I am just trying to survive and once we get to a point where we can settle into our life, maybe then I will know." Her hands balled into fists. "Did our parents demand you escape, too?"

Aiden's jaw pulsed at the question. He nodded curtly. "They wanted to ship me off to our cousin's keep already. I told them I would melt that far south - from the shame of abandoning our people more than the heat."

She huffed a laugh. "They forget we are their children. Our parents cannot shoo us away so easily."

He pressed his lips together in a tight smile, but said nothing further. They had made it to the dining entrance, last to arrive. Everyone else was milling about, clumped up in small groups and chattering.

Aiden made a beeline for Darryn and Johann, the latter looking refreshed and back to his usual swagger. Darryn was disheveled and his shoulders were set as if he was carrying something heavy.

Linneya's stomach twisted at the sight. His gaze locked onto hers and a familiar warmth flushed up the back of her neck. Their attraction cut through everything, even the strain of life-or-death decisions and impending wars. Darryn gave her a nearly imperceptible nod, as if to say they would discuss it after dinner.

Shailyn bounded over and grabbed her hand. "We have been talking to Alayne. Catching up on all the gossip." Her sister-in-law's eyes sparkled with gleeful malice as she leaned in to whisper. "She is still furious she had to settle, but at least she appears to be learning her place." Shailyn giggled as if the woman's misfortune was the highlight of the season.

Linneya bit back a smile and mumbled back. "Well, if she has learned her place, let us at least be friendly."

Shailyn smirked and pulled her to their corner. Chrysa was giggling at something and Alayne's grimace looked painful. Linneya braced for whatever awkward situation the women were putting her in.

Chrysa motioned to her and spoke to Alayne. "Lia met your mother at the reception."

Alayne blinked. "She came? I was surprised she ventured out."

Linneya nodded. "She did. I was introduced to her celestial storytelling abilities."

Alayne raised her eyebrows. "My mother gave you a prediction? She is eerily accurate with her celestial storytelling. What did she say?"

Linneya bit her lip. She did not want to announce Duchess Jenyce's predictions, especially not in the same room as Aiden. Linneya thought back to the woman's words - the crown would pass to her. Not her brother. The ever growing tension in her chest squeezed again.

Linneya schooled her face into an impassive expression and shrugged, offering a half-truth. "She said there were those who would not be pleased with my union to Darryn. It was all very cryptic and easily dismissed."

Alayne narrowed her eyes. "That is unusual. Most of her predictions are more clear. Many walk away unnerved by whatever they did not want to hear."

"My sister is always looking for ways to seem more important than she is." A voice snipped from the doorway. Despite Eleanor's sharp tone, Linneya beamed as her sister walked into the room.

Her hair was pinned back in a tight bun, accentuating the sharp contortions of her features. Her lugubrious expression hurt Linneya's heart. Gone was the bubbly presence. In its place stood a woman hardened by betrayal.

Eleanor did not look at her. She walked to Alayne and stood at her side, arms crossed. They wore a similar pinched expression, two women fighting against whatever invisible enemy threatened them next.

Linneya's shoulders dropped at the sight. Of course her sister was still angry, but she had hoped that a full season away would have softened things. She took a deep breath and tried to act as normal as possible. "I am glad to see you. May I introduce Shailyn, Darryn's sister, and Chrysa, one of our close friends?"

Eleanor grabbed Alayne's arm as if the woman was a shield and nodded at the rest of them. Something simmered beneath her expression, a deeper power that hummed. Linneya blinked at the realization. Something was... different.

"It is great to meet you." Shailyn held out her hand and Eleanor hesitated. Alayne nudged her forward and finally she acquiesced.

Alayne piped up. "Eleanor has been training. The four of us should spar sometime. You will be impressed."

Alayne gestured to the other women, making it clear Linneya was not invited. Eleanor's eyes met hers and another surge of power came through. She opened her mouth to ask, but Eleanor shook her head and turned away.

At that moment, the butler announced dinner. Her mind was spinning. So much had changed and so much was at stake. She wrung her hands together, resisting the urge to hug herself and broadcast how much anxiety was building inside of her. Somehow, even this dinner was beginning to feel like a battle.

A warm, strong hand pressed into her lower back and she sighed with relief. Darryn's grounding presence alleviated the pressure she felt. They walked into the warzone together and she held her head high.

Chapter 33

To her surprise, the dinner was perfect. Conversation remained light and Queen Altheia had curated a meal with all of the family's comfort foods. Waves of nostalgia broke over Linneya at the beginning of each course. She beamed when the dessert arrived. Her favorite: multi-colored berries, slightly chilled and served with a creamy cheese sauce.

The butler walked in and whispered to King Varilon. Linneya tensed as the color drained from her father's face. Rarely had he been this disturbed. He set down his utensils, took a sip of wine, and stood.

All conversation ceased and everyone shot to their feet. The king stared at one of the tapestries that depicted his ancestors conquering this land. As a child, Linneya had thought the scene showed their strength, the power of a mighty lineage. Now she wondered how her forebears had been viewed by those who were invaded.

Queen Altheia laid a hand on the king's arm, breaking him of his reverie. He cleared his throat and patted her hand. "Please, everyone continue. Caelin, Linneya, Darryn, come with me. There is a... a visitor that you must meet."

Lord Caelin scurried to his side and the two men stormed out of the dining hall. Darryn's eyebrows shot up and Linneya looked at her mother for answers. Queen Altheia nodded, gesturing discreetly for the two of them to follow.

Linneya shrugged and turned to Darryn. "I guess we are being summoned." Darryn grunted and they followed the men down the hallway, into King Varilon's study.

The king stood close to a hunched-over man with dark hair. "Come in you two. I believe this is an important matter that both the Falorian knights' leader as well as our flame-talker need to discuss."

She inched toward the figure. His unusual black hair stirred a memory. The man looked up and Linneya inhaled a sharp breath. Ice crept into her veins as his locks fell back and a white streak revealed itself. This was the ground-tamer from her last dream.

Lord Caelin urged the man to retell his story. Linneya shivered as the ground-tamer recounted the assassin's attack. Darryn squeezed her hand. She could not look at him, for fear of what she might read on his face.

The ground-tamer's details were vivid, identical to what she saw in the dream. The man balled his hands into fists as he finished. "I think I killed him. I did not stop to check but he also did not come after me. It would have been easy to catch up before I had the boat back on the river."

Linneya pressed her lips together, trying to keep an impassive expression. She had seen the assassin crawl out of the hole and follow him. What happened after she woke up?

The ground-tamer continued. "My power was drained. I have not been able to use it since." His hands shook as he held them up. "This has never happened to me before. I cannot feel my connection with the soil any longer."

Her eyes went wide at the confession. Darryn shifted uncomfortably beside her. The idea that an elemental could encounter someone and their power be completely tamped down was terrifying.

King Varilon moved to the door and spoke with a guard for a few moments before turning back to the ground-tamer. "If you will follow my guard, they will take you to the infirmary. Speak with Wralion once you are there. The healer has an uncanny knack for helping elementals. He may be able to see what must be done to restore you."

The man stumbled over himself, thanking the king and bowing over and over as he backed out of the door. As soon as the door clicked shut, the king settled behind his desk, motioning for them to sit. "What do we make of this? We have had almost a dozen stories of this assassin. If he was trying to collect the elements to claim himself the prophesied, he has already succeeded. How did he drain this man without killing him?"

Lord Caelin nodded and stared at a crack in the ceiling, thinking. "If we had more time, I would send emissaries into fae territory. I believe the scribes at Mount Varsha will have answers."

Linneya leaned forward. Falryn's tales of the vast number of scrolls and tomes at the mountain had piqued her interest. The thought of having unfettered access to so many accounts of healing powers was exciting.

Darryn huffed in frustration. "That does not solve the issue of what this may mean for us now. There is no time to make that treacherous journey if we need answers before King Shumor's attack."

King Varilon nodded. "Thus the conundrum. I worry that whatever power they are using will come out against us at the battle. We are not Varsha, but the library here is vast. Do you have anyone you trust to help you research our archives?"

Darryn's face darkened and he grinned. "I will bring my best men to help me research. Trotyn is especially clever at understanding new enchantments."

Linneya piped up. "I will help as well. I know this library better than anyone else." Darryn reached for her hand and squeezed. Her cheeks heated, from his touch or the excitement of a project, she was unsure.

Her father nodded. "It is decided, then." He waved them on "You should go back and join the rest of the family. Oh, and ask Eleanor to come. Lord Caelin and I must discuss some things with her."

Linneya raised her eyebrows. "What exactly has happened with Eleanor? There is something... off. I worry something is wrong."

Lord Caelin inclined his head. "Your sister is more formidable than she lets on. She may yet have a role to play."

Linneya clamped her mouth shut. Eleanor had never been one for the outdoors or learning to fight. Something significant had happened while she was gone to change things so drastically.

Darryn placed a hand on her back and led her back into the dining hall. Linneya relayed the message to Eleanor, who huffed and slunk off. Then, she and Darryn made their way to say goodnight to her mother.

Queen Altheia wrapped Linneya into a hug. "I shall go with you and make sure there is nothing else you need as you get settled in." She motioned toward the door and started out into the hall before anyone could argue.

Darryn raised his eyebrows and Linneya shrugged. Her mother was being a bit odd, but Linneya had also not expected to have to visit her childhood home as a married guest. Maybe this was more normal than she realized.

Linneya almost stumbled as Queen Altheia turned left instead of right. Darryn caught her upper arm and kept her upright. The gesture was brief, but his touch sent a wave of chills spiraling down her spine. The past few days had been... delicious. Linneya blushed at the memories of their more intimate moments and he placed a warm hand on her lower back, adding to the sensation.

They turned down another hallway, even further away from the family wing. She had expected to go to her old room, the same place she had always slept, but her mother seemed to have other plans. Linneya finally asked, "Where are we going? I have not been gone so long that I have forgotten the way to my rooms, have I?"

The queen turned to her with a mischievous smile, gesturing as she walked. "We thought you might want more privacy than being in the family wing. It gives you more room to come and go as you please. After your father and I married, we were grateful that my parents found us an out-of-the-way area for our... activities."

Heat crept up Linneya's cheeks and Darryn rubbed the back of his neck. He took a deep breath before replying. "Thank you for being so thoughtful. I know this marriage was unexpected, but I am grateful you have welcomed me so graciously."

The queen waved her hand, not even bothering to look back at them. "Nonsense, we are happy that the two of you mended fences. I have a knack for recognizing when people should be together. After seeing you two dancing, there was no doubt in my mind you would be a perfect match for my daughter."

Darryn cleared his throat. "Yes, it is my fault that we did not have a smooth start, but I plan to do everything I can to make up for it."

The queen stopped in front of a door and cocked her head, looking suspiciously like Aiden plotting. "I doubt it was all your fault. Sometimes my dear daughter is more stubborn than is good for her. I am glad she has you."

Darryn grinned and nudged Linneya with his elbow. Linneya sighed and rolled her eyes. She would never hear the end of this.

"Anyway, here we are." Queen Altheia motioned to the door and stepped aside to let them in.

They walked into their chambers and Linneya's eyes widened as she took in the luxury of the space. A light smell of rosemary wafted, the dark green walls matching the color of the scent. A set of recessed bookcases accented one wall and the opposite wall sported massive windows with a magnificent view. The sound of a small waterfall echoed from the washroom and a fire crackled in the inglenook.

Her mother stepped through the doorway. "Will this do alright for your stay? If so, I will direct the butler to have your things brought to the room. We can always put you in your old suite if you prefer."

Linneya grinned and turned, wrapping her arms around her mother. "If I had known we had something this nice right down the hall, I would have demanded to move."

The queen laughed and brushed Linneya's hair out of her eyes. "Why do you think we always told you the guest wing was off limits? It was not just to keep the place clean. We have always believed in saving the best we have to offer for visitors."

Darryn bowed at the waist. "Thank you for your generosity."

"There is no need to be so formal, dear!" Queen Altheia took his hands in hers and pulled him in for a hug. "Your mother would be proud of the man her son has become." She choked a bit as she said it.

The queen then turned and wrapped Linneya into her embrace. Linneya could have sworn Darryn turned away and wiped tears from his eyes. Her mother gently reached out and tucked a stray strand of hair back behind her ear and whispered, "Do not waste time being angry, Lia." Linneya nodded and the queen turned and left.

Darryn began wandering through the space, but Linneya made a beeline for their bed. It was plush and draped in wools and furs. She ran her hands through the soft pelts and scratchy blankets, inhaling the woody aromas wafting from the bedding. The lighter throws were piled in an armchair beside the bed, a sign that the spring season's warmer nights were ahead.

Darryn walked to the recessed bookcase and ran his fingers over the spines. "Your parents know how to entertain, that is for sure."

Linneya shook her head. "I had no idea we had this much space. This is grand." She grinned, a laugh rising in her throat. "They were right to hide this from us. Aiden and I would have snuck into the wing and played as much as possible. Eleanor would have demanded this room on the spaciousness alone."

Darryn smirked. "I would have taken you lot as more clever. I cannot believe you never snuck in here."

Linneya giggled and walked to the other bookcase, making a note of some of her favorite novels. "They kept us focused on exploring outside. It never occurred to us to go into out-of-bounds areas inside. There was too much else to do."

He came up behind her and snaked his arms around her waist, kissing the top of her head. "Wait until you see the washroom." The excitement in his voice made Linneya spin around.

Her gasp was audible as she took in the large bath. The entire area was covered in light gray stone with elaborate detailing. One wall was lined with high windows. Beneath them was an inside waterfall, a stream of warm water cascading into a large pool. Steam rose off its surface, the space looking as if it could comfortably hold six people.

She leaned back into Darryn and he murmured in her ear, his voice rough, "What do you think? Do we need to upgrade?" He squeezed her closer. "Should we try it out and see?"

The need in his voice sent waves of warmth up her neck. Citrus and cedar wafted around her, grounding her after the chaos of the day. She sighed. It was a lovely bath, but she missed their home.

Her breath caught at the realization. Home - sometime in the past twelve mooncycles, their mansion in Enthor had solidly become home. Or, rather, the life she was building with this man was home. She twisted around, facing Darryn and placing her hands on his chest. "It is lovely, but I miss ours. I am surprised at how much I miss our home already."

He stiffened in surprise and his brows raised. She rose up on her toes and gave him a gentle kiss. He stroked her hair and pressed her close for a moment. They stayed there for a few breaths before he wandered back to the bookshelves.

Linneya sighed and stared out the window, watching a strong crimson aurora dance across the sky. Usually, spring auroras were yellow and green. An Arduin deity, Burdur, was said to paint omens in the sky. A red aurora in the spring season was considered a warning - a condemnation on all who could view his masterpiece.

Darryn finally broke the silence. "The ground-tamer that arrived, you knew him. His story sounded eerily like your dream." The statements were more question than fact.

His hand on her shoulder caused her to start. "Sorry, Darryn. My mind is racing." She rubbed her face and turned into his chest. "Yes, he was in my dream. His story matched what I saw."

"It unnerves me since I do not know how to tell which ones are real. Several have been, I think. The ones where the assassin sees me at the end and it wakes me up... those seem the most vivid."

He sighed, wrapping his arms around her. "Once this is over, we will talk to Falryn. Dream-walkers can be powerful in their own right. Combined with your elemental affinities... fate has placed a heavy burden on your shoulders."

Linneya worried her bottom lip. Would she even have the chance to meet with the healer again? In her dreams, the assassin had made eye contact with her enough times that she was concerned he might have actually seen her. What if he knew who she was? What if he was already hunting her, maneuvering so he could murder her at the first opportunity?

She shivered at the thought.

Darryn squeezed her tight and pressed a kiss to the top of her head. "Do you think we should tell your father?"

She pulled back to meet his gaze and shook her head. "No, I think we should keep this between us. He is going to be more adamant that I leave if he finds out I am sporting a Creators-blessed power as well."

Darryn's jaw pulsed. "His plan was tempting. I would do anything, give anything to keep you safe."

But Linneya did not want to be kept safe. She wanted to help her family in whatever ways she could. She stepped back, pressing away from him and shaking her head. "No, you cannot ask that of me."

He closed the distance and brushed a hand through her hair, settling at the nape. "I would not ask, princess." He growled. "If it was up to me, we would just go. I would put you to sleep and you would not wake up until we were at the southernmost island."

She shivered at his tone, but he dropped his hand and sighed. "Lucky for you, I cannot bring myself to force you on anything. Too many times my judgment has made things harder." He looked at the ceiling, a vein twitching in his neck. "As long as you say no, we will stay."

Linneya crossed her arms and nodded. "Thank you." Then she sighed. "What do you make of the rumors of Serathor's powers?"

Darryn rubbed his chin and shrugged. "I am unsure. I do not know how we will fight. Strategy is a shot in the dark with so many unknowns."

"I could just -" she waved her hands around and made explosion noises, mimicking her power's eruption that saved them from the ambush at the Raelin crags.

He narrowed his eyes, thinking. "It is one thing to blast away fifty scouts while Tiuthan shields us. It is another to destroy an entire army while keeping all of our soldiers safe."

Her jaw dropped. "Tiuthan what?"

Darryn grinned. "What did you think happened?"

Linneya shrugged one shoulder. "I had not thought about it much. I guess I figured I annihilated those who needed to be taken out. You mean to tell me that I do not have all powerful, omniscient explosive capacity?"

He threw his head back and laughed. Light danced in his eyes. "You should ask him about it when he arrives. It's a fascinating elemental power."

Linneya chewed on her lip. "Mother says the fae have already refused to join us."

His face fell into a somber expression that told her what she already knew: without them, the battle was as good as lost.

The next week was filled with a flurry of preparation. During the day, Linneya stayed busy with the life-tenders, stocking supplies and foraging for wound-healing plants. She spent afternoons in the infirmary, using her affinities to heal what the other life-tenders could not. She settled into a nostalgic rhythm, sometimes even able to forget the dull ache of impending doom.

Darryn spent much of his time in the barracks with the Falorian knights. Graisor and Trotyn sparred with anyone who had elemental affinity and Darryn critiqued the fights. Shailyn regularly showed off her powers, besting anyone who challenged her. Occasionally the auxiliary units would join, Aiden and Johann included.

Linneya and Darryn spent some evenings with subjects who had requested to meet with Aelor's legendary flame-talker and her powerful husband. Some came seeking healing, others seeking advice for a family member with elemental affinities. Other evenings, the two of them scoured the library for any sign of powers that could drain elementals without killing them.

King Varilon sent scouts to strategic locations to keep watch and signal any suspicious movement. If Serathor's armies arrived sooner than expected, the palace would have almost a full day to prepare. The king spent most of his days locked in the study with Lord Caelin and other advisors. They turned it into a war room, complete with terrain maps and figurines of soldiers.

At dinner one evening, King Varilon half-heartedly invited both Darryn and Aiden to join him and his council. Linneya chuckled, suspecting that her father was not ready to admit the next generation was competent enough for high level strategy. She was certain her mother had demanded he try to involve the men.

Luckily for the king, the two men read straight through his facade. Darryn quickly suggested his leadership role within the knights would make him worthless on large battle strategy. Aiden mumbled something about the Enthorian auxiliary unit needing training for the hilly Aelorian terrain. The king looked pleased, his wife less so.

Queen Altheia was helping subjects evacuate the cottages found around the capital. Many of the farmers that supplied Loraen with grain and meat stayed outside the city's walls, opting for living on their farmland. This meant that homes had to be found for them within Loraen, places that they could stay safe for mooncycles if necessary. With dragons, it was possible that all the cottages would be razed by the end of the battle - victory or no. The queen was directing the evacuations herself, even going so far as to personally entreat with some of the more stubborn farmers who did not want to leave their homes.

The queen had taken Chrysa under her wing and dragged the woman with her everywhere. Chrysa was slowly warming up to the arrangement, arriving every morning with parchment full of questions she had thought of the night before. Linneya's mother beamed every time, thrilled to share everything she could with the woman.

Aiden spent his days sparring with the auxiliary unit. He was gone well into the evening most of the time, and Linneya began wondering why he appointed himself their Aelorian emissary. His demeanor had shifted to something heavier over the past season, but there were moments where his lightheartedness shone through.

Eleanor was another story. She was still sulking. Most days, she snuck out to spend time with Alayne. Sometimes, she invited Shailyn, which was the closest Eleanor got to civil conversation with any of the Enthorian visitors.

One morning, a cold snap accompanied dreary weather. Linneya took the opportunity to stay inside, letting the patter of rain lull her into a stupor. She was lounging on the couch and daydreaming whilst staring into the fireplace. A knock on the door caused her to sit up, but Darryn was already halfway to answering it.

He grunted in surprise. "Lord Caelin, do come in."

She stood, smoothing out her skirts and hair. Her father's advisor shuffled through the door, wringing his hands out of habit. He bowed to Linneya and nodded to Darryn. "I thought you would both like to know that we have received word that the fae will be here today after noonrest. It would seem Prince Tiuthan has answered your call for his battalions to join us."

Linneya's stomach lurched in anticipation. A wicked grin spread across Darryn's face. Her parents had been wrong, after all. So much fear around their allies refusing to join - all for nothing. The strength of the fae would surely give them an edge. Serathor's armies might be large, but the fae had fierce battle tactics and were known for winning against forces ten times their size.

Darryn snorted. "I wonder what Tiuthan did to change his father's mind."

Lord Caelin inclined his head thoughtfully. "I came to ask you the same thing. Were any promises made on our behalf? This is highly unusual and I would like to know what we are up against. The fae have never offered their armies so freely."

Darryn shrugged. "Tiuthan is a close friend. No promises were made, though you can speak with Graisor. He was the one that delivered the request. Perhaps he can shed light on the situation."

Lord Caelin bowed and left for the barracks. Linneya and Darryn hurried to dress. The ring on her finger felt warm, as if it was responding to her enthusiasm. Her heart pounded in her chest, a newfound excitement that perhaps this battle was not the end. A molten flame burned in Darryn's eyes and she was certain he felt the same.

They made their way downstairs, just in time for King Varilon to debrief them.

Chapter 34

The gray skies were dreary, but the welcome party was cheerful. This time, everyone's smiles were genuine. Linneya's breath caught as fae battalions began pouring through the palace gates. She had imagined Tiuthan might offer a few units, something to match the numbers offered by Enthor and the Falorian knights. Instead, he came with almost five times as many warriors. Her head swam as she tried to comprehend how they would handle the logistics of such a large force. She laughed to herself; it was such a wonderful problem to have.

Their battle armor glimmered in the muted sunslight. Sigils were carved in the breastplates of almost every warrior. Many were modern, but Linneya spotted the occasional ancient Kworish script. A rainbow of banners suggested dozens of battalions had joined them.

The fae rode in on *dumumi*, horse-like creatures with iridescent scales across their rib cages. Some had wings, others sported an extra set of legs. There were many rumors around their magical capabilities, but Linneya thought the fae chose them for their gracefulness above anything else.

Most brought some sort of sword, though the elite forces carried whips or bows. The curved blades and intricate weaponry had always fascinated Linneya. Their advanced tactics were lost on her, but the aetherial beauty of their fighting style was almost like a ballroom dance.

More fae filed through the gates. Tiuthan's blonde, curly hair stood out against the others. His *dumumi* had no wings, no extra legs. Without the scales, she might have mistaken it for one of their horses.

He slid off his mount and strode toward the royal family. He held his head high, a proud look on his face. Linneya's heart soared with hope. She reached for Darryn's hand and squeezed as the fae prince approached.

He bowed to King Varilon. "Your Majesty, I present the best of Bachael's forces. We are at your service in the fight against this great evil rising from the south."

The king inclined his head slowly, as if he was still in shock that the fae realm had come to help. "We are grateful to see you all." He motioned toward Aiden. "The prince will be in charge of helping your troops get settled."

Aiden strode to Tiuthan's side, the two princes clasping each other's forearms. Aiden whispered something in his ear and Tiuthan smiled and nodded. He gestured toward some of the leaders and Aiden clapped him on the back. Linneya's brother strutted toward the group and began introducing himself to the other fae.

Tiuthan approached Queen Altheia and kissed her outstretched hand. "Your Highness, it is good to see you again."

The queen dipped her chin, smiling. "And you. Of course, you know our eldest daughter and her husband."

Tiuthan bowed slightly to Linneya and grasped Darryn's outstretched forearm. The fae prince smirked. "Glad to see you both have made it this far in one piece." Darryn grinned and clapped the male's shoulder.

The queen motioned to her youngest daughter. "And this is Princess Eleanor."

The prince straightened up and locked onto Eleanor's slender frame. Something in his eyes shifted, a passing shadow. Linneya craned her head to see the exchange better, fascinated by the fae's sudden interest.

Eleanor's hands flexed, as if she would throttle the prince if he came within reach. The fury written on her features was a loud, clear threat. She clenched her teeth and barely acknowledged him with a nod.

The side of Tiuthan's mouth curved into a small smile and he stepped toward her. She let out a soft hiss as he took her hand and brushed his lips across the back of her knuckles. "Princess, it is an honor to make your acquaintance. I hope we can see more of each other once my battalions have led your armies to victory."

Eleanor seethed through her gritted teeth. "We are grateful to have you, but you should not mistake our gratitude for worship or adoration." A gust of wind whipped around her, accenting her icy demeanor.

Tiuthan grinned. "I see." He lowered his voice and leaned in close. "Well, perhaps it is I that will do the worshipping, *mahuchav*."

Eleanor ground her jaw and took a step back, dismissing him. Darryn snorted and Linneya turned to him, raising her eyebrows. He mouthed "*later*" and she narrowed her eyes.

There was no time to press the point, as the fae prince turned back to Darryn. "What is being done to prepare? How can I best be of service?"

Darryn motioned him toward the gardens. "Walk with me. We need to discuss shielding against the dragons. Rumors suggest King Shumor has more than we had anticipated."

Tiuthan crossed his arms and wrinkled his brow before following. They walked off together, deep in serious discussion regarding aether affinity and warding the skies over the city. Linneya's heart swelled with hope. The fae prince had not only surprised them by showing up, he came ready and willing to do whatever to support them. Now if only Eleanor could find a way to not completely insult the male who had possibly saved them all from destruction.

She sighed and turned to her sister, but the woman was already halfway up the palace steps. Linneya rolled her eyes. The next few days were bound to be long and frustrating.

Almost a week later, Linneya snuck out before the suns were up to harvest some bark from the oak trees. It was still cold enough that sap had not begun to rise, making it easier to collect the astringent bits without having to separate the sticky pieces.

Retracting her steps through her old haunts was peaceful. She passed elyre bushes that were beginning to bud. The birds were singing their usual tunes, although she occasionally thought she heard strains of Darryn's lullaby. The scent of everblue trees and early blooming flowers brought peaceful memories from childhood.

A rustling sound coming from the caves made her jump. Her panic was short lived when Aiden and Johann emerged. They were cackling at some joke and Johann cuffed Aiden on the arm.

Linneya stepped into the path and crossed her arms, trying not to laugh. "I know you are not giving away our secret lairs to some Enthorian noble with no honor."

Johann's face flushed and he rubbed the back of his neck. Aiden blinked in surprise at her sudden appearance. He stepped toward her, waving his arms like he did as a kid when he was trying to come up with a lie. "We were just -"

Linneya held her hand up to stop him. "Whatever you were about to say, you and I both know it was going to be a fib." She smirked as his face turned an embarrassed shade. "Shall we head back? Mother will demand we are all there for noonrest tea. She is becoming more antsy the closer we get to the expected arrival of Serathor's soldiers."

Johann bowed toward her, a disappointed look on his face. "Princess, I will leave you both to it and head back to the barracks."

Linneya cocked her head and glanced at Aiden, who was studying his friend's face. Johann seemed unusually subdued and something about it pricked her heart. She reached for his arm. "You can come with us. There is always more than enough to go around and Mother will be happy to have you."

He raised his eyebrows and looked to her brother. Aiden nodded. "Lia is right, you should come. After all, how many more days do we have before Serathor arrives and the world turns upside down?"

Johann grinned. "Alright, but I cannot stay long. Straion is coming this afternoon to spar and I want to be there."

Linneya linked her arm with Johann's and they made their way back to the palace. The three of them sauntered into the king's private stateroom, windblown and flushed. Eleanor, Alayne, and Chrysa were by a window, leaned over and chatting quietly. Darryn was seated with the queen. King Varilon had just picked up some biscuits and was headed for the door. He grunted in surprise at their swift entrance and Queen Altheia jumped to her feet.

Darryn shifted in his chair, something dark painting his expression. Linneya met his gaze and he raised his eyebrows at her. She smiled and he stood, stalking toward her.

The queen scurried over, making over Aiden and greeting Johann. Linneya dropped Johann's arm and approached Darryn. He growled and brushed his lips over her cheek. "I never want to see you on another man's arm again."

Heat crept up Linneya's neck at his admission. She pinched his side and leaned in. "Unless you want to renounce our titles and shun my family forever, you will have to get used to it, my warrior." Darryn raised his eyebrows and smirked, but said nothing else.

They settled back on the loveseat and Linneya began making her plate. The queen sat across from them as Johann and Aiden found a small table further down. Darryn made small talk with Queen Altheia while Linneya nibbled on a pastry, enjoying the bland domesticity of it all.

A page knocked on the doorframe and stepped inside, bowing first to the queen and then the rest of the royal family. His blue eyes were wide, uncertain. "Your Highnesses, I bring news from the posted watch. Serathor's troops have been seen on the fjords. Based on the timing of the first warnings, they are expected to arrive by tomorrow morning."

A dread settled heavy on her chest. The dark tides of war threatened to wash everything away. Darryn pressed a kiss to her knuckles as Queen Altheia thanked the messenger. Everyone waited in silence until the man had left. Then, chaos.

Aiden and Johann exchanged a look and stood, hurrying from the room before anyone else could be consulted. The queen paced the length of the stateroom, chewing on a knuckle and muttering under her breath. Alayne fanned herself, her face turning a mottled purple. Chrysa was a whirlwind, chattering at Eleanor while rummaging for something to help Alayne. Darryn had jumped up and assumed a defensive posture, surveying the room.

Linneya locked eyes with Eleanor, both of them motionless and pale. The stillness between them was like a pond whose surface had not been disturbed by wind or wildlife. A moment of clarity passed between the two sisters and a lump rose in Linneya's throat, regret and disappointment. It was unlikely that their friend circles would be left unharmed. For that matter, odds were against the family coming through the battle unscathed.

She could not focus on the inevitability of the carnage. Linneya rose to her feet and motioned toward her foraging basket, announcing to no one in particular. "Since we have less than a day, I must get to the infirmary with these supplies. Life-tenders will be up all night preparing them for the battle." She shivered and Darryn reached for her hand.

The wicked look in his eyes said he was ready for this fight. She wished she had the same confidence, though she supposed it came from annae of warrior training. He ran his thumb over the back of her hand, soothing circles that calmed her brain before it boiled into panic. Linneya squeezed his hand once and then made her way out of the stateroom, through the main entrance, and toward the infirmary.

From the mayhem unfolding around the clinic, Linneya could tell they had already been made aware of the approaching armies. A life-tender met her at the front, the woman was wiping her hands on her tan apron and breathing heavily. "Oh, princess, thank you so much! Take those inside to the preparatory room. Wralion needs them for the styptic powder he is finishing."

She nodded and pushed through the front door. Inside, healers were hurriedly packing things, moving people, and wrestling with boxes of supplies. The usual stagnant smell was heightened with adrenaline and sweat.

Linneya had worked with many of these people, and her heart hurt. She may have been in disguise, so they never became close, but she knew many by name. Mathera struggled with both of her pregnancies and raised her two children alone, but they were the light of her world. Shullen was a farmer, but he worked the early shift at the infirmary to combat his loss of crops from the worsening droughts. Ayurana was snippy, but Linneya had learned it was from chronic pain that wore on her, day after day. These people would struggle to survive in the face of war. She tamped down the worry around what the upcoming battle would mean for her former colleagues and elbowed her way through the crowds to enter the preparatory room.

The healer with reddish brown hair and hawk-eyes grinned as she entered. "Your Highness, how may I help you?" He bowed slightly, but continued grinding whatever was in the mortar and pestle.

She held up her foraging basket. "I have oak bark. The woman at the front said Wralion would need it."

"Ah!" he exclaimed. The man stopped grinding and wiped his hands on his apron. "I am Wralion, I shall take that for you, Princess."

She blushed at her gaffe. "I apologize! I did not realize we had met before."

He grinned. "No worries. Thank you for bringing these supplies. If there is anything I can do to be of assistance to you, please let me know."

She hesitated. Lord Caelin had indicated he had an uncanny ability to help elementals. Perhaps he would know something about Creators-blessed gifts as well. Linneya turned to him. "Actually, I could use your advice. I have heard you may be able to see what an elemental needs for their future."

Wralion raised his eyebrows. "I do have some visions. Other times, my mind plays nasty tricks. Hallucinations. I have had to learn to watch for warning signs so that I do not share the wrong thing or lead someone to act based on my internal anxieties. With the upcoming battle, I am not sure that I would be able to give you direction for your future." He busied himself transferring the bark into a clay pot, then placed the pot on top of the stove.

Linneya wrapped her arms around herself. Things felt precarious enough with everyone knowing about her elemental affinities. The wrong person learning she could dream-walk could be devastating. Still, she was going to have to trust someone at some point. "I am not in need of having my future read. It is actually... well..." She took a deep breath. "If I think I am dream-walking, how do I tell the difference?"

Wralion's brow knit together as he handed her the basket back. "What do you mean you think you are dream-walking?"

She dropped her voice low. "Sometimes, my dreams seem..." He leaned in and she waved her hands, trying to grasp for a better word. "They seem... real. I have this recurring figure that threatens elementals and want to know if I should pursue figuring out their motivation."

Wralion nodded thoughtfully. "That is an unusual situation. However, many dreams can be vivid without happening in the real world. For that matter, many dreams can even feel prophetic and turn out to be nothing. I have known many a dream-walker who lose their minds chasing their own imagination."

Linneya chewed on her lip. She was unsure if it was safe to tell the life-tender that she recognized the ground-tamer from her dreams. She took a deep breath. "I am certain that some of them are real. Evidence has emerged and now I need to know more about how to differentiate. How can you discern what is a vision? How do I know if I am dream-walking or if it is just my mind?"

The healer's face twisted in thought. "It can be a bit different for everyone. For me, my visions have sharper edges and my dreams look more blurred. If I am overly stressed, I am more wary of anything that seems like a vision. Pressure, anxiousness, fear... all of these things can lead to muddled discernment and I try to stay away from acting on anything that comes forward."

She wrung her hands. "Okay, thank you." She wished there was more time to discuss this, more trust built so she could share about the assassin. However, preparations for the battle had to continue. Perhaps after, Linneya could come back and they could talk more. If there was an after.

Wralion dipped his chin. "Look for something in your dream world that does not translate to the real situations you are visiting when you dream-walk. That will help you differentiate. Then, look for someone who can teach you how to control the dream-walking. You can do powerful things if you know how to utilize your talents."

Linneya thanked him once again and headed back toward the palace, her head spinning.

The eve of battle brought with it an emotional turbulence. Excitement that their allies stood with them. Terror over the unknown. Hope that they could prevail. Dread over what might be necessary to win.

Linneya and Darryn took dinner in their suite. Her mother had looked disappointed, but agreed that having the evening to be together was valuable. She had a lavish spread sent to their rooms, the best wines they could find in the cellars, and a note to ring for dessert when they were ready.

Linneya picked at the assortment of food, but found her stomach wound into too tight of a knot to eat much. She wandered to the bookcase, her satin evening gown flowing around her. She hummed, twisting the ring Darryn gave her around her finger and looking for a tale that she could reread. Getting lost in a fictional world seemed as good a way to soothe as any.

Darryn coughed and she whipped her head around. He was engrossed in a missive that detailed tomorrow's final plans for the Falorian knight units. He was shirtless, his muscles rippling as he made notes. Her eyes ran over his scars and she bit her lip. His forehead wrinkled in concentration and she had to resist the urge to walk over and smooth it out.

As if he could feel her gaze on him, he looked up and grinned. Everything shifted, the waves of conflicting emotions washed away and he anchored her in the moment. Linneya's mouth curved into a smile. "Are you going to spend the evening going over plans you already know like the back of your hand?"

He picked up his pile of parchment and tapped it on the table, letting it settle into a neat stack. Then he stood and crossed the room, placing the papers on the shelf next to her. "You are right. The facts help my brain stay focused, but I do not need to look at the strategy again. What is on your mind?"

She wrapped her arms around herself and drew in a breath. "I do not know what I will do if I lose you tomorrow."

His mouth tugged up on one side and he stepped closer, placing his hand on her cheek. "Do not kill me off yet, Lia. I have survived against worse odds." He brushed a wild lock of hair out of her face, tucking it behind her ear.

Linneya ran her hands up his chest. "I hear the dragon shields are in place?"

Darryn grinned, pressing his forehead to hers. "Yes, Tiuthan and I were able to capture aether into some stones. We have strategically placed them about to reinforce the original enchantments. I am confident that whatever dragon shows up will not be able to fly its way into the city. Nothing will burn inside Loraen tomorrow."

She smiled and leaned into him, savoring his citrus and cedar scent. His hands went to her waist and he pressed into her, hardening as she ground her hips into his. She buried her head into his neck and hummed a sigh.

Her knight twisted his fingers through her hair and pulled back, holding her gaze. "You move like that and I want nothing more than to consume you." He angled her head and began running his lips down the column of her throat.

His hands moved over her stomach. He was too high, too low, seductively close, but not close enough. Her breasts ached for his touch and a slick sensation gathered between her thighs.

"You move like *that*, warrior, and I want nothing more than for you to consume me."

A deep rumble escaped his chest. His fingers dug into her hips, pleasure on the edge of pain. She raised up, grabbing the back of his neck and arching her body into his. He pressed his lips to hers, dark and greedy. Taking what was his, in spite of tomorrow.

Warmth spread through her limbs and her breath hitched. Darryn teased her mouth with his tongue and ran a hand up her torso, squeezing her breast through the light material of her gown. She parted her lips and he tasted her, leaving behind a soothing flavor of sweet mint. Whatever may come, she wanted tonight to be memorable.

She broke the kiss and pulled him to the bed. She sat back and wrapped her legs around him. He waggled his eyebrows and leaned forward, pressing his hands onto the blankets and caging her with his arms. "I love how eager you are tonight."

Linneya huffed a laugh and shook her head, planting a soft kiss on his cheek. "Something about facing my doom brings out a feral part of me."

She sighed and looked toward the ceiling, releasing her legs. "But perhaps we should go to bed, get some rest. A good night's sleep will help us be better prepared for whatever tomorrow brings."

He groaned and dropped his head, pulling his hips away like he was bowing and stretched his shoulders. She ran her fingers through his hair and he hissed an encouraging curse. When his eyes met hers again, they were pitch black.

Darryn sank to his knees and ran his hands up her legs, sliding the hem of her gown up and resting his fingers dangerously high. One thumb made circles close to her center and she gasped at his touch. Any further and he would feel how ready she was. Her knight grinned as if he knew what she was thinking and squeezed into her soft thighs. A warmth throbbed through Linneya and she stifled a moan.

"Are you sure sleep is the answer?" Darryn teased, a wicked glint in his eye. "I could rejuvenate you in other ways, love." He pressed a kiss to the inside of her knee, sending a tingling jolt to her core.

"You drive a hard bargain, warrior," she joked, stroking her fingers up his arms. Her fingers trailed over the ridges of his scars and he made a low, dark sound in the back of his throat.

Linneya wanted to demand he splay out on the bed, let her finally take him and ride him until her desperate energy abated. But her knight had other plans. He grabbed her, a shriek escaping her mouth as he pulled her forward.

"Let me feast on you, Linneya." He draped her legs over his shoulders and wrapped his hands around her hips, pinning her. She was bared to him, her gown scrunched around her waist, and he muttered his approval at the sight.

Burning intensity shone in his eyes as he licked and nibbled the inner parts of her thighs. He dragged his thumb through her wet center and made a feral noise like a starved beast. Linneya whimpered as he pulled away, leaving her desperate for the pressure that would finally take her over the edge.

"If I am to die tomorrow, let me die with the taste of you on my lips."

He scraped his calloused fingers down the inside of her legs. Waves of sensation traveled up her body and she gasped, unable to talk. The sight of him knelt before her, opening her wider, savoring her thighs like they were the main course nearly undid her.

Her legs trembled and he paused, leaving her aching for more as he lifted his head to meet her gaze, his eyes dark with need. "Well?"

"Yes, oh please, Darryn."

With a growl, he dove between her legs, devouring her. She failed to stifle her moan as he flicked his tongue over her swollen apex. The sound seemed to make him more eager and he massaged her entrance with his fingers. Her hips undulated with his hand, a frenzied tempo.

He stopped and parted her soaked center. She gasped at the cool sensation on her overheated sex, moaning his name. Her knight ran one hand under her gown, palming her breast before rolling her nipple in between his thumb and pointer finger. He slowly dragged his flattened tongue over her exposed center and she murmured his name again.

"That's it, love. I want you so wrapped up that my name is the only thing you can manage."

Her hips arched as he ran his tongue over her, setting a slow, torturous pace. Release built in her, a deep and aching promise. He pressed her legs wider, angling her hips, and plunged his tongue deep. She writhed and hissed her approval, his chuckle sending warm vibrations through her core. Her knight moved faster, pumping and curling his tongue into her.

Just as she thought she would lose her mind, he wrapped his lips around that sensitive bundle of nerves and *sucked*.

His tongue beat a fevered rhythm against her bud and a strangled noise wrenched from her throat. He pushed two fingers inside of her, stretching her as the sensation shattered her. Linneya writhed, his name a scream of ecstasy as she rode out the pleasure.

She fell back onto the bed, breathless. He crawled next to her, kissing her deeply. Something about tasting her pleasure on his lips stirred a warmth in her chest. She ran her fingers across his abdomen and he shuddered at her touch. His hardness strained against his sleep pants and she gripped it, earning a guttural moan from him.

He pulled her up from the bed, breathing hard. "Shall we try for number two? We need to christen this tub." She grinned and her knight gestured around the magnificent room. "I say we lay our claim on this suite for every time we visit."

She giggled as he led her into the washroom and down the stairs into the bath. They tangled together, a mess of tongues and limbs, and his touch washed away her fear of what tomorrow would bring.

Chapter 35

Her legs burned with soreness as they climbed the stairs to the parapet, but at least she was sore in all the right places. The memory of Darryn's hands on her, of them feasting on each other, was a warm anchor in the face of the nightmare that would be today's battle.

She looked to him. His armor hugged his body, accenting his shoulders and hips. A strip of leather pulled his hair back into a tight bun. He wore a wicked grin that had built as they prepared for the day. He had even hummed a traditional battle hymn to the war goddess Zhaifa as he braided her hair back. Darryn lived for war, ached for the bloodthirsty battles. Today, he would shine.

They got to the top of the stairs and trudged onto the parapet. A red light bathed everything as the smaller sun rose first. Eleanor and Shailyn stood, heads together, whispering about whatever their plans were for the day. Shailyn was dressed in battle attire and a multitude of bottles hung around her neck. Eleanor was in little more than a dressing gown, unapologetically bleary eyed.

King Varilon was already outside the walls, inspecting the troops. Queen Altheia was close behind, a bow and arrows slung over her shoulder. Darryn kissed Linneya's forehead and broke off to meet with Trotyn and Graisor. She shook off the beginnings of an anxious chill and looked for the fae prince.

The male was leaning against a statue, polishing a studded club. His armor glinted orangish red in the early morning light. His curly blonde hair was intricately braided and one side shaved, showing off ancient warrior rune tattoos. He looked up and nodded as she approached.

"How might I help, princess?"

Linneya raised her eyebrows and looked at Tiuthan. "I wanted to thank you for your help with the shields. Lord Caelin says they are powerful."

Lord Caelin had ensured that the elemental shields that had been placed around the city walls would hold. With Tiuthan's help and Darryn's scrolls, they had devised a system for repelling the dragons and their flame. Something to do with certain energies that aether-weavers could remove from the air and condense into a hard dome along the perimeter. It created a barrier and a vacuum, making it impossible for the dragons to shoot flame or fly within the airspace around the capital. Linneya barely understood the theory behind it, but was grateful for it.

The fae prince shrugged. "I have rare elemental abilities - Void affinity. It allows me to act as a shield against other elemental powers and seems to have translated well to the barriers here."

Linneya shook her head. "Void? But that does not fit the elemental structure. Are you sure it is elemental and not Creators-blessed?"

He nodded absently and rolled his eyes. "Yes, yes, this is the same conversation I have with everyone who finds out about my affinity. Maybe someday we will have time to debate this, but for now just know it will save everyone's asses today the way it saved everyone's asses while you indiscriminately blasted a crater and nearly killed us all."

Hot shame crept up Linneya's face. Eleanor crossed her arms and scoffed from a few feet away, not trying to keep her voice down. "From what I heard, you barely did your part whilst my sister was the one saving everyone's asses."

Tiuthan stood up and stalked toward her, a duocentury of polished, predatory skill honed in on the woman. "It is more than you did."

Eleanor looked unphased by his dramatics and opened her mouth to snark back. Linneya walked away, letting them bicker as Shailyn giggled at the debacle.

Graisor and Trotyn were leaving for the field and Darryn hurried back to her side. They watched the units on the battlefield through a notch in the wall. She shivered again and he placed an arm around her shoulders. Overwhelm began to set in and Linneya could barely sense him beside her.

They stood there, silently awaiting their fate as more people filtered outside. Teams dragged catalpults onto the field. Others erected large life-tender tents. The larger sun rose just as an insistent mist fell across the capital. Slowly, their friends and family members trickled down and toward the battlefield. Linneya struggled to dismiss the foreboding sensation of doom. A dark blur appeared on the horizon and some of the soldiers began to take notice.

Linneya ground her teeth as murmurs shot through the ranks. The Aelorian army and its allies were formidable. However, it was already clear the Serathanian military would be a force to be reckoned with.

Darryn squeezed her shoulders. "Shall we head down to the commanders' tent?" Linneya jerked a nod and they followed the stairs back to the ground floor. The guards at the front gate saluted and let them pass. She held her head high, hoping that no one would notice how wobbly her legs were.

A cackle met them as they arrived at the commanders' tent. Shailyn was comparing her studded club to Tiuthan's, bragging about the inventive mechanisms she had added to hers. "No, but see, if you add a latch here, it becomes easier to refill the poison. You do not risk it slinging out on you during battle because of the springs holding the valves of each nail in place. The club must tear into flesh to seep the substance into a person's body."

Tiuthan threw his head back and laughed. "This is brilliant. What kind of mad scientist are you? What even prompted you to create such a mechanism?"

If Shailyn had feathers, she would have preened. As it was, she looked thrilled with the praise. "I dabble in both botanical healing and devastation. It keeps me well rounded." She smirked and motioned to her necklaces. "These bottles are different antidotes, including one for this club's poison. I may be proud of my work, but I take no chances. I want to guarantee that I will live to experiment more."

Tiuthan chuckled, but Darryn shook his head and crossed his arms. "And you will not be using the club during this battle, Shay. I have arranged for you to stay in the life-tenders' ranks with Eleanor. There is no reason to risk either of you."

Shailyn huffed and tried to argue, but her protests were drowned out by a higher voice.

"No, I will be fighting. No peasant knight will tell me otherwise." Eleanor pushed back the tent flap and walked inside. She must have gone back to the palace - she was now fully battle-ready. Linneya raised her eyebrows at the sight of her dainty sister lugging an axe and decked out in armor, in the same breath she wanted to yank her sister's perfect braids for insulting her husband.

Tiuthan turned and dragged his eyes over her body. A bit too slowly, but Linneya would not interfere. Her sister had made it clear she could hold her own against the male.

The fae prince smirked. "How kind of you to finally show. I was beginning to think you would nap straight through the battle."

Eleanor pointed her weapon and snarled. "Stay out of my way. I am here to fight."

Tiuthan leaned in, snatching her axe and holding it to her throat. "You think you are going to make a difference on the battlefield, *Mahuchav*? Attitude counts for little in the face of steel."

Darryn snickered and Linneya shot him a look. He grinned back at her, unphased by the warning behind her expression.

Eleanor lifted her chin, ignoring the steel pressed against her neck. "These are my people. You know nothing of my training or what I am capable of."

Tiuthan shrugged and stepped back. "Better you show up last minute rather than cower in the safety of your tower, I suppose. Still, you are going to end up roasted meat today. Better to stay with the life-tenders." He flipped the axe and handed it to her, handle first. His shoulders straightened and he drew himself up to his full height as she touched the handle.

Eleanor snatched it and matched his body language. "If you are that worried, you can protect me yourself. Prove yourself a great warrior and fight while keeping me from becoming roasted meat."

Tiuthan's mouth split into a grin. He leaned forward and brushed a curl off her forehead. "Alright, *Mahuchav*. I will do that. My shields will be yours today."

Eleanor's face went red and Linneya had to suppress her own snicker. Her sister practically spat at the fae. "If you are going to curse me, you could at least do it in a language I understand."

Tiuthan cocked his head, smirking. "Oh, but where would be the fun in that?"

Eleanor scoffed, turning a deeper shade. "I did not emerge from ash and flame to have some egotistical, bratty... *freak* talk down to me."

Linneya narrowed her eyes at her sister's wording. What had happened to her over the past season? Why was she interested in fighting now? There was no time to discuss it, but she wished that Eleanor had been willing to talk to her. Lives would be lost today and it was hard to have that cloud hanging over their relationship.

Tiuthan rolled his eyes. "We may have the advantage, but Serathor's dragons will burn everything if they get through our defenses. I will talk however I need to in order for you to be safe."

Eleanor looked ready to blow, but Shailyn elbowed her way through the arguing pair and stood in front of Linneya. Darryn towered behind them and Linneya could feel the anger radiating from him. Anger that came from the same fear she held: their younger siblings needed to stay safe.

Shailyn huffed. "Tell Darryn I can hold my own."

Linneya shook her head. "No, I believe Darryn is right about this, Shay. It is safer if you focus on your life-tending skills today."

Shailyn began to twist her features into the same expression of frustration as Eleanor. Before she could protest, Linneya held a hand up. "Listen, I know you want to prove yourself a formidable foe, but today is not the day for it. You promised that if I advocated for you, you would do whatever was required when it came time for the battle. Stay alive today, there will be plenty more opportunities for you to get in the middle of the fight."

Shailyn's hands balled into fists and her eyes became watery with tears of frustration, but to the woman's credit she nodded. "I will go to the life-tender's tents immediately." Darryn let out an audible sigh of relief and she could feel him relax a bit.

She wrapped her sister-in-law into a hug. "We will find you afterward. Just, do everything you can to keep yourself safe." Darryn hugged her as well, whispering something into her ear.

Shailyn stalked out of the tent, just as Aiden pushed in. "Darryn, Tiuthan, you will want to see this."

The men jumped up and Linneya followed them out. Muttering through the ranks created an uneasy atmosphere. No one was prepared for what was coming. Linneya squinted, watching the distant shadow of armies headed toward them. There were more soldiers than they had predicted. Many of them moved faster than she expected for such a large group.

The rumbles of curiosity turned to shouts of horror as the first line of soldiers became more clear. Shadows billowed and a musty stench permeated the air. The blood drained from Linneya's face. The wolf-like creatures with stag horns were appearing and advancing at an unnatural pace. The reverberations of their forces shuddered through the air.

"*Sharvach.*" Darryn's fists tightened at the word. "King Shumor must have sent emissaries to promise them a cut of Aelor's lands."

Linneya clung to his arm as the skies darkened. Both suns were hidden behind the incoming wave of dragons. They circled overhead in a show of force, coming dangerously close to the city walls. Some had Serathanian warriors or *sharvach* on their backs. Many more were riderless. More than one Aelorian soldier shouted in terror as the dragons swooped.

They landed, scattered in between the advancing platoons. The dragons with riders had bejeweled harnesses that sparkled in the sunslight. Linneya worried her lip at the sight. If the jewels were real, so were the rumors that King Shumor had experimented with giving dragons other elemental powers.

There were dozens with riders. More than she could count. Her legs shook as their screeches filled the air. A sulfuric stench singed her nostrils and Darryn leaned toward her. "Do you smell that? They starve the poor beasts and it creates a dank odor. They think it makes the dragons more vicious."

Her blood ran cold. King Shumor claimed to be a savior to the human realms, but how could anyone believe him with the way he was treating these animals? A person could be judged based on the way they acted toward creatures. It was terrible enough that the king had spent time prematurely waking dragons to harvest and nurture more eggs. It was worse knowing he tortured them.

They looked vicious. This many could do so much more damage than Linneya had anticipated. She took a deep breath. With any luck, the city's shields would hold and the dragons' damage would be confined to the battlefields.

"I would rather go to the *sharvach* than go through that, freak." A shrill, biting voice told her Eleanor and Tiuthan had arrived. She closed her eyes and rubbed her temples as Darryn chuckled.

Tiuthan bit out a reprimand. "Stay away from the *sharvach*. Their bite is lethal for many, but if you survive you will be driven mad from the venom in their saliva."

Eleanor and Tiuthan stopped beside them. She crossed her arms and huffed. "You cannot scare me with your fantastical tales."

He leaned toward her. "I may be a freak, but I know what I am talking about. You should be afraid. By the twins, I am afraid. Just, agree to it, will you?"

Eleanor's face drained. "Fine. If we make it out of this, I will gladly let you walk me through the gardens."

Darryn and Linneya exchanged a look, trying to keep from smiling.

"It's a date, princess." Tiuthan grinned, a darkness simmering just beneath the surface.

Linneya took a deep breath and looked for their friends. Queen Altheia was making her way toward the main life-tender's tent. Shailyn and Chrysa were right outside, stacking supplies into the carts the life-tenders would use during the battle. Linneya did not see Mariel or Straion, but guessed they were inside the tent, preparing.

A few paces away, Trotyn was bouncing on the balls of his feet, twisting his whip in his hands as if he would take off running toward Serathor's front lines at any moment. Graisor was calmer, stoic even. He watched the advancing troops with a somber expression.

The rumbling became more crisp. Drums became distinct as the soldiers drew near. The Serathanian army stopped a gross of paces from the Aelorian lines. There was a moment of hesitation on both sides, as if no one quite knew how to start.

"Shumor! Let us find peace!" King Varilon stepped onto the balcony of the highest watchtower at the city gates. Aiden appeared beside him, the two making an inspiring sight.

No one answered. Her father spoke again. "If your king is not here, who here has the power to treat with me?"

"Of course the cowardly bastard is not here," Darryn ground out. "He never has known how to face adversity. The man will always hand it off to anyone else."

Linneya shivered at his tone. Until now, the whole affair had felt like a thought exercise. More like the war games of the Falorian knights instead of a deadly serious battle that threatened her parents' country with destruction. If Loraen fell, the rest of Aelor would be unable to stop the advance of King Shumor's troops.

No one answered the king. Her father and Aiden stood for several more breaths, waiting for someone to take charge. Linneya chewed on her lip and gripped her sword so hard her knuckles blanched.

After what felt like an eternity, King Varilon coughed and nodded to Aiden.

Her brother stepped forward and raised his arms. A single shout and the dam broke. Arrows everywhere, screams and clanging metal.

She was not ready.

Linneya tried to steady her breath as they began to run forward.

She was not ready...

The battlefield was a blur. A rainbow of smoke billowed as those fighting activated their affinities. Thoughts were fogged by panic and her instinct took over. Linneya grunted, trying to match the advancing soldiers blow by blow. The first man was struck down easily, but the second came forward with more bravado. She spun, narrowly avoiding his strike, and tumbled into the mud. Darryn cut him off as he swung at her head, slicing the soldier's neck.

He knelt down beside her and lifted her chin. The screams and crashing of the battlefield fell away. "Love, use your affinities. This is what you have practiced for."

Linneya inhaled, a wild energy coursing through her veins. The chaos felt tamed, she could direct it and step into her own. She nodded and he lifted her up by her arms. They turned just in time to dive back in as a soldier swung an axe at her neck.

She dodged him and flicked her wrist. Flames shot into the man's armor. She did not wait to hear his screams or watch him fall before turning to meet the next soldier.

Mariel and Straion were not far away. They were further back and fighting one or two soldiers that broke through. Mariel carried a small cart with several supplies for life-tenders who were nearby.

Aiden and her father had made their way out of the city gates and were side by side, swinging weapons in a coordinated dance. Tiuthan and his unit were nearby, slicing through *sharvach* fighters like a warm knife through butter. Eleanor was shakily waving her axe, occasionally landing a hit but making more work for the fae prince in the interim. Trotyn's whip cracked and Graisor's sword shimmered as they moved with the other Falorian knights. Linneya could only pray to the Creators that Shailyn had stayed back as requested.

Darryn fought next to her, a vicious sight. If she had been able to step back and watch, she was certain his massive yet lithe form would have been magnificent. If they were to die today, at least it would be together. No one would write of them like Luthin and Payera, but they would die knowing they did their best.

As the thought ran through Linneya, a screech overhead made her look up. A dragon was circling, swooping lower with each pass. All the bravado drained from her body. Her chest buzzed with a primal need to run, to hide.

Linneya blocked an advancing soldier's attack, pulling flame from the embers falling around them and sending it underneath his armor. The man's face twisted in agony as he fell to his knees. He swung his sword a final time, nicking her calf as he collapsed.

She hissed at the sting. The trickle of blood began running down her leg as they pressed forward. She refused to give in to the thoughts that a deeper cut might have incapacitated her.

Beside her, Darryn slashed and cut his way through the enemy. He sucked the air out of one soldier, suffocating him. The next, Darryn blocked an overhead blow while sharp vines sprung out from the ground and slashed, disemboweling the soldier before he knew what was happening. His face was contorted into an expression of pleasure at the darkness. Sweat and blood flew, his muscles pumped, and a deep tug squeezed in her chest once again.

This man was powerful. Brilliant. If she had to die, she was glad it was by his side.

A dragon with dark blue scales stomped forward. The brown leather harness was speckled with blue and purple gemstones. Its rider cackled as the

Aelorian soldiers backed away. Even the Serathanian soldiers had retreated, giving the beast a wide berth.

Linneya's heart pounded in her chest, begging her to run as far away as she could. Darryn stepped in front of her, as if he could shield her from whatever destruction the beast would unleash. The ground shook with its steps, its feet sinking into the mud and spraying a dank bog smell into the air. Gray smoke and hissing sounds suggested the dragon was somehow heating up the dirt. Sure enough, molten lava glowed in its wake.

The dragon stopped and turned toward them. The beast huffed at Darryn, the telltale glowing at the base of its neck suggesting it would attack. Heat rose in her veins, as if it could protect her from the inevitable flames. She cringed and raised her sword, for all the good it would do.

Linneya held her breath, waiting for the attack, but the dragon's neck cooled and returned to its natural dark blue color. It turned away, uninterested in the fight. The rider screamed, hurling insults at the majestic beast. He began beating at the animal, as if his riding crop could command it better than words.

The dragon grumbled, a deep noise of discontent. The rider continued his barrage of abuse, turning to grab a sensitive spot in the beast's scales. It bellowed and snapped its neck back toward its rider.

Linneya grabbed Darryn's arm and pulled. "We need to go. Now."

Darryn shook his head. "If we run, the creature's prey drive will cause it to follow. Stay behind me. Back away slowly. Maybe it will become distracted by something else."

The fighting continued around them, no one able to see the predicament they were in as the dragon locked back onto them. "Where is Tiuthan when you need him," Darryn huffed. Linneya would have laughed, if her stomach was not twisted into knots. The fae prince's void powers would be a welcome relief, but at least he was somewhere protecting Eleanor.

The base of the creature's neck was glowing again. Before they could run, the flames unleashed, a white hot stream of fire aimed directly at Darryn. He stumbled backward, as if surprised by the beast's attack, but the dragon's flame followed. It engulfed him and Linneya screamed. Another soldier ran forward and she turned to wrap him in thorny vines, slicing his skin and choking him until he fell to the ground.

Darryn fell to his knees, shaking. His armor was melted in places, as if the dragonflame had reforged the metal. The beast took another breath in, preparing to finish the job. Darryn looked up, trembling in pain, but unwilling to cower in the face of his death. Linneya doubled over, retching at the sight of her husband accepting the end.

This man had upended her world in the course of a few mooncycles. She should have hated him for taking her from her family, should have walked away and never spoken to him again. His pride, his ridiculous angst, all of it was infuriating and she still did not understand everything that had happened.

However, that tug to be by his side had been so strong. He had a fierceness with which he would protect those under his charge. A sob caught in her throat as she thought of their friends, the close and easy relationships that had been built because he gave them space to exist. She clenched her chest at the memories of how the Falorian knights under his command honored his word and respected his strategy.

But most of all, his laugh. His wicked tone as he seduced her. The way her breath would catch at his whisper. They had a connection that was irreplaceable.

She closed her eyes, a sigh escaping her lips. She would never again care for a man like she had cared for this enigma of a warrior. The pain mixed with denial.

How could this be their end?

Chapter 36

A horn sounded and Linneya's eyes popped open. The dragon and its rider took off toward a different part of the battlefield. Gone, just like that. She froze, unsure what had just happened, until Darryn collapsed to one side. Linneya let out a breath she did not know she was holding.

She scrambled to reach the place where Darryn was sprawled out on the ground. Over half his body was charred, but his chest was still rising and falling. His armor was melded to his skin in places. There was no way to remove it to see the extent of the damage.

Tears burned in her eyes. She tried to turn him onto his back and he vomited, a mixture of blood and bile. Linneya gritted her teeth. The sooner she could start the healing, the more likely it would be that she could fix this.

"Khreth aeki raewi." She held her hands over his body and chanted the words over and over. Red light glowed around her and the warmth of her healing powers flowed through her hands, but Darryn did not move. Did not make a sound.

Her brow furrowed. This burn was different. Almost as if traces of elemental magic had been used to create it. She chewed on her lip, willing the healing to continue, trying not to lose hope. Linneya did not understand why her power was not healing him. There was a missing piece of information that was keeping her from saving Darryn's life. Her chest tensed at the thought, winding so tight she felt it could crack a rib.

Shouts made her stop. With the dragon moving on, soldiers were once again advancing. It meant she had to turn and fight. She grabbed her sword and spun around, panicked at the sight of the massive men charging.

Her eyes darted around, beseeching the Creators to send her help. The longer she had to wait to heal him, the harder it would become. If she was dead, there would be no hope. She tried to shove the dastardly thoughts away, twisting her hands around her weapon's handle. She took a deep breath and lunged forward, focusing on fighting and conserving her elemental abilities to heal Darryn.

A familiar shout caused Linneya to start and whip around. Aiden and Johann sprinting towards them. The two were blocking and parrying as if they had choreographed the battle in advance. Aiden would aim high and Johann ducked low. Johann's whip moved as if it had a mind of its own, sometimes shooting flames at the same time it struck an enemy, and Aiden would finish them with his skillful swordwork.

Her shoulders dropped in relief and tears burned at her eyes. Aiden countered another soldier's attack and Johann snapped his whip across the man's throat. The soldier stumbled back, clawing at his neck as if the flexible weapon had collapsed his airway. He slowly dropped to the ground, tears in his eyes - from pain or grief no one would ever know.

The two of them ran up to her, checking her over for injuries. Everything became muffled and her vision went glassy as she took in their appearance. Aiden was streaked in ash and blood. His hair was almost black from the grime of fighting and a chunk of his scalp was grazed. Johann's pupils were blown, no signs of the golden eye color she was used to.

Aiden hissed through his teeth as he saw Darryn, nearly lifeless, on the ground. He grabbed her shoulder and shook her. "Lia, focus on healing Darryn. We will fend them off."

Linneya began shaking. "I cannot - it is - there is something wrong." She gulped for air, fighting the sensation of her world crumbling and dragging her down with it. This was not where she was supposed to be. She should be with Mariel, with the life-tenders, not in the midst of a fight when she could barely hold her own. Now Darryn was dying. He was leaving her unprotected, ungrounded... Everything froze and for a moment a blissful numbness enveloped her.

Aiden smacked the back of her head, hard enough to surprise her. "Quit it. Now, focus. We can fall apart later. Right now your husband needs you."

The sudden shock jolted everything back into place. The battle sounds became almost overwhelming and she bit her lip. She stared down at Darryn's body. He was no longer moving. Her shaking resumed.

Johann grunted, wrapping his whip around the ankle of a *sharvach* and throwing them to the ground. "Hurry, Lia. We need him to keep fighting. We need both of you if we are going to win this."

Johann's words stung her heart. The hopelessness of their situation threatened to consume her. Darryn was lying on the ground, helpless. Her family was facing ruin, countless lives lost to Serathor's troops.

Aiden yelled her name again. She shook her head, clearing her thoughts. There was no time to dwell on this.

Darryn needed her. At least she could fix his burns, if she hurried. She dropped to her knees beside her husband, brushing his hair off his face. His eyes fluttered open and she tried to smile. "Darryn, I am here. Stay with me." He wheezed, struggling to focus on her face. "Shh, stay still, give me a moment, I can heal you. I can fix this." Linneya panted as she tugged on her affinities, trying to draw the energy to focus on healing.

Darryn grimaced and tried to bring his undamaged hand to her cheek. "Lia, it was always meant to be you. I never would have lasted if I had known. He cannot have you." Her eyes burned as tears welled up at the gravelly sound of his voice. He rasped, "at least I get to die with the taste of you..."

She laughed through her tears. Something was still wrong with her affinity. Her healing flame-talker abilities were moving too slow. She chewed on her lip as part of the armor came loose from his skin healing underneath.

"Shumor's experiments worked." He grunted and coughed. Linneya shushed him, continuing the healing enchantments, but his comment brought hope.

The dragon, it had been covered in a jeweled harness. Its flame had been almost white. That combined with its smoke...

It had used elemental power, superheating its natural fire with flame-talking abilities. Linneya's heart warmed at the thought. This, she could work with.

It would take longer, but she was certain she could heal him. She called in her mist affinity, not as familiar with its healing, but certain that it would speed the process along. Its green light mixed with the flame healing light as she worked.

Slowly, Darryn's breathing became more normal. The battle raged around them, Aiden and Johann keeping Serathor's soldiers beat back as she worked. He finally sat up, rubbing his face with his hands.

His hair was tousled and caked with mud. His armor hung at odd angles, misshapen from the ultrafire of the dragon. But when Darryn looked at Linneya with clear eyes and a wicked grin, she fell against him and sobbed.

He grunted, but laughed. "I always knew you could do great things, love." His arms wrapped around her, a buffer against the evil that sought to destroy everything. For a moment, Linneya did nothing but breathe in, hints of his citrus and cedar scent still there underneath the sweat and grime of battle.

Shouts of celebration came from Aiden and Johann as they began to realize Darryn was conscious. Aiden slammed into an advancing *sharvach*, sending the beast plummeting toward the ground, then drove his sword through the creature's skull. With that, there was a lull in the fighting.

The two men came forward, helping them off the ground. Darryn was still slightly unsteady, but able to stand and pick up his sword. Aiden clapped Darryn on the shoulder as Johann swept Linneya up in a hug and spun her around. The lighthearted moment came to an end when another of Serathor's horns blasted.

Aiden's jaw pulsed. "We need to get back to our unit. They have been overwhelmed and need us." Johann nodded his agreement.

Darryn clasped both men on their shoulders. "Thank you for the part you played in keeping us safe." The three of them stared at each other, silent bonds of brotherhood strengthening. The camaraderie that had formed during the shadowland raids shone through and Linneya wished for more time for Darryn and Aiden to grow closer.

The two men took off toward their unit and Darryn gestured for them to fall back toward a life-tender's cart. They slowly made their way toward the nearest healers and one woman helped them make it back to the tent.

As a life-tender checked Darryn's almost fully healed wounds, another healer brought Linneya a cold tea. She nodded in thanks, eyes turning back to the fights. Linneya's limbs were shaking as if she would collapse at any moment. She scanned the battlefield and her heart sank. The Serathanian forces outnumbered them, four to one. Even with the powerful fae on their side, the *sharvach* beasts evened things out. A smoky haze was settling over the battlefield, making it harder to see. She inhaled the acrid fumes and rubbed her burning eyes.

Aiden roared nearby, locked in close combat with a *sharvach* soldier. The two wrestled ferociously, locked in a sort of stalemate. Linneya gasped as the shadow wolf swept Aiden's ankle, jaws clamping around his neck, and forced him to the ground.

She cried out and dropped her tea, screaming his name as if the sound alone could save him. Fate could not take him. Prophecies be damned, she would not wear the crown. Linneya left the tent and started running toward the *sharvach*, all thoughts of using her affinity or battle training lost. Darryn stumbled behind her, his body still unsteady after being brought back from the brink.

Before she could reach Aiden, the stench of sulfur and burnt ash filled her lungs. A crimson dragon without a rider swooped in between them and landed directly in her path. Its bright yellow eyes had specks of red, as if the suns were combined and seared their power onto this creature's iris. Darker patches of red dotted its wings and its tail. It was a smaller beast, but obviously quicker witted than some of the larger dragons. Possibly more fierce. She raised her sword, shaking, and Darryn bellowed for her to stay back. She could not look away. The animal would have been majestic if not for the crazed hunger blazing in its eyes.

The creature looked at her with an intensity that made Linneya recoil. Whether sizing her up for dinner or looking deep into her soul, she could not tell. Serathor's horns blasted a new set of sounds and the dragon looked for the source. It huffed, bared its teeth at Darryn, then turned toward a group of fae, screeching. Linneya's legs wobbled like jelly and Darryn caught her before she could fall.

Linneya reoriented herself. Aiden. He was hurt. She wrenched away from the knight and tried to make her way to her brother through the chaos. It was slow going; more Serathanian soldiers advanced and progress became dependent on multiple dead bodies.

Through the crowds of fighting soldiers, she caught a glimpse of Aiden's lifeless body. A newfound wave of fury pulsed through her. Linneya raised a hand and allowed her mist element to drown a man from the inside out. He dropped and she had a moment to evaluate their situation before the next wave of soldiers. She stepped forward and raised her hands, envisioning which soldiers needed to be immobilized. With a pulsing motion, she allowed ground to move through her. A fine wisp of rust colored vapor swirled around her.

Everything shook. Darryn shouted as men and *sharvach* began dropping into the soil. She allowed herself a grin of triumph before turning to survey the battlefield. The treeline was on fire. Some of the evacuated cottages were a flaming inferno. Ash fell around them, silent and white like a heavy snow. Aiden was unmoving in a puddle of his own blood, surrounded by humanoid-sized sinkholes. Linneya's heart dropped and her shoulders slumped at the destruction. Even if they won this battle, it would not be a victory.

The ground shook, followed by a growl so deep it sounded like clicking. The threatening noise caused her to straighten up and turn. The blood drained from Linneya's face as she looked into the flaming orange eye of a gigantic dragon, not five paces away. It swiveled its head and its nostrils flared as it huffed. Her hair flew back from the force of its breath. Scars littered its gray scales, the tales of numerous fights won. A sensation like creeping insects gripped the back of her neck. The creature's neck glowed, a visible threat that it would incinerate them whenever it so chose.

Her legs locked up from resisting the urge to run, the muscles seizing and creating sharp pains that radiated in her calves. The beast bared its teeth, the noxious sulfur scent billowing around Linneya. It was larger than she had ever imagined a dragon could be, its wings nearly blocking out the sun. Its harness had no jewels. Then again, what ancient beast would require assistance from the elemental powers?

She jumped as Darryn placed a hand on her upper back. His lips were set in a thin line and his fingers curled dangerously around his sword handle. "Get behind me, Lia," he muttered.

She tightened her grip on her sword and hissed back. "No, you will not do this alone."

He looked toward her to argue, but the dragon lunged forward a single step. Darryn and Linneya stumbled back, the force of the beast's stomp shaking the ground.

She looked around, wondering if she could cry for help. The creature roared and took a deep breath. Tiuthan was fighting, Eleanor by his side. If only Tiuthan could get to them to shield...

Tiuthan... his shield...

If Tiuthan could shield with his void power, was it possible she could do the same? It was too late to wonder. She threw her hands up, just as the dragon huffed a pillar of flame to consume them both.

The blistering heat rushed at Linneya and Darryn. She did not know which flame enchantment to use, so she began invoking them all. Her affinity glowed around them in a ball of red light and smoke as the dragon's flame billowed forward.

Darryn hacked, choking as the air superheated. The strangling noises turned into laughing and whooping. Linneya looked over her shoulder and grinned at the wild excitement in Darryn's eyes.

Finally, the onslaught of fire stopped. Linneya dropped to her knees, panting. Darryn sank down beside her and wrapped his arms around her, kissing her forehead and crushing her to his chest. "Are you burned anywhere? Are you okay? That was brilliant, love."

She shook her head, unable to speak. The dragon was watching them, its eyes slightly narrowed in confusion. It huffed and sat back, as if answering the creature with fire had earned her respect.

"Creators, how did you do that?" A cloaked figure was perched atop the beast, too high for her to make out any features. Darryn released her, growling under his breath at the opponent.

Linneya was in no mood to brag about her tactics to the enemy. She scrambled to her feet, raising her sword. "Face me you coward! Come down from there and fight. Win and I will tell you all about my powers." Her throat burned from screaming into the smoky air.

Darryn stood beside her, weapon at the ready. She sent a silent petition to the Creators that they would live to see another day. She wanted nothing more than to walk away from this and start her life with this man.

The figure perched atop the dragon seemed to consider her offer. Finally, he grabbed a sword and slid down the side of the monstrous beast. As he marched toward them, blood drained from Linneya's face. She knew the man's appearance, his walk, even the way he tilted his head. The assassin from her dreams was storming toward her.

The silver trillin mask glinted in the muted sunlight. Linneya's stomach knotted as the man grinned. His hooded cloak whipped around him.

Her gaze never left the approaching threat, but she reached for Darryn. He squeezed her hand, his voice a dangerous threat. "I know. He will answer for the elementals he has killed. He will suffer for the torment he released on you."

The assassin strode toward them, the promise of evil glinting in his eyes. Linneya's teeth ground together and she braced herself for the fight. Underneath his cloak, glittering gemstones lined his vest. At least one elemental killed for each stone. Fury flooded her veins, a sharp sting of heat. She would exact revenge on this man, destroying him through whatever means necessary.

The man opened his mouth to speak, but Darryn stepped forward and hissed. He flicked his wrist so fast Linneya barely saw the movement. A whirlwind started and within another half second she raised her arm, inviting flame to dance in the swirling air. Combined, they directed it toward the assassin.

The decision was so fast, so intuitive, it surprised her. Their affinities fit together, a perfect complement of color. There was no time for their enemy to react. He would undoubtedly be injured - if not fatally wounded.

Before she could complete the thought, their opponent held a hand up, fingers splayed wide. He closed his hand into a fist and the whirlwind disappeared. Darryn coughed, as if his air had been choked off. Ice flooded Linneya's veins.

The assassin chuckled. "Now, now, Darryn. Your wife issued a challenge. Surely you know better than to interfere. This is between the two of us." He motioned toward the dragon. "You go sit with old Grinnyn. He is sure to appreciate your company."

Darryn rolled his eyes and lowered his sword. "Really? That is the best you have for us? Try to sideline me over my wife's taunt? Pitiful."

The assassin wiped his mouth before charging forward. Darryn tightened his fingers around his sword handle and pointed with it, a villainous threat. He ducked as the masked man swung wildly.

Linneya cried out and pushed her flame element toward the assassin. Without looking, he waved her flames to the side. Vines grew up around her feet and she hacked at them with her sword. "Stay there while I deal with your husband, you bitch."

She struggled as the vines laced around her arms, stilling them at her sides. Linneya blinked back tears and tried to look anywhere but the fight between Darryn and the assassin. She could not bear to see the struggle for fear of watching Darryn fall yet again.

The battle was reaching a fever pitch, a bleakness beginning to settle over Aelor's defenders. Johann was running toward Aiden's body. He collapsed beside him, sobbing and swinging at anyone who got near. Her heart squeezed, knowing her brother was gone.

Her eyes scanned for signs of Eleanor. Her sister was proving she had some training. Linneya gasped as Eleanor grabbed a *sharvach* by the horns and slapped it across the face. The beast fell and did not move. She silently cheered as Eleanor and Tiuthan continued moving toward the advancing soldiers, holding their own.

The relief was short lived as she laid eyes on Shailyn. The woman had abandoned her healer's cart and was going toe to toe with a rider and dragon. The dragon was writhing, Shailyn shaking as she held her arms high. A bright light and thick plume surrounded them and Linneya's jaw dropped as the dragon collapsed, the rider obliterated.

But that was the only dragon that had been killed. The dragon Linneya witnessed earlier was stomping through a section of fae fighters, liquefying the ground into magma. Its rider was cackling mercilessly at the fleeing soldiers. The unluckiest were becoming trapped in the superheated soil, their screams of agony cutting through the air.

Trotyn fought a rider with a smaller dragon, his whip pulling the rider off his seat. Graisor stepped forward, rocking back and forth as if he could keep the dragon watching him instead of Trotyn. Chrysa was nearby with a life-tender's cart, eyes frozen on the scene.

A scream tore from the assassin, bringing her attention back. Blood dripped down his chin, as if Darryn had managed to connect with his mouth. The assassin held his arms up. "I am the prophesied! None who stand against me shall prevail!"

Darryn spit toward the man. "You have no natural born affinity, you beast. You cannot fool many for long. As soon as the real prophesied is revealed, your armies will flee. Your king will be ruined."

The prophesied grinned. "My king? No, once we have conquered the human realms, Shumor will bow to me. I will never surrender to the likes of him. Anyone who is wise will stay out of my way."

Linneya began calling her flame affinity, subtly burning through the vines. She called on the mist element, directing it to condense around the assassin, making it harder for him to breathe. She pushed her ground element, adding divots and tripping hazards around him.

Vines began falling away from her as the small fire burned through them. She only let one or two go at a time, hoping to get free without the masked man noticing. She chewed on her lip, pressing down the bile rising in her throat. If she could catch the man from behind, hit him with everything, they stood a chance.

Darryn growled. "You are a pitiful excuse of a leader. No one will bow to you. No one will see you as worthy of the title of prophesied. By the shadowed void, your own *dragon* ignores you!"

The prophesied snapped his fingers and a vine shot up from the ground, twisting around Darryn's leg and snapping the lower bones. Darryn's scream rattled Linneya to her core. She began to shake, her affinities begging to be unleashed on this evil bastard.

The assassin snickered, a sound of malignant greed. "You believe whatever you must. I will end both you and your wife, taking your powers as my own. You will die knowing that I prevailed. I won." He lifted his hands, muttering several enchantments under his breath.

Wind whipped, fires grew, and chaos reigned. Linneya glanced at the assassin's dragon. The creature seemed to be taking a nap, completely unbothered by the scene in front of it. She had to take her chances now or risk them dying anyway, whether the beast retaliated for its master's death or not.

The last few vines broke free. She raised her arms, calling on everything she had learned. The prophesied turned and directed his attacks at her.

Stars streaked in her vision as she strained the limits of her power. She heard Darryn roar, calling on vine and aether, as she fell to her knees. Linneya was shaking and she looked around, desperate for another option, another choice point, anything that might stop this horrid man from leading them all toward mutual destruction.

The prophesied trudged forward, barely hindered by the combined power of their elements. One flick of his wrist sent her flying. Her head smashed into a fallen soldier's helmet, her arms jerking up instinctively.

Hot, thick liquid began streaming into her eyes. Blood. The hit must have split open her scalp. She scrambled to try to stand, but the nausea and spinning caused her to drop to her knees.

The prophesied's dragon shifted, his deep growl clicking across the battlefield. He huffed forward, shaking the ground as he stepped toward Linneya. She grimaced as the musty heat from his breath gusted over her. The beast moaned, almost as if this was not the outcome he had hoped for, but turned away and settled close by, watching the fight play out.

The prophesied's voice burned through her, his taunts searing into her skull. He raised his arms and pointed directly at her, as if they were in another one of her dreams.

Screams were amplified alongside metal on metal screeching. A burning in her chest as her breath was being sucked out of her body. Fear boiled up, a cornered animal fighting to break free. Linneya tried to think of the words, tried to find the enchantments that would stop the suffocating sensation. Just one more, just one more...

Her vision tunneled and she fell back, limp. There was no more fight to be had. An odd calm washed over her body as a numbness took hold.

Everything faded to black. Linneya's last thought was that she wished to smell his citrus and cedar scent one last time. She mindlessly brushed her thumb across her ring as her consciousness disintegrated in waves.

Then, peace.

Chapter 37

A few minutes earlier...

Eleanor was livid. A season ago anyone could have asked her what she wanted out of life and she would have given a trite answer about running her own household and securing some lord's succession with babies. Lots and lots of babies.

Her blood boiled at the thought. She wanted to go back. The realities that had shaped her world in the last several mooncycles were infuriating. Now she was on a battlefield, the stench of burning bodies and tangy blood forever seared into her experience.

Maybe she should not have let the fae prince get under her skin. She could have stayed back with Mariel and Shailyn, working with the life-tenders. She ground her teeth and gripped her sword as another wave of soldiers advanced. Glancing toward Mariel's cart, she huffed a laugh.

The cart was surrounded by *sharvach*. Lord Straion and some other soldiers were fighting to keep them beat back. Even Mariel was swinging a sword and throwing small clay pots that exploded on impact. The woman dodged incoming swipes from the beasts' paws with an impressive, uncanny precision.

Eleanor shuddered. No, staying with the life-tenders would not have stopped this inevitability. The fight was everyone's today. Holding back would not have changed this outcome. Serathor's armies were too massive. Their allies, too strong.

And the dragons... so many dragons. Eleanor thought there would be only one or two. She nearly collapsed in fright when the suns had been blocked out by their advance. She prayed to the Creators that the shields would hold and the capital would still be intact once this battle was over.

Eleanor grimaced and pressed forward, dodging a swing by a *sharvach*. She managed to grab the wolf-like creature's horns and slapped a hand across his muzzle. He dropped instantly, dead. Tiuthan grunted his approval, cutting down another with a swift stroke of his blade.

When Lady Alayne suggested she might have Creators-blessed powers, Eleanor had laughed so hard she almost vomited. The absurdity of her - Eleanor - having a role to play beyond pretty princess was the funniest thing she had heard in annae.

She did not want this.

She did not need it.

Another swing, another block, this time she grabbed the soldier's arm and watched him drop. She grimaced and turned to the next opponent. The celestial storytellers had not foretold battles in her chart. Eleanor's destiny was supposed to be in comfort, in enjoying the easy life her parents had created for them.

A destiny that her sister had never understood. Linneya would blather on about duty and responsibility, an interminable lecture that made it impossible to enjoy anything. She missed out on so much joy because she was caught up in her head. Eleanor rolled her eyes thinking how her sister would haughtily raise her eyebrows and yammer on about the importance of their roles.

Eleanor had no role, no special place. That suited her fine. So when her new friend pressed the idea that she could be Creators-blessed, it was hilarious.

But quickly it became evident that Alayne had a knack for recognizing power in people. They started scouring the main library together, searching for mentions of shadowchildren, eclipse births, and what to do when your power can convince anyone of anything at the slightest touch.

Including convincing them that they are already dead.

A wry smirk crossed her face as she dropped another *sharvach*. The trick was getting close without getting injured. Her Creators-blessed power did the rest.

Eleanor spun round, sinking her axe into a soldier's neck. Something deep in her gut wrestled to come alive as his blood sprayed across her face. In those moments in the library, when she and Alayne bonded over their mutual annoyance of researching nebulous ideas that had no apparent origin, she felt a similar lurch. A spark of destiny - some greater force telling her that she had a place in this story.

Another *sharvach* lunged and she tripped. Her hands slammed on the ground and the invocation words tumbled from her mouth, almost an instinct. "*Raegow aeki raewi*." Vines shot out of the ground and wrapped around his legs, cementing the creature in place. More plants reached for his arms, but the *sharvach* snapped and chopped at them, making it impossible for Eleanor to get close.

Tiuthan huffed a laugh. "*Mahuchav*, you are fierce. What else are you hiding in that pretty little head of yours?" He swung around, embedding the spiked club into the *sharvach*'s skull with a satisfying crunch.

She grinned at him and turned back toward the advancing units, gasping for air. Her muscles ached, a metallic taste coated her breath. Eleanor rotated her axe in her hand, trying to steady her racing mind. She had never trained for a scenario like this. Her parents always pressed for their children to focus on the light, the healing abilities. Even after falling into the bonfire at Meðon and emerging unscathed, she had only asked for self-defense lessons. Not once was there a reason to think a battle would come to their doorstep.

Her vine affinity had emerged accidentally during those lessons. Once she realized Alayne was right about her Creators-blessed powers, Eleanor had marched to the armory and demanded to speak with anyone who might agree to train her on weapons. After several bewildered looks, one man stepped forward.

He was a nobody. Handsome, young, but no one of consequence. Barely starting his own smithwork. Still, he knew his way around all the weapons and was willing to train a princess. His lessons were tedious, rote movement over and over. Now, she was grateful that her body knew where to go without much thought.

She swung her axe, parrying the attack of an advancing soldier. Somehow, soldiers had begun maneuvering to attack from behind them. Eleanor slammed her hands down, pulling bushes and brambles up into a formidable barrier. Tiuthan shouted his elation at her cleverness and pressed forward.

Sweat dripped into Eleanor's eyes and she wiped her face, grimacing at the sting. That first lesson, the smithy had tripped her. Her hands hit the ground and she saw red. She wanted to strangle the man, furious that he had bested her. A choking sound had brought her back. Vines were wrapped around the man's neck, his eyes bulging. She had sat up, panicked, and immediately the plants wilted back into the dirt. Now, the vines on the battlefield held, a testament to her growing strength.

The haze that enveloped the battlefield was growing thicker. The taste of burnt foliage seared her tongue. Everything was on fire. Dragons were hidden in the sky, the suns blotted out by the smoke. Trees glowed with orange webbing, their inner wood burning while the bark remained intact.

Linneya's screams rose above the clamor. She was calling for their brother. Eleanor's head whipped around, searching for his unit. She could not see Aiden, but Linneya was close to the life-tender tents and was being approached by a maroon-colored dragon.

Blood left Eleanor's face as the beast leaned in and splayed its wings, showing off its unusual spotted pattern. She braced as if the creature was in her face instead of Linneya's. Watching her sister die was *not* on her list of expected things in her future.

Serathor's horns blasted across the battlefield. Tiuthan grabbed her arm and yanked her toward him. "*Mahuchav*, we need to fall back. We have to get out of here before the dragons sweep back this way."

She wrestled away. "No! I cannot see Aiden. We need to help - we need to find him."

Tiuthan pulled her behind his back and stabbed a soldier with the end of his club. He turned back to her, wide-eyed with what looked like worry. Eleanor was breathless as she nodded her thanks. She knew that she was more of a hindrance than a help, but she was grateful to be doing something. Anything. At least the fae prince seemed to enjoy the challenge of protecting her in the midst of the chaos.

She looked towards him. The man moved with the grace of a predator, weaving and bobbing as if the fight was a ballroom dance. It was a performance for him, flourishes and unnecessary spins adding a cocky bravado to his kills.

Something unwanted churned in her gut as she watched him. There was a pull to be near him, more to scratch his eyes out than do anything pleasurable. Her hands heated with the flame element at the thought, an orange light pulsating from her fingers, and she shook her head.

Hints of other affinities had popped up over the next couple of mooncycles. Any time she became angry, some elemental power would emerge. And Eleanor was angry a lot.

Her mother finally called Lord Caelin to the palace to discuss what was happening. Words like "prophesied" and "talent" were bandied about, making Eleanor cringe. The sudden weight of responsibility had pressed on her, as if it could smush her deep underground.

Tutors came and tried to teach her the nuances of the elements. Serious looking men joined her father and evaluated her abilities. All walked away disappointed. Eleanor could not figure out how to project any of her power.

No matter what she tried, she had to be able to touch the source. Eleanor grabbed another soldier's arm. The man screamed before going limp. She huffed, smiling through the sweat and mud accumulating on her face. The ground shook and Tiuthan stumbled into her. He grabbed her waist, keeping them both upright. As soon as the quake stopped, she spun around, taking stock of her family.

Her father was a powerhouse. King Varilon slashed through the enemy alongside Aelorian soldiers. One would never realize he was quickly fading, as if the surge of energy from being on a battlefield brought back the vigor of youth.

Even more surprising, Queen Altheia fought like fury personified. Eleanor had never seen this vicious side of her mother and was, frankly, impressed. She wielded a bow with the skill of a seasoned archer. As each wave of soldiers grew closer, she drew her short sword and dropped almost as many people as the king.

Aiden was still nowhere in sight. Eleanor cracked a knuckle and craned her neck, looking toward the battlefield. Ash and soot smothered the air with a burnt tinge. Linneya and Darryn were pointing toward an area where the ground had opened up and swallowed most of the enemy. A body, bloodied and broken, lay in the center.

A grunt made her jump and she turned as Tiuthan blocked another blow that might have killed her from behind. "Watch yourself, *Mahuchav*. I may be skilled but I am not infallible."

Her breathing was labored from what little she had done. "I already told mother, if I do not make it out alive they are not to blame you." She motioned around the battlefield. Elemental affinities were being tossed about with next to no effort from almost every soldier. "There are too many forces at play."

Tiuthan grimaced, looking around for the next wave of soldiers. The fight continued, blocking, parrying, Eleanor occasionally grabbing someone and making them suffer. Then, the prince's eyes widened.

"At this rate, none of us may make it out alive." He nodded toward a colossal dragon, possibly the largest Serathor had.

Eleanor followed his gaze and the blood drained from her face. A man in a dark hood was standing in front of the beast, striding toward Linneya and Darryn. Her fists clenched as her sister and her husband spun up a fiery whirlwind.

Eleanor's heart pounded in her chest at the show of their combined powers. The formidable column of whirling flame stretched into the sky, roaring and twisting. A primal urge to join them heated her body and she shook at the force of the impulse.

The hooded figure raised his hand, clenching it into a fist. Almost as fast as it appeared, it was gone. Eleanor turned back to the soldiers advancing toward her, placing her hands on the ground and calling her vine affinity. A surge of cold went through her, a light wisp of green, and plants erupted all around. They spun out of the ground, reaching for any soldiers within an archer's aim, rooting them to the spot and twisting like snakes.

She flicked her wrist and they squeezed. Tiuthan dropped his club to his side, panting and watching her work with a glimmer in his eyes. The soldiers' choking and squelching quickly stopped as the plants constricted around them, crushing out their lives.

The fae prince strode to her side, an icy fire in his expression, and brushed the hair out of her face. She stepped back wrenching from him as if he had held her captive. His eyes narrowed and Eleanor pointed across the field. "No time for your theatrics, freak. We need to get to my sister."

He nodded and strode toward the massive dragon. Eleanor's stomach twisted as they made their way across the battlefield. Occasionally, they stopped and fought a stray *sharvach* or Serathanian soldier. Eleanor struggled to pay attention to anything other than the action ahead.

Darryn collapsed, his leg splayed at an unnatural angle. Linneya was fighting with a white-hot flame, shooting it toward the cloaked figure with a ferocity that left Eleanor breathless. Her sister had not let on, but clearly she had been training more than Eleanor this past season.

Wind whipped around Eleanor and Tiuthan as they drew closer. Darryn bellowed and thunder rumbled as Linneya fell to her knees. He began crawling to her, dragging one leg behind him.

Panic rose in Eleanor's throat. Her heart beat a frantic rhythm and her chest squeezed. Linneya was tossed by the cloaked man's power, knocking her into the ground. She clambered to rise and the gigantic dragon shifted toward the fight.

Tiuthan growled and he and Eleanor picked up pace, breaking through the last couple of soldiers and stumbling into the clearing just in time to see the blood streaming down Linneya's face. The breath left Eleanor's body as she watched her sister wobble. Linneya's arm lifted, reaching for her husband who was still crawling as if his presence could stop the inevitable.

But then her eyes rolled up into her head and she fell backward, squelching into the mud. Eleanor could feel her sister's power draining before she even hit the ground. Darryn's roar stopped everyone fighting nearby as he made it to her side and grabbed her body, cradling her.

"No!" Eleanor screamed and ran toward the hooded man, blinded by rage. The man's silver *trillin* mask covered his features, but she did not care. Let him die an anonymous death.

Tiuthan ran beside her, lifting his club as they got close. She threw her arms up, calling aether, hoping to smother the attacker and end his life. "*Raeshio aeki raewi.*" Nothing happened but sputtering smoke and she grimaced. Aether-weaving had been the most unpredictable of her talents. She cursed under her breath.

The cloaked man cackled and spread his arms wide. "None shall stop the prophesied from his ascension!" His raspy voice held a hint of mania, a sound of unhinged ego.

Eleanor's teeth ground as she took in the scene. Tiuthan stepped in front of her, half shielding her as if he could stop her from having to experience the wrath of this imposter. She shoved him out of the way and hissed toward the man. "You will pay for this. You will die for these atrocities."

He raised his hands in reply, an evil grin widening beneath his mask. "I suppose you think you will be the one to pass judgment?"

Shockwaves radiated out of the prophesied's hands. She braced for the impact, but just in time Tiuthan yanked her back, throwing up his shields. He tucked her under one arm and held their ground while the man threw wave after wave of elemental attacks. The prince groaned at the force, sweat dripping off his forehead and blood draining from his face.

Her stomach turned at the sight. She had to do something. The prophesied kept up a barrage of elemental forces, an unnatural stream of damage. She slapped the ground, willing to pull deeper than Tituhan's shields could reach. Her head swam as she touched into all five of the elements, all of the power of their world. With a whisper, she moved enough soil to knock the man down.

The prophesied huffed and puffed, as if the air had been forced from his lungs on impact. Tiuthan patted her cheek and turned around, ready to fight. The masked man sprung to his feet, but this time Tiuthan was ready. His void power swallowed attempt after attempt. Eleanor watched, a strange excitement stirring deep.

A soft shuddering sound caused Eleanor to break her attention away from the fight. Darryn was hunched over Linneya, shaking her and commanding her to wake up. The sight was almost too much. Eleanor's shoulders sagged and she curled inward, as if the motion would protect her from the heartbreak.

The irritating sound of the prophesied's cackle caused her to turn. He was advancing on Tiuthan, circling him like a *trillin* ready to pounce. She took advantage of his distraction and knelt down, pressing her hands into the dirt and calling her vine affinity.

The plants shot up, tangling themselves around the prophesied. He struggled, but seemed contained. She leered at him, stepping forward to grab his head and kill him.

Tiuthan grabbed her wrist. "No, do not risk it. Get Linneya's body. I will help Darryn. This is our chance to escape." Eleanor's breath caught. Linneya's *body*. Even the fae prince thought it was too late.

No. No. NO.

The man smirked at their exchange. "Escape?" He wrenched his arms, an invisible force slicing through the vines. "Oh, no, you will never escape me. I am here to rule the entirety of the human realms." He threw his hood back, revealing sandy blonde hair, and tossed the cloak to one side. The man yanked his mask off as he pulled at his collar.

No - not at his collar. At his brooch.

The brown gemstone set in gold glinted in the sunslight.

Orrain.

Chapter 38

Time stopped.

He was... alive.

The man she mourned.

An entire season wasted, despising the wrong people.

Eleanor's mouth dropped open. "You - you were dead."

Orrain just laughed. A deep, hateful roar of mirth. Flames burned inside of her as emotions clashed. The battle raging around them was nothing compared to the fury she felt.

"You bastard! You conniving wretch!" Eleanor stormed forward, hair wild and eyes blazing. The shadow realms could take her, as long as she got a chance to get inside his head and boil his brains.

His dragon only opened its eyes and huffed. It had barely moved, as if it was bored of the fighting. Eleanor's blood boiled as a gust of wind knocked her back. "How are you even here? What are you doing?" She bit out, glaring at the man that she had dreamt of for mooncycles.

The man pulled a knife from his belt and twirled it between his fingers. "I told you at the ball. I have the grandest ambitions. All will bow before my might. I am the prophesied and am here to unite the human realms underneath my rule!"

A hissing noise rose behind her. Darryn had looked up from her sister's body, his eyes locked on Orrain. "No one will bow before you, you snake. Once King Shumor hears of your plan to usurp him, your life will be forfeit."

Orrain stepped toward Darryn. Eleanor moved to stop his advance, but Tiuthan grabbed her arm. He pressed her to him, wrapping one arm around her waist, and whispered, "Stay with me. Darryn can handle himself." The fae prince's body radiated heat and the scent of the open ocean. Safety. For a moment, she allowed herself to slump forward, tears springing to her eyes.

Orrain leaned down over Darryn, leering at Linneya's broken form. "I suppose you will be the one to tell King Shumor? Are you willing to walk into his court and declare me a traitor? Do you want to answer his questions? Have him learn your secrets? Have him break the enchantment?"

Darryn's jaw pulsed. Orrain straightened up, his face contorted into a sinister expression. "I did not think so." He gestured across the battlefield, smoke and ash still rising around them. "This is only the beginning. Anyone who stands in my way will meet these armies - *my* armies - and perish."

Eleanor blinked back her tears, anger washing over her grief. "These are not your armies. You have no right to claim power from anyone." The fae's arm tightened around her waist, as if he could keep her safe in his arms. She knew better.

Orrain spun around and shouted a command at his dragon. The beast huffed, not even bothering to raise its head. He rolled his eyes and turned back toward Eleanor and Tiuthan. "No matter, I do not need that overgrown mutt to roast you all." Without warning, flames shot from his arms.

The fae prince spun Eleanor behind him and threw his hands up, blocking the blaze. The heat radiated through his void shield, beads of sweat running down his neck. Eleanor cried out in frustration just as the flames stopped. He spun around, wild eyed and reaching for her. Tiuthan patted her down, checking for injuries but not saying a word. Their eyes met and she placed a hand on his arm, nodding her reassurance. "I am okay."

Orrain scoffed. "I see you have found a loyal fae lapdog." He cocked his head, scraping his eyes over her frame like he was evaluating an animal to be sold. "Tell me, how fast did you try to pull him into your bed? Did you hope to trap him before he found out you were worthless?"

She shook at the accusation. Tiuthan tried to step in front of her, but she shoved him out of the way. "Did you even like me or was that a ruse too?" Eleanor spit her question.

Orrain snorted. "*Like* you? I had you picked out as the easiest target. You would have done exactly as I asked."

Eleanor's face turned hard and a muscle pulsed in her neck. "I see." She felt no shame, no embarrassment at his admission. Undoubtedly, that would come later. If there was a later.

For now, her pulse quickened and her eyes darted, looking for a way to survive. The longer the battle raged, the more people died. The more destruction would be wrought. The more likely the shields around the city were to fail.

If she could just get close enough to touch him, perhaps she could end this. Or at least avenge her sister. She needed to keep him talking, distracted.

As if Tiuthan read her mind, he cocked his head and asked, "How did you manage to get so many power stones?" He waved his hand, gesturing across the battlefield and the myriad of soldiers wielding stolen affinities. "Our people have no records that suggest there are this many stones."

Orrain smirked, picking a piece of lint off his uniform. "It was easy enough once I realized I could walk between our worlds. I have brought back piles of untracked gemstones. My men are loyal to me, to the man who created their power. The prophesied who wields all affinities."

A hysterical, bubbling laughter rose to Eleanor's throat. Orrain ruffled with indignation at the sound. She wheezed, turning to Tiuthan and gesturing toward Orrain like the fae prince should be in on the joke. Instead, the man cocked his head and raised an eyebrow.

"I am more likely to be the prophesied than you, Orrain." She gasped, trying to catch her breath. "No one will follow you when they see what I am capable of." She slammed into the ground, calling on plants to wrap his body, calling on the fires that scorched the field to concentrate into his lungs and burn him alive.

Tiuthan lunged at Orrain, activating his void power and sucking the man into a vortex of darkness. He went screaming, covered in flames and restrained by rope-like tendrils. A sucking noise hissed as the last of the fire disappeared.

"So much for the prophesied," Eleanor huffed, her body aching, muscles that she did not know existed burning. They grinned at each other, pleased that the impromptu elemental attack had winked Orrain out of existence. The battle was far from over, but perhaps this would be a turning point.

Tiuthan stepped toward her, holding out his hand. "*Mahuchav...*"

She reached for him, but a murmur and a puff of wind made her turn. Sky blue light pulsed from Darryn's hands. She looked behind her to see the man still hunched over her sister, cradling her lifeless body. He was whispering in her ear as if he could draw her back to life with his aether. As if he could turn back time and make her whole once more.

Eleanor knew it was too late. She had felt the shift.

Her heart seized, a deep seated pain for her sister's death. Linneya was supposed to be the person who grew old with her, with recollections of all the bizarre things their parents did. They were supposed to get together at the solstices and complain about no one remembering how chaotic certain previous family events had been. A shudder went through her body and she barely registered Tiuthan's hand on her shoulder.

Her chin wobbled and her jaw ached from holding back the grief. She and Linneya were supposed to be the two with shared memories that went back to childhood.

Memories of pranks and games.

Of caretakers, advisors, and long lost friends.

Of being the spares, living in the shadow of their brother.

No one else would know. No one else could possibly understand.

She took a deep breath and looked around, blinking against the burning tears in her eyes. An unnerving, twisting sensation sank into her back as the battle continued to rage around them. Surely someone would see them soon and send a life-tender for Linneya and Darryn. Maybe one of the healers would have an idea of how to bring her back. Maybe she was not completely gone...

A popping noise startled her. Hissing grew stronger. Tiuthan growled and squeezed her shoulder. "Get behind me, *mahuchav*."

A charred, bitter stench overwhelmed Eleanor. Orrain fell forward from nothingness, unwinding from the vines and sloughing off burned skin. Her jaw dropped as his body rejuvenated itself, fresh skin knitting over his burns within a few breaths.

He raised his arms, a triumphant gleam in his eye. "Your aether power cannot hold me beyond this world! I am a world-walker, imbued with the affinities of dozens of elementals." He pointed to Eleanor. "All who stand before me will perish."

She shook, eyes darting around for the backup to her backup plan. Eleanor tried to ignore the stitch growing in her side. How were they to fight such unadulterated evil? She racked her brain for ways to stall the bastard.

"How did you manage to kill so many? There are not that many humans with elemental powers anymore." Eleanor tried to look interested, possibly in awe.

Orrain grinned. "I was not limited by humans." He gestured to the plethora of stones on his body. "Dwarves, merfolk, fae, faun... everyone sacrificed to raise me up to lead humans to unity."

Tiuthan growled and raised his club. "How dare you harm my people!" Orrain put up a fist, opened it, and a force knocked the fae prince backwards. Eleanor's heart jumped into her throat and she ran to the male.

Orrain huffed and turned to Darryn, a snarl on his face. "I never properly thanked your wife for giving me the stone that completed my collection." Orrain held up his right arm, a green stone gleaming on his gauntlet. "She found one of the mythical *bathow* gems on our way to Enthor. Remember the swim you all took?" He smirked. "I will never forget how you fumed as your wretched tart tried to buy her way into my good graces."

Darryn vibrated with fury. "Lia did not need to buy her way in with anyone. She was the jewel you could not see for the mud in your eyes."

Eleanor's heart squeezed, a sharp prick struck it as if thorns were its noose. Even in a rage, he spoke of her sister with such tenderness. She wrapped her arms around herself, shame creeping in from the damage she had done. She had lost so much time, so many opportunities to mend her relationship with Linneya. All for this pile of manure.

Orrain sneered at Darryn. "What worthless words. Did you ever confess it all to her? You may have married a princess, but she undoubtedly found you to be an unworthy prince."

The light was fading from Darryn's eyes. Eleanor knew it well - the defeat, the overwhelm was setting in. He turned to Orrain and shrugged. "Your jealousy has always been your downfall."

Orrain scoffed. "Jealous? No. Surely you have figured it out by now. I hated her. I hired the bandits to attack our caravan."

Darryn nodded numbly and Orrain continued. "Mercenaries were easy enough to find. I just walked away from camp and returned before moonwake. They attacked the caravan but did not have the mettle to finish the one person off I needed gone."

Eleanor's heart sank. Would he have done the same to her? How did she manage to pick the most evil man on this planet to fall in love with?

"I did not think it would be so hard to get rid of her, but it matters not." Orrain motioned to Linneya's lifeless body and smirked. "I have finally succeeded."

Eleanor's vision went black. Instinct rose within, the fire and ash around her spinning with the force of aether. The flame energies pulsed through her arms. Rain began to fall and the ground shuddered.

She threw her arms out and screamed, pointing at the evil bastard. He dodged the first attack and they exchanged volleys. Eleanor slammed her hands into the soil and he sank into the mud. Orrain whipped the wind into sharp strikes, cutting her cheeks as if the gusts were knives. Tiuthan tried to step in, absorbing some of Orrain's strikes and giving Eleanor an advantage.

She strained against the energy it took. Her breaths came in heaving gasps. Even with Tiuthan's void affinity, they were at a stalemate.

Orrain realized it at the same time Eleanor did. He glared at her and dropped his arms, huffing. She watched him trying to decide what to do next. Tiuthan eased in front of her, a silent promise that he would protect her if she needed it.

A strangled sound made Eleanor break Orrain's stare. Darryn covered Linneya with a torn banner and stood, a dark fury burning throughout his countenance. Eleanor's heart sank. If Darryn was giving up, it was over. Linneya was gone.

She turned back to Orrain, heat flooding her veins. The man was marking Darryn's every move with a smirk on his face. Eleanor's stomach clenched. No matter the outcome of today, she had lost. Her sister was gone and she had never apologized to Linneya. She wanted the chance to tell her that no person would ever come between them again. She shivered as the rain turned ice cold.

Darryn's eyes were pitch black. Storm clouds built, lightning cascading above them. Orrain laughed, a triumphant burst of mockery. "I told you before and I will tell you again, you never could learn to stay out of my way. What now? What will you do since your beloved princess has met the fate she deserves?"

Darryn raised his sword, the wind whipping around his body. Tiuthan grabbed Eleanor, forcing her to step back. Darryn growled and stood, a whirlwind of sky blue aether tightening around his broken leg, as if it were a cast. "My beloved has found me in this lifetime. She saved me from a fate worse than death and I will be there to protect her in the next life." Darryn hissed as he placed weight on his leg, testing its strength. "You, however, will be thrown into the shadowed void and your soul left to rot, hopeless and isolated." He pressed forward, limping slightly as his power adjusted to hold his leg better.

Orrain's face contorted and he lunged. The two men locked into a battle of elements, the enchantments so fast she could not keep up. Darryn held his sword up, absorbing a lightning strike, then shooting it at the evil man.

Orrain tried to suck the air from Darryn, but the knight conjured an aether shield and stopped him.

Tiuthan joined in. He dodged and swiped, dark swirls of the void affinity dancing as he moved. Eleanor collapsed to her knees as the men clashed. She shook, her body threatening to give out after such strain.

She scrambled back, bumping against her sister's dead body. Her eyes were locked on the battle in front of her, but she could feel the vacuum of emptiness in her heart. The stirring whispers of wind, the warming of flame, a rumble in the ground, none of those things could touch her in this moment of grief. Eleanor turned to embrace her dead sister one last time...

Her heart jumped into her throat. The torn banner was moving. She screamed as Linneya's body sat up. Her sister pulled the cloth off her face, glaring.

Chapter 39

From the nothingness, black swirled up to meet her.

The harsh juxtaposition between the peace of oblivion and the world was too much.

The first thing Linneya felt was searing pain from her senses being flooded. Clanging sounds. Bright light. Acrid, pungent scents.

Everything came rushing back. Darryn, her family, the prophesied. A surge of power rushed through her body, dancing along her spine. She gasped for breath and clawed out from under the thick cloth that covered her body.

Eleanor shrieked and Linneya cringed. "Creators, you have always had the largest set of lungs."

Her sister tackled her, tears streaming down her face and laughter in her voice. "Thank the deities. You are here... But how? How did you come back?" Eleanor tried to brush the matted hair from Linneya's face. Linneya winced in pain as the hair pulled on the sore spots of her scalp.

Before she could respond, a man's voice cut through. "No - it is not possible. I finished you. You bitch!"

She stood trembling and blinking. The battlefield was still full of smoke, fire, and screams of pain. A shock ran through her body. His sandy blonde hair came into view and she stumbled back. "Your body. You were dead. Straion saw it floating downstream."

Orrain shrugged. "I knew they were coming. Knew it would be easier if someone reported seeing my body." He held up his arm and gestured to a bright blue gemstone. "A quick bubble of air under the water and I was safe to float downstream like a corpse."

His lips tightened into a smirk, pleased with his own ingenuity. Her brow wrinkled, another jolt of sensation shooting through her. Her body shook from the force of the energy. She needed her husband. She needed his grounding presence.

Linneya's eyes scanned for her anchor. Darryn was standing only a few paces away, his eyes wide. She froze, overwhelmed. His chest heaved with each breath and an odd whirling movement caused her gaze to drop to his leg. She shivered at his power. His affinity was keeping his mangled leg locked into place so he could stand.

He took a tentative step toward her, reaching out a trembling hand. The motion cracked through her panic and she ran, stumbling into his arms. He cried out, a broken sob. "Lia, oh blessed woman!"

Orrain hissed, but Tiuthan slid in between them, holding his club at the man's throat. Eleanor stood behind the fae prince, leveling her axe at Orrain as well.

Darryn wrapped his arms around her and tears streamed down his face. "You made it, you came back." He was shaking and she ran her fingers through his hair trying to soothe him. "I felt you go, I felt you slip, I -"

She crushed her mouth to his, an act of desperation. She needed to feel him, to know that she had really returned. He moaned into her mouth, pressing her close.

She pulled back as another wave of energy shot through her, a scene of a firemountain eruption filling her mind. Smoke billowed. She was connected. Risen from ash and flame.

Her eyes widened and she looked at Darryn. His jaw was set and he cocked his head. "What is it, love?"

In response, she sent a small gust of air across his neck. His pupils blew and his mouth dropped open. She could feel... everything.

The resonance of the trees as they spoke to each other, crying out for the ones who perished.

The breath of the birds as they fled for quieter spaces.

The dwindling powers of the dragons.

The souls slipping away.

Everything.

Darryn cradled her face in his hands. She looked up, locked eyes, and the burning sense of his gaze consumed her. Fire rushed through her veins and her hands heated with a bright red glow. A small smile grew on Darryn's face, but she motioned for him to stay quiet.

Orrain huffed. "Whatever you two are doing, wrap it up. This battle needs to be over by noonrest. Tell me, Linneya, what do you think of my handiwork?"

She turned around and stared. Her mind was whirling, connecting to the rhythms of life. This man broke them. This man destroyed everything, risked the vitality of the world.

Orrain gestured to his collection of stones. "I could feel your essence watching me. You saw how hard I worked for my title. You saw how much I am willing to sacrifice for this honor. Tell me. What do you think?"

Linneya's blood surged with flame. Mist filled her eyes. Her bones connected with the ground. Vine strengthened her muscles. Her voice lit up with aether. She pointed, a condemnation.

"I think you invoked my true title, my birthright, in order to harm others. I think you must face the consequences and suffer in the shadowed void."

A tremor rumbled across the battlefield at her declaration. Shouts from others told her the groundquake was felt by all. She raised her arms, a pillar of fire burning around her.

Orrain's dragon screeched, shooting into the air. Several others took off from the battlefield, circling around the column of flame and shrieking. Linneya pointed at the man and the flame mixed with a mist, burning and boiling.

Orrain scrambled backward, throwing his arms up, trying to fight. The stones on his gauntlet disintegrated with rapid cracking sounds. Linneya pressed forward, intent on stripping him of all his power. Every time one of the gemstones cracked, a burst of light shot into the clouds.

She loomed over him, the power in her veins throbbing with a sharp pulse. Orrain laid there, limp as a threadbare rug, as if his own terror had consumed him. A powdery sheen coated the mud around him.

Linneya snorted at his pitiful cowering and raised her boot over his face.

She stomped and he howled, blood gushing from his nose. Vines wrapped around his body, holding him in place as she walked to retrieve her sword. His coughing and sputtering faded into the background as she surveyed the damage to her people.

Everything was on fire. Cottages, trees, even catapults and wagons. Her heart warmed to see that Tiuthan and Darryn's shield had kept the city from harm, but a wrenching grief in her gut threatened to consume her as she looked at everything outside the city walls.

She had to stop the damage. Her arms raised and she poured her fury into the clouds, summoning a deluge. Hissing sounds carried across the battlefield as massive fires were extinguished. Soldiers began slipping and sliding in the ever deepening mud. Someone nearby shouted and pointed at her.

"The prophesied! The princess has risen!" A small cheer came from a few battleworn Aelorian soldiers. She turned and laid eyes on the *sharvach* that were attacking them. One of the beasts had a soldier by the throat.

Like Aiden.

She broke. No longer Linneya, the woman channeled the wrath of the Arduin and began tossing enchantments at anyone and everyone attacking her people. *Sharvach* were tossed in the air, bones breaking and crumbling to their deaths. Soldiers were thrown into vacuums where all mist and aether was sucked from their bodies until they collapsed as desiccated, ghoulish corpses.

Serathor's armies began to run. At first it was just one or two fighters, as if they had gone mad and could not stomach any more. Linneya continued throwing all five elements at the front line until blood leaked from her nose and her lungs burned as if they were filled with dragonfire.

More witnessed her power - the full prophecy completed. Risen from ash and flame, the princess claimed all five of the elements. Fear rippled through Serathor's ranks, rising to a critical mass. An occasional gemstone cracked and a flash of light would rise. Orrain was outed as an imposter. No one could believe his claims any longer.

Linneya raised her arms again, aiming toward the sky. Fire shot out from her hands, meeting the wind and turning into a spinning mass of heated destruction. The roars of fighting soldiers pitched upward, into a higher range of panic. A wave of men, dragons, and *sharvach* began to retreat.

Orrain was screaming. His face turned purple from the strain. He faded from her vines and reappeared halfway across the battlefield. The man began grabbing at his fighters, trying to pull them back towards the battle. Wave after wave of soldiers passed by, until someone conked him over the head with their hilt and began dragging him backwards.

Linneya stopped and watched the chaos. Aelor's fighters cheered at the receding forces. Her body released the shattering energy of wrath and she took a deep breath, feeling herself settle back into her own.

A warm hand on her shoulder steadied her. His citrus and cedar scent made her smile before she ever turned around. Darryn groaned in pain and she spun to face him. "Your leg!"

He nodded and began to sink towards the ground. She settled with him, unwilling to leave his side until she knew he would be safe. He fingered one of her braids, his eyes glassy and unfocused.

Eleanor knelt beside her and hugged her again, blood and sweat streaked across her face. "I am so sorry, Lia, I am sorry. He was so evil, I had no idea."

Linneya shushed her sister and pulled her close. A numbness crept in, exhaustion combined with knowing the emotional toll the next few days would take on all of them. As long as everyone was there, everyone in one piece, she was sure they would all eventually recover.

Tiuthan stood nearby, lingering and looking a bit lost. A few of the fae leaders wandered up and spoke with him. The somber tone of their voices sent chills down Linneya's spine. She was certain they were reporting injuries and deaths. So many had sacrificed so that Aelor could remain safe.

Healers began making their way across the battlefield, looking for injured people. She raised both arms and waved as one life-tender with shock white hair drew near. The woman nodded and began picking her way through the carnage, huffing and puffing. She was one of the volunteers that came out of retirement to be on the battlefield. Tears sprung to Linneya's eyes as the woman diligently drug her supplies to Darryn's side.

Another group of life-tenders made it to Johann. The man was kneeling over a body, Linneya suspected it was Aiden. Her stomach twisted, expecting them to move on in a matter of moments. Instead, they picked him up and placed him on the stretcher.

Eleanor shrieked in relief at the sight and ran toward their brother. She grabbed Johann's arm and the two of them followed the life-tenders back toward the city. Tiuthan trailed at a distance, as if he had not quite realized his duty to Eleanor was finished.

Darryn hissed as the lifetender poked and prodded his leg. She shook her head and wagged a finger at him. "You had no business standing on this. It will take us the better part of the afternoon to get it set and mended well enough for you to be on it again."

He grinned at the woman, a softer expression than he usually held. "It was either that or die. I chose inconvenience over leaving this beauty." Darryn squeezed Linneya tight to his side and the life-tender laughed.

Linneya was standing outside one of the healer's tents waiting on Darryn when she spied Graisor. Relief washed over her as he stepped around a cauldron and swept her into a hug. Tears sprang to her eyes. "You made it! Thank the Creators."

He smiled, a tight expression. "We were not all so lucky. Your friend needs you." Graisor blanched and gestured back toward one of the healer's tents. Linneya's heart dropped into her stomach. Graisor's face was pained and he looked away, as if he could not come to terms with it.

She squeezed his hand, unsure what to say. After a moment, he bowed and shuffled into the tent to speak with Darryn. Her husband's voice rang stronger as he greeted his brother and part of Linneya's fear subsided.

Taking a deep breath for courage, she trudged toward the healer's tent he had indicated, unsure if she was ready to face whatever tragedy she had missed during the fighting. So many of their friends and family had been involved. She knew it was impossible for everyone to walk away unscathed, but the thought of even one person missing from their group burned like bile.

She lifted the flap and her chest squeezed. Mariel was cradling her husband, his lifeless body gray and limp. His head was at the wrong angle and Mariel kept trying to set it right as she rocked him.

Linneya approached and knelt beside her best friend. Mariel's face was flat. No color dusted her cheeks. She stared into the distance, as if her soul had fled the scene. Her voice trembled as she spoke. "I - I tripped. My cursed foot caught on a divot in the ground and I fell. Straion was trying to protect me."

The blood drained from Linneya's face and her stomach sank. Straion did not deserve such a fate. Neither did Mariel. No words could make up for such a loss, no comfort could be found in such a shocking moment.

Instead of trying to say anything, Linneya slid to the ground beside her friend and stroked her hair.

Mariel gasped, her breaths short and ragged. "We were just finding our stride, two odd personalities that had chosen to love each other. We had not had time to enjoy any of it. He is dead because of me." Tears ran down her cheeks, creating streaks in the blood and dirt smeared across her face.

"No, love, not because of you. Because of the wicked King Shumor." Linneya hummed her sympathy. "What do you need right now? Can I get you water? A warm washcloth?"

Mariel took a deep breath. Something in her body language shifted and her eyes cleared a bit. "Stay with me?"

Linneya nodded. They sat together, just being with the moment. Occasionally Mariel would cry. Scream. Curse the Arduin and the Creators.

Linneya let her do what she needed, two friends with a bond so old there was no need to discuss it. Her heart tore watching her friend sob. But for luck, their roles could have been reversed.

Mariel's pain from blaming herself was raw and ragged. She kept repeating her self-condemnation. Linneya kept responding, putting the rebuke on Serathor's king, for that is where the blame belonged.

Slowly, they settled into silence, both women lost in thoughts of the violence and shock of the day.

Linneya startled back into her body as Darryn's voice rumbled through the tent's door. "Lia, whenever you can, Wralion is asking for you. We have more wounded than the life-tenders can handle."

Linneya bit her lip, but Mariel turned to her. "I think I am okay to be alone. You are needed. The dragons were numerous and I suspect many will need your flame-talking light."

Linneya squeezed her friend's hands. "If that changes, you send for me."

The woman gave her a tight smile, but some of her brightness had returned. Still, Linneya hesitated to leave her alone.

Graisor poked his head in. "Mari, do you want me to stay with you?"

She nodded and Linneya's shoulders relaxed. She gave Mariel a final hug and rose to meet Darryn. Graisor dipped his chin as he moved to take Linneya's place, his eyes as raw as Mariel's.

Darryn was waiting for her as she came out of the tent. His leg had been mended, though he still leaned as if it was tender. Tears burned at the sight of him alive and relatively whole.

She fell against him and he wrapped his arms around her. She sobbed, leaning into the strength and warmth of his presence. He drew soft circles on her back, murmuring gentle words as she bawled. In relief, in guilt, in pain, she was unsure. The catharsis was sharp and stung, but it washed away with her tears.

Finally, Linneya was able to straighten back up. Darryn watched her carefully, as if he would rather pick her up and carry her back to their suite. She sucked in a deep breath and nodded to him.

He took her hand and threaded his fingers through hers. "Shailyn is safe. I've heard from Chrysa as well. Your parents are heading cleanup efforts and we have been asked to help the life-tenders, if you are up for it."

She bit her lip, grateful for the news that some of their friends were safe. "Well, let us go see Wralion so he can direct us to where we might help."

He nodded and fell into step as they headed to the main life-tender tent. Some cleanup had started and Linneya blanched at the carnage. A Falorian knight was harvesting scales and talons from the dragon carcass. Others were still removing stones from the Serathanian troops' uniforms. Some of the life-tenders were still picking soldiers up from the ground. Healing affinity glowed in many different colors, like lumescent signals across a barren land. An occasional scream pierced the air as the healers shifted the wounded onto stretchers.

Linneya and Darryn stepped into the life-tender's tent, searching for Wralion. His keen gaze found them first and he exclaimed. He made a beeline for them, bowing as he approached. "Prince, princess, thank you for coming."

Darryn started to correct him, but Linneya shot him a look and he clamped his mouth shut. There was no point in worrying about titles or propriety when people were dying. She inclined her head. "How might we be of assistance?"

A muscle pulsed in Wralion's jaw. "As you can imagine, many are burned from the dragons. Your flame-talking skills are needed. But we have also heard rumors that your husband has some abilities himself."

The healer turned to Darryn. "Is it true that Falryn shared the aether enchantments with you on how to still death?"

Darryn grunted his assent and Wralion nodded. "There are many people you may be able to save today, if we work wisely. I will spread the word, but if you will start with this nearest tent and make your way around the circle, that should get to people in the order they were brought in."

They moved from tent to tent, checking to see where her skills were needed or where Darryn might be most useful. In between each patient, more and more people stopped her to speak. Rumors were beginning to spread about Linneya's resurrection and it seemed that everyone wanted to have a moment with the prophesied.

Trotyn was in one tent, but, some minor burns aside, the man was in good spirits. They found out from the healer-turned-farmer Shullen that Aiden had been moved to a suite in the palace for privacy. Shailyn came back down after dinner and aided the life-tenders with whatever she could.

Darryn stayed by Linneya's side, using his aether-weaver abilities to freeze those at the brink of death so the life-tenders had more time to work. Some made it, others were unable to rally. Every time one of their people did not sit up, Darryn's shoulders slumped a little more.

They worked through the evening, through first sleep, and finally took their leave around moonwake. Neither of them spoke as they picked their way across the muddy battlefield.

The funeral pyres scattered across the battlefield cast an eerie glow as they trudged toward the city gates. Some were attended by family members, the wailing of grief ebbing and flowing. A low hum of songs, laments sung by the fae, drifted across the war-torn lands. The stench from the burning bodies wafted by and roiled Linneya's stomach.

As she and Darryn got to the city gates, she stopped and turned to survey the devastation. Linneya's heart wrenched at the sight. So much death, so much pain. All for cheap vengeance and petty ambition.

Chapter 40

Linneya woke up and stretched, wincing at the aches that had settled into her muscles.

The red sun peeked over the horizon first. The world was bathed in brick tones, as if an ominous tribute to the fallen. She groaned and rolled over, her eyes landing on her sword and armor spilled across the armchair.

As the previous day's events finally flooded her memory, she grimaced at the heartache. The aftermath of war left scars deeper than she anticipated. Striking down soldiers who would have rather been home with their families brought no joy.

How could anyone consider yesterday a victory?

Orrain had fled. She had chosen to end the battle instead of exacting her personal revenge, and as far as she knew he was still alive. Straion was not. A hollow pit formed in her stomach at the injustice.

She should not be alive, either. Linneya shivered, not ready to face the memories of her rebirth. She had chosen to return, to take up her place as the prophesied, but her recollection of her time in the realm of spirits was fuzzy. Some part of her unconscious told her she would be happier if it stayed that way.

A hand pressed into her upper back and she let out a sigh. Darryn's warmth grounded her into a feeling of safety. His arm possessively circled her waist and a contented moan escaped his mouth as he squeezed her close.

Linneya rolled back over, snuggling into his chest. This was real. They were safe. She breathed his citrus and cedar scent and pressed her forehead against his breastbone.

He ran his fingers through her hair and guided her head back up. Darryn's eyes eased open and a small smile curved his lips upward. She placed her hand on his chest and he brushed a knuckle across her cheekbone. "Good morning, princess."

"Good morning, prince."

He grimaced at the title and she laughed. "Well, you are technically prince consort. The council would probably even ratify you as a prince of Aelor if we wanted to press the point."

His shoulders relaxed and he buried his head into her neck, pressing his lips to her pulse. "I do not care what we are called. I am just grateful you came back. I cannot imagine what I would have done if that was the end."

A shudder rocked his body and she wrapped her arms around him, holding him close. "But I did come back. I am here now." She pulled back far enough to look into his eyes. "Which, I want to know what you did. You pulled me back, I felt it."

Darryn smirked like he was proud of his handiwork. "Falryn had read that more powerful aether-weavers could bring life back if it was lost in the course of evil action. The legends suggest balance must be maintained, so one could not resurrect a person dying of natural causes. However, murders and war deaths were reversible if one knew the right enchantments and could get to the person quickly."

He ran his hands up and down her arms, as if he needed the reassurance she was real. "Part of what Trotyn brought me was the resurrection enchantment. I was only going to study it, practice calling the rite, but when I saw your body limp and broken..."

He shuddered again and she brushed the hair out of his face. Darryn's eyes were filled with tears and her heart shattered. This man had lived her worst nightmare - watching his spouse leave this plane of existence.

Linneya cupped his face in her hands and leaned in. She brushed her lips to his, a soft invitation. His tears spilled over as he kissed her back. Her eyes began to ache, her own tears welling up. So much heartache, so much pain...

"But we made it through." She sighed and brushed the tears from his cheeks. "And, frankly, I am impressed you stayed focused after Shailyn defied all orders and went to swinging at the cursed dragons."

He chuckled and made a face. "She is going to be the death of me." They laughed for a few minutes, relief in knowing that she was safe, despite her impulsive decision to take the beast on.

Darryn sombered and brushed a lock out of her face. "When you stood and I felt the air on my neck..." He hummed a sound of victory. "What do you think happened? You showed no signs of aether or vine affinity less than a mooncycle ago."

She shrugged, not wanting to tell him her wild theories too soon. "I am unsure. I want to talk to Falryn about everything. I experienced..." she worried her lip, looking for the right words. "...unusual things, but part of me is afraid to dredge it back up just yet."

Linneya drew in a shaky breath and tried to steady herself. She had spent so much time dreading her darker side, worried that embracing the destructive abilities of her power would drive her to ruin. Her beliefs had solidified around one point: the light energies, the healing forces she wielded, would be able to prove her worth. She ran so far away from any sort of balance that, when the time came, she almost did not survive.

Now it was undeniable - she was the prophesied. Linneya resolved to find harmony between the light and dark. If the prophecy was true, she could no longer hide behind meekness. She had been reborn of ash and flame and now she would be the one to determine the fate of humankind. The burden of responsibility pressed against her chest, but she could still draw a deep breath.

Darryn studied her expression, watching her steel herself. He cupped her face in his hands. "No matter how this plays out, I am with you. I do not care if you are raised up as the prophesied or if you are stripped of everything. Every day, I will choose you. The two of us are stronger together. Not from some mystical force or some unfulfilled mythos. It is because we have each other's back."

Linneya smiled. "And as long as I am the prophesied, I can heal whatever nightmarish injuries you get next."

He huffed a laugh, sitting up. "You healed more than just yesterday's burns." He pulled the blankets off his torso and her eyes went wide.

"That is amazing." She sat up and leaned in for a closer look. Most of his childhood scars were still there, but some were less severe and others were completely gone.

Darryn grinned and ran one hand over her collarbone. "You are amazing. Your power is just a bonus."

She lightly brushed against the remaining scars. "Do you want me to see if I can heal the rest?"

He laid his hand over hers, pressing it into his side. He smiled and shook his head. "No, Lia. Thank you, but I do not want them gone. They do not hurt often and they are a reminder of my mother's love. I would not have you remove a tangible memento of how she cared for me."

She nodded and a warmth flooded her chest. This man may have an insatiable bloodlust on the battlefield, but he cherished his family. All of his family - related and chosen.

Linneya stretched, her sore muscles pulling in protest. More of yesterday's battle flew through her brain. She shivered at the memories of the dragons and their riders, at how terrifying the horde had been to witness. Especially when she had realized there were *sharvach* riding some of them.

She hugged herself. The wolf-like beasts were formidable on their own. Why did they need the dragons?

For that matter, why were they fighting King Shumor's battles? Darryn had said that the king had likely promised them some of Aelor's land's, an offer that could quickly double the size of the shadowlands. A low ache settled in her gut at the thought.

The *sharvachs* had terrorized humans. The legends told of the damage that these creatures could inflict. Why someone would risk helping the creatures to rise again was beyond her comprehension. The *sharvach* would make it likely that they would be fighting a war on two fronts. She wondered what Luthin and Payera would do in the face of the renewed threat.

Their renewed threat... the thought pricked a memory. Linneya sat up straighter and Darryn cocked his head. "What is it, love?"

With everything else going on, she had never read through the scroll Falryn gave her as they left Enthor. Legends or no, the healer gave her the story because it could help. Linneya slid out of bed and padded over to the bookshelf, pulling it down. "The *sharvachs* - why were they here? What caused Serathor to ally with one of humanity's worst threats?" She waved the parchment, imitating Falryn.

Darryn stood and stalked to her side. Linneya opened the scroll and started reading. He watched over her shoulder, hissing after a few paragraphs. Linneya blanched and a growl rumbled through Darryn. She rolled the scroll back up and looked into his eyes. Shivers crept up her spine at the storm gathered there. "We need to show this to my father."

He dipped his chin once in agreement. She set the scroll back on the shelf and they both scrambled to dress. Linneya rang for a maid, directing her to relay the need for the meeting to her father.

As soon as Darryn was finished lacing her up, she snatched the parchment and they rushed to the king's study. The doors were shut, her father in a meeting, so they waited in the dark corridor. Darryn bounced on his toes and Linneya tried to steady her breathing.

Finally, the door opened and a guard stepped out, motioning for the two of them to enter. Linneya straightened her back, trying to look more regal as they approached her father.

Linneya and Darryn bowed and she bit her lip, worried. Her heart twisted at his appearance. Dark circles under his eyes and pale skin suggested the king had been up all night. He had aged annae in one day, a haggard look to his countenance.

Lord Caelin and the hawk-eyed healer, Wralion, were standing to one side, their faces twisted underneath the pressure of the battle's aftermath. Linneya sent her thanks to the Creators for protecting them from worse devastation, but she wished there had been some way to stop the events altogether. Darryn wrapped an arm around her upper back and squeezed her shoulder, silently urging her to speak.

She cleared the grief from her throat and passed the scroll across the desk. King Varilon's eyebrows raised as he took it. She launched into an explanation of Falryn's gift and why she had not read it sooner. All three men watched them as Darryn added a bit of context from his work with the Falorian knights.

Lord Caelin stepped forward. "So, you believe that Serathor's war will unleash the *sharvach* on the humans once again?"

Linneya wobbled her head from side to side. "Partially." She pointed to a section close to the end of the writings. "But if you read on, it indicates that part of the prophesied's ability to bring harmony will come from facing the *sharvach*'s leader and stopping the threat."

She sucked in a deep breath and looked at her husband. Darryn nodded, eagerness shining in his eyes. She turned back to the men. "I do not know how, but this battle is the start of something important. This scroll suggests Luthin and Payera have to bring together the three origins in order to restore peace and the prophesied must face the dragons to overcome that which is sealed away." She motioned to the end. "If we believe this source, we must tread carefully or we will all burn."

King Varilon stroked his beard, his eyes darting between the two of them. Lord Caelin shifted on his feet, a dark look passing over his eyes. For a long moment, everyone mulled over the scroll's contents.

Wralion drew in a breath and hissed, stepping forward. "I believe the two of you must go to Mount Varsha. The fae will have more information on these three origins. You may also be able to find more on the full prophecy, glean more of an understanding of what this means for our realms."

The king raised his eyebrows. "I am not sure that it is wise to go and request these legends. The fae are concerned about upsetting the balance of political power in our realms. They may be hesitant to turn over details of prophecies to royals."

Darryn narrowed his eyes and cocked his head in thought. "The Falorian knights have a secret collection of manuscripts that we have debated donating to their archives. Perhaps it is time to make that trip. It will take my men a few weeks to catalogue everything when we arrive. Lia can spend the time innocently reading, as she so loves to do. I can talk with the head of our order, Noryo, when we return to Rathen."

Linneya bit her lip. She was unsure if Noryo would be willing to release control over the vast knowledge collected in the vault. He had made it clear that he thought it was foolish to release the archives to the fae. Even though he had acquiesced to Darryn diverting some of the knights here, she was unsure how the old man would take being forced into another scheme.

However, King Varilon seemed satisfied with his son-in-law's plan. He nodded and waved, dismissing them. "Please tell Altheia I will be along in a bit for tea. Lord Caelin and I have a few other matters to discuss." The king turned to the healer. "Wralion, thank you again."

Wralion, Darryn, and Linneya all bowed, backing their way out of the study. Once in the hallway, Wralion grabbed Linneya's wrist until she turned to face him. "Your Highnesses, if you are going to Mount Varsha, I would recommend taking the comet path and meeting with the seer."

Darryn growled, drawing himself up to his full height. "That trail is a death wish. No seer is worth the risk."

Wralion nodded. "I will not deny it, the path is treacherous. The fae in the holy order that lives on the consecrated mountain consider her presence a nuisance, especially when they have to send supplies, but she continues to insist on her location. However, with your wife's dream-walker abilities, I would advise you to visit. It will go well."

Darryn hissed, but Linneya placed a hand on his chest. "If Wralion says it will go well, then it will go well." She nodded to the healer. "Thank you, we will make sure to visit her."

The man bowed, turning to leave. Darryn's eyebrows scrunched together and she shook her head. "He has some foresight and is careful with his instructions. I trust him to lead us the right way."

Her husband nodded and offered her his arm. "Then let us go before your mother sends a search party." She giggled, laying a hand on his forearm, and they made their way to the stateroom.

The mood was somber when they arrived. Everyone was staring into their cups, barely touching the noonrest food. Shailyn and Chrysa were sitting with Mariel and Alayne, both now war widows. Darryn kissed her temple and moved toward Trotyn and Graisor.

Linneya filled her teacup and took a slice of elyreflower bread. She made her way to where Eleanor stood in the corner of the room, as still as the statues that lined both sides. "How are you?"

Eleanor would not meet her gaze. "I am sorry for blaming you for trying to steal that man from me. I see now that my taste in men is flawed. To think that I was taken in by such an evil being..."

Linneya grabbed her hand and squeezed. "Oh, no, you cannot think that way. He had us all fooled. I was convinced I had done something terribly wrong when he first tried to hurt me. If he had not disappeared down the stream, I dread to think how far things could have gone."

She placed her hand on her sister's shoulder. "I am so grateful you stalled him. Yesterday could have gone much differently if you had been unable to wield your affinities as well as you did. You saved us."

Eleanor stepped away, her hands clenched into fists. "For today. He is still alive, he can come back and finish us off. If I could have gotten my hands on him, he would be dead. That bastard does not deserve the air he breathes." She was shaking, fury flushing her cheeks, her eyes getting that faraway look.

Linneya balanced the teacup and saucer down on their great-great-something's foot and grabbed Eleanor's shoulders, meeting her gaze with raised eyebrows. "We will. He will pay for what he has done. To you, to me, to all elementals. We are going to find him and he will answer for his crimes."

Eleanor inclined her head, a wicked gleam returning to her eye. "I will be the one to send him to the shadowed void. That man's life is forfeit."

Linneya grinned, crossed her arms, and leaned against a pillar. As long as that fire was still there, her sister would be alright. "So what exactly is your power? I saw you dropping soldiers with a mere touch."

Eleanor's mouth curved into a bitter smirk. "I can manipulate anyone or any creature into believing anything. It seemed likely that I could make someone believe they were dead and it would shut down their mind." She shrugged. "It was a gamble, but the only place to try it out was on the battlefield."

She launched into an explanation of how Alayne found out she was a shadowchild, her training with the smithy, and the subsequent revelation of multiple powers. Linneya leaned back and crossed her arms. Eleanor's tenacity was impressive.

"If you desire it, perhaps you can return to Enthor with us. Meet Falryn. They will be thrilled to train another talented elemental."

Eleanor's shoulders hunched forward. "I am unsure that is wise. Falryn will want to spend more time with you, now that you are our prophesied. Their talents should not be wasted on me. I am unable to keep myself safe from evil men, much less anyone else."

Linneya pursed her lips. "There is no need to be so dramatic, hun. I will gladly share my mentor. I do not need to spend every moment of every day with Falryn. Come with us. Stop worrying about that abusive jerk. No one saw it."

Eleanor shook her head. "I should have been able to see it. He was a foul creature and I was swept up. I cannot trust myself to choose a man, not that any would have me with my wild ways and chaotic power."

As if on cue, Tiuthan sauntered up. He was dressed in a dark blue tunic and pants, almost the same color as the fae healers' garb. It turned his grey eyes into a stormy promise. "*Mahuchav*, we survived." He grabbed Eleanor's hand and brushed his lips across her knuckles. "I believe you agreed if we made it that you would walk with me in the garden."

Eleanor's eyes narrowed and she leaned away. "I do not think that would be wise. I should not be alone with any male. Not after everything that has happened. You would be subjected to ridiculous rumors."

A small pang of guilt shot through Linneya's chest. It was only a season ago that she wished she had Eleanor's lack of hesitation. She may have been envious, but she did not want Eleanor to hurt, especially not if it meant her sister pushed away any possible happiness.

The fae prince cocked his head, studying Eleanor's reaction. "Ah, yet you promised." He leaned in, baring his teeth in a way that seemed half-threat, half-jest. "We fae take promises seriously. Come."

Eleanor snarled through gritted teeth. "Do not twist this, freak. There was no binding agreement."

The fae prince smirked as if his nickname was a challenge. Linneya bit back a smile. The male seemed more than able to handle Eleanor's fury.

"There is no bind, but your word is only as good as your action."

Eleanor hissed an exhale through her teeth like a wounded animal and Linneya snickered. "Oh, go on. It is not as if one walk will tether you to him forever."

Tiuthan's lips curved upward and he held out his hand, a triumphant gesture. Eleanor balled hers into fists and walked toward the garden exit. Tiuthan raised his eyebrows at Linneya and she shrugged. "At least she is headed in the right direction? You had better catch up with her."

He shook his head, sighing, and jogged in her direction. Linneya grinned. If nothing else, maybe interacting with the fae prince would help Eleanor stop her self-deprecating monologue.

A familiar heat bore into her back. Fingers slipped into hers and she turned, smiling. "Hello, you." She gestured with her chin. "Did you see Eleanor's new beau? Think she can fight her way away from him?"

Darryn rolled his eyes and kissed her cheek. "I have no comment on that. In better news, the healers say we can visit Aiden now. Are you ready?"

Linneya sombered at the news. Her smile tightened and she fell in step as Darryn guided them back into the hallway and toward Aiden's rooms.

Her stomach dropped with every step, her heart pounding a frantic rhythm in her chest. She wanted to ignore the worry that this might be the end for her brother. Instead, she almost expected to walk into the room and see him sitting up, smiling.

She made to open the door, but jumped back as another person wrenched it open. Johann staggered through, his red-rimmed eyes staring into nothingness. She exclaimed in surprise and he blinked as if bringing the two of them into focus.

Darryn clamped a hand on the man's shoulder. "How are you holding up?"

Johann's mouth was set in a hard line and his jaw pulsed. "I should have been there. He fell because I had gone to help a soldier who was being attacked by a dragon rider. I should never have left."

Darryn shook his head. "*Should* never works in the aftermath of a battle. You know that as well as I."

Linneya nodded her agreement. "You would be welcome to stay here until he recovers, if that helps. My mother will be happy to put you in a suite. I can ask her at dinner."

Johann's shoulders slumped. "I failed to protect my prince. I am named brother to a traitor, to the false prophesied. There is no place for me here."

Linneya patted his arm. "You cannot blame yourself for any of that. I know as well as anyone that it is impossible to keep younger siblings in line." Darryn grunted in amused agreement.

She gave her husband a small smile and turned back to Johann. "As for Aiden, I know the two of you have fought side by side before. You know how difficult it can be to stay safe in a normal battle. The *sharvach* are a formidable enemy and you could not have predicted this."

The man could not be consoled. He nodded to her, a shell of his usual self. "If you will excuse me, I must pack."

"Of course." Linneya watched his retreating figure, saddened that he shouldered such guilt. He could not be held accountable for her brother's misfortune or his brother's bad decisions....

Darryn placed a hand on her lower back. "We can come back later, if you would prefer."

"No, it would only make it harder to follow through. I would avoid this until it was too late." She took a deep breath and pushed open the door. Ice snaked through her veins at the sight of her brother. Aiden was covered in a fevered sweat, twitching and thrashing in an otherworldly manner. His teeth were gritted, lips pulled back in a snarl. The loud hiss of his breath through his clenched mouth was unnerving.

Two life-tenders were changing his bandages. The sour smell that radiated from his open wounds caused bile to rise in Linneya's throat. A pulsating void seemed to wind around his aura, its shadowy tendrils reaching out slowly before snapping back.

Linneya's legs turned to jelly. She collapsed into the chair next to his bed, her mouth slightly open at the sight of the formidable warrior writhing in pain. This was her brother, her fearsome protector. Her eyes burned as tears threatened to spill over onto her cheeks.

Darryn nudged her arm and gestured to a bowl of water with a cloth on the nightstand. She took the washcloth and squeezed it out, dabbing Aiden's forehead. Linneya was grateful for something to do, some agency in the face of overwhelming dread.

Aiden's eyes snapped open and he grabbed her wrist. She gasped, pulling back, but his grip was unyielding. He pulled her close and whispered. "They are coming, the hive approaches."

Darryn growled, wrenching himself around the bed. Before he could do anything, Aiden's eyes rolled back in his head and he began convulsing. Linneya shrieked and Wralion burst in the door with another life-tender. The healers began reciting enchantments and her brother's body relaxed, his breathing slowed.

She trembled, sinking back into the chair. "Wralion, what is this?"

Wralion sighed. "Traditionally, it is said that the *sharvach* curse can drive a person to madness. In my limited experience, it seems to be more nuanced than that. He may heal and be fine. He might be bedridden the rest of his life. We will know more if he survives the next mooncycle."

Linneya blanched. Her brother would be devastated to lose the ability to walk. She sent a silent petition to the Creators on his behalf and a few tears spilled over.

Wralion patted her shoulder. "If he wakes, he may be imbued with unusual powers. Some have visions of the future, others are plagued with an ability to see beyond our physical world. Many go mad from the debilitating mind warping that happens. If he does face these curses, I will be here to guide him. For now, he needs rest."

She managed a small smile as she stood. "Thank you. I am glad to know he has you to help." She took Darryn's hand and they walked into the hallway. King Varilon was leaning against a panel, his face white as wool.

Linneya opened her mouth, but could not think of a thing to say. Her father placed his head in his hands. "I never expected to outlive a child. The thought is unbearable."

Thorns twisted, stinging her heart. She ran to him, throwing her arms around his waist. The king wrapped her in a hug and shuddered. "I am sorry. The last two days have taken their toll."

Darryn walked over and placed a hand on the man's shoulder. "You should rest, Your Majesty. Shall I walk with you back to your chambers?"

The king nodded, but the ghostly look on his face remained. Linneya mouthed her thank you to her husband and the two men strode in the direction of the family wing.

She took a deep breath and hugged herself. There was only one place she wanted to escape to. Perhaps finding a favorite story in the library would help distract her. She turned on her heel and made her way toward the room that felt most like home.

Linneya pressed open the door, the sweet scent of the old tomes greeting her like a long lost friend. A sniffling sound caused her to turn.

Mariel looked up, eyes hollow and face blank. Linneya's heart shattered again at her friend's grief. She had been through so much already. Linneya worried losing Straion might destroy her.

She crept over and sat down beside the woman, patting her hand. Mariel sighed. "He would have wanted to be set out to sea like his North Isle ancestors. Not burned on our pyres."

Linneya nodded. "I am sorry that was not possible."

Her friend shook her head, as if clearing her thoughts. "Tell me, what happened to you? We saw a dragon stop in your path, but then we lost sight of things after that."

Linneya recounted her experiences on the battlefield. She skimmed over her death, trying to save her friend from more devastation. Mariel seemed unsurprised at Orrain's resurrection. She nearly grinned when Linneya described coming into her full power.

Linneya had not realized how badly she needed to talk. The words spilled out of her, a catharsis of information. She talked through realizing Aiden was injured, all the life-tending she and Darryn did, and how the destruction stung her soul.

She ploughed on, telling Mariel about the upcoming journey to Mount Varsha. She gave her the bare details, skimming over the seer and their treacherous journey. As she ended, Mariel grabbed her hand. "Let me come with you, Lia."

Linneya rubbed her thumb over the back of Mariel's hand. "Are you sure? You could stay here with your parents and Shailyn can look after your home in Enthor until you are ready."

Mariel shook her head. "No, I mean I want to travel with you. I know I cannot be helpful in a fight because of my foot, but let me spend time in the archives at Mount Varsha. Let me be a part of what stops the evil that took Straion."

Linneya smiled at the tiny glimmer of light she saw rekindled in her friend's eyes. She would not deny her this. "Absolutely, you are welcome to join us."

The next few mornings were filled with visits throughout Loraen. The king and queen would send Linneya and Eleanor on different assignments, usually to offer aid or hear petitions from those affected by the battle. Darryn and Tiuthan accompanied them, much to the excitement of many of the citizens.

Linneya and Darryn met with King Varilon and Queen Altheia at noonrest each day. They wrestled with protocol and expected tradition, weighing it against the responsibilities Linneya would face as the prophesied. The mood was sour, no one wanted to be making these plans as if Aiden would not pull through. Still, the council demanded a clear path forward and the royal family would oblige.

The afternoons were spent at the infirmary. Linneya and Darryn worked side by side as she taught him some of the basics of life-tending. Wralion introduced them both to healing techniques for their affinities. Darryn's death-halting enchantment saved more than one life, but the resurrection enchantment did not work again.

A week later, Aiden seemed to be stabilizing and the council was no longer worried about the line of succession. King Varilon had rested, regaining some of his color. Things were slowly returning to normal, and it was time to return to Enthor.

Linneya was relieved when they were given permission to head home. She was eager to get back and begin planning for their trip to Mount Varsha. She and Darryn made their way to the front courtyard and the sight of everyone bidding each other farewell made a lump rise in her throat. Her mother and father stood in a receiving line, giving everyone final goodbyes and blessings before the caravan left.

Alayne and Mariel were huddled together, faces downcast. Linneya was glad her friend had someone who could mourn with her, but she wished it was someone other than Alayne. The woman still sent chills down Linneya's spine and she did not trust her.

Shailyn and Chrysa were more lively. They were thrilled that Eleanor had decided to come to Enthor to train with Falryn and were gushing over all the things the three of them were going to get into once they were home. Eleanor looked a bit too pleased at the ideas that the women were suggesting, but Linneya resolved to try to stay out of the way and let her heal.

Johann had joined Graisor and Trotyn as if he was one of the Falorian knights. His eyes were hollow, but he still managed to laugh when Trotyn flipped his red hair back and flourished his hand, making some joke. Graisor was more subdued. He kept glancing at Mariel, as if he wished he could find some way to fix what had happened.

A warmth enveloped Linneya as Darryn crept up behind her and snaked his arms around her waist. She sighed contentedly, leaning back into his strength and letting the tension wash away. She twisted around to kiss him. As he crushed his lips to hers, she smiled.

As long as they had each other, they could get through anything.

Thanks for Reading!

Want more?

Bonus scenes available at
www.elliefowlerbooks.com

Bonus Scene 1: Eleanor and Tiuthan after the battle

Bonus Scene 2: Darryn's POV as they head back home after the battle

Sunday Side Quests Series:

Follow King Varilon and Queen Altheia's love story by signing up for
the Sunday Side Quests at

www.elliefowlerbooks.com

Acknowledgements

Thanks to everyone who came with me on this journey! To my husband for wrestling the more nuanced parts of the magic system and the artwork, my literary friends for chewing over ideas together, and my animals for holding vigil as I edit.

Special gratitude to my alpha readers, including:
Courtney Sokolowski
Lara Spell-Worsham
Amanda McKannon
Katie
Marci Sosdian Jackson
Samantha Vathmi
Cassandra Boswell
Allison R

And to my beta readers, including:
Carriebooksandart.
Tammy
Shayna Gunn-Crosson
Maura
Donna
Renate Sacks
Whitney Wenthold
Lexy
EJ Lindell
Krysia Fadden
Whitney Cox

Content Notes:

This book is written for an 18+ audience and has several potentially difficult themes. Please note the possible triggers below:

On page depiction:

- Attempted SAs (not between the two main characters)

- Violence and gore

- Intimate partner violence (not between the two main characters)

- Death of characters

- Accidental outing of LGBTQIA+ character

- Substance use disorder

- PTSD, dissociation, schizophrenia, and other mental health concerns

Mentioned but not explicitly described:

- Cult activity

Book Two

A Battle of Wings and Talons

Coming April 2025!

www.ingramcontent.com/pod-product-compliance
Lightning Source LLC
Chambersburg PA
CBHW070655010826
48975CB00013B/1332